THE WISH-EATER

CLAIRE LUANA

Cover Design: BookFly Design
Editing: Amy McNulty
Map: The Book Cover Bakery

For anyone who's ever felt the pain of a wish unfulfilled...

CHAPTER 1

BAUMAI

*E*lodie was surrounded by movement and color and light. The parade was a riot of rich hues, each wagon adorned with an embarrassment of flowers cascading over its wooden sides. The Baumai celebration in her little town of Lunesburg was growing more elaborate each year—more blooms, more drink, and certainly more carousing as the sun slipped out of sight.

Elodie understood. It was the beginning of summer, a time of warmth and plenty, promise and coupling. It would take a heart of stone to greet this joyous season with anything but a hearty welcome. Elodie pressed one hand to her chest in a vain attempt to banish the heavy feeling nestled there.

"Give the wee ones a smile," Elodie's mentor, Agathe, called to her over Maven's tan haunches. "We're almost to the church." They walked on either side of the cart-horse, Agathe holding the reins in her firm but gnarled fingers, turning him up the narrow cobblestone street that led to the village center. They would soon pass over the Weiss river that snaked through the center of town, glistening like a satin ribbon fluttering in a maiden's tresses.

Elodie smiled woodenly at the school children who lined the parade route, bouncing and waving in the hopes that a stray piece of peppermint might be flung their way. The sight of their cherubic faces and glossy curls froze her breath in her lungs.

She placed a steadying hand on Maven's warm side and pulled another fistful of ivory blossoms from the cart, focusing her attentions on tossing the elegant blooms into the crowd. The flowers would be gathered with those thrown from the other wagons and woven into crowns to be worn by village girls or into nosegays to be gifted to favored lads. She herself had given Willum one of those little bouquets five years ago to the day—the most beautiful combination of magenta oleander and rare cerulean hollyhock, woven with mint leaves and velvety sage. They had danced until the pads of her feet had burned in her slippers and then kissed until her heart had burned with a different kind of fire. The universe had stretched wide above them that night, every winking star a possibility—a wish waiting to come true. These days, the indifferent faces of those same stars mocked her. She could not find peace even in solitude.

"You didn't have to come," Agathe said softly.

Elodie shook her head. "Nonsense. I'm fine. And what would people say if I didn't attend?" *And what would Willum do, if I was not there to keep him from the bottom of the cider flagon?*

"I don't give a fig what they say, and you shouldn't either." Agathe's lined face was kind. Her skin was tanned and wrinkled from her days in the sun tending her garden, but her body was still strong, her tongue stronger still. Her hair was the quicksilver of fish scales, but for a streak of snowy white at one temple. Today Agathe had twisted her tresses into a crown of braids decorated with baby's breath—a look favored by little girls and not entirely appropriate for an octogenarian. But Agathe cared little for propriety. Sometimes Elodie envied her that.

Their conversation was forgotten as Maven made the final turn into Lunesburg's main square. Their town was undeniably lovely. Quaint, half-timbered buildings crowded together in bright colors, decorated with matching lacquered shutters and windowsill flowerboxes. The whole town had turned out in their finest clothing, waiting for the parade to end so the real celebration could begin.

Maven trundled around the fountain at the center of the square, his bulk momentarily shadowing the graceful statue of the Daughter dipping her pitcher down for a drink. Elodie glimpsed the familiar faces of her family as she passed, her younger sisters, Sidonie and Josephine, her father, Frederick. Sidonie held her month-old daughter in her arms, while her older son, a rambunctious three-year-old, sat atop his father's shoulders. Josephine smiled and waved when she caught sight of Elodie. Elodie waved back, her eyes scanning the crowd. Where was Willum?

There. He leaned against a building near the back of the crowd, flanked by two other faces she unfortunately recognized as well: those of her mother- and father-in-law. Their little town was nestled in the hills of Astria, a verdant region known for growing juicy apples, sweet creme dairy cows, and war. Umbria on the west and Frieland on the east had fought over Astria for generations—only in the last three decades had they returned to Umbrian rule. Elodie's husband and his parents favored the Frieland coloring—they were broad and tall, with dark brown hair, olive skin, and eyes the color of warm chocolate. Though Willum's eyes had been anything but warm lately.

Agathe pulled Maven to a stop as they passed into a shady alley behind the square where the wagons from the parade were lining up for the day. Elodie grabbed three bundles of herbs wrapped in seafoam ribbon and followed Agathe the short way back to the main square. Before they rounded the corner, Agathe spun and grabbed Elodie's hand.

She flinched in surprise.

"You will get through today." Agathe's cornflower blue eyes bored into Elodie.

"Of course." Elodie examined her leather slippers peeking out beneath her dress. The soles were so worn she could feel the contours of the cobblestones beneath her feet. "It's a day to celebrate." Agathe had a keen way of seeing to the heart of a person, and that insight could be inconvenient at times. She looked up and met Agathe's gaze, willing the old woman to see a show of strength. Fortitude. Even if she felt anything but strong inside.

Finally, Agathe nodded once, releasing Elodie's hand. "Blessed Baumai," Agathe said, offering the traditional greeting for the holiday.

"Baumai blessings," Elodie responded, giving Agathe a quick peck on her leathery cheek before she turned and plunged into the crowd.

Elodie longed to join her sisters and father and pull her nephew, Rolo, up on her hip, but she directed her steps toward where she'd seen Willum and his parents. A wife's place was with her husband on this day of fertility—in hopes the couple would be seen by the Daughter and blessed by the goddess with a child. A surge of emotion flooded through her at the thought and Elodie was too ashamed to name it for what it was. Bitterness. Four and a half years she and Willum had been married, four and a half years trying to conceive. Her sister Sidonie had married and birthed two children in the same time.

"Blessed Baumai," Elodie said brightly, pasting on a smile as she found Willum.

"Baumai blessings," Willum murmured, his eyes barely flicking to her. His handsome face was tight with pain, and he leaned against the nearby building for support. It was a bad day—after almost five years, Elodie could tell from the set of his jaw alone.

It all came rushing back, those horrible weeks. Willum had been apprenticed to a stonemason, set up to have a comfortable life and lucrative trade. Until one day, a month before they were to be wed, a stone had fallen on Willum, partially crushing his hip and leg. She still remembered the agony on his face as they'd moved him, trying to save his life. His mobility. She remembered her terror at what it had meant for their lives together. But how could she leave him? Refuse to marry him after his accident? What kind of woman would that have made her?

"Elodie." Her mother-in-law, Eugenia, acknowledged her with a sniff. Her greying hair was pulled into a rigid bun, her marriage shawl wrapped around her as if a bracing wind bit at her, rather than the sun's soft rays.

Corbitt, Willum's father, nodded his welcome, before turning his eyes back to the church, where Lunesburg's Alder was taking the steps. Corbitt stood nearly as tall as his son, both broad of shoulder with square jaws and strong, graceful eyebrows, but the corners of Corbitt's mouth were turned down in an expression of perpetual disapproval. When Elodie had married Willum, it had astounded her how such a cheerful boy had sprung from such dour stock. These days, the similarities between father and son made her mouth go dry.

"I brought a nosegay for you each," Elodie said, distracting herself as best she could from her spiraling thoughts. She handed one to Willum, who absentmindedly tucked it in the pocket of his threadbare shirt.

Eugenia took hers with a frown. "What are these sad little flowers?"

Elodie struggled to keep her tone light as she replied, handing the last to Corbitt. "They're not strictly flowers. Agathe and I decided we'd do herbs this year, as she's been letting me grow them in her greenhouse for cooking and healing. The blossoms are chamomile and cone-flower, with holy basil and winter savory greens. If you smell them—"

"Smells like medicine," Corbitt said, wrinkling his nose.

"Agathe... Is that the strange woman you insist on working for?" Eugenia asked. "Willum, why do you let her work for that kook? She's no doubt filling her head with all sorts of strange thoughts."

Elodie ground her teeth together. She worked for Agathe because the money was the only thing keeping a roof over their head. Not to mention the leftover vegetables and provisions Agathe gifted Elodie had seen them through several winters. "Agathe is Lunesburg's most respected healer. This town would have lost many fine folk over the years without that *kook*, including..." Elodie swallowed her next words as Willum's eyes whipped to hers, his finely-wrought lips pressed into a tight line. Once Elodie had dreamed of kissing those lips every night, of those lips being hers alone. Gods, she missed those days.

Eugenia *harrumphed* and turned back to the church.

"Would you like to find somewhere to sit?" Elodie asked quietly, placing a hand on the small of Willum's back.

He shook his head. "I'm fine. Look, *Alder Landry* is calling for attention." Willum couldn't say their town leader's name without a tone of mocking.

"How that man ever beat you still astounds me," Eugenia muttered, crossing her chubby arms under her bosom.

No one responded. Elodie turned to regard the figures that stood on the steps of the church. Elodie knew precisely how Dion Landry had won the election. The alderman was tall and well-built, with the reddish-blond hair that many Astrians favored. He had the green eyes of an Umbrian, and a face that must have been designed by the All-father solely to make women's knees weak. He was charismatic and funny, and he seemed surprisingly competent. The contest between him and Willum had been hardly a battle at all. Perhaps the Willum she had once known could have bested Dion Landry—her Willum had been just as cocky and charming and genuine, with the innate confidence of a man who knew the world could be his. But that had all changed after his accident.

"Welcome, all! Welcome, summer," Alder Landry called out in his smooth baritone, his arms open wide. His suit was made of well-tailored tan wool, no doubt new for this year. Elodie resisted looking down at her own jade dress, the same she'd worn the last two years, and tried not to think of how different their lives would have been if Willum had won the Aldership. Dion's wife, Delphine, stood next to him, her thick, brunette hair pulled into a braid over one shoulder, her hands demurely resting on her extremely pregnant stomach. On her other side stood Justus Gregoire in his white robes, the triangle of the church hanging from the gold chain about his neck.

Elodie tried to focus on the Alder's words, then on those of Justus Gregoire, but she'd heard them so many times before. Thanking the All-father for bringing them through another winter. Honoring the All-father's Daughter for blessing them with new life, new unions. Banishing the Un-brother, the All-father's wicked sibling, who sought to mar their happiness with curses and trickery. Soon it would be time to name the Baumai Queen, a tradition she had delighted in as a girl, and which she now dreaded with every fiber of her being.

Her eyes slid over the crowd bordering the church steps and stopped as her gaze met another. Sebastian Beringer—the owner of the town's largest apple farm and new cider brewery. He was a handsome man, with golden hair and the loveliest hazel eyes ringed with blue. He was kind, too. She worked for him some days tending his trees when they showed sign of ailment, and he'd hired Willum for the picking season, paying him the same wages even though he was slower than the other men. She smiled and Sebastian answered with his own before turning back to the church. He must have been scanning the crowd, just as she.

"And now it's time to crown our new Baumai Queen! Let those married ladies hoping for blessings this year come forward!" Alder Landry announced.

Elodie stayed frozen to her spot, her feet as heavy as stone. It was elegantly said, but everyone knew what the Alder meant. Married women who wanted children. They would gather and each select a berry tart, biting into it. Baked inside one of the tarts was a little wooden stork, the symbol of Astria and a sign of fertility. Legend said the woman selected as Baumai Queen would have a baby in her arms the following spring. Which Elodie knew was a load of horse manure, as she'd been selected two years ago, and her womb was still as empty as her pantry.

"Elodie." Her mother-in-law's voice cut through her troubled thoughts. "Why do you not go?"

"I thought...maybe I'd skip this year..." she managed, wishing the stones would swallow her up. To stand out there before their town for another year—without even a swell in her belly—it was to bare her greatest shame to everyone she knew.

"You selfish girl," Eugenia snapped, making Elodie recoil. "You don't even ask for the Daughter's blessing? You will deprive us of our only chance to have a grandchild because you cannot be troubled to walk across the square? Go, and pray the Daughter did not see your disrespect."

Elodie's feet were moving before the force of Eugenia's words truly hit her. She stumbled into the center of the square, falling in with the other married women who were clothed in pastel dresses and crowned in flowers. Most she knew. She offered them smiles, even as her thoughts raged within her. Was she selfish to seek respite from this horrible tradition? To avoid having her failures paraded before her in the guise of celebration?

But...perhaps she was being too proud and needed to humble herself before the Daughter. It wasn't about her, after all. It was about the joy of bringing new life into this world. She was willing to do anything, to try anything, if it meant she would be a mother. Even if it felt like she'd already tried everything a hundred times over.

Elodie's thoughts consumed her as the tray of tarts passed from hand to hand, as she took one topped with a pastry rose. As she took a bite and felt her teeth make contact with the undeniable wood of a stork.

CHAPTER 2

SOJOURNER

The crowd watched in rapt delight as the potential Baumai Queens bit into their tarts.

Sebastian watched with them, though his eyes gravitated toward one particular woman. As they always did. Elodie Mercer. He had every inch of her memorized. He could draw her with his eyes closed —if he could draw, that was. The image he held of her when he closed his eyes was as full of life as Elodie herself—from the way the sunlight filtered through her curls, highlighting the faint copper in the blonde, to the blue of her eyes, a color pure enough to make a perfect summer sky envious. He drank in every angle of her, from the regal set of her slim shoulders, enduring this mortifying tradition—again—to the lean curves of her body, far too lean of late. Yes, he knew it all—the graceful arch of her neck, the sweet apples of her cheeks, the pink flesh of her lips, which were now frozen in the act of chewing.

"No," Sebastian breathed out, little more than a whisper. Surely the All-father would not be that cruel. Wasn't it enough that He had deprived Elodie of the one desire of her heart? Did He also have to flaunt the fact before the entire village? Again? He still remembered Elodie's delight when she had bitten into the stork two years ago, followed by her bubbling laugh of triumph. She'd had faith then in the providence of God, so sure the stork meant that long overdue blessings would indeed visit her home that year. Sebastian tried not to think of the other who lived in that home, the towering brute that shadowed Elodie's sun. No, Willum Mercer hadn't deserved her back then, and he didn't deserve her now. Perhaps it was a blessing that the man seemed intent on drinking himself into an early grave.

As soon as the thought surfaced, Sebastian chided himself for it. The All-father hadn't been kind to Willum, either.

"Elodie has it!" someone cried from the crowd.

Sebastian winced. No one else's eyes rested on Elodie quite as often as his, but it was inevitable that some callous villager would spot her halted chewing and call her out as their new queen. But Daughter, for her sake, he wished it weren't so. As the news traveled on a whispered wave through the crowd, a quiet fell over the square, a collective discomfort at the awkwardness of the moment. A recognition that this was an unfortunate turn of fate indeed.

At last, Elodie fished into her mouth and pulled out the little wooden stork. "Perhaps someone else would like to be queen this year?" she offered with a rueful smile.

Dion leaped forward as Delphine elbowed him in the side. "Nonsense, the All-father has chosen! Come, Elodie, and be crowned our queen! Let's give her a hand." Dion boomed the words with such good cheer that people seemed to almost believe them.

Scattered applause followed.

Dion placed the flower crown upon Elodie's flaxen hair and hung the shawl of the Baumai Queen, embroidered with hundreds of flowers, about her shoulders.

Elodie smiled and waved, but Sebastian could see from the tightness around her eyes that she was holding back tears. He wiped his hands on his trousers as his body flushed in sympathy. He would give anything in that moment to take away her discomfort. To redirect the watching eyes that must be burning into her.

Sebastian's feet were moving before he realized what he was doing, pushing through the crowd and up onto the stage. Dear All-father, what in the Light was he doing?

Dion raised an eyebrow at him as he passed, and Sebastian shrugged at him helplessly, shooting his friend a look that he hoped communicated *I don't know what the hell I'm doing, but let me do it.*

Sebastian held up his hands as his face grew warmer, willing his voice to hold strong. He was terrible in front of crowds; it had only been in the last year or two that he could manage to talk to small groups without his knees turning to jelly and his words to gibberish. "Good people."

The crowd quieted, and Elodie shot him a questioning look. He gave her what he hoped was a reassuring smile. He had wanted to take the attention off her, and now he had. *Be careful what you wish for, Sebastian.* He cleared his throat. "In honor of this year's queen...I'd like to...donate...a cask of my finest cider to the celebration. It'll be brought to the feast tonight!" He muddled through the words, but they had their effect. The crowd went wild, ebullient at the promise of free alcohol.

He nodded his head to Elodie, but she was already slipping off the stage, safely out of notice.

Dion strode to Sebastian's side, leaning in. His friend was shaking his head, but he held a smile. "That was an awfully nice thing you did. A tad obvious, perhaps, but nice nonetheless."

"I don't know what you're talking about," Sebastian replied. "Donating a cask is just good business. They'll get the taste for it and be back for more."

"Uh-huh." Dion nodded, his green eyes sparkling. "Good business. Nothing to do with distracting the crowd from Elodie Mercer's unfortunate crowning, I'm sure."

Sebastian said nothing. Dion had kept his secret for years, other than a bit of good-natured teasing.

Dion and Justus Gregoire needed to finish the ceremony and so Sebastian hurried back down the stairs. He was met at the bottom by hands grasping his shoulders and clapping him on the back. He smiled and shook hands with the mass of townspeople around him, searching the crowd for Elodie. She was gone. He was glad that she'd been able to make her escape. Now it was time to make his. The square would be clearing out soon to allow long tables to be set out and the feast to be served. He better be back with that free cask by the time it was.

THE CELEBRATION WAS in full force when Sebastian returned to the town's center with the cask on his handcart. He ducked beneath a cascade of pink and white flowers spilling out of a low-hanging second-story window box as he rounded into the square. Elodie would know what kind of blooms they were. She knew everything there was to know about plants and flowers and herbs. His heart twisted sharply at the thought of her. Elodie, Elodie—always Elodie.

Sebastian maneuvered the cart through the crowd toward the front of the tavern and was surprised when a stranger leaned down to help him lift it onto the table that had been set out.

Sebastian straightened.

The man who aided him was as unusual a fellow as Sebastian had ever seen. Freckles covered the man's face like a burst of rain on the surface of a lake, but it only made him more striking, Sebastian thought with a sliver of envy, especially when combined with his straight, white teeth and shocking copper hair. By his feet stood a fine-looking shepherd dog of brown and black, its bushy tail wagging rhythmically.

The man was a sojourner, Sebastian was certain of it. Sojourners were traveling folk—moving from town to town in their brightly painted wagons. But they were more than that. They were said to be magicians—purveyors of arcane arts both ancient and mysterious. And more than a little dangerous. Sebastian had never actually met one.

Realizing his mouth was open and he was staring like an imbecile, Sebastian gave himself a little shake. "Thank you...for your help."

"I was hoping I could get a free drink out of it." The man chuckled.

Sebastian nodded and grabbed one of wooden cups the tavern

owner, Mikel, had set out. There was already a line forming behind them of people eager for free cider. "You'll have the first."

Sebastian poured a cup for the sojourner and they both stepped aside, out of the way of the flood of people. "What brings you to Lunesburg?"

"It was just a short detour from my path," the sojourner said, "and I've heard tales of the beauty of this city...and its inhabitants." He winked at Sebastian, letting out an easy laugh.

Sebastian offered a smile, though the man's words made his skin crawl. "It is a very pretty town," he managed. Sojourners were also known for preying on helpless young women, though some of the tales of their misdeeds seemed far too wild to be anything but hyperbole. Besides, the man before him surely didn't need to bewitch anyone's daughter. No doubt plenty of women would line up for his company voluntarily.

"Piers is the name."

Sebastian took the man's wrist in his hand, giving it a firm shake. "Sebastian."

The dog sat down between them and leaned against Sebastian's booted leg.

"Corentin likes you. He's a good judge of character."

Sebastian leaned down and scratched behind the dog's sizable ears. He supposed a man with a dog couldn't be too bad a fellow.

They made polite small talk as Piers sipped his cider. The sojourner was from Genovese, Umbria's neighbor to the northeast, but had traveled as far as his wagon could take him in three directions, selling trinkets and rarities, trading songs and information. No mention of spells or potions, though Sebastian doubted he would be advertising that particular aspect of his wares. The man had lived with other sojourners for a while, but they had settled in the eastern Firrin Mountains, and he had wanted to keep moving. "I'd like to go all the way to the Cerene Sea, someday," Piers said. "The tales say the sand is as white as snow, the water as clear as crystal. I'd like to put my feet in it."

"Me too," Sebastian agreed. "I hope to travel someday."

"You haven't?"

"Not yet. I've been focused on growing my business."

"Makes sense. Besides, it would be hard to leave this place. It's like a painting," Piers remarked.

"It was badly damaged after the last war. There was only rubble and grey. The townspeople decided to rebuild it with more color than ever. My mother called it a tribute to life."

"A tribute to life. I like the sound of that. And there is another tribute to life," Piers murmured, eying a female form navigating the crowd and moving steadily toward them. Sebastian recognized her—it was Josephine Ruelle, Elodie's younger sister. Josephine was a head taller than Elodie and as slender as a reed.

"Mister Beringer. Are you going to introduce me to your friend?" Josephine's eyes were bright, fixed upon Piers' unfairly handsome form. All the Ruelle sisters had those blue eyes as bright as sapphires, though Elodie's were undoubtedly the loveliest, topped with long, sweeping lashes that shone like tiny golden feathers in the sun.

Piers took Josephine's hand and bowed over it, gracing it with a kiss.

"Piers, this is Josephine," Sebastian said.

"You'll have to come visit my wagon," Piers said. "I have a bolt of silk that would thank its lucky stars to clothe a figure as lovely as yours."

Josephine's delighted giggle sounded painfully like Elodie's.

"Perhaps you can go with your father or sister later." Sebastian placed a gentle hand on Josephine's shoulder and did his best to shepherd her away from the sojourner. The girl's feet seemed as heavy as stones. "She is only seventeen, you know," he said meaningfully to Piers, "so she shouldn't make purchasing decisions without consultation."

"Mister Beringer! I can too." Josephine scowled at him, her hands on her hips. She looked so much like Elodie in that moment that his heart nearly seized in his chest. Sebastian sucked in a deep breath to get it working again as he searched for any reason to get her away from Piers. "Besides, your father is waving you back to their table."

"He is?" Josephine turned and craned her neck, her smooth brow furrowed. Sebastian seized the moment and ushered her back into the crowd.

"Nice talking to you," Sebastian called back to the sojourner, who watched the scene with amusement.

"Josephine, I do hope you come visit my wagon. I have all manner of delights I could show you." Piers' mouth curved into a wolfish smile as Sebastian looked at him in disbelief.

"I will!"

Sebastian tightened his arm around her, keeping her moving.

"Sebastian Beringer, you had no right," Josephine said as soon as the crowd had swallowed them up. She threw off his arm and stormed away.

He just shook his head in disbelief. Looks was where Elodie's and Josephine's similarities ended, it seemed. The girl had the temper of a tea kettle.

He looked longingly across the square at where Piers was now holding court by the cider barrels, attracting the attention of half the town. It was too bad. He could really use a drink.

CHAPTER 3

THE WISH-EATER

*E*lodie itched to take this cursed flower crown off and crush it beneath her feet. But that wouldn't be a very queenly thing to do. So she held her head high, smiled, and bore the mortification of being crowned Baumai Queen yet again. At least Sebastian Beringer's generous gesture had taken the worst of the attention off her. That had been a pleasant surprise.

She sat amongst her family at one of the long tables that filled the square like the neat rows of a field. Her nephew, Rolo, squirmed in his seat across from her, refusing to sit still and eat his supper.

"Rolo." Elodie addressed him as Sidonie let out a sigh of exasperation. Elodie's new niece, Chantall, was firmly latched to one of Sidonie's full breasts, and her sister seemed to have little patience for the tyrannical whims of a toddler. "Do you know what a queen is?"

The little lad nodded. "She's in charge."

"That's right." Elodie nodded severely. "I am the queen of this day, and by royal decree, I order you to eat two bites of your supper. If you do not, I will be forced to punish you. There will be no bredele flowers for you to eat tonight."

Her nephew's eyes widened with horror at the thought of being deprived of the evening's cookies, and he dug in just as Willum thunked heavily onto the bench beside her, his cider sloshing into her lap like a cold slap. "More like queen of nothing," Willum said as his drinking partners Bellamy and Marsaint sat down too, straining the bench. "Queen of a barren land. Nothing but dust."

Elodie's face burned at his words. Sidonie's expression blackened across the table, and she opened her mouth, no doubt to give Willum one of her signature tongue lashings. Sidonie could take the hide off a hare with her displeasure.

Elodie shook her head sharply. It wasn't worth it. Not here, not now. There were three stages of Willum's drinking. The first stage came after one to three drinks and was in fact quite pleasant. Willum was happier, kinder, sometimes almost cheerful. The pain in his hip and leg was numbed, and he was so much like his old self that it pained her. Stage two came at four drinks or more. Willum became truthful to a fault, bristling with barbs that would put the thorns of a blackberry bush to shame. At eight and above, her husband staggered into blessed unconsciousness. Willum and his friends were on their fourth cup of Sebastian's free cider, putting her husband firmly in stage two. No good could come from engaging.

Her brother-in-law, Hugh, put a gentle hand on Sidonie's shoulder, soothing her outrage on Elodie's behalf. Sidonie pressed her mouth into a firm line, turning her attention to her daughter, brushing a tender stroke across the babe's fine dark hair. Hugh, a tall, quiet man with spectacles who kept the books for a merchant conglomerate, was a fountain of calm in the chaos of their family. Elodie was more and more grateful for his presence in their lives each passing year. She'd thought Sidonie out of her mind when she had announced her plan to marry the mousy bookkeeper, assuming her sister had only wanted someone to boss around. But now she saw the wisdom in it.

"El, Sid!" Josephine appeared at the head of their table, her face flushed. "There's a sojourner here! He has goods to sell. Will you come look with me?"

"A sojourner?" Elodie's father, Frederick, snorted around his bite of pork. "They carry naught but trouble and turmoil in those wagons. The Un-brother's lot they are. You stay away."

18

"Pepa." Elodie chided. "Don't be so prejudiced. I'm sure there are good and bad folk amongst the sojourners, like any people."

"Problem is you can't tell the difference till it's too late," Frederick replied. "Besides, there's no good where magic's concerned. I won't have you anywhere near that stuff. Now sit down."

Josephine threaded her way onto the bench with a long-suffering sigh.

Later, Elodie mouthed and then she winked.

Josephine pressed her lips together to hide her answering smile.

The celebration continued as the shadows grew long. Lanterns were lit around the square, gilding the townsfolk with flickering light. Sebastian's free cider had run out hours ago, but there was plenty more for sale, together with Umbrian brandywine and stout ales imported from Frieland. Music bloomed to life, fiddle and mandolin and pipe. Rolo was asleep in Hugh's arms, his golden curls askew and a smear of jelly on his face. Sidonie's eyes were fluttering, her head nodding against Hugh's shoulder. Tiny pink Chantall rested in the crook of her elbow. Elodie tore her hungry gaze from the scene of domestic tranquility, fighting down the surge of jealousy that buffeted her. She *was* happy for her sister. Of course she was.

The quicksilver strum of a lute accompanied by a honeyed male voice drew her attention. She craned her neck to see the source. It must be the sojourner. Elodie had never seen someone quite like him, painted in such rich hues. He wore a loose tunic shirt the color of an eggplant tucked into a wide leather belt, scarlet pants, and brown knee-high leather boots. On anyone else, the colors would look garish, but they suited the sojourner well. From the copper of his hair and neat beard to the startling gold of his irises to his white teeth that shined like pearls—the man was a royal treasure come to life.

Now the sojourner was serenading Delphine at the head table. Elodie pursed her lips. Why was she not surprised? Delphine laughed in delight at the attention, seeming to glow with life, one hand upon her swollen belly.

Elodie's eyes lingered on that belly. There was nowhere she could look that was safe. She was surrounded by happy families. Mothers.

Children. She swallowed thickly, pulling in a deep breath to work free the knot in her chest. It was heavy, this feeling. Like a weight pressing down on her, growing heavier with each passing month. Some days she swore there was no space or lightness left in her soul, only the wish. This dream that had become a millstone.

The sojourner finished his song with a flourish of strings and called out in a loud, clear voice. "I'd like to tell a tale, if you would care to listen. Gather 'round." With the firelight limning the planes of his handsome face, he looked like an angel. Or a demon.

Elodie began to stand.

"Where are you going?" Willum's hand clamped around her wrist. He was close to stage three, but she had a little more time.

"I'd like to hear the story," she said lightly, pulling free from his grip.

The sojourner's voice drifted through the air like a blanket of new fallen snow, dusting the square with the quiet hush of new possibility, transforming their familiar town to something otherworldly.

Elodie shivered and wrapped the embroidered shawl of the Baumai Queen tighter about her shoulders.

Once upon a time, there was a man who was born as poor as they come. He was the sixth son of a cabbage farmer, and a sickly boy at that. There was never enough food to fill all the hungry bellies, and never enough wood to keep their hovel warm. When he was just six, he began helping in the fields, carrying and pulling weeds where he could. But he knew no other way.

One day, while the boy was working in the fields, three men on horseback rode by on pure white horses atop stamped leather saddles inlaid with silver. The men's clothes were the finest thing the boy had ever seen, velvets in bright colors topped with thick cloaks lined with warm furs. The boy looked down at his own linen rags, too small for his growing limbs and too thin to keep out the chill and for the first time, he realized life could be different.

"Who are they?" the boy asked his father, whose face was lined and streaked with dirt, as it always was.

"They are rich men."

Rich men, *the boy thought. That was what he wanted to be.* "How does one become a rich man?"

"You must have money," his father replied before cuffing him and telling him to get back to work.

But it was too late. The dream had planted in the boy's heart—its roots growing deep and strong, watered as it was by the child's imagination. He asked everyone in the village how one becomes a rich man and how to make money. "Work hard and the All-father will bless you," many said, but the boy already worked hard, and he wasn't rich, so he knew this couldn't be true.

"Rich men are born rich," one man in the village told him. The All-father had not blessed him in such a regard, so the boy would have to find another way.

"Education," another man told him, "you need learning." But then the man told him that one needed money to buy the education, so the boy saw that route was closed to him as well.

"Marry rich," one of the village girls suggested with a giggle, but the boy did not know where he would even find a rich woman, let alone one who wished to marry him. And he was not entirely sure he wanted to marry. So he dismissed this as well.

It was his mother who gave him the sagest advice, as mothers often do. "For a boy of your stature, your best hope is to learn a trade. Apprentice to a master and follow all of his teachings. You will not become a rich man, but you will become a comfortable one." This seemed the most sensible advice, and so he begged his father to travel to the nearest town and find him a trade. His father, seeing his boy's ambition to better himself, took pity on him and took him to town, arranging to apprentice him to a blacksmith.

For years, the boy labored, growing strong and sturdy. As he grew into a man, the lad saw his mother had been right. He was not rich, but no longer was he laboring in cabbage fields for coppers. He met a beautiful maiden and they fell in love.

Elodie's mouth was parched, hanging open in anticipation. But she refused to surrender her spot to go find a dram of cider. This man was an uncommon storyteller, his words and the strumming of his lute melding together to create visions that came alive. The sojourner continued.

But sickness came to the town, sweeping through with hungry fingers. The lad's love fell ill, until her very life hung by a breath. The lad summoned the doctor to her bedside and pleaded with him to save her. The lad had heard there was medicine that could cure the sickness in some cases.

"The medicine is rare and expensive to concoct. I have so little left," the doctor said apologetically.

"Name your price," the lad replied, but when the doctor did, the lad knew there was no way he could pay it. The sum was more than he would make in a year, and more than he had saved. He begged the doctor, but the man left, leaving only empty platitudes behind.

The lad refused to leave his love's bedside, even after she slipped into the afterlife. Finally, her family came to collect her body, and still he wept. For all his prayers and hard work had meant nothing. Without riches, he couldn't save her. Being a comfortable man wasn't enough. He needed to be rich.

Heavy with sorrow, the lad, who had grown into a man, returned to work at the forge. His thoughts were consumed by his lost love and ways to make his fortune. One day, an old man came to the forge with a strange request. He sought to commission the blacksmith to make two cuffs of iron that would be strong enough to hold a giant. "I must ask," the blacksmith said, overcome with curiosity. "What are these for?"

The old man had a gleam in his eye when he responded. "I hunt the Wish-Eater."

"The what?" the blacksmith asked.

"The Wish-Eater is a creature as old as the All-father, as devious as the Un-Brother," the old man replied. "It has great power. If you capture it, it must grant you a wish."

The blacksmith laughed, but the story nestled deep inside him, finding that same fertile soil the wish once had so many years ago. "I will make you these cuffs, on one condition."

"That is?"

"You let me come with you to find the Wish-Eater."

The old man agreed, provided he get his wish first.

The blacksmith labored for three days and nights making cuffs strong enough to restrain the All-father himself. Then they set off. The old man had a map to the Wish-Eater's cave, though he kept it to himself. The blacksmith understood, for men were treacherous, especially when it came to treasure. They traveled together amicably, through green countryside, up into the hills.

Hills became mountains, and soon their horses were trudging through thick snow. The old man said they were close and so they left their horses beneath the boughs of a stand of evergreen trees. The blacksmith kept himself warm by dreaming not of his forge, but of the castle he would return to when his wish was granted, filled with wide, roaring fireplaces and thick, bearskin carpets.

Near nightfall, they came upon a cave. The old man took the heavy cuffs from the blacksmith and told him to wait at the entrance. "I go first. We had a deal."

Unease filled the blacksmith, but he agreed.

The blacksmith passed a frigid night at the mouth of the cave. When the morning dawned, the old man had still not reappeared. "I will go find him," the blacksmith decided. "Perhaps the cave is empty, and he broke a leg." But when he entered the cave, it became clear that the space was not empty. He saw first the iron cuffs, strongest he had ever made, crushed into a little ball, lying on the floor. Then he saw the old man, lying prone on the dirt. The blacksmith rushed to him, and when he felt for life, he found that the man had turned to stone.

Elodie's breath caught in her throat as the sojourner's words echoed in her ears. The man had paused in his story and his golden eyes caught hers—they seemed to bore into her—stripping her down to her soul. As if he could see the dark, hard weight where her joy had once been. She shivered. It was just a story. People turned to stone in stories all the time. It was as common as hens that laid golden eggs or giants who guarded great treasures.

As the crowd began to cry out for the story, the sojourner rubbed his throat, a lazy grin illuminating his handsome face. "Throat's a bit scratchy. Will one of you fine folk buy me a famous Astrian cider?"

"Buy the man a cider!" someone called, and there was a quick scuffle as a drink was acquired for the sojourner.

He took it with thanks and tipped it back for a long pull. "My compliments to the brewer!" He nodded to the crowd, and Elodie spotted Sebastian leaning against a table, his hands in his pockets. He gave a quick nod in return, looking discomforted by the attention. Elodie wondered what had prompted his uncharacteristic decision to leap onto the stage and offer the free ale. Whatever the reason, she was grateful for it, as it had taken the attention off of her.

"The story!" a woman called, and the sojourner's smile widened. "Right, the story!" And he began again.

Something moved in the darkness. The blacksmith stood quickly. "Who goes there?" He first heard the sound of shuffling footsteps, then he saw the gleam of yellow eyes in the darkness.

"Do you come to enslave me too?" a rasping voice asked.

"No," the blacksmith said quickly—honestly. "I...I have a wish. I heard that you grant them."

"I do, after a fashion," the creature said. "They fuel me, the desires of men. So much energy and power within them."

The blacksmith voiced the secret wish of his heart. For his wish had changed. "I wish you to bring my lost love back to life."

"And what would you give as payment for your wish?" the Wish-Eater replied. "Would you give the thing you love most dear?"

"I have already lost the thing I love most dear. I have nothing else to offer. Just my wish."

The man could have sworn the Wish-Eater sighed. "You do wish strongly. It courses through your blood. Very well. Because you have already lost that which you love most, I will take pity on you and accept your wish without payment. It will be as you desire."

And with that, the blacksmith felt a strange magic pass through him, and a weight lift from his shoulders. "Thank you," he cried and then he hurried from the cave, back down the mountain. The blacksmith rode like the wind back to his village. When he returned to his forge, he pounded up the stairs to the apartment above. And when he opened the door, he was shocked to see his lost love alive and well, as beautiful as the first day he had seen her. The man fell to his knees on his sheepskin rug and wept. For the vision of his wish realized was the most beautiful thing he had ever seen."

Piers' final words rang out, dropping like a falling star into the velvet night. A moment passed before someone started clapping, as if no one wanted to be the first to dispel the magic that dusted them like dew. Elodie rubbed her arms to banish her goosebumps as the gathered folk burst into cheers and applause. It had been a very fine story. But something about it bothered Elodie.

When the throng of admirers surrounding Piers thinned, Elodie walked to face him.

He dipped into a graceful bow. "Your Majesty."

Elodie was dumbfounded for a moment. Then she remembered the crown on her head. Her cheeks heated and she waved a hand. "That's hardly necessary."

"How can I help you?"

"The story, sir—"

"Please, call me 'Piers.'"

"It's too good to be true." Elodie crossed her arms before her. "He didn't have to give anything up for his wish to be granted."

"He had to go on the journey," Piers countered. "And he did give something up. He offered the energy and power of his wish."

Elodie snorted. "But that didn't pain him or cost him."

"Some might say he had already suffered enough. But I would say, can't a man receive good fortune *without* suffering for it?" He regarded her shrewdly. "Or a woman?"

Once Elodie might have thought so, but no longer. "In real life, nothing comes for free."

"Well. It *was* just a story," Piers said with a laugh as warm as a nip of brandywine on a cold night. "Though all stories hold a grain of truth. This one especially."

Her heart seized. "What do you mean?"

"The Wish-Eater is real, my queen. There really is a mythical creature that grants wishes by eating them." That sounded a lot like blasphemy, but her own thoughts had crossed over the line of blasphemy many times in the past years. Four and a half years with an empty womb would do that to a woman.

"The creature's tale is told in this book." Piers flourished a little volume before her. He hadn't been holding it a moment before, she was sure. Where had it come from? But Elodie couldn't help herself. She leaned in to examine it. It was bound in blue leather stamped with gold, the edges of its pages trimmed in gilt as well. Other than the All-father's holy Dialogues, she'd never seen a book decorated so extravagantly.

"How much?"

"Ten pieces of silver."

"Ten pieces!" She took a hasty step back. That was enough to feed them for half a year. "Why would I pay ten silver for a book with a story you just told?"

"Because the book isn't just the story." His smile widened. "It contains the map, too."

"You lie," Elodie said, but her words were unconvincing, even to herself. Her eyes affixed to the leatherbound book in his hand. Could he be telling the truth? Could the Wish-Eater be a real creature? Could that book contain the key to its whereabouts? She allowed herself to imagine for a moment finding it, offering it the energy of her wish. Like the blacksmith from the story, her wish filled her so full sometimes she feared there was no room for anything else. It was crowding out all life and joy, strangling her like mistletoe on a host tree.

"I never lie about my merchandise. I have a reputation to uphold," Piers said.

"Elodie!" Willum called harshly through the crowd.

Elodie briefly closed her eyes, pulling in a steadying breath. She turned to find Willum staggering through the crowd of people, his expression as black as thunder.

Willum drew up beside her, his tall form shadowing her like the impenetrable branches of a holly tree. His face was red with drink, and his eyes were narrowed at Piers. "Keep your vile magic away from my wife." His deep voice carried over the crowd.

Elodie cringed, doing her best to ignore the meddlesome gazes already swiveling their way. "Willum." Elodie laid a gentle hand on his bicep. "I was just complimenting the man on his fine story."

"This man is dangerous, Elodie. He could be bewitching you this very moment."

"I would no such thing, good sir. I apologize if I have upset you,"

Piers replied, the very picture of politeness. "Your wife speaks true. She was just paying my story an innocent compliment."

"I'm tired, Willum," Elodie said, pushing at him gently. He was nearly impossible to move when he was this drunk. "Take me home?"

Willum seemed to register her request and nodded.

Relief flooded her as he draped a possessive arm around her shoulders.

"I see why you wish," Piers muttered under his breath as they turned to go.

Willum froze. "What did you say?" Before Elodie could stop him, Willum unraveled his arm from about her shoulders, drew back, and punched Piers square in the jaw.

The sojourner fell back into the crowd and townspeople swarmed in to hold Willum back. But her husband was the tallest man in the village and still strong, even after his accident. It took Bellamy stepping into his path to stop Willum's forward progress.

Piers sat on the cobblestones, rubbing his face and looking balefully at Willum.

"Stay away from my wife!" Willum shouted at him before grabbing Elodie's hand and yanking her forward.

I'm sorry, she mouthed to the sojourner, hoping he would forgive her husband's brutish behavior. Though she would never have enough money to buy that book, she had enjoyed the story, and imagining, for just a moment, that her life could be different.

Willum dragged her through the square as people dodged out of the way of his limping form. The Baumai crown fell from her hair and she looked back at it, pink and white blossoms abandoned in the dirt.

This was her life. Not a queen, not a mother, not a seeker of a magic beast. Just the impoverished wife of a lame drunk. That was her story. And there was no escaping it.

CHAPTER 4

CLEAVED

*E*lodie woke up the next morning wrapped in a blanket on the floor, her neck stiff and protesting. Their bed was a narrow, lumpy thing, and Willum took up most of it even when he wasn't sprawled out drunk. When he'd been drinking, not even a sliver of space remained.

She stood and pulled the blanket around herself more tightly, padding to the kitchen to start the fire in the stove. Their little flat was tiny and dark, with few windows, but it was dry and it warmed up fast on chilly nights. It was more than many people had.

Elodie let the tea kettle whistle a bit longer than necessary, hoping the noise would rouse her hungover husband. No such luck. She filled an earthen mug with boiling water and a blend of black tea leaves that she and Agathe grew and dried, breathing in the scent of peppermint and fennel. When the tea had steeped, she strained out the leaves and went to sit next to Willum, shaking him awake.

"Early," he grumbled.

Elodie shook him again. "It's an hour after sunup. The day's begun." She left the tea on the little bedside table and started to work on breakfast. It was one thing if Willum drank the night away, but she'd be damned if she let him sleep his days away, too. He needed to be out there looking for work every day, or the few opportunities that presented themselves would pass him by.

Elodie set a pot of oats and water on the stove to boil. Her stomach growled for bacon or sausage, or even bread and a little jam, though she'd never admit that to Willum. One of them had to stay positive if they had any hope of reaching brighter days ahead, and it sure as hell wasn't going to be Willum.

She sat at their rickety table while the water heated, watching him over her shoulder. Her husband was still the handsomest man she'd ever laid eyes on. He had thick, dark hair and arching brows that framed striking, walnut eyes. Three days of scraggly stubble covered his square jaw, but it hardly marred his fine features. Before they'd wed, he'd been a man too big for life—exuberant, bold, confident in his place. He'd always gotten what he'd wanted and when he'd made it clear that he'd wanted Elodie, she'd marveled at her good fortune. Willum Mercer, the most desirable man in the village, wanted her. Those days had been the brightest in her life—even now, they shone without tarnish. The day he proposed he'd stood atop the church and shouted down to all the village that if Elodie Ruelle did not marry him, he'd be forced to jump, for there was no life without her. Delighted and mortified by his public declaration, she'd called up to him that of course the answer was *yes*. Willum had climbed down and spun her around in a circle while people had applauded and cheered around them. It had felt like a dream, even then.

Willum slumped into the chair across from her and rubbed his face. "My head feels stuffed full of wool." He groaned.

Elodie pressed her lips together, holding in her comment. What did he expect? This wasn't exactly his first night of heavy drinking. She retrieved the tea from the bedside table and placed it before him. "Drink your tea. Agathe and I put together a special blend to help with your head. And the pain in your leg."

Willum pushed the mug away with a grimace. "Agathe. Agathe, Agathe, Agathe. She's all I ever hear about in this house."

Elodie stifled her sigh, considering her words carefully. "She's my friend, Willum. And she's helped us. She gives me something to do, and

29

I feel useful." *Not to mention the money from my work for her has kept us from starving,* she wanted to add. But such a comment would set Willum off. What was it about men and their pride when it came to money?

"She's beyond strange, always trying to push her odd-smelling potions."

"Those *odd-smelling portions* keep people healthy. The village would be lost without her. There's not a doctor within two days' ride. Just think..." She trailed off, realizing her mistake almost before it was too late.

"Just think what?" Willum's eyes narrowed.

"Nothing. Just think how hard a time the women would have birthing without her around." She had been about to say how Agathe had saved Willum's life after his accident. She had certainly helped him since, managing pain and regaining function. Or she'd tried to. Willum was so damn stubborn. He wouldn't hear any mention of his accident or his disability. Like acknowledging it gave it power somehow. That was madness. It had far too much power as it was.

"Maybe. But you can't go wandering through the woods during the full moon without spooking a few good folk. It's no wonder she never roped a husband or had a family."

It was pointless to explain that some of the herbs Agathe gathered bloomed under a full moon. Willum's eyes glazed over when she spoke of plants. "Well, I think it's admirable that she's made something of herself. It's not easy for a woman alone to support herself, but she's done it well. Besides, not everyone *wants* to be married."

Willum snorted. "Deep down, every woman wants to be married."

Elodie arched an eyebrow and swatted him with her dishcloth. "Are you such an expert on the female species now? You know what we all want more than we do?"

Willum captured Elodie's waist as she tried to walk around the table, encircling her with his arms and pulling her down onto his lap. "I only claim to be an expert on one woman." He threaded a hand through her hair and tilted her chin, dusting a row of kisses along her neck, the stubble on his chin scraping against her sensitive skin. "For instance, I know that you make those soft little noises when I kiss you here…"

A shiver of pleasure wended its way through her as his lips traced along the line of her chin. Willum's affection may have been rare these days, but he still knew how to make her knees weak.

His deep voice tickled her ear, "And when I kiss you here—"

A noise on the stove pulled her attention from Willum's ministrations as the porridge threatened to boil over. She pushed against his chest and freed herself from his grasp. "Alas, the porridge knows how to capture my attention even better than you do." She set it on the table and retrieved the bowls.

Willum groaned as she placed a bowl before him. "As if I needed more reasons to resent porridge. Is there any honey?"

She shook her head. "Too early in the season. It's boring, but it fills the belly. So eat."

"Yes, sweet summer." Willum gave her a little salute.

She smiled, sitting down before her own bowl. It had been Willum's nickname for her, from the very beginning of her courtship. He'd said her blue eyes and bright hair reminded him of a summer day. But for far too many months, she'd felt more like the depths of winter. Grey and numb and doubtful that the air would ever be warm and sweet again. But she tried not to let Willum see that. She tried not to let anyone see that.

ELODIE WAS MAKING deliveries for Agathe that day, and her last of the afternoon was to Sidonie. Sidonie and Hugh lived in a beautiful cottage five minutes outside of the village. The cottage was bright with windows, and the midday sun spilled into the kitchen. Elodie kept a bevy of plants happy on the ledge behind Sidonie's kitchen counter, and a patch of vegetables growing in their generous backyard. In exchange for the space, Sidonie and Elodie split the harvest. For some reason, Elodie and plants had always gotten along. It was as if they had an understanding. They would speak their woes to her, and she would listen. It suited everyone just fine.

Sidonie and her children were in the garden when Elodie arrived. Rolo was attacking a poor squash plant with a stick while Sidonie rested on a bench with Chantall, her face upturned to the sun.

Elodie gave her a kiss on the cheek. "Don't get up," she said as Sidonie opened her eyes and started to rise. Elodie settled in next to her. "How are you feeling?"

Sidonie sighed, rubbing her face. Deep shadows smudged the smooth skin beneath her eyes. "Promise me I'll sleep again someday?"

"Promise," Elodie said, her eyes resting on Chantall. It was a strange thing, how something women complained so fiercely over, Elodie would give anything for.

Sidonie saw her gaze and straightened. "I know I have no right to complain. It is a blessing."

The words had just left Sidonie's mouth as Rolo sprinted by and whacked both of their knees with his stick. "Rolo!" Sidonie screeched. "You come back and apologize to your aunt!"

But Elodie just laughed, rubbing her leg. "A blessing, right?"

Sidonie shook her head ruefully. "So I keep telling myself."

Chantall chose that moment to wake, her tiny pink fists balling in outrage at being disturbed. A wail escaped from her that startled Elodie with its power.

"My, she has a lot to say," Elodie remarked.

"You have no idea." Sidonie closed her eyes briefly.

"I can hold her—" Elodie offered, but Sidonie shook her head. "I think she's hungry. She'd be a demon for you. Let me feed her first."

Elodie nodded, turning her sights back to the garden as her sister unbuttoned her dress so Chantall could eat. She adored being an aunt, but it was different. It would always be different. Motherhood was a secret hall of the feminine that she couldn't enter. It was cold here, on the outside.

They settled into silence as Chantall ate and Rolo played.

"I'm sorry about yesterday," Sidonie said quietly. "Baumai Queen. It's a stupid tradition."

Elodie shrugged. "It's over. I wasn't even going to go up there, until Eugenia made me."

Sidonie pressed her lips together. "That woman... I don't know how you haven't told her off by now."

"They're family. Unfortunately. And Eugenia holds a grudge like no one I've ever met. However good it would feel to lay into her... I'd pay in the long run."

"But it would feel really, *really* good, wouldn't it?" Sidonie flashed a devilish grin.

Elodie laughed. "Daughter, yes."

Sidonie's smile faltered. "It's no surprise Willum turned out sour, with parents like those."

Elodie held back her knee-jerk defense of her husband. She could be real with Sidonie. "I don't know. No one starts out sour, do they? They turn slowly. Then all at once. Like milk."

"Those two have curdled long ago," Sidonie said. "I wish you hadn't married him. You could have avoided all of this."

"I couldn't refuse to marry him after his accident. What kind of woman would that make me?"

"A practical one. You signed up for a happy husband who could care for you—financially and emotionally. You ended up with a thunderstorm of a man who's too hungover to find a real job."

"He's struggling. This wasn't the life he wanted, either," Elodie protested. "I see how it eats at him. The pain. The fact that he can't do what other people do. He feels like half a man."

"He *is* half a man," Sidonie said sharply.

"Sidonie." Elodie recoiled. It was a cruel thing to say, even for her sister.

"Not because he's crippled." Sidonie shook a finger. "Because when that stone fell on him, he stopped living. He gave up."

Elodie swallowed down a lump in her throat, looking out at the field of green fluttering in the breeze, letting the verdant freshness soothe her. It would be so much simpler to be a plant. Her only troubles would be water and soil and light.

"Maybe it's for the best if he cleaves you." Sidonie's voice was soft.

Elodie's gaze whipped around, shock lancing through her.

The cleaving was an ancient Umbrian tradition that allowed a husband to set aside his wife after five years if she had not borne him children. Annul their union, as if it never was. As if a marriage was a contractual exchange wherein a wife's failure to perform her one obligation was grounds for calling off the whole thing. To toss out five years like yesterday's hedge trimmings. The cleaving hadn't been invoked in decades. It was archaic and antiquated and downright cruel.

"How could you say such a thing?" Elodie hissed.

Sidonie tried to grab her hand, but Elodie pulled it back. "Because I want you to be happy, dear sister, don't you see? And you won't ever be happy with him. Not with who he's become."

Her and Willum's marriage was by no means a perfect thing, but at least as his wife, she had status in their village, a place to live, and a chance at the truest desire of her heart: to be a mother. Without Willum, all of those things crumbled. She would be a pariah. Elodie pushed to her feet. "I wouldn't be happy as a cleaved spinster, either. Willum has never spoken of it. And I would ask you to do me the same courtesy."

She turned on her heel and marched out of the garden, her face flushed. She didn't think that Willum was capable of such a terrible thing, at least the Willum she'd once known. But he was distant now. Some days she hardly recognized him. And she knew Eugenia whispered the idea into Willum's ear, planted the idea like a worm in a crisp, red apple. Would he truly consider such a thing?

Most of the time, she appreciated her sister's ability to speak the unvarnished truth, no matter how painful. But after the mess of yesterday, after *years* like yesterday, she felt thin and brittle. She didn't want the painful truth. She wanted soft lies she could wrap herself in like a sheepskin blanket.

CHAPTER 5

SPECIFIC GRAVITY

The cider sparkled like fairy dust as Sebastian dipped his ladle in to take a sample, sending tiny effervescent bubbles streaming toward the surface. He closed the vat's lid, backing down the three stairs to the warehouse floor.

"Knock, knock," a feminine voice called across the space, and Sebastian jumped, sloshing a few drops from the ladle onto the floor.

Elodie stood hesitantly at the threshold, a faded lavender dress cinched around the hourglass of her form. A beam of morning sun slanted through the warehouse's high windows and landed only upon her, as if the heavens themselves conspired to make her even more lovely.

"Elodie," he managed, fighting to slow his racing heart. He must have done some good deed for the All-father to bless him this day with the light of her presence.

"I'm sorry to startle you. Did you spill?" She smiled, her dimples puckering her sweet cheeks.

"This floor has seen many a spill in its day, don't you fear." Sebastian wiped his palm on his apron. "Will you follow me into my workshop for a moment? I need to deposit this."

Elodie followed him obediently, two empty clay flagons in her hands. He knew why she'd come—to get a refill on his cider. No surprise that her husband had gone through two flagons in as many days. His drinking had been getting worse as of late.

Sebastian's workshop was a wood-paneled room built into the side of his warehouse. A desk and filing cabinet sat on one side of the room, with his ledgers and accounts neatly recorded, and a tall workbench lined the far wall, backed by a bookshelf where he kept the chemicals and tools of his trade.

As they walked through the door, a black-and-white cat darted between his feet.

Elodie watched the cat go. "Someone's in a hurry."

"That's Grincheaux. He kind of adopted the warehouse. Doesn't like people much."

Grincheaux had patrolled for the better part of a year, and in that time, he'd only let Sebastian pet him twice. It was a slow friendship, but Sebastian was confident the cat would come around eventually.

He pulled out a glass flask and poured the cider into it, grabbing his notebook to record the measurements.

"What is that?" Elodie asked, peering at the glass cylinder with its bobbing weight inside. She smelled of rosemary and he breathed in her scent as unobtrusively as he could. A man could drown in that scent. In those dimples. In those eyes.

"Sebastian?" she repeated, nodding toward the flask.

"Right." Sebastian pulled his thoughts back from where they had wandered—to an impossible future where he ran his fingers through her silken hair and pressed his lips to her plush mouth. He hated himself for those thoughts, even as he longed to linger in the daydreams. She was a married woman. She would never be his, however much he wished for it. "This measures specific gravity."

"What?"

"It measures the density of liquid. It's a tool by which I can determine how much alcohol the cider has. That way, I know when it's stopped working and is ready for casking."

Her blue eyes widened in understanding. "It's important to deliver a consistent product, I imagine."

"Exactly." Sebastian nodded. She got him all the more when he saw glimpses of her intellect. She would make an excellent business-woman, if her brute of a husband got over himself enough to let her loose. He hesitated for a moment but then pulled his glasses off the shelf and put them on quickly to record the figures in his notebook.

"I didn't know you wore glasses." Elodie's tone was amused.

He looked up, his face heating. He pulled them off hastily. "Just for reading. Writing."

She smiled, that knowing curve as gentle as a crescent moon. "Nothing to be ashamed of. I think they look good on you. Very scholarly."

"I think they make me look like my father," Sebastian admitted.

"If I recall, he had quite a way with the ladies." Elodie laughed. "So perhaps that's not such a bad thing."

"Don't remind me." Sebastian groaned. His father had been much older than his mother, and when she'd died of a fever when Sebastian was three, his father had cheerfully taken every advantage of his widower status. His father's antics and skirt chasing had mortified him as a teenager, but after his father had died, and as he'd grown older, Sebastian wondered if he didn't recognize the true motivation behind his father's actions. Loneliness.

"Are you finished?" Elodie nodded to the notebook. "Could I trouble you for a refill?" She held up the two flagons.

"Follow me." Sebastian led them to the front of the warehouse, where he kept the casks for sale. Willum seemed more and more inclined to drown his sorrows lately. He often saw the man at the tavern with Bellamy and Marsaint. From his vantage point, it seemed that Elodie bore the brunt of their financial woes, growing thin, selling her herbs to get by, running errands for Agathe. It wasn't right how the man turned a blind eye to his wife's plight. Certainly, his accident had been terrible, and Sebastian couldn't begin to under-stand what it was like to live with that kind of pain, but at some point, the excuses wore thin. Elodie was living with a different kind of pain. Was he was the only one who saw it?

Sebastian took the flagons from her hand and filled them,

wracking his brain for a way to keep her at his side for a few more moments. She was so pleasant to talk to and an insightful listener. He wished—not for the first time—that it was appropriate for a man and woman to be friends. He longed for any bit of Elodie in his life. Whatever bit he could have.

But the flagons filled quickly, and so he handed them back to her.

"How much do I owe you?" she asked brightly, but he—who knew every one of her inflections and mannerisms by heart—could hear the strain there, see the worry.

"Actually, I was hoping I might be able to trouble you for a moment of your time, rather than payment. I have a few trees that are looking a little peaked, and I want to make sure it's not something to worry about." Elodie's innate knowledge of plants took his breath away. She always knew just what was troubling them, and just what to do. Some days, he swore her simple presence was enough to make them bloom all the bolder. She truly had been invaluable to the health of his orchard over the last few years.

"You know I would be happy to look at them for no charge."

"Yes, but I could not think to prey upon your kindness. A trade would be my preference. Especially if you throw in some more of that pepper garlic herb blend you make." Last year, Elodie had started growing herbs for cooking. Sebastian had watched with pride as her little side business had taken off. The bakery was selling bread baked with rosemary and lavender, and savory tarts with dripping cheese and chives. He knew the innkeeper and tavern owner bought her herbs too, as did many of the village's families, who used them for flavoring roasts and sausage.

"You've used yours up?"

He nodded. "It makes for the best roasts."

She raised one curving eyebrow. "I didn't know you cooked."

"Perhaps not well, but a man can't live on sausage and cabbage alone."

"Tell that to half the men in this village." She rolled her eyes. "You are a surprise, Sebastian. You'll make some woman very happy when you finally settle down."

His cheeks heated, his tongue tripping over a response to her compliment.

"Shall we go look at the trees now, or are you busy?" she asked.

"Now would be fine."

Elodie tucked her flagons away in the shadow of a shelf and they headed outside into the sunshine. These were his favorite moments, her and him in the orchard. The only time it was appropriate for them to be alone. Beneath the emerald canopy, he could almost see the two of them stretched out on the grass for a picnic, the warm breeze fluttering her curls. He searched for a topic that would safely pull his thoughts away from where they lingered. Where they always lingered. Elodie. "I'm thinking of building a tasting room onto the warehouse," he said. "A place where people could gather, with tables and food. An alternative to the tavern. Do you think people would come?"

"Absolutely!" Elodie stepped through the gate he had opened for her, out into the orchard. "It's a fantastic idea. The tavern's always too crowded. You could even set out tables on the lawn when the weather is warm. Parents could bring their children and let them frolic about while they enjoy a drink and a meal."

"I hadn't thought of that, but it would be perfect. And would take very little effort."

"Who will build the addition for you?"

"Trastille, no doubt. If I can get him to give me a fair price."

"Just threaten to get someone from Oberhaven, and he'll drop the price right quick," Elodie said. She hesitated. "Perhaps if you need help with some of the less...technical work...you could hire Willum? He's still as strong as an ox. He could help you with whatever you need."

Willum, Willum. He hated that with Elodie, there was always Willum. Everyone in town pitied the man—Lunesburg's prodigal son brought low by tragedy. Sebastian was the only one who envied him. He'd thought many a lonely night about whether or not he'd trade places with Willum, given the chance. Would he give up the ability to walk comfortably and subject himself to daily pain if it meant living with Elodie at his side? Every time, he reached the same conclusion. It was not even a contest. He would give anything he had for Elodie. His wealth, his success, even his body. She was worth it.

But…she'd asked him a question. He brought his thoughts back to the present moment. She'd asked him to hire her husband. Willum was slower than the other men, and more surly, too. But he did work hard and stayed till the job was done. And for Elodie, he would do anything. "It's a fine idea," Sebastian said. "He's done good work for me in the past."

A smile broke across her face like the sun from behind a cloud. Hiring Willum would be worth it. It would make her happy and help with their financial situation. Elodie and her husband were both too proud to take handouts, so he'd had to devise ways to help her indirectly.

"Oh," Elodie breathed, shielding her eyes from the sun. "I can see my mother's greenhouse from here." The far edge of Elodie's family's land bordered Sebastian's.

"You used to play over in that garden all the time," Sebastian said. It was where he had first seen her, when he'd been just seven years old. He had loved her even then, though he hadn't recognized it for what it was. It had been just a few months before her mother had died.

"That seems like a lifetime ago."

"It's leaning a bit this year. I'm not sure it'll last another winter." He knew it bothered her, seeing her mother's legacy like that. He could see it in the way she pursed her lips, how she crossed her arms before her. After loving her for so long, there was little about her that he couldn't read. "Why don't you fix it up? You could use it for your herbs. You need to expand your operation."

She nodded. "I fear I am crowding Agathe out of her greenhouse. But Pepa forbid any of us from going in the greenhouse after mother died—from going near any of her things, really. I think it was too painful for him to be there, and we couldn't come all the way out here unsupervised."

"I don't discount his grief, but your mother died, what, seventeen years ago? Perhaps his sorrow has faded. You could ask him."

Elodie shrugged, still gazing at the dilapidated building. "I don't know. He's stubborn. I worry even asking would set him off. But…I do wish I could restore it. To grow things in the place she grew things… I think I'd feel closer to her." She let out a rueful laugh. "If that makes any sense."

"It makes perfect sense."

Elodie turned to him, chewing on her lip. "Were you there at the festival when the sojourner told his story?"

"About the Wish-Eater?" Sebastian asked.

"What did you think of it?"

"A tall tale if I've ever heard one. Death isn't a thing to be trifled with." Or love.

She nodded curtly, displeased with his answer. *Stupid!* Of course she would find comfort in a tale of wishes come true. Of lost loved ones come back from the grave.

"I do believe," he added hastily, "in the type of wishes we grant ourselves. Through our actions. For instance, if you wish to restore your mother's greenhouse, I have no doubt that you could make that wish a reality."

"You're right, of course," she added softly, "but what of the wishes in the All-father's hands? Those wishes that we have no control over, no matter how much we do?"

The leaves let out a soft shivering sound as a breeze slipped past. An apple blossom drifted gently, landing in Elodie's hair. It was moments like this that she took his breath away. That the warmth nestled inside his heart turned to an ache so profound that he wanted to double over from the pain of it, to reach inside to be sure his heart was not collapsing in on itself.

He had no answer for her, no wisdom to offer. All he could do was murmur into the wind. "Yes. What of those wishes."

CHAPTER 6

LARKHAVEN

*T*he flat was blessedly empty when Elodie returned that afternoon. Elodie would bet the Un-Brother himself that Willum was at the tavern with Bellamy and Marsaint. For once, she didn't feel angry. She just felt resigned.

The trip to Sebastian's had been the perfect distraction from her troubled thoughts. Sebastian had a lightness about him that made it easy to forget the weight of her worries. His troubled apple trees had showed little sign of disease, and he had admitted that perhaps he was being overcautious. Even after she'd checked the trees and assured him of their health, she'd found herself lingering in the brewery, chatting with him about everything and nothing. She admired him for his business sense, and for his kindness, and for the way his soulful eyes crinkled at the corner when he smiled. But most of all, she loved how talking to him made her feel like the most important person in the world—as if the weight of his attention was a cozy cloak about her shoulders. She knew it was just his way. Sebastian was like that with everyone. But it was a welcome warmth nevertheless.

Elodie stashed the cider flagons in a cabinet in a vain hope that it would take Willum slightly longer to realize that they were full and set to drinking them. And then she looked around, pulled one of the flagons out, and poured herself a small glass. She stood by the window, in the apartment's sole patch of sunlight, looking at the town beneath her. She sipped her cider, enjoying how the bubbles tickled her nose. Somehow, the cider felt optimistic. Carefree. Like Sebastian himself.

But then an aching pain twisted through her abdomen and her hand flew to her stomach. Elodie looked down, any semblance of a good mood shattered. She knew this feeling intimately—the cramping that signaled that her monthly courses were imminent.

Every month, it came, a grim harbinger of her failures as a wife. As a woman. Every month, she wondered how she would bear it, wondered whether this would be the month when the weight of it finally crushed her. Each month, each failure, was like a rock placed upon her, suffocating her, blocking out the light. After four and a half years, she was well and truly buried.

A sob ripped from her, and Elodie keened into the quiet afternoon, her shoulders shaking, hot tears leaking down her cheeks.

It wasn't fair, none of it. Not how other women obtained so easily what she had worked for and prayed for so diligently. Not how the Daughter had abandoned her and turned a deaf ear to her prayers. How the All-father had robbed her of the happy life she had envisioned, with Willum laughing at her side, tossing his son into the air, another babe on her hip. It wasn't fair how everyone seemed to recognize Willum's pain—how he was allowed to fall apart, to drink himself into a stupor—while her pain was a silent, hushed thing. She was expected to smile and coo and hold their lives together, when all she wanted to do was fall apart. Elodie wanted to meet oblivion at the bottom of a cider flagon—but she couldn't even do that, for drinking hurt her chances of conceiving.

She gazed into the liquid gold of the glass, the story of the Wish-Eater bubbling to the surface of her mind. She had been just feet from the book, had seen the wizened pages and worn binding. A story, yes. But even the wildest stories contained a grain of truth. What if that book had been her only chance at conceiving, and she had let it go without a fight?

43

Elodie wiped a stray tear from her cheek and downed her last swallow of cider. It was foolish to long for the book. She never could have afforded it. It seemed only the rich were entitled to their wishes.

Willum wouldn't be back until late, and it would do her no good to sit here in this dark apartment feeling sorry for herself. She grabbed a gnarl of licorice root to chew on the way, the only cure to her monthly cramping, and headed out the door.

Elodie walked north through town toward her family home. As she turned down the lane, she paused, straightening one of the letters on the sign that marked the property. Larkhaven. It was strange, how the All-father cast his blessings on some and withheld them from others. Her father, a lowly soldier in the last Umbrian-Friedland war, some thirty years ago, had saved a famous general in an important battle. When the war was over, the general had rewarded him with a plot of land. He had farmed for a time, but it was the timber on the land that had proven the more lucrative investment. He now allowed others to harvest it for construction and heating for a tidy sum.

And then there was Willum's brother, Zander, who hadn't even survived basic training in the Umbrian Army during peacetime. She shook her head. How did the All-father decide? Or perhaps he didn't decide at all but let fickle luck and the Un-Brother's twisted plots rule the lives of mortals. Elodie didn't know which was worse.

"Hello," Elodie called out as she let herself in the front door.

Pepa appeared toward the back of the hallway, a sheaf of paper in hand. "Elodie dear, a pleasant surprise."

She hurried down the hallway and kissed him on the cheek. They had taken to calling him "Pepa" when Josephine had been just two and could not say "Papa" for the life of her. Her clumsy efforts had caused the older girls no end of delight, and the name had stuck, much to their father's consternation.

"What are you working on?" she asked.

"Just going over some accounts."

"Well, don't let me distract you. I thought I'd stay for dinner, if it's all right?"

Her father's substantial brows furrowed, and she braced herself for impact. *"That lout* out drinking again?"

Elodie forced a smile. "That lout is my husband. And yes, he's spending time with his friends. He needs to decompress sometimes." She'd long since given up sharing her woes with her father. It only served to make him angry. He'd have it out with Willum, who would then have it out with Elodie for airing their dirty laundry. She'd learned it was best to avoid the whole business.

"Not every bloody night," Pepa said. "Drinking you out of house and home. If I'd known how things would have turned out, I'd have never said *yes* when he asked for your hand."

Elodie sighed. "None save the All-father know the future, right?" *And He sure as hell isn't talking.*

"All I'm saying is—"

Elodie forced her voice to stay strong. "Pepa! I didn't come here to get lectured about Willum. I'm doing the best I can with the situation I've been given."

Pepa deflated a bit at that and patted Elodie's shoulder. "I know, I'm sorry. You're doing a fine job. I just worry, that's all."

"Well, you're my father. That's *your* job."

"Full time one with you three," Pepa said.

Elodie rolled her eyes. "We're not so bad. Now, back to your papers. I'll find Josephine and entertain myself until it's time to prepare dinner."

"She'll be happy for the help. If the girl spent half as much time cooking as she did grousing about having to cook, the supper would make itself! All-father help her husband someday."

Elodie laughed. "She's seventeen. Besides, I don't think Jo will ever want to do anything that takes her away from her wheel." Josephine had spent much of her time the last two years spinning pottery.

"Don't know where she gets it. Your mother was an angel." His lined face grew wistful, as it did in the rare instance when he spoke of their mother.

"If it didn't come from her, there's only one other possible culprit." Elodie raised an eyebrow.

"Oh, be gone with you." Pepa shooed her away with his papers. "I'm fine breeding stock. Look at how you and your sister turned out."

Elodie shook her head with a final chuckle, heading through the hallway to the backyard, toward her sister's workshop. After her lessons were done, Josephine could usually be found in the little outbuilding.

Elodie stood in the doorway for a moment watching her sister work. At the potter's wheel, Josephine seemed much older than her seventeen years—regal and serene. Her long, strawberry-blonde hair was tied in a kerchief, and the sleeves of her day dress were rolled up, leaving her hands free to work the clay. When had they grown so strong? So mature?

The shelves of the workshop were lined with bowls and plates and beautiful pitchers, some unfired, some painted and glazed. Against the far wall, a long table held paints and brushes clustered like a neat row of daisies. Josephine was the baby of the family, and Pepa refused her very little. He had built her this workshop and a kiln and had bought her all the supplies she needed. The only thing he refused her was permission to actually sell her work. According to Pepa's outdated beliefs, trade-work was man's work, and it wasn't proper for Josephine to sell her wares. But Josephine kept spinning, so all of their family's cupboards were busting with dishes fit for a king's table.

Josephine finished with her bowl and used the thin wire to free it from the wheel. She stood to put it on the shelf but then caught sight of Elodie and screeched in fright. The bowl slipped from her hands with a plop.

"Oh no, Jo!" Elodie stooped down to examine the mushed pile of clay. "I'm so sorry. I didn't want to disturb you."

Josephine shrugged, retrieving the bowl.

"Can it be salvaged?"

"Not this one," she said. "But there are plenty of others. Don't feel bad."

"I do," Elodie admitted.

"Nonsense! Come on. Let me wash my hands so I can give you a proper hug." Elodie followed her outside to the water trough and pumped while Josephine washed. She dried her hands on her apron and then opened her arms to Elodie. "You here to help me make dinner?"

Elodie laughed and wrapped herself into her sister's embrace.

"You smell of licorice root," Josephine said.

Elodie stiffened. Josephine herself used the root Agathe prescribed for the cramping that accompanied a woman's monthly courses. She would know what it meant that Elodie had been chewing it. "Yes," she managed.

"Oh, El." Josephine sighed and pulled her in tighter.

The unexpected affection was like a chisel against the tough surface of her facade. A crack snaked through. A sob escaped from Elodie, and she tightened her grip, leaning into her sister. Elodie couldn't talk to Sidonie about her woes; she didn't want to make her sister feel guilty for her own good fortune. But Josephine had always been her confidante, from her first kiss with Willum to how he'd proposed. Josephine had wanted to know every bit. That hadn't changed, even when her stories had changed from those of stolen kisses to those of hidden tears.

Elodie finally pulled back, wiping her eyes quickly. "It's okay. I'm just emotional from my courses."

"It's not okay." Josephine took her hand and led her to the over-sized bench nestled against the house. "But you will be."

"When did you get so wise?" Elodie asked, though her sister had always longed to be older than her years. She didn't like being left behind.

"You try living alone with Pepa for a year or two!" Josephine rolled her eyes and shoved a lock of hair out of her face. Elodie studied her. Josephine was always something of a ray of sunshine, but today she looked even more radiant. Her face was glowing with happiness.

Elodie cocked her head. "You look different. What's going on?"

Josephine's smile faltered. "No, I don't. What do you mean?"

"Come on. Spill. You can't keep anything from me," Elodie said.

Josephine struggled to keep the smile off her face, hiding behind her hand for a moment before she finally let it free. "Promise you won't tell Pepa?"

"This sounds good." Elodie sat up straighter.

"I sold some of my pottery to Piers," Josephine whispered, her blue eyes as bright as sparkling sapphires.

"The sojourner?" Elodie had promised to go see the sojourner's wares with Josephine, but the idea had been lost to the bustle of the night. Josephine must have gone on her own.

Josephine nodded. "He buys merchandise from all over the world. He had the most beautiful blue and white bowls—so I asked him if he'd consider some of mine."

Elodie's eyes went wide. "You clever little fox!"

Jo grinned. "I took him some of my samples after the festival. He bought a set of plates, five bowls and two pitchers! He said it was the most beautiful craftsmanship he had ever seen, and that he was sure I would become known throughout Umbria and Frieland!"

"That's amazing!" Elodie said. "You've worked so hard, you deserve some recognition." It sounded like Piers might have been laying on the flattery, but she'd never say so. Jo's workmanship was exquisite—maybe he was truly being genuine.

Josephine beamed, her hands clutched to her chest.

"He paid you for the pieces?"

"We agreed that he would pay me half of wholesale, and the other half when he came back through town and had sold them off." Josephine bounced on the bench.

Elodie struggled to keep her smile from faltering. "That's wonderful." She prayed, for her sister's sake, that the man would come back through town and keep his word. It would be a hard lesson otherwise, though perhaps a valuable one.

"He was so handsome, wasn't he?" Josephine said, her eyes distant for a moment.

"Who, Piers? The sojourner?"

"Yes! All the girls were swooning over him. And that story! I felt like I was right there, ready for my wish to be granted."

"He was quite a storyteller," Elodie agreed. "But...wish-granting creatures aren't real."

"Maybe not, but that doesn't mean wishes don't come true," Josephine countered dreamily. "My wish was granted."

A warning bell rang in Elodie's mind, and she opened her mouth to ask more, when a shadow fell over them. It was their father, his big arms crossed over his belly. "What are my two best girls so excited about?"

Josephine looked at Elodie with barely-veiled panic on her face.

"Um." Elodie wracked her brain. "I was actually telling Josephine about something I'd like to try. But I needed to talk to you about it."

"Out with it then," Pepa said. "Anything that has my daughters in a tizzy is something I need to hear about."

Elodie cleared her throat and looked at her father. "I'd like to restore mother's greenhouse. To use for my herbs."

Josephine let out a little gasp, and Elodie kept herself from wincing. She hurried on. "I'm outgrowing my space in Agathe's, and Willum could help me with the repairs. You wouldn't need to be involved at all—"

"Absolutely not," Pepa thundered. "I've said my piece about that place. You're to have nothing to do with it. That place is cursed." He turned on his heel and stormed inside.

Elodie and Josephine both flinched as Pepa slammed the door behind him. Josephine let out a shaky laugh. "Well, that's one way to distract him."

Elodie shook her head, playing over what had just happened.

"Whatever made you think to say that? You know how crazy he gets over talk of Mama," Josephine asked.

"I was actually thinking about asking him tonight," Elodie said. "It's been seventeen years. I thought maybe he would let me fix it up, so long as he didn't have to see it or be involved. But now I'm just confused. What's this about it being cursed? Have you ever heard anything like that before?"

"No, nothing. But you know he never speaks of her."

"Maybe I'll just take a page from your book and do it behind his back," Elodie said, a flare of rebellion streaking through her.

"It's your funeral. He'd disown you if he knew you touched her things without his permission. He's not rational when it comes to her."

Elodie deflated. "You're right." It seemed even this one little wish was beyond her reach. What hope did she have for the others?

CHAPTER 7

VELVET

*E*lodie sat before the stove in Agathe's workshop, stirring a pot of nettle tea. She hummed a tune that her mother used to sing, though she couldn't remember the words. Agathe was perched by the long, wooden workbench, pulverizing herbs with her marble pestle in its matching mortar, humming in harmony with Elodie's tune. It had always been easy between them, even from the beginning.

"I asked Pepa about letting me fix up the greenhouse," Elodie said as she came to the end of her song.

Agathe looked up sharply. "I'm surprised I didn't hear the thunder from here."

Elodie let out a hard laugh. "He was not pleased."

"Your father is a stubborn man. He doesn't like to be pushed around, especially by women."

"Well, I don't like to be pushed around, either. Especially by men."

Agathe snorted. "And people wonder why I'm not married."

"He just stomped off. He wouldn't even talk about it."

"Your mother always used to say that the way to move him was to find a way to make him think it was his idea."

Elodie smiled. That sounded like something her mother would have said.

Agathe had been close with Elodie's mother; Agathe had said they had bonded over their mutual love of all things green, despite the fact that her mother had been thirty years Agathe's junior. Elodie remembered their friendship through bright snatches of childhood memories—the buzz of bees and flicker of hummingbirds, the cool press of shaded grass on her bare feet. When her mother had died bearing Josephine, her father had forbidden the girls from seeing or even speaking to Agathe. Elodie had lost a mother and a grandmother that awful day. But Frederick had been inconsolable—he'd blamed Agathe for his wife's death. In truth, Pepa had blamed everyone in those early years—the All-father, Agathe, Elodie's mother, even tiny Josephine. And most of all, himself. In his grief, he'd turned hard and turned inward, leaving Elodie to care for her sisters at the age of seven.

In the end, it was Josephine who'd healed the wound in their family. Josephine was beautiful and sweet, with wild strawberry-blonde curls and eyes as blue as a summer lake. Those eyes were striking, even for a Ruelle. Giggling, pudgy Josephine had softened even the ice in her father's heart, and soon he adored her, spoiling her rotten. When she'd fallen ill with a case of rheumatic fever and had almost died, it was Agathe who'd saved her. Somehow, that had brought them full circle. To forgiveness. Elodie had started training under Agathe the next month.

"Whatever gave you the idea to ask about the greenhouse?" Agathe asked.

Elodie shrugged. "I don't know. Sebastian."

"Sebastian Beringer?" Agathe raised an eyebrow.

Elodie hurried to explain. "I was out in the orchard looking at a few trees with him. I saw the greenhouse. It's falling over. It was just so sad, to see mother's legacy like that. And I could use the space."

"That you could," Agathe said. "You know, that Sebastian Beringer must have the most well-tended orchard in Astria."

Elodie's cheeks heated. "It's his livelihood. Besides..." Her voice lowered. "I think he knows we could never pay off our tab at his brewery, and so he invents little jobs for me to hide his charity."

"He has a sweet spot for you."

Elodie shook her head. "He would do the same for anyone. He's a kind man." *The kind of man I should have married*. The thought surfaced so suddenly, it shook her. Guilt flooded in next, hot and powerful. How could she think such a thing? She loved Willum, despite all his faults.

"Willum has been drinking more, has he?" Agathe asked. "Is the pain worse?"

Elodie turned to Agathe, her shoulders slumping. "Everything's worse. He can't sleep from the pain unless he passes out from drink. He's moving more slowly, more stiffly. He's too stubborn to do the exercises you showed me, or even to let me massage it with the poultice you gave me. Sometimes I do it while he sleeps just to work the muscles and the scar tissue, but I don't know what to do. If it gets much worse, he won't even be able to do the odd jobs he manages to find. He'll have to walk with a cane. If that happens, I fear he'll give up completely. He's not himself as it is." Her throat grew tight with unshed tears as her woes bubbled forth. Her worries were like stones, dragging her down into the deep.

"Hush, hush, child," Agathe said. She pointed to the pot. "Keep stirring."

Elodie let out a choking laugh and turned back to the pot, resuming her stirring.

Agathe brought her stool over and set it beside Elodie. "I will brew something stronger for the pain. I didn't want to because it can become addictive, but he's already addicted to the alcohol, so we're over that bridge. I'll give you something that should help him sleep, too. Keep up the massage, even if it's while he's asleep. Nag him about the stretching, but most importantly, you must remember this is not your fault." Agathe reached out and grasped Elodie's chin gently, forcing her to look into the woman's wise, blue eyes. "Willum is his own man. How he handles this challenge is a sign of his character, not yours. You can lead a horse to water, but you cannot make it drink, you hear? You are not to feel guilty about his condition."

Elodie closed her eyes, weariness overcoming her. "I can't help it. I feel guilty about everything."

"Welcome to womanhood. But you must fight it. You can only be responsible for yourself. He has to do the same."

Elodie nodded.

"You stopped stirring again." Agathe released her chin.

Elodie smiled and started again. Admitting the truth of her situation left her feeling raw and exposed. She knew that Agathe spoke the truth—she was not to blame for their predicament, for Willum's drinking, or even her own melancholy. But her guilt always twisted her thoughts, made her feel that she should have been able to handle it all on her own. If she were only a better wife, she'd be able to help shepherd Willum out of his depression. If she were only a stronger person, she'd be able to find her way out of her own.

Agathe returned to her mortar and pestle. "Do you need any other refills?"

The lump in her throat returned. When she spoke, she was proud that her voice was clear, unwavering. "Licorice root."

Agathe's pestle stopped scratching. "Oh, child." Agathe would know, of course she would, what it meant that she was out of licorice root. That her monthly flow and its companion cramping had come. That yet again, she wasn't with child.

Agathe crossed the room in a blink, her strong arms around Elodie's shoulders, her wrinkled hands rubbing her back. Agathe's firm touch broke the makeshift dam Elodie had cobbled together around this part of her, holding back the hopes and disappointment and guilt. A sob escaped her and Elodie pressed her face into Agathe's wiry shoulder.

"Hush," Agathe cooed, rocking Elodie back and forth. "Hush, my dear." The sorrow came like a summer storm, in sudden bursts of rain so heavy, they sent her darting for the nearest shelter, wondering how there could ever be so much water in the sky. And how there could be so much sadness in a person—more than enough to drown in. She tried and tried to hold back the tide, but it seemed her sorrow was cleverer than she was. It always found a way to spring free. The water was always rising.

It was some time before the storm of Elodie's grief cleared, leaving her rung out and Agathe's tunic damp with tears. She leaned back and took Agathe's offered handkerchief, blotting her face. She must have looked frightful.

But there was only kindness on Agathe's face. Understanding. "You have handled the challenges you've been given with grace and faith. I'm proud of you."

Elodie shook her head. "You only say that because you don't know my thoughts. Inside, I rage at the All-father. I want to scream at him."

"Then scream."

"Sidonie spoke of the Cleaving yesterday." She could barely whisper the word. As if by voicing the name of the horrible tradition, it might gain some power over her life.

Agathe was silent for a moment before she pinned Elodie with her powerful gaze. "If it did come to pass, you would be fine. In fact, you would be better than fine. You would thrive. Because that is who you are."

Elodie pressed her lips together into a thin line. First Sidonie, now Agathe? "He won't do it," she snapped. "He would never do it."

"You know I was married once?"

Agathe's comment cut through the red coloring Elodie's vision. "What?"

Agathe nodded. "When I was younger than you. He was handsome, and charming, and wealthy. His father was appointed the governor of our county, and they'd moved to town shortly before I'd turned eighteen. I loved him the moment I saw him. When he turned his attention on me, I thought I was living a dream. Every other girl in the village was green with envy."

Elodie sat perfectly still, enraptured. She knew next to nothing of Agathe's youth. She rarely spoke of the past.

"We married quickly, before I truly knew him. For if I had, I never would have said *yes*. It turned out he was spoiled and had a nasty temper. He believed I needed to obey him in all things, never speaking my thoughts or opinions. When I opposed him, he beat me."

A little gasp escaped her. She couldn't imagine fierce, fearless

Agathe under the thumb of a cruel husband... It didn't fit. "What did you do?"

"I did what any good wife does. I tried to be better. Kinder. I twisted myself into knots to please him, to avoid his triggers. I wanted to be married and I wanted children. I was convinced that if I was perfect, that perfect life could be mine." Agathe shook her head. "But it was not to be. His abuse continued. Worsened. It took me longer than I care to admit, but I realized that anywhere was better than there. So I decided to run away."

"Are you still married to him?"

Agathe's face grew stony. "He came after me and caught me. He dragged me back and beat me so badly, I was in bed for a week. I was his property. I was not allowed to leave. So I made the best of it. I started studying herbology and medicine to heal myself. And to keep myself from falling pregnant, for I knew that I couldn't bring a child into that home. We were married three more months when he grew very ill. A healer came to tend to him, but he was too far gone. I didn't even put his body in the ground. I convinced that healer to take me as an apprentice, and I never looked back."

Elodie closed her mouth, realizing it had been hanging open. All-father, what a horrific tale. "I'm so sorry, Agathe."

"I'm not." Agathe's voice was as hard as stone. "It made me who I am. I know that Willum is not a villain like my husband was, but I also know you are not living the life you had dreamed for yourself. Sometimes being alone is better than being married to the wrong person. You always have a choice."

Elodie's voice was a whisper. "You know I don't, Agathe, a woman can't cleave her husband. Besides, why do I have to go without, when others have it all? Happiness, kindness and comfort, children running about. What did I do to deserve this?" She was just as devout as Sidonie. More so, even. Why did Sidonie get happiness and she only sorrow? Her stomach soured as the thought surfaced. What kind of wretched person begrudged her own sister's happiness?

Agathe reached out and stroked her cheek softly. "You did nothing to deserve this. But the All-father only gives us what we can handle."

"Then He was wrong. Because I cannot handle this."

"Yes, you can. You are. There is strength in you. But…there is stubbornness too. You get that from your father. You'll stand your ground just to prove the All-father wrong."

Elodie let out a bark of laughter. True.

"But, Elodie…too much stubbornness freezes a person. You need to be open to unexpected paths. Trying new avenues. That is true faith."

"And when there are no paths?"

"There is always a path, if you look hard enough. For instance, I wish you would reconsider the medicine I told you about. For Willum."

Elodie sighed. She and Agathe had been around this topic many times.

Agathe stood and crossed to the cupboards, pulling out a white glass bottle with a stopper. "I know I've already said this, but I'm still convinced Willum's accident is the reason you struggle to conceive. The rock crushed his hip and leg and likely damaged his reproductive organs. Some damage might be too much to repair, but other types could be helped by herbs. This elk antler velvet is known for increasing male fertility."

"Oh, no. I barked up that tree once and I've never seen him so furious. He already feels like half a man because he can't walk or provide for us. If I keep suggesting it's his fault we can't have children, too…" Elodie shook her head. She worried it would break the last bit of spirit he had. And without those flashes of sunshine—the old Willum shining through when she least expected it—their marriage would truly be lost.

"That's why I made it tasteless this time." Agathe wiggled the bottle at her. "If you're going to stay with him, the least we can do is try to heal him as best we can."

Elodie thought on that. What Willum didn't know wouldn't hurt him. And she was willing to try anything. She opened her hand for the bottle. "Fine. What could a few drops hurt?"

CHAPTER 8

CAGE

Sebastian hesitated on the doorstep, his fist raised to knock. What was he doing here? He didn't want—

The door flung open, displaying Delphine in her extremely pregnant glory. "Sebastian!" she trilled. "Darling, Sebastian is here!" She stepped forward and threaded her arm through his, pulling him bodily over the stoop into the brightly-lit interior of the house.

"Delphine—"

"No. I absolutely will not tolerate any cold feet."

He held back a sigh, his mind searching for a way out of this without offending her. "I don't think arranged courtships are a very good idea."

Delphine crossed her arms over her swollen stomach. "Sebastian Beringer, I never will understand you. You've made a life for yourself. Don't you want someone to share it with? Don't you want children? Life isn't meant to be lived alone."

"I'm not alone—I have you two, my other friends," Sebastian protested, though his argument sounded weak even to his own ears. He did want to share his life with someone. Just not the particular someone who would be sitting across from him at dinner this evening.

Delphine softened and laid a gentle hand on his arm. "I cannot pretend to understand your hesitation, but I'll honor it. Don't think of tonight as a date. It's...a dinner with dear friends. Talia is very enjoyable company, even if you never fall in love with her."

Sebastian bit his lip. He *was* hungry.

"And..." Delphine added the final nail in his coffin. "I made my famous glazed roast."

Sebastian groaned, but a grin escaped him. "All right. You win."

"I always do," she breezed.

He handed her the flagon of cider he'd brought. "You should have led with the roast."

"Why do you think I made it?" She flashed a devilish smile.

Sebastian walked through the long, graceful hallway of Dion and Delphine's home. It was the grandest house in Lunesburg and belonged to the village, maintained as a residence for the sitting alderman. He turned into the salon to find Dion and Talia perched on the plush couch, Talia flipping a card onto the polished table before them.

"Sebastian!" Dion strode over, clapping him on the back. "You remember Talia." Sebastian held in a wince. Did his friend's introduction have to sound so opportunistic? He might as well have paired it with a waggle of his thick eyebrows.

"Good evening." Sebastian nodded to her.

She gave him a little curtsy. "Always a pleasure."

He'd seen Talia around the village many times before, though he didn't know her well. He'd grown up with most of the women in the village, witnessing their transformation from knobby-kneed feral children to the women they were today. But Talia's family had moved from the lake town of Rothleston just a few years ago. She *was* lovely —tall and voluptuous, with rich brown hair and eyes the color of loamy soil. He sometimes heard her from across the tavern floor or even the village square, as she had a bold voice and boisterous laugh that carried. She was everything Elodie was not. And Elodie was everything she was not.

"What do we have here?" Sebastian gestured to the cards displayed on the coffee table.

"Oh!" Talia clapped her hands, raising one strong eyebrow. "I was telling Dion's fortune."

"His fortune?" He leaned closer. The cards were painted with colorful images, quite unlike a normal card deck.

"Yes, my eccentric aunt sent these to me from the palace at Arandel. They're all the rage there. Queen Theodoria supposedly has a seer who uses these cards to help the monarchs decide and ascertain all sorts of things. What trade agreements to make, how harsh the winter will be, who's looking to stab them in the back."

"Don't let Justus Gregoire see these," Sebastian said. The holy man would be none-too-pleased that someone other than the All-father professed to know the future.

Dion waved a hand. "It's just a little fun. What the Justus doesn't know won't hurt him."

Delphine briefly came into the room with a tray of glasses and returned with the cider flagon. "It's best if you keep that chilled," Sebastian advised.

"I'm confident it'll be gone before it has a chance to warm up." Dion laughed. "You should have brought two."

"I can run back for another," Sebastian offered, seizing the opportunity.

"Nonsense," Delphine said. "We have plenty to drink. You're our guest. Now sit down. Talia can have a go at your fortune."

"That's not necessary," Sebastian protested.

Dion grabbed a glass and pressed it into Sebastian's hand before maneuvering him down onto the sofa next to Talia. "Lighten up. Have a little fun."

"Fine." Sebastian threw up a hand. "Fine."

Talia picked up the cards and started to shuffle. "It's really just a bit of fun. No need to be nervous."

"I'm not." Sebastian set the glass down and tucked his hands beneath his knees. "What was your fortune, Dion?"

Dion looked at Delphine, his eyes bright with the vision of her. "Good fortune and new life."

"It hardly takes an oracle to predict that!"

"Oh, hush, ye of little faith." Talia's smile softened her words. She stopped shuffling and set down three cards on the table.

Sebastian's stomach twisted. They were just a bunch of stupid cards. It wasn't like they had any real power or meaning.

Talia flipped the cards over one by one. Flip. Flip. Flip.

They all leaned in to examine the pictures. Sebastian licked his dry lips. The first card depicted a birdcage with a yellow canary inside. The next was a man swathed in a thick cloak, seeming to be lost in the wilderness. The third card showed a snowy forest, silent beneath a heavy blanket of snow.

Talia frowned.

Sebastian didn't like that twist of her lips. Whatever she saw—it was bad. He cleared his throat. "What's the verdict? Am I doomed to die a horrible death? Or will I discover a hidden treasure trove of pirate's gold?"

She chuckled, but it was a far cry from the exuberant laugh he'd heard from her before. "The cage means you're trapped by something. Bound, or tied somehow."

"That sounds bad," Sebastian offered, doing his best to fill the words with a tone of levity.

"It's not bad in and of itself, but with these other cards..." She pointed to the card with the cloaked man. "This is the wanderer. It indicates that you can't make up your mind. Perhaps your inability to choose a path is what is keeping you trapped. The third card represents winter. Together, I would say they mean that if you do not choose a path to escape whatever binds you, you will find yourself in a time of darkness and cold, a winter for your soul."

No one moved. Talia's words were as heavy as the snow on the third card, smothering the room. Her prediction was...unwelcome in its accuracy. He knew his love for Elodie tethered him—he seemed unable to move on. But it was the winter card that filled him with disquiet. He'd been doing fine. He had found a way to endure his unrequited love and still live his life. The open wound of seeing her with another man ate at him sometimes, but it had become such a part of him that he hardly noticed it most days. Everything was going well.

His business was booming, he had his health, and he was liked and respected in the community.

Talia scooped up the cards, startling him out of his spiraling thoughts. "Like Dion said, it's just a bit of fun."

"Right. What do a bunch of cards know?" Dion said.

"Besides," Delphine chimed in. "If there was something of truth to the reading, now you know. Our paths are not set in stone, are they? Sebastian merely needs to choose a path, and he will find his way to a blessed summer."

"Very true," Talia said. "The cards only show a possible future. One that can be avoided if corrective measures are taken." She patted Sebastian gently on his shoulder.

"Refill?" Delphine asked, hoisting the flagon. But as she did, she gasped, her hand flying to her stomach. She staggered against Dion, her normally rosy cheeks gone a deathly shade of pale.

"Delphine? Are you all right?" Dion was out of his chair in a flash, lowering her into it.

Delphine's plush lips opened and closed, her brow scrunched in pain. "I...don't know."

"Is it the baby? Is it time?"

"You still have two weeks to go." Talia knelt at Delphine's other side, placing a hand on her belly.

"Babies do come early," Dion said.

Talia nodded. "Yes, they tend to have a mind of their own."

"Is that it?" Dion asked. "Is the baby coming?"

Delphine shook her head, hissing out through her teeth, doubling over. "I don't know. I don't know what it's supposed to feel like."

Sebastian jumped to his feet. "Should I fetch Agathe?"

"Yes." Dion seized upon the suggestion. "She'll know what to do!"

Sebastian dashed out the front door and down the steps, jogging down the lane toward Agathe's house. She lived on the outskirts of town, but Sebastian made it there soon enough. He banged on the door, his other hand on his hip as he struggled to regain his breath.

The door opened to reveal Elodie, an apron around her waist, her curls pulled into a messy knot atop her head.

Sebastian's heart ground to a halt at the sight of her—her easy beauty, the surprise in her blue, blue eyes.

"Sebastian. Is everything all right?"

He couldn't find his voice. He couldn't stop staring. He hadn't been prepared to see her, hadn't braced himself as he normally did. He hadn't had time to place the armor around his heart—piece by piece—the shield necessary to endure the blessing and curse of her presence.

She stepped forward and gave his shoulder a little shake. "Sebastian?"

Her touch lit him on fire. He was a pyre, blazing across the night sky, all-consuming. Under her touch, he would burn happily, until he was nothing but ash.

But no...he was here for a reason. He forced his mind to turn from where her small hand rested on his shoulder, warm through the linen of his shirt. "Delphine." He shook his head, trying to rally a coherent thought. "Delphine is ill."

Elodie's hand flew to her mouth. "The baby?" He nodded, trying not to mourn the absence of her touch.

Elodie disappeared inside the house, giving Sebastian a moment to compose himself. When Agathe appeared, he had managed to pull himself together. "What are her symptoms?"

He hesitated. "Pain in her belly. She just doubled over."

"What else?"

Sebastian shrugged helplessly. "She wasn't sure if the baby was early, or if it was something else."

Agathe hissed her frustration and disappeared back into the house. Two minutes later, both women bustled out the door, cloaks on. Agathe clutched her dark medical bag in one hand.

Sebastian fell into step beside Elodie. "You're coming too?"

She nodded. "We're not sure what's wrong. I'll come until Agathe makes her diagnosis. Then I can run back and grab any additional medicine or herbs, if it's something we didn't think to bring."

That made sense.

"Don't worry. Agathe has done this a hundred times. Delphine will be fine."

When they reached the Alder manor, Sebastian let them in. "Dion?" he hollered.

"In the bedroom," his friend yelled down the stairs, and the two women hurried up, leaving Sebastian lingering on the landing, not sure if he should follow.

In the end, he went back to the salon. It would be crowded in the bedroom. Agathe and Elodie would need space to work. He sat on the sofa, draining a last swallow of cider from his glass. The deck of cards sat quietly on the table before him. He reached out and retrieved the top one. The cage. He examined the golden bars, the little bird inside. Was it such a bad life, for the canary? Perhaps it preferred the domesticated life. Three square meals a day, safety from predators. Warmth and ease. Was the cage so bad if you chose it?

His shoulders sagged. But he hadn't chosen it, had he? It had chosen him. And the golden shine had dimmed as of late. He was weary of only looking at the bars. Part of him wanted another view.

He looked up to find Talia standing by the door, watching him. He hastily returned the card to the deck.

"How is she?"

"She's still in pain, but Agathe thinks it's false labor. She's doing more tests."

"False labor? Isn't real labor bad enough?"

Talia laughed. She came to sit beside him. "I hear the tribulations of motherhood are great indeed."

He sensed she was leaving an opening—perhaps she wanted him to ask her if she wanted to be married or have children—but he didn't take the bait.

"I'm sorry about your reading," she said, when the silence stretched long enough. "Sometimes it can be personal."

"Nothing too personal to share among friends," he said, though in fact he felt just the opposite.

"You know..." She hesitated. "You know what your cage is, don't you? The look on your face..."

He didn't answer. This *was* too personal.

"It's none of my business," Talia said. "But, as your unofficial fortune teller, I'll give you one free piece of advice."

"And that is?"

"Don't wait too long...to make your escape. Or you'll forget what it feels like to be free."

CHAPTER 9

TARTS

*E*lodie pressed herself into the corner of the room, trying to stay out of the way. Agathe stroked Delphine's brow, speaking to her in hushed tones. The woman was in false labor. Now that Agathe had given her some herbs to numb the pain and quiet reassurance that the baby was healthy, Delphine was drowsing into sleep.

Elodie cast her eyes about the room, searching in vain for something to fix her gaze upon. Nothing was safe. Not the rich mahogany paneling, nor the beautiful gold-framed table and vanity nestled against the wall, nor the fine tapestry depicting a scene of the All-father and Daughter in the Sacred Meadow, where they were said to reside. Certainly not the massive four-post bed filled with goose-down blankets that cradled Delphine like a cloud. Elodie and Willum's whole flat could fit inside this room. Her gaze flicked to Dion himself, but that wasn't safe, either—the worried husband, so handsome and fair. It wasn't that she was attracted to Dion, though many women in the village found him quite agreeable, his prettiness wasn't quite her type. But it was the kind of husband he was—the kind of man. A man who was confident and hale and...whole. In body and spirit.

So, she found herself watching Delphine, though that was worst of all. She couldn't look away. It was the same with Sidonie. The mere presence of a pregnant woman was a potent fertilizer to her jealousy, which already raged out-of-control within her. It was like a bramble vine, eager and opportunistic—reaching tendrils into the deepest corners of her heart, caging her with its thorns. Objectively, she knew she did not wish for such pain as Delphine suffered. She should not long for her body to be stretched and morphed until it was a watercolor painting of its former self. But she couldn't be objective. Not with this. Perhaps that was why she found herself unable to stop thinking about a certain children's tale.

"Elodie."

Elodie blinked, surprised to find Agathe before her.

"Let's head downstairs. Delphine should rest."

Elodie descended the stairs after Dion, following him into the salon, where Sebastian and Delphine's friend Talia sat. Elodie's face flushed as she took in the two of them side by side on the couch. It appeared that Delphine's false labor had interrupted a double date. Talia seemed an odd match for Sebastian, a touch too brash, with a laugh that Elodie suspected was more show than genuine. As if the woman wanted the world to know she was amused. But who was she to judge? Sebastian was her friend; she should be pleased that he was courting someone. He deserved happiness.

Sebastian and Talia stood as they entered. "How is she?" they asked in unison, then exchanged a glance and a nervous laugh.

"Delphine and the baby will be just fine," Agathe said. "Though I'm going to stay the night, just to be here in case anything changes."

"That would be tremendous." Dion ran his hand through his flaxen hair. He looked older when he was worried, without his mask of self-assurance.

"I'll stay as well," Talia offered. "I'd be happy to assist Delphine tomorrow, make sure she has everything she needs. If that's all right with you?"

"Of course," Dion said. "She'd be pleased to wake and find you here."

That was Elodie's cue. "I'm going to make my way home. I don't want Willum worrying."

"I'll walk you," Sebastian said.

Was that a look of disappointment that flitted across Talia's face? Had she hoped for a sleepover, then? She and Sebastian beneath the same roof, perhaps an illicit kiss before they retired to their separate rooms?

"I wouldn't want to impose," Elodie protested.

"Nonsense. It's too late for you to be walking about alone. I'd be happy to."

"Very well." It would be nice to have company on the short walk home.

"You shall have tarts!" Dion's face lit up. "Yes! As a thank you for coming and attending my wife at this late hour. Wait right there!" He strode from the room, leaving the rest of them bemused in his wake.

"Delphine's tarts are legendary," Talia said. "I believe she uses some of your herbs, actually, Elodie. She does a mint raspberry that's delicious. And a lemon rosemary."

Elodie's stomach rumbled in response. "I'm happy to hear she's made such a creative use of the herbs."

Dion reappeared with a brown paper package. He thrust it into her hands and gave her a kiss on both cheeks. "Thank you."

Elodie blushed. "You're welcome. Agathe, I'll see you tomorrow?"

Sebastian extended his arm for her and she threaded her arm through his elbow. What a gentleman. Willum hadn't offered an arm for her in years. Though she understood why—he needed to focus on his own limping gait.

She paused. "Dion, might I ask you a question?"

"Anything."

"The sojourner who stayed here on Baumai. Do you know where he hails from? Or where he's headed?" Elodie realized how that could sound and hurried on. "He bought some of my sister's pottery. I'd love to receive word of how it sold."

"He's pointed toward Wouraux, I believe," Dion said. "I imagine he'll continue on the western road after that."

Elodie pressed her lips together to hold back the grin. He was close, then.

They said their goodbyes and stepped out into the cool night. The stars were brilliant above them, the inky black sky a velvet tapestry. Elodie couldn't help but breathe in the fresh air, the brisk night feeding the barely-restrained glee within her. It was silly. It wasn't like she could even afford the Wish-Eater's book. And even if she could have, to spend so much on a children's story would be irresponsible. But...her father had plenty of money, and she knew where he kept it. Perhaps she could take a loan. Pay him back some day. After all, he'd tried plenty of times to give her and Willum money. It was only Willum's stubbornness and pride that had forced her to turn it down.

"Is it too late for a tart?" Sebastian's voice cut through her whirling thoughts. She looked from the paper bag in her hand to his amused smile. He walked with his hands behind his back, as if he had few cares in the world.

"It's never too late for tarts." It was a treat to see him twice in two days. Normally, she didn't see him for a week or more at a time.

She retrieved one of the flaky, buttery pastries and handed the bag to him. She bit into it, bending over slightly to avoid the shower of flakes that rained down. The filling hit her tongue, sweet raspberry with the cool aftertaste of mint. "These are extraordinary!" she said around a mouthful.

"Don't tell Margery that. She won't be pleased the bakery has competition." Sebastian took a neat bite of another tart and his eyes fluttered closed as a moan of happiness escaped him. He had the longest golden eyelashes. "This lemon rosemary is even better."

"Let me try."

He passed it to Elodie, licking his fingers.

Elodie bit into the second pastry, savoring the tart of the lemon and the earthy flavor of the rosemary. She handed it back and nodded, chewing. "That *is* good. But I think the raspberry mint is my favorite."

"What? Have you no taste buds, madam?" He shook his head and took another bite. "More for me."

Elodie chuckled. A squirt of lemon filling had escaped the tart and

decorated the corner of his mouth. "You've got a little something—"
She reached out and wiped it from the corner of his mouth before she
realized what she was doing.

He froze, as still as a waiting breath.

She forced her hand to her side as her cheeks heated. "Sorry."

Sebastian wiped his cheek where she'd touched him, his eyes
shining with starlight. Elodie looked down, her mind racing. What had
she been thinking? She'd just touched another man. She hadn't been
thinking—that was the problem. Being with Sebastian made her forget
herself. Her problems, her worries, even the space that should stretch
between them. It was just so effortless to be around him. Comfortable.
There was something about him that made her feel unbound.

"Is it gone?"

She looked up to find Sebastian had smeared a dollop of lemon
filling across his nose.

She burst out laughing, her mortification draining from her.

He chuckled too, wiping the filling from his nose and sucking it
off of his finger. A fantasy flashed through her mind, unbidden, and
the imagined feeling of Sebastian's lips around her own finger sent a
bolt of desire through her depths.

She grasped desperately for a safe topic of conversation. Something to distract her from her sudden awareness of Sebastian's easy
sensuality. "Have you ever thought about putting herbs in your cider?
Some new flavors?"

Sebastian slowed.

Elodie turned. "What?"

"That's an excellent idea. There's only so much you can do with
apples. I was thinking about expanding into other fruit—berries—
apricot, perhaps. But I could try infusing other flavors..." He strode
forward again; his mind was clearly working.

She smiled. It was a gift, to have found what you love to do. What
you were made for.

"What's that smile for?" Sebastian asked as he came back to the
moment and realized she was watching him with bemusement.

"You're so happy when you're talking cider."

He let out a rueful laugh. "I do have a bit of a one-track mind."

"So...did we ruin your date?" Elodie asked. She knew she shouldn't pry, but she couldn't help herself.

He waved a hand. "Hardly. You were helping Delphine. And...I'm not sure it was a date. Or...maybe it was, but I'm not sure I wanted it to be." He sighed. "Delphine seems intent on finding me a wife."

"And you're opposed to that?"

"No...it's just, I'm busy with the brewery right now, and I suppose I always thought I would find her myself. I would see her, and I would know." He met her eyes in the dark, holding them with a peculiar intensity. "Does that sound daft?"

"Not at all. So tell Delphine to back off."

He let out a bark of laughter. "You've clearly never met Delphine once she's gotten hold of an idea. She's like a hound dog with its favorite bone."

Elodie popped the last of her tart into her mouth and brushed her hands off on her skirt. They were passing the main square with the church, almost back to her flat. She couldn't seem to pass it these days without glaring at it.

"You seem less-than-enamored with our immortal lord." Sebastian nodded toward the church.

Elodie looked at him sharply. Were her thoughts so plain? Or perhaps Sebastian was particularly adept at reading people.

"I'm sorry. I didn't mean to pry."

She sighed. "It's no secret. My contention with the All-father is regular village news."

"That's not true," he said, though she wasn't entirely convinced.

"Do you ever wonder why the All-father gives you a dream and then doesn't fulfill it?"

They had reached her door.

Sebastian turned to her. "All the time."

"It just seems...cruel." Elodie shrugged.

"I agree completely."

"Justus Gregoire says the All-father is infinitely good. Some days, though, I don't see it."

"You can't fault yourself for evaluating the All-father's character based on your life experience. People can tell you a man is good, but if he cheats you in a business deal, you're going to form your own opinion. It's only natural."

That made sense. "But isn't faith believing in what we can't see?"

"Don't tell the justus, but I don't put much stock in a faith that requires me to disregard the truth before my very eyes. If the All-father wants to be known as good, let Him do good in the world."

Sebastian's words were borderline blasphemous, but they struck a chord within her that pealed loud and strong.

"You know..." He hesitated. "It took my parents five and half years before they got pregnant with me. Don't give up hope."

She swallowed the retort rising hot within her. Everyone had a sister or an aunt or an old neighbor who had been miraculously impregnated. She had always believed in miracles. But somewhere along the way, she'd stopped believing they would happen to her. Elodie and hope had parted ways long ago.

But that wasn't Sebastian's fault. He was trying to cheer her in the only, if misguided, way he knew how. So she said, "I believe *you* are good, Sebastian Beringer. Thank you."

"Anytime, Elodie." He gave her a little bow. "Good night."

CHAPTER 10

TEN SILVER

ouraux was less than a day's ride to the west, the closest large town to Lunesburg. It also happened to be where Agathe traveled to once a month, to tend to the children in the town's orphanage. Elodie had made the trip with Agathe a few times several years ago, but Willum didn't like her gone for such long days, so she had stopped. This time, there would be no stopping her.

A week ticked by, each day as interminable as the rest. What was it about waiting for something that made time rebel like a petulant child —digging in its heels against each passing minute? But Elodie was well-acquainted with waiting. The best remedy against it was hard work. So she threw herself into her daily tasks—working with Agathe, harvesting in Sidonie's garden, scraping together passable meals from nothing more than root vegetables and greens. It would have been a week like any other but for two clandestine activities that set her heart racing like the Weiss River after the spring thaw. First was the elk antler velvet. Elodie diligently placed the drops in Willum's cider each night, breathless with the thought that he might notice something out of the ordinary. But Willum seemed none the wiser.

Her other, more criminal activity, was not so simple.

The sounds of the All-father's organ tickled her ears as she flitted through the shadows, making her way to Larkhaven. Everyone was at Sunday service, but she had begged off on account of a "terrible headache." Willum had grumbled about having to attend despite his pain, but in the end, she had made such a show of rolling about on the bed moaning that he'd grabbed his coat and ambled down the stairs. Well, she'd attended church alone when their roles had been reversed many a time.

Elodie hurried down the lane to her family's home, slipping around into the back garden, where she knew a key was hidden beneath an old log. She wouldn't let the Wish-Eater's book pass through her fingers again without making it hers. And that meant acquiring ten silver pieces, through whatever means necessary. Ten pieces of silver may have been an outrageous sum, but alternative was paying a far higher price. The lightness of her very soul.

Elodie knelt down and retrieved the key, wiping one sweaty palm and then the other on her skirt. She summited the three steps and stood frozen, key poised at the lock. Was she really doing this? Stealing from her father? No—borrowing. She would return the money someday. And it was part of her inheritance, after all. If she wasn't able to scrape together the money to pay him back, she would tell her sisters, and it would come out of her inheritance. Yes. That would be fair. She wouldn't steal from anyone.

Her hands shook and the key slipped through her fingers, hitting the stone with a ping. She huffed and retrieved it. She could do this. This was Larkhaven, after all. She'd grown up here. It wasn't like she was breaking in.

The house was still as an inhaled breath.

Elodie padded into her father's study, closing the door behind her. His curtains were drawn, leaving only a sliver of daylight visible. She let her eyes adjust to the dimness. The less she touched, the better. Her father kept a cache of spare coin hidden in a box under a floorboard. He had told her, as the eldest, of its location. So she would know where it was, if he should ever pass. *Not so you could steal it to go on a wild goose chase for some mythical creature.* She squeezed her eyes shut and flicked the thought aside. It was money for a rainy day—for an emergency. Well, this was her emergency. She wasn't sure when the idea to take the money had coalesced in her head, only that once it had firmly lodged there, she couldn't deny it.

She knelt down and pulled back the rug, feeling around the smooth floorboards for the notch her father had shown her. There. She dug in her fingernails, pulling up the board, exposing the dark space beneath. A metal box glinted dully within. She maneuvered it out carefully and quietly, setting it on the rug. The lid creaked as she opened it, and she winced, freezing for a moment, holding it still.

She chuckled at herself. She didn't even need to be quiet. There was no one here.

Elodie had broken the law only once—before she and Willum had been engaged, back when she'd been desperately in love with him— the kind of young love that had no patience for reality or common sense. Willum, Bellamy, and Marsaint had gotten the bright idea to steal Mister Verta's prize calf and deposit it in the church, to be discovered at Sunday service. She'd agreed to be their lookout. She hadn't even gone over the fence into Verta's pasture. In the less than ten minutes the boys had been gone, she'd thrown up twice from the sheer nerves. When she'd arrived at church the next morning to see the tile floor of the altar covered in manure, she'd thrown up again. Pepa had thought it was the smell. She'd never told him the truth.

Her lips pressed into a thin line as she counted out ten pieces of silver. It was more money than she'd ever held in her hand, though there was plenty more in the box. She didn't feel nearly as nauseous as she had that night, though her stomach still tumbled like a butter churn. She wasn't that naive girl anymore. Life had changed her into someone else. Something else.

The coins were heavy as she slid them into her belt pouch, though not nearly as heavy as her conscience. Pepa could never know about this. It would break him, to see how desperate his little girl had become.

Elodie replaced the metal box, then the floorboard, then the rug. She pushed to her feet. She'd surely be able to haggle down the price of the book. First offers were always negotiable, especially with a sojourner. It was just a loan. One she'd pay back in full when the spring of good fortune had returned to her life.

She stepped into the hallway. And was greeted by a shadowed form, weapon raised to strike.

Elodie screamed.

The shadow screamed—a high-pitched sound. A familiar sound.

Elodie collapsed against the doorjamb, her hand pressed to her chest as if to keep her pounding heart inside. "Josephine?"

"Elodie?" Josephine lowered the cast-iron pan she had been holding over her head. "What are you doing skulking about in the dark?"

Elodie's mouth went dry. The coins, heavy in her belt-pouch, jingled softly against each other as she moved. She stilled. *Traitors.*

"Elodie?" Josephine repeated.

"What are you doing here? I...figured you'd be at church."

Josephine's hand drifted to her stomach. "I wasn't feeling well. I stayed home."

Elodie's alibi flooded back to her. "Me too." She licked her lips. "I have a terrible headache—that's why I didn't open the curtains."

"But why are you here?"

Why was she here indeed? "I...gave Pepa a tincture of white willow bark and...valerian root...for his arthritis. I was out. So...I thought... I'd see if I could borrow his."

"Did you find it?"

Elodie looked down at her empty hands. "He must have used it all."

"I have some of the white willow bark, if you want that," Josephine offered. Concern was etched across her smooth brow.

"Okay." Elodie couldn't refuse, not without blowing her cover. She followed her sister into the large stone and tile kitchen, where Josephine retrieved a bottle from the shelf. She handed it to Elodie and sagged against the counter.

Elodie frowned. "You said you aren't feeling well, either?"

Josephine waved a hand. "If you have a headache, you should get home and rest."

Elodie feigned a pained look. By the Daughter, she hated lying to

Josephine. She was seized by a sudden urge to tell her sister the truth. Of all her family, Josephine would be the most likely to understand. To be excited by the prospect of adventure and magic. But Josephine also wasn't particularly good at keeping things from their father. She couldn't risk it. "At least tell me what's wrong. Perhaps I can help before I go."

"I just feel nauseous. Like I might vomit at any moment," Josephine admitted.

Tell me about it. Elodie turned to the shelves behind her, rummaging around. She had stocked Larkhaven with remedies over the years. "Peppermint tea." She handed the box to Josephine. "A few times a day. Should help until it passes."

"Don't tell Pepa, okay? You know how he frets over me like I'm made of glass."

"If you promise to do the same?" The only thing worse than lying to her sister was making an unwitting accomplice out of her, but if Pepa knew she'd been in his study, he might get suspicious. Especially because he'd refused to ever take the remedy she'd claimed she was looking for.

"Deal." Josephine gave her a gentle hug. "Now go home and get back in bed! Make Willum wait on you for a change."

Elodie snorted, then pretended to wince. "I won't hold my breath."

Josephine opened her mouth to say something, then seemed to change her mind. She clutched the tea to her chest.

Elodie hesitated. "Jo—you saw the sojourner's wagon, right?"

Josephine straightened. "Why are you asking me about him?"

She searched for an excuse. "I was just curious. I'd heard the decorations on their wagons were sometimes symbolic to the sojourner."

"Oh. Well, I saw it. It was a round, wooden thing painted grass green with a border of red roses."

"Hmm." Elodie chuckled. "Think he has thorns?"

"How would I know?"

Elodie cocked her head at Josephine's forced reply. "Just a bad joke, Jo. Feel better."

"You too."

Elodie glided out the front door, making every effort not to jostle the coins in her pouch. She ducked around back to return the key and then hurried back down the lane. She needed to be back to the flat before service let out.

When she was out of sight of Larkhaven, an elated grin bloomed across her face. She had done it. She had the money to get the book. The map. Despite the weight of her crime and her lies, she felt lighter than she had in weeks. Buoyed by something she'd gone so long without that she almost didn't recognize it any longer. Real, genuine hope.

CHAPTER 11

WOURAUX

*W*ouraux was a town of narrow, winding streets and gravity-defying half-timbered houses. A wall of sandstone hugged the city center, which was crowned by the Alder's fortress sitting high on a hill with a bird's eye view of the lush valley. Elodie had never liked coming here—twice she had gotten lost in the maze of streets and shops. But that was the furthest thing from her mind today. Today, there was nowhere in the world she was more eager to be.

The orphanage was housed in a converted school near the town's southern gate. The building was at least a hundred years old—long and low with rows of leaded windows. Elodie and Agathe parked Maven and the wagon on the shaded street behind the orphanage and retrieved their medical supplies. The squeals and cries of children playing could be heard from the courtyard inside.

Elodie planned to help Agathe for a few hours, before excusing herself to head to the market. She'd thought her story through—if Agathe asked. She was shopping for a present for Pepa's birthday, which was coming up in less than a month. *Let the sojourner's wagon be close*, she prayed. Too long an absence could draw suspicion.

The day passed quickly, filled with a whirlwind of grubby hands and hopeful faces. The children loved Agathe. She was like the grand-mother they'd never had, far warmer and more inviting than their Headmistress.

Elodie fetched remedies for Agathe, cleaned and bandaged cuts and rashes, and handed out pieces of peppermint candy they'd brought for the most cooperative patients. But her thoughts were elsewhere—fixed on the sojourner. And the Wish-Eater. Not to mention the pilfered ten silver pieces weighing her down.

When the flood of patients slowed, Elodie stood and stretched. "I wanted to pop over to the market to pick something up for Pepa."

Agathe looked back, raising a silver eyebrow. "By yourself? If you wait another hour, I'll be done. We could go together."

"That's not necessary. By then, we'll want to be back on the road, to make it home before dark. I'll be fine."

Agathe paused but finally nodded. "You know the way?"

"I do. And if I get turned around, I'll just ask for directions." She forced a smile.

"If you're sure."

"I am." Elodie turned on her heel and slipped out before Agathe could ask any more questions.

Her retreat took her by the open door that led to the nursery. In prior visits, she'd spent hours in that room, singing to the children, rocking them. The sight of those abandoned babes had filled her with longing and fury in turn. That anyone could abandon such an inno-cent... She picked up her pace, hurrying past. Willum had made his thoughts on adoption quite clear. He wasn't raising anyone's child but his.

Elodie felt lighter as she passed from the dark of the orphanage into the afternoon sunshine. She held her face up to it for a moment, letting it warm her. Then she looked left and right, gauging the direc-tion. The market should be to the left. Right?

Elodie only had to ask directions of two kind passersby to find her way to the market. Rows of colorful canopies stretched as far as the eye could see. She swallowed. This could take much longer than she'd anticipated. Better to ask.

She slipped into the crowd of people, making her way toward a plump spice vendor wearing a marriage shawl embroidered with grey vines. "Excuse me."

The woman turned, taking Elodie's measure in a sweeping glance.

"I'm looking for a sojourner passing through town. Is there a particular area of the market where they park their wagons?"

The woman spit on the ground, causing Elodie to jump. "Alder doesn't let those devils in town. You can find them in a camp outside the southern gate."

The southern gate. Back where she'd come. *Great.* Elodie forced a smile, swallowing her criticism of the woman's prejudice. "Thank you kindly."

Elodie trudged back toward the orphanage, trying to find the silver lining. At least she'd asked, rather than wandering the market aimlessly for an hour. At least she wouldn't have to hike to the other side of the city. She'd be able to find Piers and get back to Agathe with plenty of time.

Elodie fought the crowd as she neared the southern gate. It appeared the bulk of people were entering the city this afternoon, not leaving. She was jostled between carts and families, merchants with piles of wares and beggars in rags. She ignored the foot that crushed hers, the elbow that dug into her side, using her thin build to slip between people and make her way forward. At last, she was under the arch of the gate, and the crowd spit her out onto a dusty path that wound through a trampled meadow. Elodie stepped to the side off the path to survey her surroundings. There. To her right, along the curve of the wall—the colors of the sojourner wagons were unmistakable, even shadowed by the stand of tall juniper trees.

Her heart soared. He was here. She could feel it.

She broke into a trot, then quickly realized she was jingling quite conspicuously. She slowed to a fast walk, and before long, she found herself in the sojourner's camp.

If the wagons were arranged in some semblance of order, it wasn't one she could discern. Elodie gawked at the brilliant color and intricate detail—beautiful images formed of both wood and paint. A bright blue wagon with clouds that looked as soft as a lamb's wool, a black wagon with its door painted to resemble the maw of a wolf, ready to gobble you up. Elodie stumbled to a stop to take in one wagon painted with fantastical creatures: a white horse with a horn like a sword and a lion with the wings of an eagle. She shook her head in disbelief, willing her feet to move again. But her eyes lingered on the wagon. Was the Wish-Eater such a beast?

The hairs on the back of her neck rose the farther she traveled into the camp. It was the same feeling she got when she stood close to a campfire but looked into the darkness beyond. The creeping certainty that there was something solid and real lurking just past her sight. If all these people were truly magicians, maybe she didn't even need the book. Maybe some sojourner wise woman could supply a solution to her problem today—

Elodie bumped into something solid.

"Watch where you put those pretty feet, madam," a gravelly voice said. It belonged to a tall man with a red cherry of a nose and hair as black as a raven's feathers. It was plain as day that the man was drunk.

Elodie shied back, scooting sideways. "My apologies. I should have looked where I was going."

He sidled forward, blocking her path, then threw up one arm, caging her against the side of a wagon. His shirt was dirty, the laces missing, exposing the hair matting his chest. Elodie's mouth went dry. The stretch of grass was shielded from view by the tall sides of the wagons. And besides her and this man, it was currently deserted.

"What brings a ripe plum like you all the way out here?" The man reached out to touch one of her curls and she ducked under his arm, freeing herself.

"I'm looking for a sojourner named Piers. Red hair? Freckles?" Her voice was breathless. "He's a good friend. If you could point out his wagon, I'd be much obliged."

His hand closed around her wrist like a shackle and he hauled her back toward him, jerking her arm near out of its socket. "I could be your good friend." He seized her chin, his dark eyes unfocused.

The smell of mead washed over her, sour on his breath. Memories flashed—times Willum had come home stumbling, his hands pawing at her. But Willum had never forced himself on her. At least that line, he'd never crossed.

Her surprised mind was rallying her defenses. *Tell him* no. *Scream, kick, hurt him—*

A deep voice interrupted her spiraling thoughts. "Oy, Claude." A younger man had appeared in the row, blond-haired and hale. "Let the lady go."

The grip on her chin loosened. "We were just gettin' to know each other."

"No one wants to know ya, least of all her," the man said, crossing muscled arms over his chest. "Come on now."

Her attacker—*Claude*—released her arm and she stumbled forward toward the other man, cradling her wrist. The bones ached as if he'd almost snapped them. Her breath came in quick gasps, her legs refusing to function.

The new fellow reached out to steady her, one strong hand catching her arm, another feather-light touch on her hip. "Easy, it's all right. Claude is a good enough fellow except when he drinks. Are you all right?"

Elodie looked at him, a lump in her throat rising with each hitched breath. No, she wasn't all right. Her words wouldn't come, her mind flitted like a hummingbird from the pain in her wrist to the stench of Claude's breath to the horror of what might have happened if this man hadn't appeared. But his blue eyes were kind, despite the scar that pulled on one golden eyebrow, and so she focused on him, willing herself to calm enough to communicate. "Piers."

"You're here to see Piers?" the man asked.

She nodded, hastily wiping away an errant tear.

"Freckled fellow?"

Another nod.

"His wagon isn't far. Come on."

The man spoke the truth—Piers' wagon wasn't far. They threaded one row over and emerged in a clearing filled with a large firepit. A woman was stirring something in a kettle over the fire. And beyond, blessed Daughter, was a green wagon painted with red roses. Elodie's shoulders slumped in relief.

"Thank—" she turned to thank her rescuer, but the man had disappeared. Elodie frowned. He'd been real, right? She shook off the strangeness of it and hurried across the clearing, pounding on Piers' wagon door.

Elodie shied back as the door swung open. Piers was just as she remembered him. Fiery red hair, those eerie golden eyes. Even his clothes were the same. Gaudy purple shirt, red pants tucked into leather boots. The shaggy head of his shepherd dog pushed through his legs, its pink tongue lolling out.

He grinned widely, showing his white teeth. "I know you. The sister of Josephine."

"You remember."

He stepped down from the wagon, looming above her. "How could I forget a girl so young with her...talents? Did she send you after me?"

Elodie pursed her lips. His tone—never mind. She needed to focus on the book. Josephine was safe at home. "Actually, I came for myself."

His eyes lit up. "Ah. I know. I thought you had that hungry look about you. You're here for the book."

"Yes." She breathed. "I'm ready to buy it."

"I'm sorry to say it's already been sold."

Elodie's heart fell into her feet. Sold? At its exorbitant price, she didn't think anyone else would be mad enough to buy it. "Don't fool me."

"I never joke about ten silver. It's gone."

"No." She'd come all of this way. Stolen from her father, lied to Agathe, nearly been attacked by a drunken predator, and now... No. This was not possible. "Another copy? There must be another copy."

"The book had the hand-drawn map. It was one-of-a-kind."

No.

"But—"

"But what?" She latched on to the word like a lifeline in a turbulent sea.

"I may have a drawing of the map. A copy."

Yes! She schooled her features into blankness. She couldn't appear too eager. Now it was time to negotiate. She let a breath pass by. "How much?"

"Ten silver."

She scoffed. "The book was ten silver! You want ten silver for a scribbled copy of *just* the map?"

Piers grinned. "The book was just a delivery device for the map. The map is where the real value lies."

She huffed. "Five silver."

"The price is ten."

Elodie ground her teeth. "Seven."

"Ten. Non-negotiable."

"Everything is negotiable."

"Not this. Do you want your wish or not?"

She glared at him.

He crossed his arms before him, picking at a piece of imaginary food from his perfect teeth with a pinky finger.

Cursed Un-Brother, he had her. He knew how badly she wanted it. She had come all this way. Obviously, she'd pay any price. *Damn it, damn it.* She didn't have the stomach for this anyway, not after what had happened. She was raw and rung out. "Fine. Ten. And I don't know how you sleep at night."

"Oh, I sleep just fine." He disappeared back inside the wagon and returned with a scroll of parchment in hand.

Elodie's eyes alit on the parchment, and a ribbon of glee laced through her. She had done it. She'd acquired the map. She reached for her belt pouch and gasped. She looked down, her hand fumbling along her belt. Her belt pouch—the silver—it was gone.

CHAPTER 12

ROBBED

*E*lodie's hands fluttered uselessly about her belt. It was gone. Gone. The money—her father's money—she had lost it. How? Where? Her mind circled like a wounded bird. Had it fallen from her belt somewhere in the city? On her trek here?

"Elodie?" Piers leaned down to look in her eyes. "Are you all right?"

"I—" She turned back to the narrow path between wagon, then back to Piers. Thinking. Retracing her steps. A featherlight touch on her hip as the blue-eyed man steadied her...realization flared in her bright as the dawn. "I...was robbed."

"Robbed?" Piers recoiled.

"Right here...that man. The man who brought me to you. He's a sojourner," Elodie said, pointing. Heat poured through her, the purifying fire of rage burning her fear away. "He saved me from that other man..." Elodie's mouth opened and closed.

"Surely, you're mistaken. Perhaps it slipped from your belt. Or perhaps you had the misfortune of running across a pickpocket on your way here. We sojourners are honest folk."

Elodie struggled to keep her features calm. The black-haired man who had attacked her hardly seemed like an honest man. "No, it was him. Golden-haired man, blue shirt. Short beard, young, handsome..."

She trailed off as Piers shook his head. Wait. Had the other man even actually attacked her? Or had it been a distraction, a bit of misdirection to send her into the arms of the other man so he could take her money? Her feet took her one step—two—back into the maze of wagons.

Piers spoke. "I know everyone in this camp. And there is no one by that description."

Elodie froze. She may not have been as good at reading people as Sidonie, but she knew a lie when she heard one. Elodie turned to Piers, meeting his strange, gold gaze. "Were you in on it?" she hissed. "Will you get a cut for your part in this little charade?"

"You're wrong. I'm sorry." He shook his head.

Elodie's fingers curled into fists at her side. This wasn't happening. The map was before her, she was here, she had found him. She'd had the money, she was so *close*. She stormed forward on the wings of some invisible madness, lunging for the map in his hand.

Piers, at least a foot taller than her, jerked it away, holding it above his head.

"At least show it to me," she cried, grasping at his arm, trying to haul it down. The man was strong.

"I'm not running a charity," Piers said. "No money, no goods."

"You people robbed me!" Elodie cried, redoubling her efforts to scramble up him to reach the map.

"Is there a problem here?" A voice rumbled behind them. Elodie faltered, rocking back a step.

A huge man stood just feet from them—his black hair and beard braided and threaded with beads.

"This lady is just leaving," Piers said.

Elodie opened her mouth to protest, but two more sojourners appeared from between the wagons, a burly woman with a frying pan and a tall, lanky lad with a hungry look in his eyes.

"My *people* don't take kindly to being accused of misdeeds," Piers said icily. "We've suffered enough prejudice from folk like you." He leaned forward, lowering his voice. "Leave now, and you may not have your coin, but you'll keep your dignity. And your life."

Elodie ground her teeth together, helplessness washing over her like the slap of an icy wave. What could she do? Stay and battle every sojourner in the camp? Demand her money back? Storm their uniform ranks? A lump rose in her throat as the burn of threatened tears stung her eyes.

She straightened her dress and turned to Piers. "I know what you did," she hissed at him.

A cruel smile flashed across his freckled face. "You don't know the half of it." But then it was gone, replaced by the expression of pleasant earnestness he had worn when she had first met him.

Elodie's stomach tightened. What had he meant?

"The lady is to be escorted safely back to the city. No harm will come to her."

The bearded man jerked his head, gesturing that it was time to go.

Elodie stood, her feet stuck as if in quicksand. She couldn't just *leave*. Not without the book. Not without the money.

"Come with me now or chance the way alone," the man barked.

A memory of the black-haired man's foul breath washed over her, and Elodie stumbled forward.

"Oh—Elodie," Piers said.

She turned, and he pressed something into her hand. Two copper coins.

"I sold one of your sister's pitchers. Her cut. I always keep my bargains."

Elodie closed her fingers around the coins. "The Un-Brother take you," she spit at him. It was the only retort she could muster, and it felt pitifully, woefully, inadequate.

THE SOJOURNER SAW her to Wouraux's southern gate safely. On that, they kept their word, at least. As soon as the bearded man vanished back into the crowd, a sob escaped Elodie—a flood of emotion she'd been holding back with every bit of her strength. She broke into a run, the tears flowing freely down her cheeks, the sobs rolling through her in great, wracking waves. The two copper pieces dug into her palm. She wanted nothing more than to hurl them at the nearest wall, but they weren't hers. They were Josephine's.

By the time she reached the alley outside the orphanage, she was a wreck, tears and snot streaming down her face, her lungs barking for air. She sagged against the wall, bending over on herself, desperate to regain her control.

Foolish. Careless. Idiot! She'd stolen from her father and had nothing to show for it. Not the book, not the map, not the money. She'd never find the creature, never get her wish, never be a mother—

"Elodie?" A shadow fell over her. It was Agathe. "Are you all right?"

She wiped her face hastily, unable to stop the flow of tears.

Agathe knelt down, placing a hand on her shoulder. "What happened?"

Elodie just shook her head, her eyes fluttering closed. Some small, desperate part of her wanted to confess it all to Agathe. But it made her sound so mad. She could never tell anyone. But she had to say something. "There was a man—"

Thunder crossed Agathe's lined face. Her hand tightened on Elodie's shoulder. "Did he hurt you?"

Elodie shook her head. "I—got away."

Agathe seized Elodie, pulling her into an embrace. "Thank the Daughter. Good for you, child. You're stronger than you know."

The tears redoubled. *No,* she wanted to say. *I'm not strong. Or brave. They stole from me and I just let them. I just walked away.*

"Let's go." Agathe hauled Elodie to her feet with surprising strength. "My work is done. Let's be gone from this place."

ELODIE'S TEARS finally dried about thirty minutes out of Wouraux. She felt strangely hollow. Empty. Agathe, blessedly, said nothing. They rode in silence, but for the gentle wuffing of Maven's breath, the soft impact of his hooves on the hard-packed dirt.

Even before twilight began to fall, Elodie felt only blackness around her. The weight of the world, pushing in on her. Brick by brick, stone by stone, a cairn of disappointments, blocking out the sun.

The lights of Lunesburg winked in the twilight before them, and Elodie nearly leapt from the seat. "Stop."

Agathe turned to her.

"Stop!" Elodie cried.

Agathe hauled back on the reins. "Why? What is it?"

Elodie scrambled down from the wagon. "I just…need a minute. Some more air. I'll walk the rest of the way."

"It's getting dark—" Agathe protested, but Elodie was already angling off the road into the underbrush.

"I'll be fine."

Elodie stumbled through the trees, clutching her shawl tightly around her shoulders. Dry branches grasped at her skirt, tangling it around her feet. She stumbled but managed to catch herself, drawing to a stop.

Around her, the trees were quiet, waiting in the dark. But for whatever reason, the dark of the night didn't scare her now. It was nothing compared to the darkness filling her up inside. Her pulse pounded in her ears, and she willed it to slow, let her eyes adjust. She was close to town and she'd been over every inch of these woods with the other village children when she was young. She wasn't lost.

She started forward, moving at a more deliberate pace. It wasn't long before she found a narrow trail that she recognized—it led from the main road down to Elliason's Lake. She couldn't explain the force that propelled her forward. She just knew that movement was good. When she stopped, it all caught up with her. The day behind her. The sorry excuse for a life ahead.

As she broke out of the bushes onto the shore of the lake, the serenity of the scene brought a wave of fresh tears to her eyes. How many warm summer nights had she spent here with Willum before his accident? Drinking in the nectar of his kisses, the honey of his compliments? She'd loved him for his boldness, and the sunshine of his smile, but most of all, she'd loved how he'd made her feel. More alive than she'd ever thought possible. She'd felt like summer when he was near. He'd made her blossom.

Those feelings were distant memories now, all the more painful for her awareness of their absence. She didn't know how to bloom on her own. A baby was the solution, she'd been sure of it. But look where that dream had gotten her.

She couldn't do it anymore—pretend around this emptiness. She was so gods damn tired of pretending. Lying to herself that the next month would be better. It was *never* better. It was only worse. Willum was worse. His pain. His drinking. Their marriage—a joke. She looked for reasons to avoid his touch most days. Her business? Who was she kidding? She was barely scraping together enough coppers to keep them fed. And all around her, families grew, bellies grew... She couldn't take it anymore. Couldn't face who she'd become. To her ears, the happy babble of a baby sounded like disappointment. A child's laughter filled her with a kind of impotent fury. What kind of person couldn't stand the laughter of children?

What would it take to make these feelings stop? She looked down in surprise as the cool water at the lake's edge numbed her feet. She took another step in. She'd do anything to make them stop.

CHAPTER 13

ELLIASON'S LAKE

Somehow, Sebastian had ended up on a date. He still couldn't quite figure out how that had happened. Talia strode next to him, her hands wrapped securely around his proffered elbow.

"I think I shall have to walk till dawn to burn off that delicious meal." Talia groaned, one hand resting on her stomach.

Sebastian chuckled. "We probably could have done without the chocolate cake."

"Or the second bottle of wine." Talia's eyes sparkled.

"Shall I take you home?"

"No, let's keep walking. It's such a nice night." Talia briefly rested her head on his shoulder, though it was at an awkward angle, as she was as tall as he.

They passed through the end of town on one of the little trails that crisscrossed the fields surrounding Lunesburg. Eventually, this one would fork—the right leading back to the main road, the left curving down to Elliason's Lake.

It had started innocently enough. Dion and Delphine had invited them to dinner at the tavern, an invitation which Sebastian had, after some debating, accepted. Like Delphine had said, there was nothing wrong with being Talia's friend. She was a pleasant enough person, even if he didn't have romantic feelings for her.

And then Delphine had pled illness, and Dion had stayed home to watch over her. It had been a ruse, Sebastian was sure of it. Designed to bring Talia and him together over dinner. He heaved a sigh.

"What was that for?"

"What?" Sebastian asked.

"That long-suffering sigh."

He paused. Finally, he admitted, "I was wondering if Delphine's illness was perhaps overblown to bring the two of us together tonight."

Talia laughed, and a bird startled out of the branches to their left. "You're most certainly right."

Suspicion bloomed. "Did the two of you plan this?"

"Was dinner with me so terrible?" The question was light, but he heard the weight hidden there.

"Answer the question, Talia," he said as gently as he could.

"No, we didn't plan it. But I confess I may have set it in motion inadvertently. I asked Delphine for advice on how to get you to dinner. I think she might have concocted the rest."

"Why not just ask me?"

"Would you have said *yes?*" she challenged, meeting his eyes.

Silence.

She snorted. "I thought not. Though I can't say I understand your hesitation, Sebastian. I'm not so unpleasant to look at. Such terrible company."

"Of course not."

"Didn't... Did you not have a nice time this evening?"

And that was the thing. He *had* enjoyed their dinner. There'd been plentiful conversation, and the time had passed quickly, filled with good food and even laughter. But...he felt nothing for her. His heart belonged wholeheartedly to another, his thoughts always with her. "I did," he finally admitted.

"Yet you hold yourself apart, even now. Why, Sebastian? Was your heart broken? Is it...perhaps..." She hesitated, her voice a whisper. "Is it not the company of women you seek?"

He jerked his head at her. "It's not that." A man couldn't remain a bachelor without it meaning something more?

"I would not judge—"

"It's *not* that." He ground his teeth. They'd reached the fork in the road, and he stopped. "Perhaps we should return."

"Do you always run from honest conversation?" She faced him, her expression fierce and bold. She was unlike any other woman he'd met. So unlike Elodie.

"Do you always assume you have the right to honest answers? To someone else's truth?"

She looked down, chastised.

Damn it. He'd been too hard on her. He blew out a breath. "I'm sorry. I'm just...a private person."

"You're right." She shook her head. "I pried too hard. I just... The reading."

"Those silly cards?"

She looked up, at the swirl of stars above them. "I'm going to speak plainly. I like you, Sebastian, and I think you could like me, if you gave yourself a chance. If you stepped out of whatever cage is holding you immobile."

"Two dinners and you think you're an expert on Sebastian Beringer?"

"Tell me I'm wrong, then."

His voice was hoarse. "You presume I hold the key."

She took his hand, searching his eyes. Her fingers were icy, but firm. "Then let me help you find it."

Sebastian swallowed, considering her offer. Perhaps it was time... to try. To try to move on. Perhaps another love—the comfort of a body, All-father, it had been *so* long... And Talia was beautiful, intelligent—

The breeze tousled his hair, bearing the sound of sobbing. He looked up in alarm. "Do you hear that?"

Talia nodded. "Someone's crying."

"The lake?"

Another nod.

"Do you think they're all right?"

"Maybe they want to be left alone—"

"But they could be hurt or need help." Sebastian tugged Talia forward down the trail. Relief flooded him. Purpose. He didn't have to decide anything now.

The trail dropped them onto a wide, curving lakeshore, the stretch of the lake cool and quiet before them. A half-moon hung bright in the sky, illuminating a figure standing by the water. Stepping *into* the water.

"What's she doing?" Talia asked. For it did appear to be a woman.

"I don't know." Unease settled into his stomach in a small, hard pit. Something was wrong. "Come on."

They hurried toward the figure. "Miss?" he called. "Are you all—" He came up short as he saw the golden curls. The dainty nose, reddened from crying. Those blue, blue eyes...

"Elodie." Talia's voice was flat.

Sebastian turned to Talia, his pulse roaring in his ears. Something was wrong with Elodie. "She's my friend, I'd like to talk to her...alone. Would you be all right to walk back to town on your own?"

Talia's eyes widened at the dismissal. She looked from him to Elodie, who stood to her ankles in the lake, regarding them warily. "Elodie again?" she hissed.

Her words stole the breath from his lungs. He looked up to meet Talia's eyes and he found them shrewd, calculating. She saw too much.

"I don't know what you mean."

"I think you do," she said softly. "I think it's all becoming very clear."

She knew. Un-Brother take him, *she knew*. And there was no telling what she would do with the information. "Talia—"

"It's fine." Then she spun on her heel and stalked into the night. He should follow—make sure she didn't do anything rash—but *Elodie*. He turned and the sight of her captured him wholly. She needed his help.

"Elodie, are you all right?" Sebastian approached warily, as if she were a wild animal. What was going on? What was wrong? Elodie was normally so composed, so *strong*, something awful must have happened for her to be so distraught.

She looked at him, tears shining in her eyes, on the apples of her cheeks. She shook her head. "Everything's a mess."

His heart seized as he held out a hand to her. "It's okay. Why don't you come out of the lake? You'll catch a cold." Was it possible to feel the pain of another, to take it upon yourself somehow? Because the sight of Elodie like this ached in his chest like a physical thing.

She looked down at where her dress pooled in the shallow water. A sob released, but she nodded. She turned and put her hand in his. A surge of energy zinged up his arm at her touch, and his breath caught in his throat as she stepped in close and buried her face in his shirt, wrapping her arms around his waist.

"Hush," he murmured as he gingerly embraced her small frame. He'd never been this close to her, he probably shouldn't be even now, but it was so clear she needed comfort. He couldn't refuse her anything, let alone this. "It's all right," he said as she sobbed. He rested his chin gently atop her head and closed his eyes. Let each sense revel in the nearness of her. The *rightness* of her. Elodie smelled of rosemary and moonlight and campfire. She fit in his arms in a way no one ever had before. Just as he'd known she would.

Elodie jerked back, and he released her, already hating the space between them. She wiped her face with the heels of her hands. "I'm so sorry, I—"

"It's all right. Do you want to sit down?" He nodded toward a downed log that lined the lakeshore.

They made their way to the log, Elodie's skirts swishing in the sand, her slippers squelching. She hadn't even taken her shoes off. She sniffed loudly, and he handed her a handkerchief. She gave a small smile before blowing her nose loudly. She folded it. "I'll wash this for you."

Sebastian let out a surprised laugh. Only Elodie, mid-breakdown, would be concerned with the propriety of laundering someone's property. "Keep it."

Elodie was looking down at her hands, turning the handkerchief in a little circle—one edge, then the next. "It looks like I interrupted a second date. I'm sorry."

"Please stop apologizing," he said. "You didn't interrupt anything. I just care that you're all right. Are you?"

She shook her head. "No, I don't think I am."

"Do you want to talk about it?" He longed to tell her that everything would be all right. That he would help her—whatever it took to dry her tears, to solve her woes, he would do it. Anything. But he didn't want to spook her.

Another shake of her head.

All right. He didn't want to pry, didn't want her to share if she wasn't ready. Perhaps he could take her mind off her sorrows in the meantime. Sebastian looked up at the velvet expanse of stars. "Do you remember coming here as a kid?"

"Of course." She paused. "I can't believe Headmaster Ristil let us play all afternoon under the guise of learning about nature."

"I think maybe there was something to it," Sebastian said. "I recall being much better behaved the week or two after one of those trips. And more endeared to him as well."

"We thought we were tricking him, when all this time *he* was the master." She shook her head, letting out a hiccup. "I haven't thought about those trips in years."

"I seem to recall you getting thrown in the lake on more than one occasion."

She was quiet for a moment, then shook her head. "Willum thought it was the funniest thing in the world to toss me in fully clothed."

"At least you got him back. Didn't he get a mouthful of mud?"

A tiny curve of a smile. "Yes. Yes, he did. I believe that was the last time I ended up in the lake."

"Until today?"

Her smile faltered.

Sebastian asked as gently as possible, "What were you doing?"

"I don't know." She took the handkerchief and blew her nose again.

Another moment passed before she spoke. "Remember floating on your back, gazing at the sky—how the world would go still around you?"

"I do."

"Maybe... I wanted to feel that way again. For a moment. I wanted everything to be quiet." She still hadn't looked at him. "That sounds crazy."

"It doesn't. I thought...I worried...maybe you were..." He trailed off. He knew it wasn't his place to ask her such intimate questions. But if there was *any* chance that she was so filled with sorrow that she was contemplating ending her own life...he had to know. Love was asking the hard question. And staying for the hard answer.

She did look at him then, her eyes red-rimmed, her face earnest. "Sometimes I think that would be easier. I'm just...tired of disappointments. I'm so tired of it all. Some days I want to lie down and never wake up."

"Don't say that," he breathed. "What can I do to help?"

Elodie gave him a sad smile. "Oh, Sebastian. Only you would ask that. There's nothing you can do. There's nothing anyone can do. That's the problem."

Seeing her like this was torture. "I know what it feels like. Wanting to lay down that burden. The wanting. The wishing. Some days, it feels too heavy to bear."

"You do?"

"Of course I do. You're not alone."

She let out a soft, "Hmm."

"What?"

"That actually does help."

They sat for a moment, looking into the night. Elodie shivered, and he took off his coat and settled it around her shoulders. He was warmed enough by her compliment.

"I tried to do something." She pulled the jacket tighter around her.

"What do you mean?"

She closed her eyes, shaking her head. "The book, that stupid book." She hit her forehead with the heel of her hand, groaning. "I just couldn't get it out of my head. The sojourner's story."

Realization dawned. "The Wish-Eater."

"I've tried everything. Everyone says to have faith, and I thought, maybe this was the All-father's way of providing me a path. Something fantastical that defies explanation and rational thought, something where all you have to go on is faith. I thought, maybe that's what He wanted from me. So I went to Wouraux, to buy the book."

"You saw him? The sojourner?" Sebastian's skin crawled. There was something off about that man. Sebastian's voice was low. "Did he hurt you?"

"He didn't get a chance. By the time I got to his wagon, I'd already been robbed and attacked." Her voice was strangled. "And he didn't even have the book. He'd already sold it." Fresh tears slid down her face. "He offered to sell me a copy of the map, but I had no money..." She brushed away the tears. "Now that I've thought about it, I doubt that piece of paper was even real. He would sell a lump of coal and say it's a diamond."

Sebastian's fingers tightened on the log, a splinter digging into his hand. *That bastard. That no good, thieving bastard.* "I'll kill him."

Elodie recoiled, her eyes wide. "Sebastian—"

"I knew the man was no good when he rolled into this town. I didn't like the way he looked at Josephine, and he—"

"Wait, what did you say?" Elodie sat up straight.

"The man was no good."

"About Josephine."

Sebastian gave a little shake. "I don't know, he just was far too friendly with her. It made my skin crawl."

Elodie frowned, then shook her head. "He said something... Never mind. Sebastian, don't do anything, all right? The man is a leech, but I'm fine."

"You're not fine, Elodie, you're walking into a lake in the middle of the night fully clothed! He did this to you!"

She put a hand on his shoulder. "He didn't. I mean, inadvertently, but..." The hand dropped, and he mourned its absence. She ran her hands through her hair. "I'm just so brittle right now, you know? I feel as thin as spring ice. Any weight, and I snap. I'm working on it, but... some days are worse than others. Today was a bad day." Another shiver wracked through her.

"It pains me to see you like this," he admitted.

"It's not my favorite, either." She let out a little chuckle. "Come on. I shouldn't keep you any longer. And I'm freezing, even with your coat."

They started back toward the trail. "I won't tell anyone, you know," he said. "About any of this."

"I know. That's why I told you."

"If you found the book somehow...would it make you feel better?"

"I'm swearing off the book," Elodie said. "Thinking about it has brought me no end of trouble."

But her words were strained. He could hear the longing in them, even now. And so he resolved himself. She thought there was nothing anyone could do. But there was. He could find that book for her. If it was the last thing he did.

CHAPTER 14

SATURDAY SUPPER

One week passed and then another. Willum found a week-long job rebuilding part of the barn on Mister Phillippe's farm, and they ate chicken and eggs for the first time in months. The work was hard, and Willum came home stiff and exhausted every day, but it raised his spirits far more than hanging around the tiny flat or drinking away his nights and their coin with Bellamy and Marsaint.

When Willum was gone during the day, Elodie did little more than sit and sleep. There was no one to pretend to, to placate with smiles and assurances. She could be herself, could feel the gaping hole within her that yawned bigger with each month that passed. What was it about a wound that fascinated a person? She couldn't help but poke it, to feel the pain, to remind herself that it was still there. Of the wrongness of it. Even when it started to heal, the urge remained to pick at the scab, to bare it to the air once again. Not that this was a wound that would ever truly heal.

When Willum was home in the evening, Elodie roused her wounded soul enough to cook and carry on passable conversation. She could never tell Willum the truth of what had happened in Wouraux, of her obsession with the story of the Wish-Eater. He wouldn't understand. Not like Sebastian had. Willum had inherited some of his parents' superstition when it came to magic; he'd likely crow that the sojourner had put a spell on her. And perhaps he had.

As the days ticked on, Elodie resolved that there would be no more thoughts of that cursed book. Perhaps her certainty about it hadn't been sent by the All-father at all, but by the Un-Brother. Her quest for the book had taken her down a road filled with darkness. She was fortunate she'd escaped with no worse than sliced purse strings. Someday, she would repay her father for the ten silver she had taken. She would make it right.

It was another week before glimmers of hope began to poke through the fog of her sadness like shoots of green through spring snow melt. Elodie diligently placed the drops of the elk antler velvet in Willum's cider each night. She went through one entire bottle, and Agathe gave her a second with an approving nod. A flash of optimism buoyed her—something she hadn't felt since before the wretched mess with the Wish-Eater. Agathe was the best healer in Astria. Her remedies had prevailed in many a hopeless case. Elodie had witnessed those miracles with her own eyes. Why not her?

So one bright Saturday morning, when Willum nuzzled at her, she turned toward him, rather than finding an excuse to slip from the bed. A lock of his hair had fallen over his forehead, and she reached out and brushed it back.

He took one of her blonde curls around his index finger, pulling it gently toward him until it slipped from his grip and bounced back. He used to play with her hair all of the time, before his accident. He used to find every excuse to touch her—her elbow, the small of her back, her chin. And she'd been the same—like each couldn't quite believe the other was real. Elodie ran her fingertips along the stubble of his jaw. She missed all those little touches. But it wasn't just his fault. She'd pulled back too.

Willum's eyes closed as she ran her fingers up his neck and around the shell of his ear. A growl of approval rumbled deep in his chest.

A shiver of desire went through her, settling low and warm in her core.

Willum captured her hand in his calloused fingers as his eyes, as dark as night, snapped open. Elodie's breath caught as she regarded the heat kindled in Willum's gaze. He pulled her hand to his mouth, kissing her palm, her wrist. "I know," he said slowly, kissing his way down her wrist toward her elbow, "that the man I am now is not the man you dreamed of."

"Willum—" she started to protest.

"Let me finish." His voice was thick with emotion. "But you have always been the woman I dreamed of. And you always will be."

Elodie pressed her lips to Willum's before the tears could come. *This.* This was why she stayed, through the fights, and the drinking, and the black moods and grey disappointments. When no one else understood. When they told her she could be better off cleaved or alone. Because this man deserved her faith. Because she still had hope. Their marriage—this family—it was worth fighting for.

Willum captured her face in his hands, his tongue tangling with hers in an urgent, breathless kiss. She pressed against him, her own hands roving over the muscles of his back, her fingers threading into his hair.

When his grasp found the sensitive peak of her breast beneath the cotton of her nightgown, a gasp escaped her, and she arched into his touch. He was hard against her thigh and she thought, not for the first time, how grateful she was that the accident had not taken this from them. Not completely. She ached for him—longed for him to fill her with the sweet heat that would wash away their worries on a powerful tide.

His other hand trailed up her thigh and parted her legs, exploring her tender nerve endings with a practiced ease. His massaging thumb sent a lightning bolt of pleasure shooting through her, and for a few breathy moments, she let him explore her, let his fingers send her higher and higher.

When heated impatience got the better of her, Elodie rolled atop Willum, her knees wide, her palms braced on the planes of his chest. His big hands encircled her waist and angled her body to bury his shaft in the slick, yielding heart of her. She gazed down upon him and as she felt the exquisite fullness of him, another face flashed before her.

Sebastian's face.

With a panicked sweep, Elodie banished the thought from her mind, tipping forward to bury her shock in the shadow of Willum's collarbone.

No, that wasn't what she wanted. *This* was what she wanted. Her husband. A baby—Willum's and hers. The heat building within her. So Elodie cleared the image and buried it deep, deep enough, she hoped, to never find it again.

AFTER THE MORNING they'd had, it didn't take much for Elodie to convince Willum to attend Saturday supper at Larkhaven.

"I can't believe you talked me into this," Willum rumbled as they approached her father's manor. His uneven gate slowed, then stopped. "Your family hates me. We'll quarrel."

"They don't hate you." Elodie turned toward Willum. "And that was months ago. Things are different now. You've been working, things are good, right?" While Willum and her father had once been friendly, their relationship had deteriorated as Willum had become more interested in the bottom of his flagon than his own wife. These days, their uneasy relationship consisted of Pepa's thinly-veiled disapproval and Willum's defensive hostility, marked by occasional shouting matches, the most recent of which had occurred last October.

Willum looked down and ran an idle hand through her curls. There was tension around his eyes, which betrayed the pain he was in that afternoon. But he was trying. For her. "Yes, things have been good. That's why we shouldn't ruin it."

"You know how much my family means to me."

Willum inclined his head with a sigh. "Lead the way."

Elodie threaded her arm through his. "Besides, you always have a good time talking to Hugh and Josephine, don't you?"

"They are both pleasant, yes," Willum admitted before letting out a chuckle. "I notice you said nothing about Sidonie."

Elodie swatted at him. "Sidonie is...*Sidonie*." Elodie prayed Sidonie would hold her tongue this evening. Her sister's fire was legendary.

But that fire was dimmed today. As Sidonie opened the door, Elodie saw that dark bags shadowed her sister's eyes, though the baby on her hip was cherubic and giggling.

She gave Elodie a quick hug, and Elodie tried to catch Willum's eye, but he was intent upon the whiskey bottle that was visible in Pepa's hand in the back room.

"Go on," she said, shooing him forward.

"May I hold her?" Elodie asked and Sidonie handed over Chantall. Elodie gave her niece a kiss on her pudgy cheek, breathing in the fresh scent of her. "Her hair is already so curly," Elodie remarked, brushing at the locks on Chantall's smooth head.

Sidonie nodded. "She's a Ruelle, all right."

"Where's everyone else?"

"The garden."

"Shall we join them?" Elodie asked Chantall in the exaggerated voice that all adults inexplicably used to speak to babies.

Chantall cooed her reply, a bright, drooling smile crossing her face.

"How is she sleeping?" Elodie asked.

"Fairly well, actually," Sidonie replied. "I've only been getting up once to feed her."

Elodie stopped at the door to the backyard, facing her sister. "That's good. And you're... doing all right?"

Sidonie's eyes fluttered shut for a moment, but when they opened, some of her usual sharpness was back. "It's just a lot...with two. There's never a moment to breathe."

"Hugh is helping?" Elodie looked to where Hugh was running through the garden with Rolo on his shoulders

"Hugh is a saint. If I had the energy, I'd marry that man all over again."

Elodie bounced Chantall on her hip. "You'll let me know if I can help?"

"Of course. But don't worry about me. It's her we need to worry about."

"Who?"

"Josephine," Sidonie said with exasperation, nodding her head to where their younger sister sat on the bench.

"Why do you say that?"

Chantall let out a cry, twisting in Elodie's arms.

"She's hungry," Sidonie said, retrieving the baby from Elodie's hip. Her voice lowered. "See for yourself."

Elodie hid her frown and took the seat on the bench next to her sister. Josephine didn't turn, her gaze fixed vacantly at a point before her. Her long hair, normally braided in some intricate fashion, was pulled back into a messy bun.

"Afternoon, Jo." Elodie threaded her elbow through her sister's. "Are you all right?"

Josephine looked at her sharply. "What do you mean?"

"You don't look like yourself."

"I'm fine," Josephine snapped, pulling her arm back. "Just feeling a touch unwell."

Still? Elodie reached a hand out to touch her sister's forehead, but she shied away. Sidonie was right. Something was definitely off. "Should I have Agathe pay you a visit?"

"I'm *fine*," Josephine said. "I need to go check the duck." She stood and hurried into the kitchen, leaving Elodie sitting, open-mouthed. Was some sort of illness going around? She would ask Agathe tomorrow.

Elodie found Willum and her father in the study. She gave Pepa a kiss on the cheek. It took all of her might not to look at the floorboard where she knew his money was hidden. The trove that she had stolen from, just weeks ago. Guilt roiled in her gut. She would repay him. If it was the last thing she did.

"It's a nice night. I think we'll eat in the garden," Pepa said. "Would you see if your sister needs help?"

But Elodie was only halfway to the kitchen when Josephine emerged with a steaming dish, her hands covered with two thick mittens.

"We've got duck!" Pepa called.

Elodie retrieved a bowl of peas and pearl onions and a basket of bread from the kitchen and carried it all to the garden. Willum had been put to work setting the table while Hugh fetched the wine, and soon the table was filled with food and family.

Pepa said the prayer to the All-father and Elodie found herself saying *Amen* with real feeling. She'd been so focused lately on what was missing from her life that she'd taken little time to be grateful for all the good still present. Truly, there was little more a person needed than family and food.

On a whim, she leaned over and pecked Willum on his cheek, his stubble prickling her lips.

"What was that for?" he asked, looking at her in surprise. But there was a smile on his lips and an ease to the tension that she hadn't seen in weeks. The lines on his face were lighter, easier.

"Just because," she replied.

He leaned in and kissed the top of her head.

Food was ladled onto plates and wine was poured. Conversation was pleasant. If not for Josephine's unnatural quiet, it would have been a perfect evening.

"Will you be at market day tomorrow?" Pepa asked Elodie around a bite of bread slathered in butter. The Lunesberg market began when the summer days grew long and ran through the fall solstice. Agathe always had a booth and the last two years, Elodie had joined her every Sunday to sell her herbs.

"I will," Elodie said. "But you know who should have a booth? Josephine."

Josephine's head jerked up at that. She had hardly taken two bites —spending most of the meal pushing her food around on her plate.

Sidonie added, "All of my friends rave about her pottery when they come over. She could sell a lot if you came out of the dark ages."

"I'm not having this argument with you girls again," Pepa said.

"Booth rental is expensive. And Josephine is not in business. It's not proper. It's a hobby."

Josephine's eyes fell back to her plate.

Elodie almost mentioned that the sojourner had already sold one of Josephine's pitchers, but she held her tongue. She'd tell her sister privately, as Pepa didn't know of that particular little deal. "Pepa, women can have businesses these days," Elodie said. "Look at Agathe."

"She's a spinster. Hardly a role model for Josephine."

"Actually," Elodie said, "Agathe was married once. She's a widow, not a spinster."

They all looked up at that. "Really?" Sidonie leaned in.

"But that's not the point. Being a wife isn't a woman's sole value in life." Elodie continued, emboldened by the cider and her frustration with Pepa's stubbornness. "I'm selling my herbs and making a fair bit of money."

Willum's face darkened a bit at that, and Elodie kicked herself. Willum saw her efforts as a sign of his failure as a provider.

Much to Elodie's surprise, it was Hugh who chimed in next. "Times are changing, Frederick. The merchant's house has started doing business with a number of female entrepreneurs in the last few years. Perhaps Elodie could put out some of Josephine's wares at Agathe's booth. That should allay your concerns over cost."

Her father looked thoughtful at that.

Elodie could have kissed her brother-in-law. "Oh, come, Pepa. Hugh's idea is a good one and you know it."

He groaned. "Maybe it's because I'm getting old, but I can't resist when all three of you gang up on me. And Hugh, I didn't peg you for a turncoat."

Hugh smiled around a sip of wine. "These Ruelle women can be very persuasive, as you no doubt know."

"So...it's all right?" Elodie asked.

Pepa nodded. "You can put out a few of Josephine's plates at your booth."

"Really?" Josephine's fork dropped to her plate with a clatter, some of the brightness returning to her eyes. But she had been silent through the exchange, and even now, her reaction was a shadow of what Elodie had expected. Something was definitely wrong.

CHAPTER 15

DISCOVERED

The smell of pork and spices filled the flat. Elodie found herself humming as she fried the sausages over the hearth. Market day had been a smashing success. Agathe's booth had been flooded with customers—Elodie had sold out of most of her sachets of herbs and Josephine's pottery had disappeared by the lunch hour. And, in the best news yet, her in-laws, Eugenia and Corbitt, who had come to town for the market, had been too worn out to stay for dinner. It was enough to make her positively giddy.

Willum sat at the table, idly flipping over a deck of cards. The glass by his hand was filled with whiskey. It wasn't his first. His teeth were clenched, the fine muscles of his jaw feathering. His pain was overwhelming tonight, likely from the exertions of walking about with his parents all day.

A hundred things to say flitted through her mind. Did he want some herbs for the pain? Did he want her to help him stretch or massage it? It wouldn't do him any good to sit idle—brooding. But she'd said all those things before, and each of her suggestions had met the same snipping retort. *I'm fine.* When the pain was on him, it was all Willum seemed to say. And it was the one thing that she was certain was a lie.

Elodie set a bowl of greens dressed with oil and vinegar on the table and went to stand at his side. She caressed her hand softly across his brow, and he leaned into her touch, just a little. "Is there anything I can do?" It was, she had discovered, the only safe question.

Willum shook his head with a heavy sigh. But he turned, pulling her into him, burying his face in her bosom, his strong hands wrapped around her as if she were the only thing anchoring him to this life. Her heart fluttered as memories surfaced. Before the accident. Before her barren womb. When they were young and carefree and wild about each other. When all she'd wanted was to give herself to him on the grass beneath a wide open sky.

She rubbed his back until he released her, reluctantly. "My sweet summer, you smell good," he murmured. He looked up at her, his eyes a touch unfocused, but still that deep brown that went on forever. Still her Willum. When he looked at her like that, he still took her breath away.

"It's the herbs." Elodie returned to the hearth to turn the sausages. "I think I'll always smell like them. Not that I mind."

Willum was quiet and she winced to herself. She wished mention of her business wasn't such a delicate topic. She longed to talk with Willum about it, like she could with Sebastian. She shook away the thought. Sebastian was popping into her mind far too much as of late.

"Did you notice anything off about Josephine the last few days?" she asked, searching for a safe topic. "She seemed quiet at the booth."

"Hmm."

She looked back and saw that Willum was considering, his features scrunched as they did when he tried to concentrate through the pain. It was the great irony of his accident. It affected him physically, keeping him from such work. But the pain lanced through his mind, too, scattering all coherent thought, making it impossible for him to hold down a more intellectual job.

"She did seem quiet yesterday at dinner, now that you mention it. And today."

"Right? I would have expected her to be over the moon about having her pottery at the market today. She barely made a peep."

"Maybe she's lovesick," Willum suggested, flipping another card. He wasn't playing anything that she could tell.

Elodie turned, her eyebrows flying up. "Why would you say that?"

He shrugged. "When a woman's melancholy, it's usually over a man."

She snorted. "You might be surprised to find there's quite a lot that goes on in our minds that doesn't involve men." But...in this case... perhaps Willum had a point. "Who could it be?"

"She was cozying up to that sojourner at Baumai, and he was slicker than a greased pig. Maybe she's mooning over him."

The mention of the sojourner chilled her blood. "That was over a month ago," Elodie forced out. "Could she have fallen so hard that she'd still be beside herself?"

"*You* did." Willum looked up at her with a crooked grin.

She laughed and shook her spoon at him. "You were always trouble, Willum Mercer."

His smile faded like a cloud passing over the sun. "Now I'm just trouble of a different kind."

One of the sausages popped and she turned back to the hearth, grateful for the distraction. She didn't know what to say.

"Maybe he put a spell on her."

Elodie suppressed a shiver. "That's just superstitious nonsense. Sojourners don't use their magic on innocent bystanders."

"What's to stop them?"

"Their magic is their livelihood. They wouldn't waste spells that they could sell." But when Elodie thought of Piers' eerie golden eyes... and the way her coin purse had disappeared from her hip like magic... She wasn't so sure. She cleared her throat. "Let's just agree to keep an eye on her? And no more talk of spells and magic."

Willum nodded. "That I can agree to."

When dinner was finished cooking, she put a plate on the table before him, retrieving his empty glass. "Refill?" she asked, knowing the answer.

Willum dug into the food, and she refilled the glass, her back to him. The second bottle of elk antler velvet was almost gone—she'd given it to him faithfully every night. Every night he'd come home, that was. She pulled off the stopper and dropped two drops into the whiskey before hurrying the bottle away in the drawer, under some towels.

"What was that?" Willum's voice behind her was cold.

She froze, her heart leaping into her chest. She did her best to school her features into nonchalance and turned. He was half-standing, his big hands resting on the table, his food forgotten.

"What was what?"

"You just put something in my drink. What was it?" He stood, coming around the table until he stood before her. Loomed above her. "Show me."

She swallowed. "It's nothing. Just something Agathe gave me—"

"Show me!" he barked, making her flinch.

He held out his hand, and she turned slowly, pulling the vial out of its hiding place in the drawer. "Willum, calm down, I—"

He inspected the bottle, glaring at it. "I told you I didn't want any of her concoctions. What's it for?"

She licked her lips. Her voice sounded small, distant in her ears. She hated it when he got like this. When she could see the flush of alcohol on his face. He wasn't himself when he was like this. "It's supposed to help with...making a baby."

"Making a baby?" His mouth opened and closed, his jaw working. When he spoke again, his voice was low. "Do you really think so little of me? It's not enough that I can't provide for you, that I'm a cripple. But how do you think it makes me feel that I can't even impregnate my own wife? That she thinks she needs some potion to make me a man?"

"That's not—"

"Maybe you should just fuck the bottle then!" He hurled the vial against the wall, shattering it in an explosion of glass shards. Elodie stood as stiff as a board, closing her eyes against the brunt of his anger.

"Is that what you want?"

She forced herself to open her eyes, to face him. He was inches from her, his chest heaving, his fists balled. He seemed to be waiting. For an answer? Her addled mind filed through his last nonsensical comment, and she forced out, "No, that's not what I want."

"Then what *do* you want?" He gazed down at her balefully. "Do you want me to cleave you? So you can take another husband, be free from the shackles of this marriage?"

Her hand shot out, connecting with his cheek before she knew what she was doing. She had slapped him.

He recoiled, as shocked as she.

"You know what I want?" Elodie sidled away from the countertop —from him—giving her space to breathe. "I want you to try."

"What?" Willum blinked.

This was dangerous territory. But she was tired of dancing through the minefield of his hurt feelings and insecurities, cowering in the face of cruelty. They couldn't go on like this. "You've given up. You won't try any of the suggestions or remedies Agathe has for your condition. You won't seek help from doctors. You know there's a doctor in Wouraux who could look at you. But you won't even try! The only place you're looking is at the bottom of a bottle, and there's no cure there."

"There's no cure anywhere," Willum shot back. "You say I've given up, but you refuse to face reality. There is no cure. None of those things will work."

"But you don't know unless you try—"

"I know! What's the use getting my hope up, and yours, when we're only going to be disappointed?"

"You don't even go to church anymore," she said. "Fine, if you don't believe in herbs or medicine. But miracles still happen. You don't—"

"Why would I have faith in a god who did this to me?" he roared, taking a limping step toward her. "How could I ever believe a damn thing said about Him? All I know is that the All-father is a cruel bastard, and I hate Him."

She shook her head. "You don't mean that—" Part of her agreed with Willum, but to think it and to say it out loud was something different. Did he want to call down the All-father's wrath? Hadn't they suffered enough of that?

"I mean it." He seized her arms and pulled her so close that she could see the red veins crisscrossing the whites of his eyes. "Do you know what it's like to live each moment through stabbing pain? Every movement an agony?" His grip on her arms tightened painfully, and she struggled, despite herself.

He was unraveling, coming unmoored from himself, from the man she had once known.

She was frozen in his punishing grip—prey trapped in the grip of a predator. She'd been angry at Willum before. Resentful. Bitter. But she'd never feared him. Not until now. "Willum, let me go."

But he didn't. "Every day, I wake up and face my failures through a haze of pain. You don't *know* what it's like."

Elodie could hardly hear through the roaring of her pulse in her ears. She twisted in his grip, breaking free. But he was upon her again, and this time, he seized her throat, driving them across the room and down onto the bed—his bulk crushing her. His fingers were tight on her neck. Those same fingers that had once touched every inch of her skin with loving caresses were now squeezing the life from her.

"The pain is a fog that suffocates everything. You can't think, you can't breathe, you can't focus on anything but making it stop. But it doesn't stop. It never stops, Elodie." His face was inches from hers, his voice distant. The throbbing pain in her neck—in her lungs—consumed her. The edges of her vision swam as she gasped for oxygen.

"Try, Willum," he cooed. "Try. Find a job. Quit moping. Make me a baby. Why aren't you trying?"

Black tinged her vision, and she clawed at his hand, unyielding as iron. She reached for his face and he shied back, but her fingers just connected, a feather-light touch. "Willum..." she wheezed.

His eyes cleared and he seemed to take her in—to realize what he was doing. He released her and fell backward to the floor, his eyes wide and wild.

Blessed air. She gasped it in, curling onto her side, pulling her knees up to her chest. Every breath burned her windpipe, raked down her throat like his fingers were still burning her.

"All-father help me, Elodie." Willum ran his hands through his hair, turning it wild. "I'm so sorry." He crawled toward her, up on his knees beside the bed, his hands fluttering over her. "I don't know what came over me... Are you all right?"

Tears leaked out of the corner of her eyes. She didn't respond. What could she say? She had seen death in the eyes of the one sworn to protect her. The man she'd loved had turned into a monster.

"I would never hurt you." He reached out to wipe the tears from her cheek.

She flinched away. "Go..." she croaked, squeezing her eyes closed. She couldn't look at him, see the regret pooling in his eyes like tears. There was no longer anything to pity in this man. Whatever Willum had once been, he was no longer. Nothing remained of him—not even as he begged for mercy. He deserved every ounce of misery coursing through him right now. He had almost killed her.

She heard him push unsteadily to his feet, heard his heavy, uneven footsteps to the door. Heard it open and close. And then there was blessed silence, but for the ragged sound of her breath whistling through her bruised throat. Still, Elodie didn't open her eyes. Because she didn't want to see. Didn't want to face the ragged remnants of her life. She didn't even want to try.

CHAPTER 16

PENNYROYAL

*E*lodie drifted in and out of her misery—her knees pulled to her chest, her hands wrapped around her delicate neck. Her wracking sobs burned her throat, but there was no stemming them. Just like she couldn't stop herself from prodding at the bruises, from tracing the contours of where Willum's fingers had tried to choke the life from her.

A banging on the front door made her flinch, her ragged breath raking across her throat like hot coals.

She sat up, as wary as a wild creature. Had Willum returned? But... he wouldn't have knocked.

"Elodie!" A muffled voice came from outside. She recognized that voice. Pepa. What was he doing here at this hour?

"Just a minute," she rasped, flying to the tiny mirror that hung above the water basin. She grimaced at the sight. Her blonde curls were wild and askew, her face red and blotchy with tears. And her neck. Daughter help her. If Pepa saw the marks from Willum's fingers, there was no telling what he might do.

Elodie frantically combed her fingers through her hair and scrubbed her face of tears. She pulled a lavender scarf from her drawer and wound it around her neck.

Her father banged on the door again. "Elodie! It's your sister."

Elodie flew to the door at that, pulling it open.

Pepa stood on the step, his face ashen. It spoke to his concern that he didn't question her about her appearance.

"What is it?"

"Josephine. She's sick. Something's wrong."

"Did you send for Agathe?"

"She's too busy birthing the alder's child to see to my girl."

"Pepa," Elodie chided. So Delphine was in labor. "Give me a moment." She turned from the door, darting about the flat, filling her traveling bag with whatever remedies she had on hand. Her stores were paltry compared to Agathe's, but maybe she had something that could help her sister until she had time to run to Agathe's.

Elodie pulled the door shut behind her, and her father looked at her then. "What's wrong with you?" he asked as he ushered her down the stairs into the street.

"Nothing." It took all her effort not to adjust the scarf around her neck. "I'm feeling unwell myself." She fell into step beside him, practically jogging to keep up with her father's long strides. She could feel his eyes on her. Examining. Deducing. She kept her own gaze fixed on the cobblestones before her.

Pepa's voice was a low growl. "I've seen this kind of unwell before, Elodie. What did he do to you?"

Elodie shook her head. For one daring moment, she wanted desperately to tell her father the truth. To bare her neck and sob her fear and pain into his strong shoulder. But what would happen then? The future opened up in a frightening tangle of possibilities. If Pepa didn't beat Willum into a pulp, getting himself jailed in the process, would he insist she leave him? Legally, she couldn't end their marriage. She'd have to run. And then what would become of her? She'd lived in Lunesburg all her life. Where would she go? Who would take her? She'd never be a mother—never have a family. She'd lose even the faint, shadow of hope she had now. And be left with nothing.

Was her marriage over? Part of her insisted it was, that small, malnourished part that somehow, despite four and a half years of denying herself for the sake of marital harmony, remained fierce and indignant. It raged at Willum, and at her for not having the courage to leave long ago. For letting it get to this point. But there was another voice. The voice that said that it was the alcohol that had done this to her, not Willum. That maybe this was the catalyst that would finally force him to change. To confront just how strong his demons had become. If he came back to himself, they could still have the future they'd dreamed of together. She needed time and space to process. Telling Pepa would deny her that. So she adjusted the scarf around her neck. "Just...tell me about Josephine. What are her symptoms?"

Pepa's brow furrowed, seeming to suggest that the conversation was not over, but he let her divert the topic. "She started doubling over an hour ago, like she's got some vile demon in her belly trying to claw its way out. She says she's fine, that she doesn't need a doctor. But you know how dramatic that girl is about being sick. It was her insistence she didn't need someone that scared me most of all."

Elodie frowned. As a girl, a stubbed toe had been enough to set Josephine wailing for hours. "That is odd. Did she eat anything strange today? Bad meat?"

Frederick shook his head. "We ate the same thing. Turnip and squash stew with a bit of ham. I feel fine."

"Does she have a fever?"

"She looks awful pale," he said, shivering. "She felt cold and clammy."

Elodie's mind whirled through the possible ailments and remedies. She had worked at Agathe's side for years, but she had never aspired to be more than an assistant. What if she missed something? This was her sister. If anything happened to Josephine because of her misdiagnosis...how could Elodie ever forgive herself?

As they turned up the lane to Larkhaven, Elodie broke into a run.

"She's in her room," her father said.

They burst through the front door. "Jo?" Elodie called, trepidation filling her as she ran through the dark house and rounded into her sister's room. Elodie stopped dead at the sight of Josephine—momentarily stunned. Her vibrant golden sister was wan and pale, her hair slick with sweat.

"Elodie?" Josephine tried to lift her head, as if that simple motion was too much effort.

"By the Daughter." Elodie fell to her knees beside Josephine's bed, her hand fluttering over her sister's smooth brow. She did feel cold, despite the sweat that coated her skin. "What happened to you?"

"I'm scared." Josephine's voice was so small. Like when Josephine was little, when their mother had first died.

Elodie pulled Josephine into a hug, her sister's body limp against her own. "We'll get you well. First, you have to tell me exactly what you feel. What you ate, whether you touched anything. It looks like you've been exposed to some sort of toxin."

Frederick hovered by the door, wringing his hands. "How are you, my darling? You look better."

"Liar," Josephine said before she doubled over, clutching her stomach. She groaned through gritted teeth.

"What does it feel like?" Elodie rolled her sister over to prod at her stomach. "Tell me if any of this hurts."

"It all hurts," Josephine cried, tears leaking down her face. "Everywhere."

Elodie continued to prod as Josephine writhed beneath her. Her organs felt fine. Where they should be. Elodie bit her lip. "Please, Jo, anything you can tell me? Anything out of the ordinary?"

Josephine opened her eyes, and there was a lucidity there that made Elodie draw back. "Just you," Josephine whispered, so soft the words were barely audible.

Elodie turned. "Can you boil some water? And bring some clean towels."

Pepa vanished, apparently grateful to be given a job.

Elodie faced her sister again. Josephine was reaching out for her, her fingers catching hold of the scarf around Elodie's throat. "El, what happened to you?"

Elodie jerked back, adjusting the scarf. "You're the sick one. You first. Do you know what's causing this?"

Josephine pushed up on one elbow with a groan and reached inside the drawer of her nightstand. She handed a black bottle to Elodie. "It's pennyroyal."

Elodie's mouth fell open. "You took pennyroyal?" The word crashed within her like waves pummeling the shore. The plant extract was highly toxic, inducing liver failure. Had Josephine tried to kill herself? "Jo, why?"

"Just a few drops," she said, groaning again. "The girls in the village told me it could...get rid of the baby."

"What baby?" Elodie asked, her mind treading slowly.

"Oh, Elodie." Josephine's face twisted in misery. "I didn't want you to know. I thought I could take care of it myself and no one would be the wiser. But now something's wrong and I don't want to die." Fresh tears poured from Josephine's blue eyes, trailing slick rivulets down her pale cheeks.

Elodie's mind was seizing, stumbling. But still, the thoughts crystallized, the horrible, undeniable facts. It was like she'd been punched in the gut, and all the breath had left her, leaving her hollow and empty. Her hand pressed to her chest and she staggered to her feet, reeling back from the bed. "I can't breathe." Her little sister—Josephine—was pregnant. Her seventeen-year-old sister was going to have a baby. And she had taken poison to try to abort it. And now she was dying. These thoughts were like quicksand, pulling her down. Elodie backed against the far wall, bending over, trying to pull air into her seizing lungs. *Pregnant. Pennyroyal.* Four long years of praying and trying and disappointment and Josephine was throwing her baby away like trash—

"Elodie, please," Josephine cried. "I'm scared."

Elodie looked up, her eyes focusing on Josephine. Pennyroyal caused liver failure. If she did nothing, Josephine would die. Of all the emotions that swirled through Elodie, she seized this last one, fighting through the despair and fury that sucked at her, trying to pull her down into its depths. Josephine was sick and Elodie needed to save her. Nothing else mattered right now.

She straightened. "I need charcoal. Father!" she ran from the room, nearly barreling into him and his pot of boiling water in the hallway.

"I need charcoal," she gasped. "From the fire. And a mortar and pestle. And a bowl!" She took the hot water from him and shooed him.

She returned to Josephine's bedside, where her sister was lying still, though her breath hissed in and out of her in rapid succession.

"Whose is it?" Elodie asked as she set the bowl down and grabbed her bag, praying she'd brought the licorice and calamus root. She rummaged through the bottles she'd tossed in. Where was it—

"Piers." Josephine didn't open her eyes.

Elodie froze. "The sojourner?" The words ripped from her aching throat. Fury stoked within her, hotter than she'd ever known. *You don't know the half of what I've done.* He'd looked right into her eyes and *gloated* about sleeping with her seventeen-year-old sister! Her fingers curled into fists. Un-Brother take that two-faced, thieving, story-telling bastard. She was going to kill him herself.

"Father can't know." Josephine rolled over, pulling her knees into her chest.

"It may be too late for that." She needed to focus, to block out all the rest. Getting Josephine well was the only thing that mattered right now. There! The tincture to induce vomiting. "You're not going to die. We're going to get every drop of poison out of you, and you and the baby are going to be as right as rain."

"Baby?" Pepa nearly dropped the items he had gathered. He filled the doorway, his face slack with shock.

Josephine groaned and tried to roll over. "Just let me die."

Elodie clucked her tongue. "Nonsense. We Ruelles are fighters. All Pepa wants is for you to get well, right?" She glared at her father.

Pepa ground his teeth together, looking at the heavens as if cursing his luck at ending up with three daughters. "Can I help?"

"Get me a bowl. A big one." Elodie handed the bottle to Josephine. "Take five drops of this."

Josephine looked at it skeptically.

"Or die," Elodie snapped. "Your choice."

Josephine grunted and unscrewed the top, taking the dose. "What does it do?"

"It'll make you vomit your guts out until there's not a drop of liquid left in you."

Josephine moaned, her arms cradled around her roiling midsection.

Pepa returned with the bowl, and Elodie handed it to Josephine. She tossed two large chunks of charcoal into the mortar to grind.

"Now what?" Pepa asked.

Elodie retrieved the pestle and started grinding. "Now, we wait."

"How long?" Her father looked between Elodie and her sister, who had turned from pale to positively green.

Elodie focused on her sister, on her patient, forcing out all other thoughts. "Not long."

CHAPTER 17

OPTIONS

*E*lodie emptied out the bucket behind the house, struggling not to gag.

Her sister had heaved and heaved until the contents of her stomach emptied to nothing. When Elodie was certain the vomiting was done, she'd forced Josephine to drink a mixture of ground charcoal and water, praying it would neutralize any toxins that had already been absorbed.

When Elodie returned to the room, Josephine was lying with her eyes closed, panting softly.

Pepa stood in the corner, his arms crossed over his barrel chest, his eyes glazed.

"How are you feeling?" Elodie asked, brushing Josephine's hair back from her sweaty forehead.

"Like I might live."

"The charcoal staying down?"

"Daughter, I hope so." Josephine blinked wearily.

"Did the poison take the baby?" Pepa asked.

The baby. Elodie shrugged. "There's no way to know tonight. It will become clear soon enough."

"If it's not gone," he said stiffly. "We'll find a way."

Elodie's head jerked up.

Even Josephine's eyes widened. "Pepa! Are you saying—"

"This will ruin you. Everything I've hoped for you. You'll never find a good husband if you have a baby out of wedlock. To some drifter," he spat.

Elodie's mouth fell open. She'd expected Pepa to fight the prospect of ending the pregnancy. And herself... She found herself desperate to convince her sister to keep it.

She knew Agathe had herbs that could terminate a pregnancy safely. She'd often been there when her mentor dispensed them to tearfully grateful women. In fact, she'd never had a problem with use of such herbs. The All-father had seen fit to gift women the blessing and the curse of childbearing, so it seemed just as natural that the Daughter would give them a choice in the matter. But not this. Not Josephine. Not her niece or nephew, a baby she could raise as her own.

"The baby is innocent. It deserves a chance." She felt numb with the truth of it. Josephine was pregnant. Josephine. After one night with a mesmerizing stranger, Josephine was pregnant. Elodie, after four and half agonizing years, still had a flat belly and an empty womb. She wanted to rail at the All-father, she wanted to scream. To cry. But none of that would help any of them. Even herself. So she swallowed it down. She needed to be rational. Calm. "It's no secret Willum and I have been trying to conceive." Elodie straightened.

Josephine opened her eyes again, misery flashing across her face. "I'm so sorry, Elodie. I didn't want to tell you. I know it's not fair—"

Elodie shook her head sharply, cutting her sister off. "It doesn't matter what's fair. This is what is. Perhaps this was the All-father's plan. We've been wanting a baby, and here one is. One that you don't want. We could take it." *Is there even a* we *anymore?* She shoved down the thought. The baby was what mattered right now.

"I thought that Willum didn't want to adopt," Pepa countered. "Haven't you barked up this tree before?"

Elodie pursed her lips. "Yes, in the past Willum was reluctant to adopt. He wanted our child. As do I. But we always talked in the abstract. Now it's a reality, not just some idea. And it's a child of someone we know. Our family. Maybe he'll feel differently."

"It still doesn't solve the problem of your sister's reputation. Even if she doesn't have to raise the babe, she'll never find a husband now that she's been spoiled."

"She hasn't been spoiled," Elodie snapped. "She was taken advantage of."

"I don't care about finding a husband," Josephine said weakly.

"You say that now, but you just wait. I'm not going to be around forever, and who's going to take care of you? Your sister? Elodie and Willum can hardly feed themselves, and Sidonie and Hugh already have two mouths to feed. Do you want to be alone, relying on the charity of others?"

Elodie flinched at her father's frank assessment of their situations.

"I want to be an artist. A craftsman. A traveler. I want to explore the world. I'll take care of myself."

"That's a fantasy," Pepa barked. "I'm taking about reality. The reality is, seventeen-year-old pregnant girls don't have prospects and can't support themselves."

"What if Josephine went away?" Elodie suggested. "What if she went away, had the baby, and came back? No one would be any wiser. We could say we adopted, and no one would need to know where the baby came from. Josephine's reputation would be preserved, we would have a family, and the baby would have a chance. It would preserve all of Josephine's options."

"Where would she go?" Pepa asked.

"I don't know, but I'm sure we could find someone. A distant relative. I'll ask Agathe," Elodie suggested.

Josephine's already sour face grew darker.

It was a far-from-perfect solution. Elodie hated the idea of forcing Josephine into hiding like she'd done something wrong, but her father was right. Josephine would suffer if they didn't. Her sister thought she didn't ever want to marry, and maybe she'd always feel that way. But what if that changed? And what of the baby? This way, it would have a chance at life. It *was* a sacrifice for Josephine, but one she hoped her sister would be willing to make.

"I still don't like it. A man lies with a woman and conceives a babe... There's a responsibility there," Pepa said. "Have you tried to find this *sojourner?*" He spat the word. Her father had been as shocked as Elodie when Josephine had admitted the truth of the father's identity.

Josephine shook her head, her eyes flicking to Elodie. "No. And before you even suggest it, I don't want to marry him. I hardly know him."

"Well, then you shouldn't have slept with him!" Pepa thundered.

"Pepa," Elodie chided. Willum's comment flashed through her mind. "This isn't Josephine's fault. How do we know he didn't put a spell on her?" She disliked the idea of further prejudicing Pepa against magic, but it was better to blame sorcery than poor Josephine. Josephine was still a girl.

"Do you think he put a spell on you?" Pepa asked.

"I don't know," Josephine said weakly.

Maybe Piers had used magic or maybe just his devilish charms to seduce her. Or perhaps she'd yielded willingly. It didn't really matter. Josephine was only seventeen, and the man was at least thirty. Could they blame her for being beguiled by such a showman? He'd taken advantage of her.

Elodie chewed on her lip. Her gut told her that the sojourner wasn't a good man. But he *was* the father. Should he have a chance to...do right by Josephine? By the baby? "He was in Wouraux two weeks ago."

Josephine sighed.

Elodie held up her hands. "Let's not do anything rash. Josephine's out of the woods. She has time. And options. We can talk to the sojourner. Willum and I could take the baby."

"If Willum agrees," her father said.

"You let me worry about Willum."

"I don't know if I want Willum to have the baby," Josephine said quietly.

"What do you mean?" Elodie recoiled.

"Look at your neck," Josephine protested. "He hurt you! What if he hurt the baby?"

"So, it's better to end its life before it even begins?" Elodie snapped. How dare Josephine suggest that life in her household was worse than death? But her hand reflexively drifted to her neck. Was it? Her stomach soured. What if Willum didn't stop drinking? What if something happened and he got violent again? How could she protect a baby from that senseless wrath if she couldn't even protect herself?

Pepa looked between them and strode to Elodie, yanking down the scarf around her neck. "By the gods, Elodie, what the hell did the man do to you?"

"Nothing. It was a...misunderstanding." Damn it all, she was not ready to have this conversation. She was too confused. It was too raw.

"No misunderstanding I can conceive of results in bruises like that." Her father's face purpled. "I could castrate the man for laying a hand on you! Let me guess, the fight was about having a baby? You always push too hard."

"So this is my fault?" Elodie bit back. She broke free from his grip and pulled the scarf back up into position. "Whose side are you on?"

"I'm on my daughters' sides," Pepa thundered. Then he sucked in a breath. "I'm sorry. I didn't mean to say it's your fault. There's no excuse for a man to be physical against a woman. And I'll flay any lowlife who seeks to hurt any of you. When your mother died, it was left to me to see you girls raised and grown and happy. I'll be damned before I fail at that."

"You haven't failed, Pepa," Elodie softened.

"Well, I'm teetering on the edge, aren't I?" He spun in a circle, his hands in his greying hair. "Maybe it would be best if he cleaved you."

Elodie hissed in a breath.

"At least you'd be safe! The man hasn't been himself since the accident. You've tried and tried, but I don't think he'll ever be the same."

"So, Josephine's too precious to be a spinster, but you have no problem dooming me to the same fate?"

"Yes, if that's what it takes for you to be free and safe. And married to that man, you are neither. It's heartbreaking to watch, Elodie. You're not yourself anymore. You haven't been for a long time."

"Do you think I don't know that?" she cried, her voice cracking. "Do you think I like being like this? It's not Willum. Or...not just Willum. It's the fact that the one thing I want most in the world is the one thing denied to me! If I could only have a baby..." She was shaking now. "Everything will be better if we have a baby." Given a purpose—a family—he'd stop drinking. Willum would find his way out of the depression that had shrouded them so long. They only needed some good news—something to go their way for a change. And if he relapsed or stumbled...she could protect the baby from Willum—she would find a way. She would do anything to protect it.

"You may think that, but it doesn't fix everything. Not the problems in your marriage."

"What?" Elodie recoiled. "You always said you and Mama were happy."

"We *were* happy. But it doesn't mean it wasn't the hardest thing we'd ever done. Bringing a child into a marriage is like pouring water into stone. It exposes every crack, every fissure. It widens them. Sometimes the pressure got to be too much, and I thought it would break us. It won't get easier. It will only get harder."

"I can handle it."

Pepa let out a sigh. "What do I know? I'm just an old man whose best years are behind him. The folly of youth is that you have to make all the mistakes yourself." He threw up his hands. "But I can't deal with the problem of your no-good bastard husband right now because I have to focus on her no-good bastard baby's father!"

Fury colored Elodie's vision. To complain about how this was affecting *him*? How many times had Elodie put aside her own feelings for her husband and everyone else? And to compare her and Josephine's predicaments...when she'd done her duty as a wife, done *everything* that was ever asked of her. More!

Elodie struggled to focus. She was done. "Do you both agree not to do anything rash? Josephine, even if you decide to...terminate the pregnancy...your body is too weak to do it in the next few days. Let's take that time to explore the other options here."

"Fine," Pepa and Josephine both said, their tone similar. Sullen.

Elodie breathed out, fighting the tempest growing inside her. *Calm. Stay calm.* "Josephine, do you feel like you're going to be sick again?"

"No."

"Drink plenty of fluids, sleep, and tomorrow get some chicken broth into you. Soft foods like squash or potatoes. You'll be okay."

"Are you leaving?" Pepa asked. "Where are you going?"

"Home." It was a lie. She didn't know where she would go, but she couldn't be here anymore. "I'll come back to check on you tomorrow."

Elodie hurried through the hallway, grabbing her cloak from the hook by the door. She stepped out into the cool night and looked up. The stars were bright above her. There was a chill in the air that she relished, but as she tried to breathe in deeply, she found she couldn't. There was something building. A pressure that she couldn't hold in—a weight that that seized her lungs and chest.

She stood in the dark, fighting against the clawing panic. She couldn't go home. She couldn't see Willum right now. Not after everything that had happened. She would unravel.

Elodie balled her hands into fists and found her feet moving. Back around the house and through the quiet garden, startling a little hare nibbling at a lettuce plant. She shooed it away and kept to the path, which had become overgrown to the point it had almost disappeared. There was only one place she could think of where no one would find her—one place where she could really feel. Face the weight of her sorrow. Let herself drown in its depths. To rail at the unfairness—at the All-father and Daughter. How could they have done this? How could Josephine be pregnant? *How. How. How.*

"Do you think this is a joke?" she hissed into the night. "Do you like toying with our lives? Seeing me suffer?" Withholding from one, giving to another. Dangling desires and wishes like fishing lures—and they the quicksilver trout clamoring for their destruction. What kind of world did she live in? Elodie tripped over a root and almost fell.

She righted herself and looked up. There it was, gleaming in the moonlight. Some of the glass panels of the greenhouse were broken, and moss and ivy crawled up the side.

She stepped inside, surveying the empty broken pots, bits of dirt strewn about. Retaken by nature. She felt like nothing more than one of those broken pots. Once holding something beautiful, full of life and possibility and growth—now a damaged vessel, empty and sad. "What do you want from me?" she cried into the unfeeling night. "What do I have to do to prove I'm worthy?"

Elodie fell to her knees, burying her face in her hands, her shawl. Then she screamed. It ripped from her unbidden. It broke free from her with such strength that she thought it might tear her raw throat apart. That throat that just hours ago had nearly been crushed by her husband's own hands.

Elodie screamed her sorrow and her anger. She screamed until she couldn't bear it anymore.

"I can't do this," she screamed. "I'm not strong enough to bear this." She couldn't put on a happy face anymore. To care about anything or anyone. Not when there was a chasm of emptiness in her heart and her life. Sorrows piling like rocks on a funeral cairn.

"I can't live like this," she rasped into the dark.

But like always, the dark was silent in reply.

CHAPTER 18

SCREAMS

*S*ebastian came to in a rush. The sound was distant but undeniable. Someone was screaming. He threw off the covers and shoved out of bed, the cool air pebbling his skin. He pressed his bare feet to the worn floorboards, listening. There. There it was again. A sound that rose the hackles on the back of his neck.

Someone was in trouble.

Sebastian hopped into pants and boots and threw his cloak over his shoulders before kneeling down and rummaging through his bottom drawer to retrieve his father's sword. He still didn't think of it as *his* sword, though it had been in his possession for the last five years—since his father had died. The weapon felt out of place in a town like Lunesburg, even with the shadow of the war that had hung over the town in his early years. But that scream... That scream made him want something solid between him and the night.

The cold slapped his face as he opened the door, a chill hanging deep in the air. It was like this, some spring nights as winter fought and clawed for the last of its domain, unwilling to give up its sovereignty.

The moon was full and bright, so bright that Sebastian took only a few steps before he turned around and left the lantern by the back stoop. The path through the garden and into the orchard was visible, and a lantern might only alert whoever was hurting that poor woman as to his arrival.

Another scream ripped through the air—keening and sorrowful. It sounded like a banshee, that restless fairy spirit who predicts the deaths of men. Perhaps she was luring him out into the lonely night to end him. *Superstitious nonsense.* He shoved the thought aside. He wasn't a child, to be scared of ghost stories of the dark. He was a man, and someone needed help.

It was mere seconds before Sebastian realized where his feet were carrying him. The sound had come from the direction of Elodie's mother's greenhouse, on the edge of the Larkhaven property. But it didn't sound again. Sebastian's stomach dropped. Was he too late?

Sebastian emerged through trees and the scent of apple blossoms into the open, where the skeletal greenhouse sat silent in the moonlight. He stopped for a moment, perking his ears. Listening. The screams had subsided, but there was a sound. A quiet sobbing. Someone was in there.

Senses firing, heart racing, Sebastian approached, his head swiveling for any sign of the attacker. He saw none. Perhaps the person was still in there. His slick fingers gripped the leather grip of the sword, its weight strangely comforting. Perhaps now he understood why his father had kept this weapon.

He stepped silently to the door of the greenhouse, taking in the darkened shapes. A woman was sprawled on the ground, her skirts splayed around her. There was no sound or movement coming from her but the soft sound of her wracking tears, the subtle movements of her shoulders.

"Miss?" he ventured softly, trying not to startle her. Which didn't work at all.

She screeched and scrambled back from him, across the dirty floor, across the broken glass strewn there. Her face was wild and tear-streaked, her golden curls tarnished in the moonlight.

His breath left him in a rush. Elodie.

They hadn't spoken since that night at the lake, since he'd found her beside herself. He'd dreamed of it in a hundred different ways—him coming upon her too late, her body floating atop the water, her pale tresses drifting, her face lifeless. Sebastian rubbed his face to clear the image.

He'd seen her in town twice since that night, but each time, she had hurried away before he had been able to get in a word. She'd been avoiding him. Likely embarrassed, though she had no reason to be. He'd worried ceaselessly that he'd ruined even their friendship by witnessing her upset that night. Now here she was again. Fate had brought him to her, at her time of need. Again.

"Easy." Sebastian raised his hands. He realized a moment later that one hand bore the sword and he hastily put it to the ground, crouching. "It's me. Sebastian."

Her wild eyes seemed to focus on him at that, the tension of her body relaxing slightly. "Sebastian?" Her voice was a hoarse whisper.

"I heard you screaming. Who was hurting you? Is he still nearby?"

She blinked at him, her face twisting. "I—" She started and stopped. Then her shoulders started to shake again, and she tipped forward, burying her face in her hands.

"Hey, hey." Sebastian inched forward and knelt at her side. "Whoever it is, whatever he did, he'll pay." He reached out a hand, cautiously, slowly. He wanted so badly to comfort her. He knew he shouldn't, but propriety was no match for the sight of Elodie's sorrow. He laid a gentle hand on her shoulder and pulled her into him.

She came willingly, collapsing against him. He pulled her tightly against his chest and let her sob into his shirt. It was like the night at the lake, but it wasn't at the same time. Something else had happened. Something worse. His heart broke for her as he smoothed the tangles in her hair with loving strokes of his fingers. How much did the Allfather expect her to take?

She pulled back from him and looked up then, a strange, sobbing laughter bubbling forth from her. Her face was just inches from his—but that wasn't what captured his attention. It was the blood that smeared her cheeks, her lovely face transformed into a macabre sacrifice in some pagan ritual.

"You're bleeding." He cupped her face in his hand, his thumb gliding across her cheekbone.

Her hand came up to cradle his, their fingers threading together for a moment as she probed at her cheek, seeming unaware of the walls that were crumbling between them. Then she held her palms between them, looking down. "I...I think I cut myself on the glass."

"Come with me." He tried to help her up, but Elodie was unsteady on her feet. She stumbled against him, trying not to touch him with her bloody palms. He swept his arm beneath her and hooked her knees, pulling her up against his chest.

"You don't have to..." she croaked, but her eyes fluttered closed and she let her head rest against his chest. She was shaking, her body shuddering uncontrollably.

"You're freezing."

She said nothing.

Sebastian had grown strong from years of hauling cider barrels about, and Elodie was a slight woman, but still his arms ached something fierce when they reached the brewery. Yet as he made it up the stairs and pushed open the door to his little flat, he didn't want to let her go. Even bleeding and nearly incoherent, he had never been this close to her, this intimate. He didn't want it to end.

Reluctantly, he set her down on the bed, the only place in the one-room flat that was soft. Part of his mind cried out how improper it was—her being here—a married woman, how very, very dangerous it was to see her on his bed, where he'd longed to find her for the last ten years. But none of that mattered. She was hurt, and he was helping her. There was nothing improper about that.

Sebastian poured water into the kettle and put it onto the stove before dipping a cloth in the water basin.

Elodie was sitting morosely on the edge of his bed, and he knelt down before her, taking her hands gently. He washed the blood away with tender strokes. Her cut looked shallow. "I don't think it'll need stitches."

"No," she said flatly. "You're right."

He crossed back to the basin and rinsed out the rag before

returning to her side. He offered her a clean handkerchief to wrap around her hand. "Here, let me." He took her chin in fingers as light as a feather and stroked the blood from her cheek. Then the dirt from her other cheek, the trails of tears. She closed her eyes as he worked, quiet and still, but fresh tears fell still. His eyes traced every part of her as he worked. The soft fall of freckles on her nose, too faint to see from afar. The long stretch of her golden lashes against her reddened cheek. The fine curve at the corner of her mouth, which longed to have a kiss pressed against it. All-father save him. He struggled to keep his fingers from shaking. Elodie was stunning from afar. This close—she was devastating.

His eyes drifted downward and it was then that he saw the shadows on her neck, the deep purple bruises in the undeniable shape of fingers.

He hissed and stood, fury blowing through him like bellows on a hearth.

Her eyes popped open and her hand flew to her neck, hiding the marks.

His question was low and hard. "Who did this to you?" He'd forgotten the sword back at the greenhouse in his hurry to get her to safety, but he had half a mind to march back out to retrieve it before hunting down whatever bastard had left that handprint. Had it been Willum? The drink finally driving him beyond reason?

"It's not...how it looks." Her voice was hoarse and grey, not at all the joyful timbre he was used to from her. She stood suddenly. "I should go. Thank you for your help."

She was leaving? His heart twisted. She couldn't leave so soon. The tea kettle whistled and he seized upon it. "Please. Just have a cup of tea, get something warm into you. Then I'll walk you home."

She wrapped her arms around herself as if considering, for the first time, how cold she was. She nodded once and sat down. He poured two mugs of tea and pulled some whiskey off the shelf, dosing both cups. Hopefully, it would help cut through some of the shock. He handed one to her and then pulled over a chair from the little table against the wall. He didn't want to sit on the bed with her. She needed space.

"You don't have to tell me anything," he said finally. "I'm sorry I asked. I just...I don't like seeing you like this."

She looked down at the earthen mug in her hands. "I know you'd never insist." She wiped her nose with the back of one hand, a gesture that was so unladylike, so unlike the regular Elodie, that he felt a strange honor to have seen it. As if he had been privy to a glimpse of the real her. "Oh, Sebastian." She shook her head, squeezing her eyes closed. "I'm so embarrassed."

"I don't know what's going on, but I'm certain you have nothing to be embarrassed about."

She took a deep breath. "No one attacked me." She pursed her lips. "Well, not at the greenhouse. The truth is...I think I went a little crazy. I was so angry...I just lost my mind. And this is the second time you've seen me unravel. First the lake, now tonight... You must think me unhinged." She let out bitter laugh then took a sip of the tea and looked at him in surprise. "Did you add something to this?"

Her blue eyes were so lovely, even red-rimmed and swollen. He nodded. "I thought you could use something a little stronger than tea. I'll make you another if you don't want it."

She shook her head. "It's good."

"I don't think you're unhinged, Elodie. You're one of the most level-headed people I know. Something must have happened to upset you so. What was it?" He wanted more than ever to ask her about the marks around her neck, but that had almost made her leave before, and he didn't want to scare her away.

"Josephine is pregnant." She said the words slowly, as if testing the truth of them, the feel of them on the air.

"What?" Sebastian recoiled. "She's only...who?"

"The sojourner."

Sebastian sat in stunned silence for a moment. "That bastard."

"Precisely."

And then it hit him. What this meant for Elodie. She, who had been longing to be a mother for four and a half years. Praying and wishing and hoping. Doing everything in her power to sway the favor of the Daughter to her cause. Anger bloomed again, hot and furious. At the exquisite unfairness of it all. He wanted to scream for her. To rage at the universe, at the All-father for what a bastard *He* was. "I understand," was all he said, meeting her eyes.

"She tried to abort the baby," Elodie said. "She poisoned herself and almost died."

The words were like a gut punch. "Is she all right? The baby?"

"She'll live. We don't know about the baby yet. She doesn't want to keep it, though. Neither does Pepa. He says it will ruin her."

"It's an innocent," Sebastian protested.

"I know. I told her Willum and I would take it. Or…if we can find that damn sojourner, maybe we can make him return and convince her to have a family with him."

"You don't want her married to that man, do you?"

"No. I don't know." Elodie shook her head. "I want her to see she has options. Josephine says she doesn't want to marry him, but shouldn't she at least have a conversation with him? Is that not even an option? Do you know how many different ways I've tried to get pregnant in the last four and a half years? And now there's a baby right here and it's like no one wants to do anything to try to give it a chance."

"Well, I might be able to help in that regard," Sebastian said. He couldn't believe his luck. After Elliason's Lake, he'd resolved himself that the best thing he could do for her was to find that damned book she was so fixed upon. He had traveled to Wouraux one week past, but the sojourners had already moved on. Word was they had circled around southeast to Rochester. He'd planned to go at the end of the week. He had a delivery to make anyway.

"How so?" Elodie asked.

"I know where the sojourner went after Wouraux. If you'd like, I'll take you to him myself."

CHAPTER 19

PLAN

*E*lodie blinked at Sebastian, his words bouncing about in her head. Despite the rawness of her sorrow, despite everything that had happened tonight, here was a shot of hope—a shooting star sparkling across a dark sky. "You really know where he is?" If they found Piers, maybe she could still get the map...

"I have contacts all over the region, as I distribute to a number of cities. I inquired about Piers and the sojourner wagons, and as of three days ago, he was in Rochester."

"How did you...? Why did you...?" She shook her head in amazement.

"I couldn't stand what they did to you. Stealing from you... cheating you. I thought...I could help. Make it right." Sebastian looked down at his hands, and in that moment, Elodie was seized by the urge to take his face and kiss him full on the mouth. She stiffened at the thought, shoving it down. *Daughter, where did that come from?* She was just grateful for his thoughtfulness. That was all.

Sebastian regarded her once more. "Maybe if we find him, we could get you that map."

She shook her head. How could she admit that after everything she'd been through, everything she'd promised herself, she was still obsessed with some children's story? "I told you I swore off the Wish-Eater. I'm done with that map. The book."

"Do you really mean that?" Sebastian cocked his head, examining her.

Elodie took another sip of tea. The whiskey was snaking pleasantly through her veins, warming her.

Sebastian was still waiting.

Finally, she sighed. "I don't know. But I should be. It's foolish to chase after a bedtime story."

"It's not foolish," Sebastian countered. "There is power in stories, especially old ones. Even if they are fables and metaphors, they are containers for something more."

"What's that?" she asked softly.

"In this case, hope," he said gently. "I don't think that's foolish at all."

"How'd you get so wise?" A smile played on her lips. Sebastian soothed her. Being here with him made her almost forget the events of this horrible night. Almost.

"You think you're the only one who's ever wanted something? Maybe I was after that book for myself." He gave a little laugh, but when he looked up, there was something in his hazel eyes that she thought she recognized. Raw and real and hungry—a yearning as powerful as her own.

She shivered. Whatever it was that Sebastian wished for, it was as all-consuming as her desire to be a mother. Somehow, she was confident he would get it. Things seemed to work out for people like Sebastian. Though she'd once thought the same about herself. And look where that had led her.

"Do you think it's real?" she asked. "The Wish-Eater?"

Sebastian shrugged. "I don't know. It seems like a long shot, but there's only one way to find out. What's the harm?"

"Ten silver."

"Maybe I'll buy it for myself. And you can...borrow it."

"Sebastian!" Elodie shook her head. His charitable offer was as plain as day. "I could never let you do that. Besides, he already has ten of my silver." *Your father's silver*, her guilty conscience corrected. "Maybe when we find the sojourner, we take it. It's the least he owes us for what he did to my sister." The sojourner had sold the book, but he'd said he had a copy of the map.

Sebastian's eyebrows rose toward his hairline. "Elodie Mercer, I would not have expected such ruthlessness from you."

"Unbecoming in a lady, I know."

"To the contrary. It's quite becoming." The look on his face was playful, as if they shared a secret.

Her cheeks heated at his words. She had been beside herself when he had brought her here, but now her good sense was returning, and she realized where she was. Alone with Sebastian Beringer. Sitting on his bed. His piercing eyes laying her bare, the lamplight casting shadows across his tawny skin.

"I should go." She jerked to her feet. "If Piers was in Rochester three days ago, he already could have moved on. I need to find him before the trail runs cold."

Sebastian's eyebrows traveled even higher. "You're going to walk? In the middle of the night? By yourself?"

Elodie paused. Perhaps she could ask Pepa to borrow his wagon. Or Agathe...it would be quicker than walking.

"I'll take you myself," Sebastian said.

"Nonsense," Elodie protested, but he held up his hands.

"I have deliveries to make in Rochester. I was going to go at the end of the week, but I could easily bump my trip up to tomorrow. I can talk to my contact."

It wouldn't be proper, a trip with just the two of them. Not when his presence set butterflies fluttering in her stomach. But she was so gods-damn sick of being proper. Where had it gotten her? "Are you sure?"

"Positive." Sebastian stood himself. He was a head taller than her—a good height. Willum was so tall, he had to bend over to even kiss her. "Do you know what you're going to do when you see him? About

141

Josephine? What if he does want to marry her? Take her away somewhere?"

Elodie bit her lip. What would she do? Say? Was there good in the man that could be salvaged? Did he deserve a chance to court Josephine, if he wanted one? "I don't know," she admitted. "But I think the man deserves to know. I suspect how he responds will give us our answer."

"Fair enough." Sebastian held out a hand. Elodie looked at it, unsure. Wanting to lay her own hand in his.

"Your mug?"

"Of course." She handed it over, her cheeks burning hotter.

He placed the mugs on the wooden countertop. "Now, let me walk you home."

"It's all right. I'll be staying at my father's. I want to check on Josephine again."

His eyes flicked to her throat, and it took all her restraint not to adjust her scarf to cover the bruises.

But he didn't ask. He just nodded. "You're sure you don't want me to walk you?"

She shook her head. "It's a short walk. You've done enough already." She paused at the door. "Sebastian, I'd appreciate it if you didn't tell anyone...about what you saw. My...behavior in the greenhouse." Even now, thinking of it mortified her. How could she have let herself come so unhinged? And to have Sebastian see it, someone whose opinion and friendship she valued. And just weeks after he'd found her distraught at the lake... "Or about Josephine. I fear the secrets I'm asking you to keep are piling up."

"Your secret, all of your secrets, are safe with me," Sebastian said solemnly. "And, Elodie...anyone going through what you're going through would be upset. Distraught. It's nothing to be ashamed of."

She pursed her lips. She wanted to believe those words, but it went against everything she'd been taught. She'd had to be strong when her mother had died, to hold the family together. She had to be strong now. She didn't have the luxury of falling apart. "It's kind of you to say so."

His face was gentle as he regarded her, opening the door. "Don't be so hard on yourself."

"It's the only way I know to keep going."

He nodded. "I know something of that." She started down the steps. "Also—" he called after her. "It's none of my business...but...if you ever need anything...I'm here. Whoever did that to your throat... if you need somewhere safe...you're always welcome here."

She nodded once, grateful that her flush was hidden in the dark. "Thank you, Sebastian. I'll see you tomorrow."

"Bright and early. I'll have the wagon ready to go an hour after dawn."

She walked slowly down the drive to the main road and back toward Larkhaven. Her mind latched eagerly on to preparations for the trip. Far preferable to thinking of anything else. She'd need to leave a message for Willum. She still wasn't ready to go home... She would leave a letter with her father. But there was another matter.

The matter of the Wish-Eater.

The story had grabbed hold of her and had not let her go in the weeks since Baumai. Even after the debacle at Wouraux, she'd thought of it. It was as if she'd been destined to see that book, to hear the story. When that bastard Piers had recited it—it had felt like a tale for her ears alone. Twice she'd missed her chance to secure a map to find the creature—first on the night of Baumai, second in Wouraux. But now, the All-father, or fate, or whatever force pulled and twisted at the lives of mortals, had brought Piers back into their lives. She would see him again—and this time, she would not lose her chance.

She would buy the map, or steal it if she had to. Demand it in payment for his affront to Josephine, to their family. Come hell or high water, she would find the Wish-Eater. And then, her nightmare would end. With a purpose and a direction, and the pride of conceiving a child, Willum would get well again. He would stop drinking, he would find a way back to himself. To her. And they would be the family they were always supposed to be.

An insistent voice nagged at her, reminding her of the bruises purpling her throat. Of the low, burning fury that still pulsed inside her. As if a fire had charred her, irrevocably altering the terrain of their marriage. Could she ever really trust him after what he'd done? Could a man who'd tried to choke the life from his wife be trusted around a child? Perhaps there had been truth in her sister's words. It had been so long since she and Willum had been happy—so long that she wasn't sure they could find their way back.

But what was the alternative? They were married. Was she truly willing to walk away from Willum, from all the years she'd struggled and held on, from the dream of the family she'd always wanted, from her very home?

"Madam Mercer," a woman's voice called in the dark.

Elodie glanced up. A woman was hurrying toward her from the direction of the village—Dion and Delphine's serving girl. Elodie wracked her mind for the woman's name. "Clarissa?"

She nodded, bobbing in a little curtsy as she stopped. "Agathe sent me to find you."

"Is it Delphine? Is she all right?"

Clarissa nodded. "Yes, she's had the babe. A beautiful little girl."

Elodie nodded, pasting a smile on her face, forcing back the tears. "How wonderful," she managed. A little girl. Now Delphine had everything. A loving husband, a comfortable home, good friends, the respect of the community, and a little heir to inherit it all. Elodie fought against the surge of jealousy that buffeted her, that bowled at her like a gale force wind. Followed, as it always was, by self-loathing. For what kind of person had such a reaction to another person's good news? Was she so selfish? So hateful?

"Agathe sent me to see how Josephine was doing. Delphine lost some blood and Agathe would like to stay with her, but if Josephine's condition is worsening, she'll come."

"Tell Agathe thank you for her concern, but I have resolved Josephine's ailment. She will be well. She should stay with Delphine."

Clarissa nodded.

"Please tell Alder Landry and Delphine congratulations from the Ruelle family," Elodie said.

Clarissa hurried off, disappearing into the night. Elodie turned down the lane to Larkhaven with heavy feet, letting herself into her father's house. A weariness swept over her, a heaviness that pulled at her like a millstone. She needed to sleep. Everything would look brighter after a good night's sleep. And tomorrow, she would go to find Piers. And secure a happy ending of her own.

CHAPTER 20

WILDFLOWERS

*E*lodie woke before the dawn. Despite all that had passed the prior night, she found herself filled with an unexpected emotion. Excitement.

She scrubbed her face in the cold water of the basin in her old room, relishing how the liquid soothed her puffy, scratchy eyes. Her throat burned and throbbed something fierce, but she riffled through the larder and found some herbs with which to numb the pain. After checking on Josephine and packing some food and a waterskin, also pilfered from the larder, she sat down in the living room to write Willum a quick letter.

Have to do something for the family. Will be back tomorrow.

She could find no more words for him, for anything she thought to say came with a host of shadows and complexities attached.

Elodie brushed her hair and donned her cloak, stepping into the summer morning. She wore a dress with the highest collar, to hide her ugly bruises. A riot of birdsong greeted her, as if the wildlife around her was ebullient at the beauty of the crisp, blue sky, the sun rising over the horizon. She pulled in a deep breath of fresh morning air and doubled over as the action traced fire down her wounded esophagus. She steadied herself, taking little sips of air. No deep breaths.

Sebastian was standing in the yard outside of his brewery, checking the harness of a handsome bay horse. He wore a fresh cerulean tunic that she already knew would bring out the rings of blue around his hazel eyes, and the sun just peeking over the trees gilded his blond curls gold. Grincheaux the cat curled around his feet, running an arching side against his boot.

Elodie's body flushed as she realized she had halted at the sight, taking it in as one views a fine work of art. She couldn't deny that she was looking forward to the prospect of spending the day with Sebastian. There was an aura of serenity and ease around him that she'd scarcely encountered with any other human being.

"Elodie." Sebastian straightened, patting the horse's rump. "Right on time."

"I know it's a long trip," she said, her feet carrying her forward. "And it's so kind of you to let me accompany you. I didn't want to keep you waiting."

"Nonsense," Sebastian said. "The first rule of this trip is that you'll cease any thoughts or worries that you are an inconvenience to me. In truth, I'm grateful to have the company. Feu here isn't much of a talker." He patted the horse again.

Elodie smiled. "Very well. I think I can subscribe to your rule." She leaned down as Sebastian's cat approached her.

"Be careful, he's temperamental..." Sebastian trailed off as the cat rubbed its head against her outstretched fingers. "Traitor. I should have known there's no one you can't charm."

Elodie chuckled, giving the cat a scratch behind the ear. "Tell that to my mother-in-law."

Sebastian gave a little shudder. He stepped forward and offered his hand to help her up onto the wagon's bench seat. When her fingers closed in his, his hand was warm and calloused. She was a touch reluctant to let it go, but let it go she did. He pulled himself up into the driver's seat beside her and flicked the reins. And they were off.

Elodie watched with interest as the landscape around them began to change. It wasn't often she got out of Lunesburg. They passed several smaller farmsteads she recognized: the Devreauxs' sheep farm and the Haringtons' vineyard, which produced sweet ice wine prized during Yule season.

And then the countryside opened up into wide meadows glistening with dew, painted with the last wisps of nighttime fog. The road turned from cobbles to rough packed dirt, which was actually much more comfortable to ride over. Though Elodie imagined it wasn't preferable during winter when the rains came in.

Sebastian seemed in good spirits too, his face upturned to the morning sun. "In truth, these trips are one of my favorite parts of the job," he said. "At home, there's always something to be done. I can nary be idle for a few moments before the guilt creeps in, nagging me about lazing around all day. But out here, there's nothing to do but sit. It feels strangely decadent."

"I know just what you mean," Elodie said. "I can't remember the last time I just sat in the sunshine. Probably not since I was a girl."

"When the wildflowers were out, you and Margery and Beatrice used to weave those flower crowns and gift them to all the boys you liked, do you remember?"

"How could I forget! I made everyone wear them. Josephine and Sidonie, Pepa—"

"They were quite intricate. I bet you could sell those at the market."

"They were just silly fun. I can't believe you remember that."

"A lad doesn't forget his first flower crown."

Elodie looked at him then. The reins were easy in his hands, his eyes before him. "I gave you one?" How could she have forgotten?

"It was nothing special. Once you girls gave them to all the boys in class. Before Baumai, I think."

"That's right! We spent hours making them. Willum wore his the entire day." Elodie laughed, and then her smile fell from her lips, a shadow passing over her.

"I'm sorry," Sebastian said, sensing her shift in mood. "We don't need to talk about him if you don't want to."

Elodie liked that about Sebastian—how perceptive he was. Like he understood what she was thinking without her needing to say it. "I'm not sure it much matters what I want these days."

"It does to me," he said, the words almost tender.

She looked at him then, meeting his hazel eyes. He looked away quickly before she could read them, before she could understand what was there. "I mean, the least I can do is avoid a subject you don't wish to speak of."

"True."

"So what shall we speak of?"

Elodie wracked her brain. "I heard Dion and Delphine had a little girl. How long do you think it will take her to wrap Dion about her little finger?"

Sebastian shrugged. "I'm sure it's already done. But..." He eyed her shrewdly. "Do you really want to talk about babies?"

Elodie let out a breathless laugh and her hand drifted to her neck as the exhalation burned her throat. "No, no, I do not. Sebastian Beringer, sometimes I think you see too much for your own good."

"I'll make sure to be a senseless lout who walks all over your feelings on our next trip."

"Is there to be another trip?" Elodie arched an eyebrow. "I've no more young sisters to be enchanted by devious magicians."

"Think bigger!" Sebastian grinned sidelong at her. "Surely, there will be some new disaster the Ruelle sisters can concoct. You just have to put your mind to it."

"You're right. The All-father will have some fresh horror for us soon enough."

"And you'll traverse it with grace and class, as you always do. And Feu and I will be here for all your navigational needs."

She shook her head at his silliness, elbowing him. "Perhaps we should just cover all of the worst topics. Get them out of the way now."

"A fine idea," Sebastian said. "What should we start with. Leprosy? Taxes? Horse manure?"

"Justus Gregoire's three-hour sermons."

Sebastian groaned. "Blacksmith Thomasen's breath."

Elodie laughed. "How is it possible his breath is that bad?"

"It's like something died down there and is just slowly decomposing," Sebastian agreed.

"Toothaches," Elodie continued.

"Your mother-in-law," Sebastian countered.

Elodie cringed. "She's the worst!"

"The absolute worst. I don't know how you put up with her."

"Do you know she still calls me *that girl*? I'll be just feet away, and she'll be talking to Willum and call me *that girl*. As if I'm a monster who might become real if she named me."

Sebastian shook his head, suddenly serious. "Inexcusable. No one should treat you that way, least of all family."

Sebastian was right, of course. Willum used to stand up to his mother on her behalf, but Eugenia seemed incapable of changing. So they'd both just...stopped trying. She'd grown used to it. That was the way of so many things.

But this was growing too serious. Elodie needed to bring back the levity. She offered him a tight smile. "Those are some terrible topics. An impressive list. But what of you? What is the subject that wakes you in the night in a cold sweat?"

"Besides your mother-in-law?"

"Naturally. Beside her."

"Oh, my bachelorhood, of course. It's like I'm the village project. Everyone sees fit to have an opinion."

"You don't want to marry?" Elodie asked, overcome by curiosity. It *was* strange that Sebastian, one of the town's most eligible men, hadn't yet married.

"Of course I do. I'm just not particularly inclined to marry the wrong person."

Elodie couldn't contest the wisdom in that. "And you think you'll find her? The right person?"

"I'm confident I will," Sebastian said, looking straight ahead. But there was something in his tone she couldn't recognize. As if she'd tread somewhere she shouldn't have.

"I'm sorry. I shouldn't have pried."

"It's all right. We're friends. And friends share things. Even the hard things," he said, turning back to her. His eyes drifted down to her neck. "Like...how you got those marks."

Elodie forced a smile. "I see what you did there. Very crafty, Mister Beringer."

"You caught that, did you?"

Elodie sighed, letting her eyes flutter closed for a moment. "There's not much to tell. Willum and I had a fight. He was drunk. I was pushing him to do more for his hip—take more medicine, try massage, stretching—"

"Don't do that," Sebastian said sharply.

Elodie drew back. "What?"

He took a breath, as if to steady himself. "I'm sorry I interrupted. Just—don't do that. Blame yourself. I hear it coming. There's no scenario you could share where it would be acceptable for him to do that to you. So just...no more blaming yourself, okay?"

Elodie pressed her lips together, fighting back the sudden onslaught of tears. Sebastian's words had touched a spot within her she hadn't realized was so tender. She did blame herself for pushing Willum too hard. But he was right. It wasn't her fault. It was his. She gave herself a little shake and spoke slowly. "He said I couldn't understand what it was like to feel that pain every day. Suffocating him." Her voice grew small. "So...he made me feel it."

Sebastian's fists tightened on the reins until his knuckles turned white. "Un-Brother take him," was all he said, low and hot.

"Sebastian—" Elodie warned. She shouldn't have told him. She kicked herself. Sebastian was as level-headed a man as she'd ever met, but she didn't want to stoke enmity between him and Willum. Especially as Sebastian was one of the only kind souls who would still give Willum work. What if he confronted Willum and it became violent? What if he told others? She didn't want to prejudice the village against Willum. It would only make it harder if she did stay, if they did try to work it out. Elodie hurried out, "Willum wasn't himself. He's never hurt me before, and he never will again."

"How do you know that?"

"I just...do," she said lamely. All-father help her, she didn't even believe it herself.

"Maybe it would be better if—"

She cut him off. "Don't you say that. If one more person says it would be better if he cleaved me, I'll scream."

Sebastian was quiet. "At least you'd be safe."

"Because being a homeless spinster is so safe?"

"Everyone loves you, Elodie. You have family. No one would let you want for anything."

Elodie felt the pressure building, the tears more insistent now. "It's not just the money, or the security. To be cleaved... I can't think of a more public failure. How could I look people in the eyes, knowing they pity me? Even my father...my sisters. How could I face people when they knew I was tossed out like garbage for being a useless woman?"

Sebastian turned to her, his eyes blazing. "There is nothing useless about you. I don't think people would think that, but if they did, the fact would speak poorly of them, not you. A society that bases a woman's value solely on her ability to bear children is backwards and wrong. Maybe we need someone brave enough to break those suppositions."

If only. "I don't want to be brave, Sebastian."

"But you already are, Elodie. Even without trying, you've created something for yourself. A burgeoning business—a skill with plants the whole village values. Josephine has followed your example, learning her own trade. The other girls in the village will too."

"It's not that simple," she protested.

"Why not?" he challenged. "Why can't it be that simple?"

She threw up her hands. "Because if Willum cleaves me, or if I leave him, I'll never have children. No one would want to marry a cleaved woman."

"But I just said—"

"You said that it's wrong if society only values me for my ability to bear children. I agree. But what if that's actually all I really want?

What if being a mother is the only thing that will bring me true happiness?"

He furrowed his brow. "Do you believe that?"

Elodie sighed. How to make him understand? Did *she* even understand? Why *was* it so important for her to have children? It was so ingrained, rooted so deep in her that she'd always taken it as gospel, but when she really dug down...

There. There it was. The tiny acorn that had grown into the oak tree choking her life. She spoke slowly, the words forming as the realization slowly crystallized. "When my mother died...we lost something. The family we were supposed to have. The childhood...the life. And I think..." Her voice cracked as tears started flowing. "I think I promised myself that I would have that perfect family someday—have the happiness that was robbed from me. I swore I'd be the mother that I grew up without. And now...if Willum cleaves me, or if I leave him... I'll have lost it again. Except this time, I'll never get it back. I'll never have another shot."

Sebastian's only response was to wrap an arm around her shoulder and Elodie leaned into his comforting warmth. Her eyes fluttered shut, and when she opened them again, she found him offering her a handkerchief.

She let out a little laugh. "I hope you have a large supply of these." But when she looked up at him, she was surprised to find unshed tears shimmering in his eyes, too. She straightened. "Are you all right?"

His Adam's apple bobbed as he swallowed. His voice was husky when he spoke. "You deserve all of that, Elodie. True happiness. A loving family. You deserve better than the illusion of it."

His unspoken words were as plain as day. With Willum, the illusion was all she'd have. Even if they managed to have a baby, even if he gave up drinking and healed and became the man he'd once been, the worry and doubt would always be there. The fear that her marriage would once again become a living nightmare. Her jaw worked as she nodded. Sebastian had a way of delivering hard truth with a gentle hand. Yet another thing she appreciated about him.

Elodie laid a hand softly on his cheek. "You are too kind for this world, Sebastian."

He smiled. "That's my line."

She let her hand fall. She'd never spoken of this with Willum. With anyone. Willum had never even asked. Yet sharing it with Sebastian felt right somehow.

He brushed a tear with the heel of his hand and she gave him back him the handkerchief. "We're a pair, aren't we?" she said.

Sebastian tucked the handkerchief back in his pocket and gave himself a little shake. "A fine travel companion I am, bringing the woman to tears. Speaking of pairs, though..." He reached into a sack between them and riffled through it before pulling out a paper parcel tied in twine. "Pear tart?"

Elodie let out a laughing hiccup. "I thought you'd never ask."

CHAPTER 21

ROCHESTER

Sebastian was sorry to see the town of Rochester spring up in the distance, the white spire with its infamous clock tower piercing the blue sky. Of all the places he distributed cider, this one was his favorite. Yet the closer Feu plodded to the town's old arching gate, the sooner it brought them to the end of this day. An entire day with Elodie. And he wasn't ready to let it go.

After their turn with a slate of unpleasant topics and Elodie's tearful confession, they'd settled into easy conversation. They'd spoken of apple blossoms and fireflies, favorite pastries and favorite poems. Whether happy or sad, to him, Elodie was like fresh air and sunshine—he wanted to close his eyes and turn his face toward her. Or perhaps she was just his sun.

In truth, he shouldn't be here at all, sitting beside her with such familiarity. It was improper and foolish. Dangerous even, to give his heart hope, even a faint hope. He *should* stay as far from her as possible. But could he help it if the All-father had brought her to him in her time of need? And that he happened to be the one person with the information she needed? True, he had sought the information out, but did that make it any less serendipitous?

Elodie clearly needed someone in her corner. Someone without an agenda. And even though he wanted her more than anything on the All-father's green earth, he wouldn't act on it. Never ask her for it. He would love her the way she needed right now. As a friend. It was why he'd stopped himself from voicing the words that wanted to burst from his lips—that if she and Willum ended, there would be someone to love her, and care for her, and create whatever kind of family the Daughter saw fit to gift them. Why he'd stopped himself from leaning in and claiming her lips when she'd laid her hand on his cheek. But it was clear Elodie was torn in two, struggling with what to do about Willum's abuse. Professing his love certainly wouldn't make the situation any clearer and could drive her away when she needed him most. He couldn't risk it.

But that didn't stop him from spending the quiet moments of the ride imagining what life would be like if she was his—if they were husband and wife. He could almost taste her lips, feel the warm velvet of her tongue. See the fair landscape of her naked body stretched out before him, limned in firelight. The image was glorious. And gut-twistingly painful, for he knew it was so desperately unlikely to ever come to be. That was Elodie. The best, and worst, thing in his life.

Rochester was a fine town, its long, winding lanes filled with bright half-timbered buildings and even brighter flower boxes. Sebastian smiled as Elodie craned her neck to take in buildings stretching above them, the tangle of shops and cafés lining the street. "First time?"

She smiled ruefully. "I don't travel much."

"Sometimes I daydream about closing the brewery for a year and traveling the world. Seeing the white sand beaches of the Cerene Sea and the frozen fjords of Montjak."

"A fine dream," Elodie said. "My daydreams usually feature decadent candies and succulent roasts."

He forced a laugh, shoving down a hot spike of anger. If Willum didn't drink them out of house and home, she wouldn't have to daydream about food. He fumbled for a safe topic. "Would you like to see the world? If you had a choice?" Often in his daydreams, Elodie was at his side.

"If I had a genie in a bottle?"

"Or a wish-eater in a cave."

Elodie looked at him sharply, and he offered a gentle smile to show it was a jest.

"I don't know," she admitted. "Everyone I love is in Lunesberg. I'm not sure why I'd want to go anywhere else."

"To appreciate them all the more when you come home, having seen how someone else lives."

"That's a fine way of looking at it. I suppose I'd have to try it out and see."

"Ah, here's the inn where we'll make our first delivery." Sebastian nodded to the Golden Lantern, a respectable three-story establishment.

"Can I help?" Elodie asked.

Sebastian slowed Feu to a stop and handed her the reins. "Just make sure Feu doesn't get any bright ideas."

She gave him a little salute, and his heart squeezed in his chest.

Sebastian turned to his work, dropping the tailgate and unrolling two barrels for the inn. He was a few days early for deliveries to Rochester, but the innkeeper didn't mind. They dropped off at three more inns and taverns before they reached their final destination, an inn called Avangeline's Hearth. The locals called it "Ava's," for the proprietor, who traded in information and less reputable items he didn't ask about.

"Ava's the one who has information about the sojourner," he explained to Elodie, offering a hand to help her down from the wagon. "I asked her to keep tabs on him."

Elodie shook her head in amazement. "I still can't believe you did that."

"It was nothing. Idle chatter between friends." No need for her to know just how many innkeepers in how many villages he'd inquired with.

"So the inn is named after this Avangeline?"

"Ava's a widow, and she changed the name after her husband died."

"She runs the whole thing herself?"

"Better than most innkeepers in the city. She's had no shortage of suitors, but she swears she'll never marry again. She likes the freedom of doing things herself." Though she didn't mind company of the male persuasion, which Ava had made perfectly clear to Sebastian on several occasions. His cheeks heated at the memory. No need to mention that to Elodie, either.

"Pepa would throw a fit at the thought of it." Elodie shook her head with a soft hiss. "I wish he weren't so old-fashioned."

"Times are changing."

"Not fast enough."

Sebastian rolled the final barrel off the wagon and into the inn's courtyard before standing it beside the front door. "After you." He gestured to Elodie, straightening his tunic.

The sprawling common room was set around a huge river stone hearth. A balcony lined the second story, filled with more empty tables. Ava's was always clean, unlike some of the other inns, which seemed to pride themselves on the stickiness of their floors.

"Hello?" he called.

Elodie was turning in a slow circle, her head craned up, taking in the huge timbered beams crisscrossing the ceiling and the two large antler chandeliers. "Where is everyone?"

"Ava's closed for lunch," Sebastian explained.

Ava bustled through a swinging door behind the bar, her eyes lighting up at the sight of him. "Bas!" She skipped to meet him, giving him a kiss on each cheek. Though Ava must have been at least forty, she was striking, with long, rose-gold curls and a figure that would make even young women envy.

Bas? Elodie mouthed at him, one eyebrow raised.

His cheeks heated.

"Who's this?" Ava asked, turning her sharp, green eyes on Elodie.

"This is my friend Elodie. Elodie, Ava."

"You have a beautiful inn," Elodie offered.

"Thank you, dear," Ava said, amused. She turned back to Sebastian, her shrewd eyes considering. "I wasn't expecting you until later this week."

Sebastian cleared his throat, reddening more as Elodie turned to him. "Yes, well, I thought I'd move up the trip. Circumstances changed...and we need to find Piers. The sojourner I asked you about."

Ava's lovely face darkened. "Ah. Why don't you pull up a stool and I'll pour you two a drink."

Elodie shot Sebastian a worried look, but they followed Ava to the bar, perching on two stools.

"Beer or wine, love?" Ava asked Elodie.

"Wine," she said. "White, if you have it. Something sweet."

"I've got it. The usual for you?" She raised an eyebrow at Sebastian and he nodded.

Ava poured their drinks and set them on the bar before shoving her hands into the pockets of her apron. "About two days back, your sojourner got in a mite of trouble. He's been parked over with the other sojourner wagons on the north end of town. There's a market of sorts over there, has been for years, and plenty of townsfolk do their shopping there for spells and trinkets. I was keeping an eye on him, like you asked. Seems he sold an enchanted brooch to the alder's daughter. A real fancy thing that was supposed to make the wearer fall in love with you. She paid a pretty penny for it, much more than even the brooch was worth."

"Let me guess," Sebastian said. "The spell didn't work?"

Ava clucked her tongue. "From what I understand, even among sojourners, love spells are frowned upon. The daughter made a fool of herself with some fellow she was over the moon for, and the truth of the supposed spell came out. The alder got all riled up and marched over to the camp to arrest the bastard. But word travels fast and the sojourners fell in defense of him. It got ugly. The fists started flying between the sojourners and the city guards and someone tumbled over a lantern. The wagons caught fire—"

"Is he dead?" Elodie blurted out.

Ava shook her head. "Sitting in Rochester jail, with a dozen other sojourners."

Sebastian blew out a breath. By the All-father... "Is everyone all right?"

"A few sojourners and guards were burned. It's a miracle the fire didn't spread across the wall and into town, though. Most of the sojourner wagons were destroyed."

Elodie's shoulders sagged and Sebastian laid a comforting hand on her back.

Ava looked between them. "He steal your best linens or something?"

"We were hoping to...acquire something in the sojourner's possession." He looked to Elodie. "We don't know if it burned."

Elodie took a gulp of her wine and slid off her stool. "You're right. We need to go see."

"And then go see Piers about..." Sebastian trailed off.

Elodie blinked, as if she had forgotten the other reason they'd come all this way. Josephine's pregnancy. "Of course."

Sebastian stood as well, taking a healthy swallow of his ale. "Ava, as always, you are a lifesaver."

She crossed her arms under her pert bosom. "Don't you forget what you promised me, now," she said with a wink.

Sebastian swallowed. Why did she make him feel like she was the cat and he the canary? "I wouldn't dream of it."

Elodie looked at him quizzically but waited until they were outside the common room to ask. "What did you promise her?"

He held a hand out to help her into the wagon's bench, unable to meet her eyes. "A date."

Elodie's blue eyes widened. "Sebastian Beringer, you sly dog."

He busied himself with the reins, clucking Feu into a walk. "It was her price, not mine. I didn't offer. It's not like I would take advantage of a lady—"

"Sebastian." Elodie cut in. "Take a breath. It's nothing to be ashamed of. She's a handsome woman. Accomplished. Wealthy. She's clearly taken a shine to you. And I don't blame her one bit. You're quite a catch."

Elodie's words sank in and Sebastian hissed in a breath. *I don't*

160

blame her one bit. You're quite a catch. His thoughts were leaves whipped in an autumn gale. Elodie had never spoken such praises of him.

She shook his arm gently, and he started. "What?"

"I said, I only wonder what Talia will think?"

Sebastian stared at her. "What Talia will think?"

"Aren't you courting her?"

He recoiled. "Whyever would you think that?"

She let out a puzzled laugh. "I've seen you together several times. At Dion and Delphine's, at the lake—"

"I'm not courting her." Sebastian ran a hand through his hair. "She just...keeps turning up. We're...friends, that's all. I'm not interested in her romantically."

Elodie's gaze turned gentle. "Have you told her so? Because I'm fairly certain she's interested."

"Actually, I think she's moved on." He hadn't spoken to Talia since she'd marched away from Elliason's Lake, fury in her eyes. But he hadn't heard rumors around town about him or Elodie, though, so it seemed Talia hadn't taken her anger out on him by gossiping. He turned Feu to the left onto Rochester's main thoroughfare, toward the outskirts of town where the sojourner camp would be. He heaved a sigh. "Can't a man and a woman be friends, without it turning...complicated?"

"Like we are?" Elodie suggested.

Sebastian stilled. Perhaps they couldn't, after all. "Right. Like we are."

"I'm afraid things are never simple when it comes to matters of the heart." Elodie tightened her shawl around herself. "Just ask Josephine."

The wagon trundled under Rochester's arching side gate, revealing an ashen nightmare. Blackened hulks dotted the landscape, remnants of their wooden frames bared like the ribs of some long-dead beast. A few sojourners sifted through the wreckage, their bright clothing grimy with soot. They ignored Elodie and Sebastian, perhaps too wrapped up in their sorrow to worry about interlopers. Or perhaps there was no longer anything to protect.

"By the All-father," Elodie breathed. "How awful."

"Those prison bars might be the only thing keeping Piers from being torn apart by his own," Sebastian remarked. "If his dispute caused this."

"There." Elodie pointed. The outline of a painted rose was just visible on the side of a charred wagon, the once green paint peeling and crackled.

Sebastian parked the wagon in the shadow of the city wall.

They made their way silently to the wagon, feet crunching on the burned debris beneath their feet.

Elodie stepped into the wagon first and he followed, his heart leaping at the close quarters. Charred wood surrounded them, the floor strewn with a tumble of detritus too badly burned to identify. She turned in a slow circle, taking it all in, her face twisted in sorrow. "No one deserves this," she whispered. "Even after all he did."

"No."

Elodie stepped farther into the wagon, kicking aside a stray piece of wood with her foot. "I think..." She cocked her head, leaning over. "Look, there was a compartment here." She knelt down and reached into a hole in the wagon's paneling.

"Wait, let me," Sebastian said. He knelt down next to her. Close. So blessed close. His fingers traced the charred opening, the splinters there. "It's like someone chopped it open."

"After the fire," Elodie agreed. "A hiding place."

Sebastian reached in gingerly, feeling about. The hiding hole was perhaps six inches deep by a foot wide—just big enough to hide valuables like jewelry or money. "Nothing." He withdrew a hand coated in black ashes. He forced himself to stand, not trusting himself to linger just inches from her.

"I'm sorry, Elodie." There was no way a map or a book had survived the fire. And she knew it.

She reached into the debris on the floor and picked up a broken handle. She held it up with a sad smile. "One of Josephine's."

He held out a hand to her. "We shouldn't linger."

Elodie placed her hand in his and he pulled her to her feet.

A low whine sounded beneath them, and they both jumped.

Elodie's foot caught on a stray board and she tumbled into his arms, her petite form flush against him.

Their eyes met and the air left him, gravity fleeing too, along with all his good sense. There was only Elodie—the curve of her waist beneath his hands, the plush satin of her lips, her scent of lavender and lemon banishing the smoke and ash.

"What was that?" she whispered, frozen.

Another whine sounded, and she melted with a shaky laugh. "It's a dog." She patted him on the chest before stepping past and down from the wagon. "Just a dog."

But it was another moment before Sebastian could move again.

CHAPTER 22

BAIL

*E*lodie and Sebastian rode back into town, the sojourner's dog between them. The poor beast had been cowering under the wagon for what looked like days, its fur coated in ash, its ears laid back on its head.

Elodie had been contemplating how to suggest that they take the dog back with them when Sebastian had turned on his heel, reappearing a few minutes later with a waterskin and the last of their pear tarts. The dog had needed little convincing to come with them after that.

"Do you know its name?" she asked, scratching the dog between its huge ears. It was filthy, but at this point, so was she. And she could use something to focus on, to steady her after the wagon. What she'd seen —her last hope at the Wish-Eater, burned to a crisp. What had happened in the wagon… Daughter help her. The second time in a day that she'd been overcome with the urge to kiss Sebastian Beringer.

Sebastian chewed his lip. "Core something… Cormorant…Coriander?"

The dog cocked its head and a bubble of laughter escaped her. "The dog's name is not Coriander."

"That's something *you'd* name a dog," he countered.

"You're not one to judge," Elodie said. "What kind of name is Feu?"

"You wouldn't believe it if I told you." Sebastian fought a grin.

"Try me."

"When Feu was a colt, he was colicky, which resulted in him... passing gas frequently. When I was little, I apparently thought it was the funniest thing in the world to...imitate the sound. I started calling him...Feu." Sebastian closed his eyes and let out a little laugh. "My mother adopted the name. Father hated it, but...it stuck."

Elodie clapped her hands over her mouth in delight. "You jest."

"I swear it on my mother's grave." Sebastian put his hand over his heart.

She laughed. "I'm afraid to ask how you named the cat."

"*Grumpy* seemed too obvious." Sebastian shot her a sidelong glance, then started laughing.

"What?" Elodie straightened.

"You have black all over your face."

No! Her hands were covered in soot, and she'd just rubbed her face. "Well, get it off!"

Sebastian pulled out a handkerchief and doused it with some water from the waterskin. "Come here."

Elodie sucked in a breath, leaning forward.

He took her chin in one hand, his fingers firm but gentle. And then with the other, he began wiping her cheek with the cloth. His eyes were bright as he regarded her, his fervent gaze fixed on the lower half of her face. "You're dirtier than Coriander," he murmured.

Elodie laughed and swiped him across the face with her dirty fingers before she realized what she was doing.

Sebastian straightened with wicked delight. "I believe that was a declaration of war—"

"Eh!" Someone hollered, and Sebastian jerked forward, grabbing the reins. Feu had been plodding forward and had almost led them into the middle of an intersection.

Elodie's heart trilled in her, even as her better judgment shouted at her to put distance between her and Sebastian. But she couldn't help herself. The man was so...everything. Handsome and smart and funny and kind and sometimes she swore he understood her better than she understood herself. And then there was the fact that his nearness set her blood boiling within her, his touch made her core tighten with need. When she'd fallen on top of him, Gods help her, she'd wanted him to pull her body tight against his, claiming her with a certainty that no amount of propriety or guilt or common sense could deny—

"We're here." Sebastian had navigated the intersection and pulled Feu to a stop before the imposing stone building that housed Rochester's jail.

The moment was gone.

Sebastian wiped his face with the handkerchief and handed it to her.

She did the same.

"Are you ready to see him?"

She shook her head. "But we're here."

It took them a few minutes to navigate their way through the guard offices into the bowels of the jail. Elodie's thoughts spiraled like water down a drain. What was she going to say to him? She'd come to Rochester for two reasons. For herself, and for Josephine. Her hopes were dashed, but this trip could still be salvaged. There could be something here for Josephine. Though what, she wasn't sure anymore.

"Some rough characters in here, madam," an officer said to Elodie before they passed through the door. "Are you sure you can't let your husband here handle your business?"

Sebastian opened his mouth as if to object to the guard's mistake, but she just shook her head. "I need to see someone myself."

Elodie was assaulted by smells and sounds as they moved from light to the darkness of the hallway between the jail holding cells. Unwashed bodies. The low muttering of voices. Torches casting garish shadows, their oily smoke staining the brick walls.

Goosebumps pebbled her flesh. Elodie buried her fingers in the fabric of her skirts, fighting the urge to grab Sebastian's hand. He hovered close, shielding her partially from the sight of the prisoners they passed.

"Here you are," the muscled guard said, coming to a stop in front of a cell that looked to house a dozen men. He knocked on the bars with his baton. "Sojourner named Piers? Visitors."

She spotted his golden eyes first, glinting in the torchlight. His face was bruised and streaked with ash, his red hair tangled. He uncoiled himself from the bench, sauntering toward them, despite a pronounced limp. Elodie took a step back and felt Sebastian's hand on the small of her back. Steadying her. Even behind bars, there was something preternatural about the sojourner. Something undeniably compelling.

"Madam of the Wish-Eater. Back again. Your dedication astounds even me." He wrapped his hands around the bars slowly. His knuckles were raw and swollen. Clearly, he'd given as well as he'd gotten.

"We went to your wagon," she said. Her voice was blessedly strong.

"Then you know there's nothing left. No book. No map. So leave me in peace."

Elodie's throat was as parched as an August afternoon. The words lodged in her throat—sticking to her tongue. *Josephine is pregnant. And it's yours.* As she stood here before him, a certainty washed over her. She was a colossal fool. Why had she ever thought this man might hold the solution to Josephine's plight? This man should have nothing to do with Josephine. Their family. The baby. The sojourner was dangerous. Feral.

She gave Sebastian a sharp shake of her head. She turned to Piers. "It was a mistake to come here. I'm sorry to waste your time. I thought you should know...we have your dog. He'll be cared for."

The sojourner's eyes widened, and for the first time, Elodie thought she saw a glimpse of the real man. "Corentin? He's all right?"

"Dirty, but none the worse for wear," Sebastian added. "Good luck to you."

"Wait—" Piers called as they turned to go. "There's something else. A way we might be able to help each other."

Elodie turned back. "Go on."

He crooked a finger, gesturing them to draw near.

Ignoring her instincts that told her to run, to flee from this place and never return, they stepped in close. This near, she could see the individual flecks of gold in his irises. "I have a secret compartment in my wagon. Where I keep my valuables. Money. Jewels." Those gold eyes flicked to Elodie. "Your money."

Elodie hissed. "I knew you were in on it."

Piers rolled his eyes. "Yes, well, you were an easy mark, princess."

"Make your point," Sebastian said through gritted teeth.

"Go there, retrieve the money for me, and pay my bail. It's twenty silver pieces. You take your ten silver back, and I'll tell you whom I sold the Wish-Eater book to."

Elodie froze.

"There's just one prob—" Sebastian began, but Elodie gripped his bicep, digging in her nails.

"What good will the identity of the book's owner do me?" Elodie said. "I can't exactly acquire a book in someone else's library."

"Because I sold the book to someone in your village."

Excitement flooded through Elodie like molten metal through her veins. "Tell us the identity, then we retrieve the money."

"I do that and you'll leave me here to rot."

Elodie exchanged a look with Sebastian, her mind racing. Someone had found the sojourner's secret compartment; the money was gone. So how could they convince him to give them the information?

Sebastian nodded his head, and they stepped into the center of the walkway to confer out of earshot. "How can we get him to tell us without the money?" she whispered.

Sebastian's breath tickled her ear. "We can't. He'll see through any ruse we come up with. Besides, he could be lying."

There was a good chance of that, in fact. But to be so close and leave empty-handed *again*... Unwelcome tears swelled within her. How many times would she fail? How many failures could a person take before it broke them? "You're right."

Sebastian pulled back, searching her face. Seeing too much. "I'll pay it. I'll pay his bail."

"Sebastian!" Elodie shook her head. "No. You can't. It's too much."

"I don't have it on me, but I'll come back. I'll come back with the money and get the information for you. You'll have the location of the book in a week."

Elodie shook her head. It was too much. Sebastian had already done so much. She couldn't ask this of him. But...that desperate part within her clawed at her excuses, her pride. He was offering. And it was the only way. She was *so* close. "I don't know." It was wrong. So wrong to let him do this. It was past time to end this whole manic Wish-Eater business. *Twenty silver pieces* for a stupid map? That would feed her and Willum for a year. How could she let him do this—

"It's for me too, Elodie," he said softly.

Her resolve crumbled. He wanted it too. He had told her, he understood. He had a wish aching deep within him, as she did. What was it? She wanted to know.

"Tick tock," Piers said, tapping a fingernail against the bars.

Sebastian strode back to stand before him, his burnished gold hair facing Piers' copper. "Someone emptied your compartment after the fire. Someone who knew it was there."

"Un-Brother's balls," Piers cursed.

"But I will return with the money for your bail. If you swear, on whatever god you worship, that the information is true."

Piers glared at him balefully. "I swear. But one more condition."

"You're not in a position to negotiate further—"

"Take care of Corentin for me."

Sebastian gave a sharp nod.

Piers stuck a hand through the bars. Sebastian looked at it. Then seized his wrist, giving it a shake.

Elodie blew out a stale breath. She needed out of this place. Away from the staring eyes, from the dank, from the sojourner's oppressive presence.

"Tell your sister *hello*," Piers called after them, the words echoing in the gloom.

Tell your sister— Elodie started to round on him, but Sebastian grabbed her arm, his breath hot in her ear. "Come on."

Elodie shook herself as she emerged into the afternoon light, trying to shed the vile feeling of the man's presence. "Horrid.

Wretched. Do you see how he mocked her? I could strangle him."
Daughter, she needed a bath.

"You did the right thing," Sebastian said as he helped her into the wagon. The feel of her hand in his was almost familiar.

"What do you mean?"

Sebastian gathered the reins. The sojourner's dog, Corentin, was lying by their feet where they'd left him. "He'd bring Josephine and the baby nothing but trouble."

"I know." Elodie rubbed her face. What a disaster. What was she to tell Josephine? Thinking Piers might hold a solution had always been a long shot, but now, it was one more door firmly closed.

"You didn't really want her married to him, did you?"

"Of course not. But I don't want her to terminate the pregnancy, either."

Sebastian's mouth opened and shut. "You think she'll still try to end it?"

"Yes. She insists she doesn't want it. She thinks it will ruin her life. I told her Willum and I will take it, but..." She shook her head. "She's not convinced that would be best. Even before"—she motioned to her neck—"he never wanted to adopt. And Pepa is worried it would still ruin her prospects. I don't know what to do. I understand where she's coming from, I really do. I just wish there was a way for her to have the baby and still have the life she wants."

She dropped her head back in her hands, threading her fingers through her golden locks. "But Pepa's right. Having a baby out of wedlock would complicate her life. It's hard enough to be an unmarried woman, even without the stigma. It would be no easier on the child to be born a bastard. If Piers were a decent man, if he'd been someone kind, whom she could have grown to love...it might have been a solution." But Piers wasn't a decent man.

Elodie sat up and pressed her hands before her mouth. It wasn't fair, none of it. Not that Josephine had to make such a heartwrenching choice, not that she had to witness it. Not that Piers was spared it all. How could the gods be so cruel? This felt more like the

Un-Brother's trickery. Had her family offended the All-father some-how, forcing him to turn His back on their plight?

"What if Josephine married someone else? Someone who would treat her well? People wouldn't know the baby wasn't legitimate." Sebastian's face was set in an expression of grim resolve, so unlike his usual open countenance that it made her blink.

"If Josephine agreed, that would solve everything. But it would be impossible to find a husband on short notice...one who would take her despite her condition—"

"I'll do it," Sebastian said.

"Do what?"

He nodded, as if deciding for himself. "I'll marry Josephine."

CHAPTER 23

PROPOSAL

*E*lodie couldn't quite believe her ears. "You'll...marry Josephine?"

Sebastian nodded, his shoulders thrown back. He looked...resolute. "You need someone to marry her. Someone who knows about the baby and doesn't care, who will help her keep her reputation intact. Someone who would be a good husband to her. I could be that person."

"But..." Why was she protesting? It was a near-perfect solution. "You don't love her. You said you wanted to wait to marry a woman you loved."

Sebastian threw up his hands. "Who am I kidding? Few people marry for love, and even if you do, it's no guarantee of happiness."

Elodie couldn't argue with that.

"I've waited for the right one, and all it's gotten me is a flurry of whispers behind my back. Josephine's a sweet girl. Perhaps we could be happy, in time. Find a way to love each other. But I know we would respect each other, and treat each other well, and raise the baby well. That's more than many get."

Elodie's stomach churned. Josephine and Sebastian. Images flashed in her mind. Sebastian cradling the baby, its tiny fingers crooked around his thumb. Sebastian chasing a towheaded toddler through the orchard, apple blossoms frosting their curls like flakes of snow. Josephine selling Sebastian's cider from the new tasting room, Josephine lying down beside him every night. Safe. Cared for. Married to a wonderful man. It was everything she should want for her sister. And more generous on Sebastian's part than Elodie could even understand. So why did the thought of it make her want to scream?

Elodie examined Sebastian as covertly as she could, the blond hair curling about his ears, the shadow of stubble on his jaw, the way his strong hands gripped the reins with expert ease. His clothing, finely crafted and well-fitted but not ostentatious—he had money, but he didn't flaunt it. His kindness and generosity. She could find nothing wrong with Sebastian, not a thing. He was, by all accounts, perfect.

"I feel like a prize brood mare at auction." Sebastian met her appraising gaze. "Would you like to see my teeth?"

An embarrassed laugh escaped her and Elodie diverted her eyes, gazing at the ruts in the road before them. "You caught me."

"I'm kidding, Elodie. You're awfully quiet, though. You think it's a terrible idea."

"No, it's a fine idea," she admitted.

"Then what's the problem?"

What was the problem, indeed? The problem was that she didn't want Josephine married to Sebastian. She would be...jealous. Her stomach turned sour. It wasn't that Josephine would find a good husband who could provide for her. That Josephine would have a baby. For Sidonie had those things, and though seeing Sidonie as a mother made her ache, it didn't feel like this. Sharp. Personal.

The problem was, blessed Daughter, she'd fallen for Sebastian Beringer. Somewhere between sharing a pear tart and braving the foul depths of a Rochester jail, she'd come to admire and want him as more than a friend. But as a man.

The air left her in a rush. The weight of the realization made her want to press her hand to her chest and sob anew. How could she have let this happen?

173

But Sebastian was waiting for her answer—was studying her, and so she had to hold it in, to shove it down with every other deceitful and wretched feeling that plagued her.

"I…" she began, struggling for an answer. "I don't want you to sacrifice your happiness. Even for a good deed. The rest of your life is a long time." Self-loathing crashed over her like a tidal wave, cresting higher than it ever had before. Was she truly so selfish that she would deny her sister a kind and honorable match because she had feelings for the man herself—feelings she could never in a million years act on? No. She wanted to seize herself by the scruff of her neck and shake. No. She would not be that type of small, petty woman. She may not be able to choose her feelings, but she could choose how she acted. Sebastian would secure Josephine a fine life—filled with comfort and joy and laughter. She would not begrudge her sister that, even if it was missing in her own life. She needed to sever these feelings, to pull them out at the root.

"I appreciate your concern," Sebastian was saying. "And it's one of the reasons I value your friendship so much. You're always honest."

Elodie wanted to let out a strangled laugh.

"But the rest of my life is a long time to be alone, too. Maybe it's time I cease holding on to a wish that will never come true. Start to live the life I've been given."

Sebastian's words were like a slap, bringing her back to herself.

"You don't believe it, do you?" she asked.

"Believe what?"

"In the Wish-Eater. The story. The map. You don't think it's real."

"What do you mean?"

"You just said it's time to give up your wish. But you wouldn't say that if you thought we'd get anywhere with the information from Piers."

His eyes softened. "You're right."

He didn't believe? He must think her mad—crazy to take him on this wild goose chase… "Then why would you agree to pay such an enormous sum?"

Sebastian worried at the reins between his hands. "I don't know. I could see how much it meant to you. And that you believed. I didn't want to be the one to take that away from you. You just...deserve to have something go right for once."

Elodie stiffened as a lump grew in her throat. And there it was. Pity. He was doing this because he pitied her. Reality slammed into place as shame flooded her, hot and powerful. It was a hard truth, but it was the truth she needed. She seized it. How she felt about him didn't matter because he saw her as little more than a charity case. Not that it mattered anyway—she was married. Her thoughts about him were nothing more than temporary madness. All of this was madness. The Wish-Eater. The book. The sojourner. It was nothing more than mist and dreams, gone with the harsh light of dawn. As if it never had been.

"Elodie?" Sebastian said. "Are you all right? I can't help but feel that I've said something wrong."

She shook her head, giving a choked laugh. "On the contrary. It was just what I needed to hear."

"Then why do you look as if I just knocked the wind from you?"

There would be no wishes, no fairy godmothers or genies in bottles. No hero to rescue her. She'd been merrily traipsing down a fairy path, and what was worse, dragging Sebastian with her. "You should marry Josephine. She'd be lucky to have you. And I won't let you return to Rochester for the sojourner's information. The man deserves to rot for what he did."

"Are you certain?"

"I am." She needed to sever all emotional ties with Sebastian, if he was to be Josephine's husband. Allowing him to make such a gift wouldn't be proper.

"It's settled then, provided the bride agrees." Sebastian reached out a hand and gave her shoulder a tentative pat.

She nodded once, her gaze straight ahead. She was resolved, despite how her heart ached. Though the pain of this new sorrow left her breathless. It was the loss of something she hadn't even known she'd had.

THE LANTERNS WERE LIT in Lunesberg when they returned, twilight a velvet cloak shrouding the night sky. "Should I take you to your flat or to Larkhaven?" Sebastian asked. There was hesitation there.

Elodie weighed her options. It felt like an eternity ago that she and Willum had fought. She didn't want to go back, to try to make peace. To hear his worthless apologies. She never wanted to see him again. But she couldn't avoid him forever. It was better to face it head on. What was a bit more misery? "The flat."

"Okay," Sebastian said slowly. "If you're sure it's safe."

She stifled a sigh. "I can't avoid him forever." Her emotions were ragged. The last thing she needed was the weight of his judgment.

"Actually—"

"I'll be fine," she snapped.

He winced at her tone.

She took a deep breath. "I'm sorry. I'll be all right. I promise."

"I could come with you—"

"No. That wouldn't help. Please, just take me home."

He licked his lips. "If you're sure."

She nodded stiffly. She was sure she needed to get away from Sebastian Beringer.

Feu trundled into the main square, and Sebastian parked the cart beneath the eaves of the church.

They walked into the square by the fountain, where Elodie paused. "Thank you, for today. And for your offer. I'll speak with my father and Josephine tomorrow."

"I could make the offer myself if it would help—"

"Beringer!" a voice boomed across the square.

Elodie froze in recognition, in horror. She knew that voice. Willum. "You should go."

"I think it's a little late for that." Sebastian turned and squared his shoulders to the shadow limping across the square, out from the bright and merry tavern.

When Willum's face emerged from the shadows, Elodie's stomach dropped. He was red with drink, his handsome features twisted into a snarl. Had he been drinking steadily the past day? He drew up just inches from Sebastian, towering over him. Though Sebastian was tall, Willum was the largest man in the village, even with the twist in his hip. "Fancy yourself a rogue, do you? Moving in on another man's wife?"

"To the contrary," Sebastian said calmly, standing his ground. "I was doing Elodie and her family a favor. A favor I'm sure she'll explain to you in private."

Drawn to the commotion, faces appeared in nearby windows and figures silhouetted in the doorway of the tavern.

"Bullshit," Willum said, poking Sebastian in the chest. "I see the way you look at her. The way you've always looked at her. Like a sad, lovesick puppy dog. And I'm not the only one who sees it. It's the talk of the gods-damn town. But guess what, mongrel? She's mine."

Elodie recoiled at the words. What was Willum saying? Who was talking about them? "Willum, he speaks the truth," she said. "Our trip was family business."

Willum's head swiveled and he took a step toward her.

Elodie realized her mistake as soon as the words had left her mouth.

"Your trip?" Willum looked between them. He advanced on her and images flashed in her mind. Willum atop her, his fingers around her throat—

"Don't touch her." Sebastian's words were low and as deadly as the grave.

Willum froze, his head swiveling toward Sebastian. His answer echoed throughout the square. "No man tells me what to do with my own wife. Say another word—"

"And what?" Sebastian stepped between her and Willum. Chest to chest. "You'll do what, strangle me? Or do you only do that to defenseless women?"

Elodie hissed in a breath. She'd told him that in confidence. He'd sworn to keep it to himself—

Willum was glaring balefully at her now. "You see what happens when you tell another man our private business, Elodie? What other private things have you been sharing with him? Have you been bedding her?" Willum seized the front of Sebastian's coat and nearly lifted him off his feet. "Have you?"

"Willum, stop!" Elodie grabbed Willum's bicep, trying to shake loose his grip. Willum was going to rip Sebastian to shreds. He'd never agree to be a part of their family now, shackled to someone as unstable and violent as Willum. She needed to stop him—

Sebastian reared back and punched Willum clean across the jaw.

Willum and Elodie both stumbled back, Willum off-balance because of his leg. But he found his footing soon enough and drove back at Sebastian like a charging bull, his head down. He smashed into Sebastian's chest with his shoulder, lifting him off the ground.

Elodie might have screamed as they both went down, scrambling and wrestling, pummeling each other with blows and kicks.

"Stop it!" she cried again, her hands hovering over her face. They'd kill each other. They'd ruin everything...

A figure barreled past her and into the fray, grabbing Willum by his shoulders and pulling him bodily off Sebastian. *Pepa!*

Sebastian, blood dribbling from his nose and above one eye, scrambled to his feet and back toward Willum.

Willum roared and lunged forward, but Pepa hauled him back, shoving him away toward the center of the square. "Enough!" Pepa roared. "You're grown men. Behaving like animals. Enough."

"He's after Elodie—" Willum started, but her father shoved him again.

"You'll never find a purer woman than my Elodie. Make another comment about her honor and I'll cleave your bollocks from your body myself! You've both known Sebastian since you were running about in diapers. You're drunk and paranoid. That's all."

Willum glowered over his father-in-law's shoulder. "I'm not paranoid," he muttered. "I'm not the only one who thinks so."

"He's going to marry Josephine," Elodie blurted out.

Willum fell back a step. Elodie could have sworn his eyes cleared. "What? Is this true?"

"It is," Sebastian said. "Not that the truth matters to you. You seem to hit first and question later."

Willum prickled. "You hit me—"

Pepa shoved Sebastian back. "Beringer! Just...turn the other cheek."

Sebastian wiped the cut on his eye with the back of his hand, turning away. "Elodie, go home with your father. Don't stay with *him* while he's this drunk."

Willum started toward Elodie and Pepa stepped in his way. "You. Go home. Sebastian's right. Elodie is coming with me. No way in hell I'm letting you anywhere near her till you've sobered up."

Willum turned his glower on her, and she shied away. Exhausted. She let her father wrap his arm around her shoulder and lead her from the square.

"Clear out, people," Pepa hollered to the crowd that had formed. "Show's over."

CHAPTER 24

DANGEROUS

The weight of her father's arm was heavy about Elodie's shoulders. Disapproval radiated from him, but he said nothing.

When they were out of the square and well on their way to Larkhaven, he released her, scrubbing his face with his hands.

He looks weary beyond his years, Elodie thought with a twinge of guilt. Guilt. It was her constant companion.

"Well, did you at least find him?" Pepa finally spoke.

"Yes," Elodie whispered, glad to speak of something besides the debacle in the square that half the town had witnessed. "But he's in jail. His wagon burned. His bail's set at twenty silver."

Pepa snorted. "Should have expected as much. Knew that man was trouble the moment I saw him. Now, the bigger question, did you tell him?"

"I was going to, but when it came time to...I didn't want him tied to Josephine. Or our family. In our lives."

"Good girl. You made the right call."

"Did I? For better or worse, he's the father. Shouldn't he know? Have the opportunity to do the right thing?"

Pepa shook his head. "Not at your sister's expense. That man would make no kind of husband. Or father. He's not the first man to have a bastard running around the world without his knowledge, and he won't be the last. Now what's this about Sebastian Beringer marrying Josephine? How'd you come up with a yarn like that at a moment's notice?"

"It's not exactly a yarn," Elodie admitted. "I confided in him about Josephine—"

"Elodie!" Pepa's eyebrows shot up. "That's Ruelle business!"

"We can trust him, Pepa. He offered to marry Josephine. To pretend the baby is his."

"That wouldn't be a half-terrible match . . ." He seemed to chew on the idea.

"If Josephine agrees. How is she?" Elodie asked. "Feeling better today?"

Her father's jaw worked, his gaze darkening.

Elodie straightened, her senses firing. "What's wrong? Is she still sick?"

"No, she's feeling better. Agathe came by to check on her."

"Then what's wrong?" Elodie asked.

Her father shook his head. "I think you should talk to her."

Elodie's heart hammered as they walked the rest of the way to Larkhaven, as she hurried through the front door. Josephine was curled before the fire, a blanket wrapped around her, a book in her hand.

At the sight of them, Josephine put the book down, her gaze flickering from her father's stoic face to Elodie's worried one. "You told her?" Josephine asked.

"Told me what?" Elodie asked.

"I thought you should have that particular pleasure," Pepa said.

Josephine wrapped the blanket tighter about her, as if fortifying herself. "Agathe came by this afternoon to check on me. I explained to her about my...situation. She told me about the herbs that will take care of it. Properly."

Elodie's mouth fell open. She knew Agathe dispensed such herbs freely. But not now. Not yet, when she'd been working on a solution. "Did you take them?" she hissed.

"Not yet. Agathe said my body is still too weak from the penny-royal. But in two weeks, I'll be well enough. And I *will* take them then."

Disbelief bloomed in her like a hot-house rose. "After everything I went through for you today—"

"It's my life. My body. Pepa understands."

Elodie's head swiveled to take him in. Pepa held up his hands. "It's the best solution. Well, I thought it was."

"For who?" Elodie shrieked. "Not the baby, certainly."

"For me!" Josephine cried, shoving to her feet. "You'd choose some...tiny blob over your own sister?"

"I asked you for a little time. Just a little time to find an alternative. You didn't even give me a day! I went to Rochester today to find Piers, did you know that?"

Josephine took a step back, uncertainty flitting across her face. She looked at Pepa.

He sighed. "I didn't tell you, Jo. I didn't want to get your hopes up."

"Did you find him?" Josephine asked.

Elodie pressed her lips together, her eyes flicking to Pepa. To the curt shake of his head. "No," Elodie said. "I didn't."

"See!" Josephine cried. "It's the right thing. I'm sorry, but I don't want you and Willum—"

"I found another solution. Sebastian agreed to marry you."

"You told Sebastian Beringer I'm pregnant?" Josephine screeched. "How dare you! He'll tell—"

"He won't." Elodie held up a finger to silence her fool of a sister. "He's been a friend to me and this family and I trust him. He's the one who took me to find Piers today. And when we didn't find him, he offered to marry you himself."

"You should think about it," Pepa said. "He's wealthy, an honorable man, good-looking... He clearly likes you if he'd make such an offer."

"I don't care. I don't want to marry him!" Josephine said. "Or anyone. I don't want to be a mother."

"Josephine, you're scared, that's all," Elodie said, taking her sister's hands. "But think about it. Like I told you yesterday, you have options. Would it be so bad to be married to him? He's kind, and handsome, you won't want for anything..."

"Then you marry him," Josephine spat.

Elodie grimaced. Was there no end to the indignities of this day? "I am already married, as you well know. If you don't want to marry Sebastian, then you could still have the baby and give it to us—"

Tears welled in Josephine's eyes. "I don't want to have to go away, El. You're supposed to be on my side. Why should I have to ruin my life just because you're desperate for a baby?"

Elodie recoiled as if slapped. Anger burned in her, threatened to devour her. At her sister's selfishness. At Willum's stubbornness. At Sebastian's damned generosity. But there was one more person she was even angrier at. And that fire burned hottest of all.

"I need to go," Elodie said, spinning on her heel. "You do whatever you want, Josephine. You clearly don't give a damn what I think."

"What's that supposed to mean?" Josephine called after her. "Elodie —" But she didn't hear the rest of her sister's sentence over the slam of the door.

Elodie marched down the dim lane to Agathe's home, her face blazing hot against the cool of the night. The part of her that saw reason, that considered the feelings of everyone else, carefully stepping around them, tugged at her from some remote corner of her mind. Agathe had sworn to help those in need. It was the same as she would have offered any other patient.

But she didn't want to be reasonable. Understanding. She wanted to burn.

Agathe's cottage was dark. Elodie marched around the back, which Agathe kept unlocked. She stepped into the dark room, her chest heaving as she stalked to the fireplace and seized the matches, lighting a lantern and the mantle candles. She tossed the box on the floor.

Where was Agathe? The rage within her needed an outlet, a course. She looked around, wild-eyed. Agathe couldn't give Josephine the tincture to end her pregnancy if she didn't have any... Elodie stalked about the room, seizing bottles from Agathe's stores. The shelves behind the workbench. The cabinet by the door. The cupboards over the sink... Bottle after bottle came out of Agathe's stores and were tossed in the fireplace. She would find them all. Some part of her knew this was madness, that Agathe could just make more from the herbs around the village, and this would not truly accomplish anything, but she was just so *angry*. She had to do something.

Like a whirlwind, she flung open cupboard doors, pulled open drawers—and froze. Elodie's breath whistled out of her, the tincture forgotten.

For in this drawer lay a book, bound in blue leather, stamped in gold. Three simple words. The Wish-Eater. She retrieved the tome with shaking fingers, gingerly opening the cover—

"What in the Un-Brother's cursed name is going on here?" Agathe stood in the doorway, her hands on her hips.

"How could you?" Elodie said. Her voice was hoarse and shaking.

Agathe's piercing blue eyes squinted at Elodie. Really saw her. "What happened to your neck?" She crossed the room in two strides, her head cocked to examine.

Elodie shooed her away. "Don't change the subject. How could you?"

"You're going to need to be more specific."

Elodie hardly knew where to start. Her grievances against her mentor had grown exponentially in the last two minutes. "Josephine! The baby!" Elodie cried, cradling the book against her chest.

Agathe stilled. "What I did was offer a patient a remedy. Something I have sworn upon my oath as a healer to do. Would you like to tell me why you're so upset?"

"It'll kill the baby."

"That's entirely the whole point. And it's not a *baby* yet."

"Do you think this is a joke?" Elodie cried, tears cracking the words like glass.

Agathe's face hardened, and she crossed her arms over her chest. "You have sat at my side as I've administered tansy many a time. What is the problem?"

184

"She's seventeen! And scared. She can't even see her other options with you dangling an easy out in front of her."

"You're not her mother. You're not her guardian. She has the right to make the decision, and I will honor that choice. I would expect you to understand that, or you haven't learned much at my side."

"This is different," Elodie hissed.

"Why, because you were planning on trying to convince her to let you raise it?"

"Would that be so wrong?" Elodie said. "For the baby to live? Grow up with a mother who loves it?"

"And what of a father? A father who drinks too much and gets angry when he does?"

Elodie hissed, spinning away. "Not you too. If I hear one more lecture about Willum, I'm going to scream."

"That's because you're not thinking clearly, Elodie," Agathe said. "Look at yourself! This isn't you! Manic, judgmental, disregarding the feelings of those you love, ignoring your own safety? This desperate need to get pregnant has consumed you. You're single-minded! Obsessed! And it's ruining you!"

"I *am* obsessed!" Elodie screamed, her cursed tears coming again. "You don't know what it's like! Every month, I hope and I pray and try every remedy and old wives' tale I've ever heard. Margery tells me that stress hurts your chances, so I try to stay calm. Justus Gregoire tells me the Daughter is testing my faith, so I pray and light candles and tell myself this is the month. Madam Roussaint says I need to spice things up at home, to lay with my husband more, to find a way to pleasure him, even though the alcohol on his breath makes my skin crawl."

Elodie clutched at her chest. "And every month, I fail. Fifty-two heartbreaks I've had. Fifty-two times I've pretended everything's all right, that next time everything will be different. And every month, I'm dying a little inside until some days I don't even want to live anymore! If all my life is to be is an endless series of heartbreaks, standing aside while almost everyone around me is effortlessly handed the one thing I want most in the entire world, then I'm not interested in living it anymore, Agathe. All right?" Elodie's shoulders shook uncontrollably, the tears flowing freely.

Agathe wrapped her arms around Elodie and Elodie sobbed into her shoulder, the world awash with her sorrow. Drowning in it.

"Hush, sweet girl," Agathe said, stroking her hair. "You've endured a great trauma. Fifty-two great traumas. There is no crush like a wish unfulfilled, like the death of hope. Even the strongest soul would struggle to bear such a thing."

Elodie pulled back, glaring at Agathe. She held up the book, spitting her next words. "Then why did you keep this from me?"

Agathe paled, taking a step back. "Elodie, that's not what you think it is."

"Isn't it?" Elodie wiped her face. "Because from the look on your face, it's exactly what I think it is. And you kept it from me? Why? Because you wanted it for yourself? Because you knew if I had a baby, I wouldn't be your apprentice anymore?"

"I kept it from you because that book is dangerous, more dangerous than you know. I saw how the sojourner's tale captivated you at Baumai, and I couldn't risk you getting tangled up in it." Agathe seemed to struggle to get the words out.

"Well, you know what I think, Agathe?" Elodie snarled. "The only good thing about being desperate is that a little danger doesn't scare me anymore."

"It should. All things have a price, wishes most of all."

"I would give anything to have a child. I would pay any price."

"Then that's what you'll pay." Agathe's words were quiet.

Elodie turned on her heel to go. She couldn't be here anymore. With Agathe's lies, her platitudes. She was a tired old woman, trying to keep Elodie trapped in her sad, little life.

"Elodie!" Agathe called after her. "Promise me one thing—"

"You don't get to ask anything of me," Elodie said from the doorway. "Not ever again."

Agathe met her at the door. "Then for you—just read the book. Before you go. Read it and decide. And if you decide to go..." She shoved an item wrapped in navy cloth into Elodie's hands. "Take this with you."

"What's this?" Elodie unwrapped a fold of cloth to reveal a long slender dagger, the blade bone-white.

"Pray you never have to find out."

CHAPTER 25

WHISKEY

*S*ebastian sat on his bed and, with a hiss, pressed a glass of cold cider to the cut on his forehead. Corentin, the sojourner's dog, lay on a rug in the corner. Thankfully, Grinchaux was nowhere to be found. He didn't relish the moment when those two made each other's acquaintance.

He ran it over and over in his mind. "I can't figure it out," he said. Corentin cocked his head, his big ears swiveling. "How in All-father's name did I get into a fistfight with Willum Mercer?"

The bastard had started it—he'd been belligerent, saying things about Sebastian and Elodie that couldn't stand. Maybe Elodie's father had been right. Maybe he could have been the bigger man, kept it from coming to blows. But gods damn, it had felt good to punch Willum square in the face.

Willum deserved ten times the bruises he'd left on Elodie, and a few more for good measure. The man had cowered behind his injury long enough. Yes, a stone had fallen on him and crippled him. There was no denying it was an unfair shake. But did that give him the right to become a miserable human being?

A knock sounded downstairs. The brewery door. Corentin let out a sharp bark. Sebastian froze. Was it Willum? Or his thug friends

Bellamy and Marsaint come to finish the job Willum had tried to start? He could pretend he wasn't here—let them beat down the door. But what if it was someone else? Like Elodie? He owed her an apology for losing his temper, for taunting Willum about the marks on her neck. He had promised her to keep her secret, and he had blabbed to the entire town square.

The thought was enough to propel him down the stairs. "Who is it?" he asked through the thick door.

"Dion," came the reply.

Sebastian's eyebrows shot up. He wasn't expecting his friend at this hour. He unlocked the door and opened it.

Dion was grinning, though shadows under his eyes spoke of a distinct lack of sleep. He hoisted a bottle in his hand. "Fancy a drink?"

"You have no idea how much."

"I have some idea," Dion replied. "News of your epic battle with Willum has spread like wildfire."

Sebastian groaned as Dion followed him up the stairs to his flat. "I can only imagine what's being said."

"Well, what's being said is that the two of you were brawling over one Elodie Mercer. Now I said that couldn't be true because my friend is far too wise to start a fight over a married woman. Please tell me I didn't make myself a liar?"

"Of course not." Sebastian retrieved two clean glasses from the little shelf above his sink. "You think after ten years of being in love with Elodie, I'd suddenly decide to battle her drunken husband for her?"

Dion spotted Sebastian's mostly empty cider glass on the bedside table and laughed. "Started without me, eh?"

"I need the hard stuff," Sebastian said, holding out his glass.

Dion obliged. "When did you get a dog?"

"It's a long story."

"Let me guess. It has something to do with Elodie Mercer?"

Sebastian huffed.

Dion went to give Corentin a scratch. "I told Delphine that the rumors must be false. That there was no way that our Sebastian

189

battled Willum for Elodie. And furthermore, that there was definitely no way that he would be foolish enough to propose to seventeen-year-old Josephine Ruelle."

Sebastian winced, taking a sip. "There might be some truth to that later rumor."

Dion groaned and fell into the chair across the room. Sebastian sank onto the bed. "Didn't I tell you?" Dion shook his glass at Sebastian. "Didn't I warn you? Elodie Mercer is your own personal siren, singing you onto the rocks. One day. One day with Elodie and you've got... what, a town scandal, a black eye, a new mongrel to feed, and a fake fiancée?"

Thank the All-father Dion didn't know about the twenty silver he'd committed in order to chase some fairy tale map. Though Elodie had said she wouldn't accept the money. "She's a real fiancée," Sebastian protested as he dabbed at his eyebrow with a finger. "If she'll have me. I haven't technically asked her yet."

"We've known each other a long time, Sebastian, and this...*engagement*...it isn't like you. Last I knew, you and Josephine had exchanged a total of ten sentences. What's really going on?"

Sebastian considered. He had sworn to Elodie he wouldn't tell anyone about Josephine's condition, but All-father help him, he needed someone to talk to. Dion could keep a secret. "Swear to secrecy?"

Dion grinned. "Ooh, I knew there was something juicy."

"Dion—" Sebastian began.

"I swear," Dion said. "Spill."

Sebastian made quick work of the story. Though Dion's eyebrows rose a bit, he stayed quiet until Sebastian reached the part where he'd agreed to marry Josephine himself.

Dion spluttered into his glass, coughing up a drink. "Are you mad?"

"I certainly hope not."

"You can't marry Josephine," Dion said.

"Why not?" Sebastian retorted stubbornly, taking a sip of the whiskey Dion had brought. All-father, this was the good stuff.

"Because she's seventeen and headstrong. Because she's carrying another man's baby. Because you two hardly know each other. *You're in love with her sister.* Shall I go on?"

"I know it's unorthodox," Sebastian said. "But she needs help, and I can give it. Isn't it my duty to help a neighbor in her time of need?"

"Your duty is to give a fellow a ride when his wagon breaks an axle. Not to marry his damn horse!" Dion exclaimed, and Sebastian couldn't help but chuckle.

"What if his horse is very handsome?"

Dion shook his head. "The handsome ones are the most dangerous."

Sebastian sighed. "I know it sounds sudden..."

"*Sounds sudden?* You've been in love with Elodie for the last decade and refused all other candidates, of which there have been plenty. Talia, a stunning, gregarious, *age-appropriate* woman, has all but professed her undying love for you. Now you're going to go marry Elodie's sister? I know it may seem like the next best thing, mate—"

"That's not why I'm doing it. Josephine and Elodie are sisters, but they're nothing alike," Sebastian said. It was true. There were similarities between them—the eyes, the strawberry-blonde hair, the freckles across their noses—but Josephine was so different. Fiery where Elodie was steady. With a head in the clouds where Elodie was grounded.

"Then why are you doing it?"

"Elodie was just...so distraught about her sister. I could help, so... I'm going to."

"You're so in love with the woman that you're going to marry her sister *as a favor?*" Dion exclaimed. "This is your life, Bas!"

"It's not just that." Sebastian stood and paced the narrow room. "I've been stuck for so long. Frozen. Unable to let Elodie go, but unable to have her."

"*Unwilling* to let her go, is the word I believe you're looking for."

"Unwilling, unable, I don't know. I've tried to put my feelings aside, and I've failed every time. Maybe I need to do something drastic. To shake them loose. To move past this."

"And marrying her sister seems like the best way to do that?" Dion raised an eyebrow. "Why don't you marry someone more suitable? Talia, for instance! She was over the moon for you before you messed it all up."

"I couldn't marry Talia knowing I'm still in love with Elodie. It wouldn't be right. But with Josephine...it's a matter of convenience. She would know I wasn't marrying her for love, and vice versa. Somehow it feels more...honest."

A loud banging on the brewery door made them both jump. "Are you expecting someone?" Dion asked.

Sebastian shook his head. He held up a finger to his lips. A muffled shout, distinctly female, reached his ears. "I know you're in there, Sebastian Beringer! I see your light!"

"Is that Talia?" Dion asked.

Sebastian closed his eyes with a soft moan. Would this night never end? "She's heard about Josephine."

Dion stood and poured Sebastian another finger of whiskey. "Godspeed, my friend. I'm here for backup if you need me."

Sebastian stood, his feet like lead weights. Down the stairs, into the dark, cavernous brewery. He'd never promised anything to Talia. She didn't have a right to be upset. He hadn't been courting her. He'd tell her as much.

She banged on the door again. "Sebastian! You coward! Come out and face me like a—"

He pulled the door open. "Good evening, Talia."

She barreled past him into the dim space. "You didn't think I deserved to hear it from you?"

"This night has not unfolded how I would have chosen, Talia. I'm sorry—"

She threw up her hands and paced before him. "I don't understand it. It's a spectacularly terrible match. She's seven years your junior. Is that what men want? A girl barely old enough to taste a Baumai tart?"

"That's not fair and you know it," Sebastian said. "I never meant to hurt you, but I never...felt about you...the way I think you felt about me. I'm sorry if I misled you."

"You're sorry if you *misled* me?" She put her hands on her hips with a huff. "Well, that's not good enough." Talia resumed her pacing. "What I don't understand is why you'd agree to marry Josephine when you're so clearly in love with Elodie?"

Sebastian's heart seized. All-father, he hadn't expected her to be so direct. "I'm not sure what you're talking about—"

"Do you think I'm an idiot? It took me...a month of paying attention to see the way you look at her. And I'm not the only one that sees it! You're not so subtle as you think you are."

Willum's words swam to mind. *I'm not paranoid. I'm not the only one who thinks so.* His mouth opened and closed. "Did you... Did you say something? To Willum? Are you the reason he was all spun up tonight?"

She crossed her arms before her. "Of course not."

Sebastian let out a disbelieving laugh. "I don't believe it. The second you don't get what you want, you take the things you learned in confidence and use them against me?"

"I didn't do that." The anger faded from Talia's face. "I wouldn't do that to you."

"You mean to tell me you told no one of your suspicions that I had feelings for Elodie?"

Talia bit her lip. "I didn't tell Willum—"

"You need to leave." Sebastian strode to the door and yanked it open.

"Sebastian—"

"Good *night*, Talia."

Tears shimmered in her eyes as she stood at the door a moment. He looked into the amber liquid in his glass.

"Goodbye, Sebastian," she whispered.

He slammed the door after her. His thoughts were heavier than his tired legs as he hauled himself back up the stairs. He hadn't had romantic feelings for her, but he'd liked her. She'd made him laugh. He'd trusted her. And she'd turned on him, on a copper piece.

Dion was dutifully waiting for him. "That sounded like it went well."

Sebastian leaned his forehead against the doorjamb. "It's been a long day, Dion. I think I need some rest." He didn't have it in him to hear any more lectures tonight.

Dion stood, setting his empty glass down. He paused, seizing Sebastian's shoulder. "All will look brighter in the morning, my friend."

A hollow laugh escaped him. "I hope you're right."

"You know Delphine and I support you whatever you do. But...I'd be remiss if I didn't mention one possibility."

Of course. Sebastian stifled a sigh. "Let's have it."

"What if Willum cleaves Elodie? They've been married what, four years? Four and a half? Delphine's heard rumblings around the village that he's considering it."

"Rumors. Just rumors. Elodie's dead set against it. She has this image of what her life should look like—this perfect family she's set on having. She won't give it up." He'd never believed Willum would cleave Elodie, but if people in the village were talking... Could the man truly be considering it? Might Elodie one day be free?

"It's not her choice. And most rumors have a kernel of truth in them. What if, six months from now, Willum cleaves Elodie, and she's free? Heartbroken, but free. It would be your chance, my friend. To be there for her. Show her she can love again. Show her what marriage is really supposed to be like. But you couldn't be there to pick up the pieces. Because you'd be married to her sister."

"What a cheerful thought," Sebastian managed, fighting his horror. He'd been so sure Willum would never be fool enough to cleave Elodie, but what if? To come so close, to have the chance to be with her stolen once again...Would he be able to stand by while some other man wooed her, dried her tears, made her laugh again? Or would it be worse if she remained alone, filled with sorrow...believing the world was such an unkind place devoid of love?

"I've counseled you many, many times over the years to abandon this unrequited love of yours. But if Willum cleaves Elodie, I'll be the first one to eat my words. You've hung in this long, my friend. Don't give up in the eleventh hour."

"I've already told Elodie that I'll marry Josephine. She's probably telling her sister right now that all her problems are solved. Could I go back on that? And all for the chance..."

"That Willum will be the colossal idiot we know him to be?" Dion said. "Yes, you can."

"Willum is many things, but he's not a fool. He has to know Elodie is the best thing in his life. He's not going to let go of that."

"Willum Mercer hasn't been himself for some time now. There's no saying what he'll do. All I'm saying is think on it. Be selfish for once in your life. Tell Elodie the truth. Show her there's another option besides her drunken lout of a husband. She could have her perfect family. With you."

"I'll think on it," he promised.

And think on it he did. Long after Dion left, through the quiet night. And as sun's rays dawned, he found no answers. Only aching knuckles and a world of trouble.

CHAPTER 26

ALONE

*E*lodie stood before the door to the flat, her hand poised on the knob. The book was tucked in her satchel. *The Wish-Eater.* She couldn't quite believe that it was in her possession. All she'd been through, and it had been right under her nose the whole time. Elodie pulled her simmering anger around her like a warm cloak. It was so much sweeter than guilt's bitter tang.

But anger wasn't what stopped her now. It was fear. What would she find when she entered? Was Willum home? Was he awake? It was late, and he'd been several drinks in when he and Sebastian had fought. He didn't last too long in that state. Most likely, sleep had already overtaken him, wherever he might be. But what if she was wrong?

It had been less than a day since she and Willum had grappled, since he'd tried to strangle the life from her. In some ways, it felt like lifetimes had passed. In other ways, she'd never left that moment. She was still there—frozen like stone—letting him steal the breath from her lungs, the very life from her body.

But she was stalling. She needed to go in. She needed to change her clothes, she needed to eat dinner, she needed to pore over the map in the back of the book. Either he was awake or he wasn't. Home or not. Standing here for eternity wouldn't change it.

As silent as a mouse, she slipped her key in the lock and turned the knob.

The sound of Willum's snores greeted her as she stepped into the dark room and closed the door carefully behind her. He was a deep sleeper when he was in his cups, so as long as she was quiet, she could go about her business and not rouse him.

Elodie untied her boots and slipped out of them, treading quietly across the floor to the kitchen, retrieving water, a hunk of bread and some cheese, and a heel of cured sausage. She took her spoils to the little table across the room, depositing them and sinking into the chair with a sigh. She lit a single candle, holding her breath as the match flared to life, as the light kissed the corner of the room where Willum slumbered.

He didn't move.

A little smile slipped onto her face, despite everything. Alone at last.

She attacked the bread, tearing off a hunk as she turned to the map, squinting in the low light. It was clear that the map wasn't part of the book; it had been sketched in after the fact. No doubt by someone who had found the creature. It took her a moment to orient herself to the rolling hills and hash-marked trees. Her eyes widened. It was Astria. Yes, she saw the serpentine path of the Weiss river's larger brother: the Rogra, the rolling expanse of the Creantine hills separating their province from Umbria. The Seleria Lakes like spots on a heifer, marking the edge of the map. The Malveille Forest marked the border between Astria and Frieland, a thick wood far from country roads and the bustle of towns. Elodie blew out a breath. Of course the Wish-Eater's telltale "X" was nestled deep in the Malveille. The stories said it was a place of dark magic and curses, thorns and shadows. It was a place where few good folk treaded.

Elodie gnawed on her salami, considering the map with a frown. The Malveille was said to be a dangerous area, past the protection of the Astrian guard, a place where wild things still roamed. It would be dangerous to take the journey alone. But who could she ask to accompany her? Not Willum, he'd think her mad, and travel always pained his injury. Besides, admitting how far she'd bought into the myth of the Wish-Eater would just give him one more reason to cleave her. Her father? No, she couldn't ask him to leave Josephine so soon after her ordeal. Plus, she couldn't imagine herself articulating to him her wild plan. Josephine was ill, and she wouldn't be any help against bandits or wild beasts. Sidonie and Hugh had the new babe. Agathe would never come, even if Elodie forgave her for keeping the book from her. Which she was ill inclined to do.

The obvious choice was Sebastian. In fact, she owed it to him. Wasn't he looking for the Wish-Eater too, for his own desperate wish? But she couldn't ask him, could she? In part because she wanted to so desperately. It was reason enough to stay away. He was Josephine's betrothed now. Well, assuming Josephine accepted the match.

Her thoughts of him flickered like fireflies, beautiful and bright. The easy day they'd spent together. The energy of his presence as they'd crouched in the wagon, just inches from each other. Being close to him had made her feel more alive than she had in years. The blue ring of his eyes, like a sky in summer, the wry twist of his fine lips as he laughed—how had she not seen him before? Growing up, he'd been one of the village boys, no more remarkable than any other scrawny, knock-kneed rascal. And as they'd grown, her eyes had fallen on Willum, always Willum. He had shined the brightest, but in the end, he'd been nothing but fool's gold. Had she ever really considered what type of man he would become? How he would handle adversity when everything in his life had always gone right? How his work ethic seemed to consist of him charming everyone into letting him skate through or carrying his load themselves?

She sighed as he let out a particularly loud snore. What girl at seventeen knew what she wanted—could make any sort of rational choice? Guilt bloomed again. Perhaps she owed Josephine an apology. Maybe her sister had shown wisdom beyond her years in refusing to marry the sojourner or bear the baby.

Elodie's hands strayed to her flat belly, her heart twisting at the thought of the babe. Its uncertain future. There had to be a way for Josephine and the baby to be happy. And her. And Sebastian. And even poor Willum. The book before her seemed to glow with dangerous promise. This was her chance. Despite the circumstances, the book and the map had fallen into her hands. It couldn't be a coincidence. The moment she'd heard the sojourner's story, it had called to her. It did still. This was a journey she must take. Perhaps she could find a way to solve all of their problems, if she was creative enough with her wish.

Elodie popped the rest of the cheese in her mouth and wiped her hands on her dress. She would go, even if she had to go alone. She wouldn't let fear cripple her. She had spoken the truth to Agathe. Some days she feared she couldn't suffer any more disappointment. Her soul was inches from lying down and giving up—succumbing to the weariness and the weight of sorrow. She had nothing to fear because she had nothing left to lose.

Elodie made quick work of preparing. She changed into a dress of plain blue homespun, cinched with a leather belt. She folded her embroidered shawl in her drawer. It would only get in the way in the woods. She braided her hair in two plaits and retrieved her fur-lined muff and thick cloak, both gifts from her father. It was May, but there was no telling how cold it would be in the woods.

She had very little of the things one needed for a journey of any length—no bedroll or tinder box or fishing line. But she rustled up some food: carrots and potatoes to cook in a little pot, stale jerky from a stag Bellamy had taken down last summer. A canteen, matches, a filet knife in a leather holster. She put it all in her pack before wrapping the book in beeswax paper to protect it from the elements, placing it on top beside the strange pale knife Agathe had given her. She could read the story, as Agathe had asked, when she stopped to rest on the journey.

The candle puddled in its holder by the time she finished packing. She looked at Willum. Still sleeping. Blissfully unaware. Her mouth tightened. It would serve him right if she left without a trace. Let him worry and think the worst. That she'd left him. That she was dead.

But good sense won out. She didn't need him tearing the town apart in her absence, brawling with Pepa or anyone else who got in his way. So she sketched out a simple note.

There's something I have to do. I'll be back within a week. We'll talk then.

She didn't want to talk then. Part of her never wanted to speak with him again. But that was tomorrow's problem. Tonight, there was only the bundle of nerves churning in her gut. She was doing it. She was going on her adventure.

Elodie closed and locked the door silently behind her, feeling strangely light despite the heavy pack on her shoulders. The night stars shone above her as she stole through the town, headed back toward Larkhaven. She padded down the lane and continued around the side of the house into the silent garden, toward the greenhouse. She didn't want to risk Willum waking and stopping her. She didn't want to risk anyone stopping her. So she would start her journey where no one would think to look for her.

Her boots crunched on glass as she stepped inside the dark space, as quiet as a tomb. She kicked the glass to the side, trying not to think of Sebastian's hands hot on hers, examining her palm as blood spurted forth. Everything seemed to make her think of him these days.

She peered into the dark orchard, in the direction that she knew the brewery to be. No lights were visible, but she didn't know if she could see them this far, even if Sebastian was up. Her heart stammered with the thrill of knowing he was there, just beyond her view, just beyond her reach. She closed her eyes to dispel the memories of him, but instead, her imagination conjured up more. How easy it would be to thread her way between the trees, to slip into the brewery and up the stairs. To feel his lips on hers, his fingers threading through her hair as he pressed her against the wall—

She took a step. There was a wildness rising up within her that she hadn't experienced in years, a desire to court danger, to throw caution to the wind. To be alive. It had been so long since she'd felt alive.

Another step, and her foot snagged on the threshold, sending her stumbling. The jolt was enough to banish the spell. She shook her head. No. She was a married woman, and a faithful one at that. There was only one thing she needed to feel alive in this life, and that was a child. That was what this was all about. *That* was her wish, not Sebastian. Besides, she'd seen the look of pity on his face when they'd returned from Rochester. What if she threw herself at him, and he wasn't interested? She would never live down the shame.

But she should let Sebastian come with her to find the Wish-Eater. She needed him. It would be too dangerous to take the trip alone. She could keep her feelings in check for a few days—keep him at arm's length. And then, when they returned, if they were both willing, he and Josephine would marry. Perhaps it would be better once Sebastian was married. Maybe then, she wouldn't be tempted.

CHAPTER 27

JOURNEY

*S*ebastian curled his hands around his mug of tea, fighting against the pounding in his head. After Dion had left, he'd polished off half of the bottle of whiskey. It had seemed like the thing to do at the time. He ghosted about the brewery, checking to see if his batches were still working. He hadn't been able to check yesterday. Judging by the lazy bubbles surfacing, the yeast still had another day or two to feast.

Faint footsteps sounded on his front porch and Sebastian froze, his ears perked. Someone knocked, soft and timid.

Sebastian pushed through the fog in his brain and made his way to threshold. He pulled the door open a crack, revealing the lovely face of Elodie Mercer.

"Hello." She gave him a tight smile. She didn't look particularly happy to see him. Had he done something to offend her? He cursed himself as the previous night came flooding back. How he'd exposed her secret to the whole town and clocked her husband in the face.

He opened the door fully and she took a step back, as if she didn't want to be too near him. The gesture pained him far more than it had any right to.

"Things got…a little out of hand last night, and I wanted to clarify."

Her words were formal. Tense. "Josephine hasn't technically agreed to marry you. If you're still willing, I think it would be helpful if you go to see her. And speak to my father."

Dion's words swirled about his mind. If Josephine hadn't agreed yet, maybe he could extricate himself from his offer without letting Elodie down too much. "Is that what you want?" Sebastian asked slowly.

She gave a wooden nod, her blue eyes brimming with tears. "Otherwise, she's prepared to...end it. Agathe will assist her."

Her words were like a punch in his gut as he thought of how hard this must be for her. "Oh, Elodie," he said. "Are you all right?"

She nodded, still not looking at him. "I don't want to speak of it. I shouldn't speak of it with you."

His stomach knotted as he realized what she was saying. They couldn't even be friends. Yesterday, somehow...a line had been crossed. He hadn't seen it then, but in retrospect...they'd grown too familiar. Well, perhaps it was for the best. He couldn't be just friends with Elodie Mercer. Being around her was a constant ache.

Through his disappointment and hurt, his eyes catalogued differences in her appearance. She was wearing a cloak too hot for this weather. And her hair, normally down in curls, was threaded into two braids. He surveyed her and then noticed a pack leaning against a tree near the road.

"You're going somewhere." The words came out more accusatory than he'd intended. "Where?"

"That's the other thing I wanted to talk to you about."

"Okay..."

She licked her lips and nodded toward her pack. They walked over together and she knelt down to pull out a small package from within. When she unwrapped it, he saw that it was a navy blue book. She held it out to him. "I found it."

He pulled the book from her grasp. *The Wish-Eater*. His breath whooshed from his chest. "What is—how did—"

"Agathe had it," Elodie said simply. "She believes. The map's in the back, marking the place where we'll find him. The Malveille Forest."

Sebastian looked up sharply. The forest was rumored to be dangerous. Filled with bandits—or worse.

"Everyone says there's magic in this forest. To stay away. But what if the magic is real? What if the stories are intended to keep people away because there's something truly valuable to find?"

"It's a bedtime story," Sebastian protested. "You can't believe..." He trailed off. Looking at her face, he saw it as plain as day. Elodie did believe, or at least she was desperate enough to believe that she was going on this mad mission.

He steadied himself, his fingers tracing the gold leaf of the title. He tried to consider it objectively. There *was* said to be something other-worldly in those woods. Normal folk steered clear. Surely, there were things in this life he didn't understand...but could this be one of them? A mythical creature that granted wishes?

He met her gaze. He saw the hunger in Elodie's eyes and felt his own answer within him. She would stop at nothing to see her wish granted. Would he? He let himself daydream about it for a moment, the idea that with a blink of magic, everything could change. Elodie could be his. Wasn't it worth the risk of finding out? If the Wish-Eater wasn't real, they would be no worse off than they were right now. No, that wasn't true. They'd have the crush of disappointment to contend with—the death of hope. But hadn't he lost hope a long time ago?

"Will you come with me?" she asked. "I know it's a lot to ask. People from the village might talk. Willum already thinks there's something between us. If you came with me...it could carry the appearance of impropriety."

Sebastian snorted. "I'm not going to let you get eaten in the woods for the sake of the *appearance of impropriety*. Of *course* I'm coming." Common sense told him all the reasons it was a bad idea. He had offered to marry to her sister. Her violent, drunken husband was convinced they were going behind his back. But none of that mattered right now. She had asked for his help. She needed it. Of course he would come.

The relief on her face warmed him like a hearth fire. "You've already done so much for me, I know, but I just thought... You said you had a wish too...."

If only she knew. He was overcome by the urge to confess everything. To tell her that he knew what it was like, to feel the ache of the wish gnawing his gut. Eating him from the inside. Like if he didn't get this one thing, he'd be hollowed out to nothing. Just a shell of a person who had once had a dream. But he couldn't bring himself to say any of that, so he simply said, "I do."

"I'd like to leave today. Now."

He frowned. "I need to see to some things around the brewery if I'm to leave for a few days. How about this? You walk on ahead, I'll gather my things and catch up with Feu." Less chance someone from the village would see them leaving together, too. The last thing Elodie needed was word getting back to Willum that they were traveling together again.

Elodie nodded at the sense in that. "The journey will be faster on horseback. Very well. I'll see you soon."

"Soon."

She strode purposefully toward the road, determination radiating from her like waves.

He stood and watched her go, soaking in the sight of her. He tested his feelings gingerly, not quite sure how to feel. Could the Wish-Eater be real? And if it was, how did its wishes work? Could it change the fabric of reality, bend it around them? He turned on his heel and headed toward the house to pack his things. It dawned on him then, that his and Elodie's wishes were at odds. If her dream came true, she would get pregnant, and then Willum would never set her aside—he'd have no grounds to cleave her. The only way his wish would be granted was if hers was not.

He frowned, then shrugged. Nothing would change his course of action. Elodie needed his protection, whether the Wish-Eater was real or not. He was going on this journey for her, not for him. Either she would get her wish and be happy, or they'd find nothing but empty forest, in which case she'd need a friend more than ever. He would be there for her either way.

CHAPTER 28

DOUBT AND HOPE

Sebastian found her two hours out of Lunesburg. Elodie couldn't help the relief that swelled within her at the sight of Sebastian's blond hair bobbing to the rhythm of Feu's gentle trot. The sojourner's shaggy dog trotted at his side. She didn't want to do this alone. She shouldn't have to. And though she didn't know how or when it had happened, Sebastian had become the one person she could count on.

"Good afternoon, madam." Sebastian tipped the hat he'd donned for the journey.

Elodie let out a snorting laugh. "What was that?"

Sebastian grinned. "Just seemed like the type of thing one should say when he comes upon a lovely woman upon the side of the road."

"I can't argue with that logic."

Sebastian swung down from his horse. "You've made good time."

"Kind of you to say so. I wasn't exactly breaking any records." Elodie leaned down to give Corentin's oversized ears a scratch.

"It's not that type of trip."

"You brought the dog?"

Sebastian shrugged. "I don't know how long we'll be gone, and I didn't want to leave him. He and Grinchaux would tear each other apart."

"We can't upset Lord Grinchaux, can we?" Elodie laughed.

"Now you're catching on."

Elodie looked up at Feu, at the saddle as high as her head.

Sebastian followed her line of sight and seemed to understand her hesitation. "Have you ridden before?"

"Not much," she admitted.

"It's easy. Though you might be a little sore by the end of the day. Here, give me your pack." She handed it over and Sebastian tied it to his saddlebags, which spanned Feu's glossy rump. He led the horse over to a downed log and helped Elodie up onto it. "Now, seize the front and back of the saddle with your hands and kind of throw your torso over it. Then you just swing a leg around."

Elodie arched a brow. "Is that all?"

"Come now. I've seen you hold a man down while Agathe reset his leg. This is child's play."

Elodie nodded. He was right. Enough stalling. She heaved herself over the horse's broad back, struggling with her skirt to get her leg over the other side. But she did it and straightened, gripping the edge of the saddle. The ground was a long way down. "That wasn't particularly graceful, was it?" Elodie remarked as Sebastian swung into the saddle with practiced ease. "It's significantly easier in pants."

He settled in behind her, his chest pressed against her back, his arms encircling her to retake the reins. "Ready?" His deep voice tickled her ear.

Her eyes fluttered closed of their own volition as she soaked up his nearness. His warm presence nestled behind her set her blood buzzing in her veins. Daughter help her, she wanted to touch him. To feel the muscles of his thighs beside her, to run her fingers along the veins of his strong forearms... She gripped the saddle tightly before her, keeping her hands firmly fixed. "Yes," she said, realizing the silence was stretching long. She could do this. She could be strong.

He clucked his tongue and Feu started to walk. She let out a little squeak and his arms tightened around her, two strong barriers holding her fixed in place.

"Try to loosen up a little bit," Sebastian said, as they returned to the road and resumed their journey, now in a very different fashion. "Move with her gait. It'll be much more pleasant. And...you can...lean back into me if you want. If you get tired."

She nodded and tried to take his advice, lowering her shoulders, loosening the straight rod of her spine so it curved into the warmth of his body behind her.

Being this close to Sebastian made her body come alive, as if her senses were waking up from a long winter. The sun on her face was as sweet as summer honey, the pine and verdant scent of the forests mingled with Sebastian's smell of apple blossoms and wood. She kept her hands to herself, but she couldn't stop her fertile mind from slipping into a daydream where she closed her eyes and bared the crook of her neck so he could trail kisses down her shoulder. One hand would grip her waist, the other sliding up to cup her breasts...Her back arched at the mere thought of it, warmth pooling deep within her—

"You're not wearing your shawl." Sebastian's voice held a throaty quality, as if her thoughts were laid bare for him to see.

It took her addled mind a moment to track his question. Her marriage shawl. She'd left it behind. "I didn't want it to get dirty or torn."

"Ah."

Was that disappointment in his voice? Daughter help her. If her mind kept skittering down forbidden trails, she might find herself asking for another wish to be granted. A wish so much more illicit. She threaded her fingers through Feu's coarse mane, grounding herself in the feeling of something solid. She needed a distraction.

"What do you think it will look like?" she asked. It wasn't the question she really wanted to ask, but it was one that felt safe.

"A twisted old woman?" Sebastian mused.

"You think the Wish-Eater will be female?" She'd assumed it would be male, if it had a gender at all.

"In the stories, it's always the women who have the magic," he said. "We males are at their hapless mercy."

"Yet in the real world, *we* are at the mercy of men."

"That's not true," he said. "Every man I know is wrapped around his wife's little finger. Or his mother's. Or his daughter's. Maybe the way women wield their power is subtle, but it's formidable nonetheless."

"Yet I would not be the one cleaving Willum, would I?" Elodie said, resentment bubbling like a kettle left on the hearth too long. "I'm his property, unless he decides otherwise."

"I'm sorry, Elodie. My comment was thoughtless."

"No, it's fine." She sighed. "I shouldn't speak of such awful things."

"But if you wish to..." Sebastian said. "You could talk to me."

"There's nothing to talk about. I don't know my husband anymore, let alone his mind. The only power that holds sway over him these days is the bottle."

"If you believe that, then why are we doing this?"

"Because...I have to believe this has all been for something," she said. "All of this pain and heartache. Willum's accident, our infertility...the Wish-Eater...my faith is being tested. We're being dragged through the fire to be purified. There's a lesson to learn here, and we will come out stronger on the other side. Prove ourselves worthy. I have to believe that if I get pregnant, it will give Willum something to live for. Help bring him back to me. Because otherwise, what is this all for?" She found her heart hammering, her skin flushed.

"What if...things just happen? What if there's no point to it? No lesson to learn, just sometimes things happen that are sad and awful?"

"If you believe that, then you should go back now," Elodie said, setting her jaw. His questions cut too deep—veered to close to her most secret fears. But surely, the pain and indignities they'd suffered hadn't been just random happenstance. The fickle cruelties of a harsh world. It couldn't have been all for nothing. "There's no room for doubt on this quest. Only desperate hope in the face of improbable odds."

"What if I have doubt *and* desperate hope?"

It was her turn to fall into silence. "Then you and I are more alike than I realized," she said finally.

"Do you want to know what I really think?"

"Of course."

"I think you're trying to learn the wrong lesson."

"Is that so?"

"Maybe the All-father isn't asking you to prove yourself worthy. But to realize you're already worthy. That you deserve better."

She let out a bark of laughter. "I wish I could believe that."

"Me too," he said quietly.

They fell into silence. The path ducked into the dappled sunlight of a stand of trees. Elodie let herself relax a bit more into him, her lower back stiff from holding herself aloft. Feu's gait was strangely hypnotic, and Elodie almost found herself dozing in the warmth of the sun and the heat of Sebastian's body nestled close.

The landscape slipped by, twisting brooks bubbling over slick, grey river stones smoothed over millennia, villages of half-timbered homes dotting green hillsides. The land began changing, as rolling hills filled with fat cattle and puffy sheep gave way to low foothills bristling with dark forests of thick evergreens.

She'd never felt so comfortable resting in someone's silence. It was Sebastian who finally spoke. "In the stories," he said, "magic always costs something. If we find it—"

"*When* we find it," she corrected.

"When we find it." He chuckled. "We'll have to give something in exchange for our wishes? What did the story say?"

She could remember every word as if by heart. "In the story, the Wish-Eater asks the man if he would sacrifice that which he loves most in the world. He says he already lost it, and the Wish-Eater gives him the wish anyway."

"Well, that seems a bit convenient."

Elodie frowned. "I agree. I told the sojourner as much, but—"

"But he's full of sheep dung."

Elodie snorted a laugh. "Exactly. We can trust him as far as we can throw him." But the discussion sent a tendril of uneasiness through her. If—when—they found the Wish-Eater, she didn't believe it would give them their wishes for free.

"And wasn't there a bit about another fellow turning to stone? Do we know what that fellow did to earn that fate?"

"He tried to enslave the creature and force it to give him a wish."

"Let's not do that."

"Agreed." She had been so consumed with thoughts of getting the book that she hadn't given much thought to the journey, or actually reaching the destination. But now that the book was in hand... "Would you give up the thing you love most in the world? For your wish?"

"I..." Sebastian trailed off. "I'll need to think on it. It might be a bit of a contradiction in my case." What did Sebastian love most in the world? She swallowed the question. It was private. Perhaps his brewery. "Would you give up what you love most in the world?"

Elodie opened her mouth to answer, and then closed it. What *did* she love most in the world? It was bitter to admit it to herself, but it wasn't her husband, not anymore. She'd already lost the man she'd once loved. The Willum she'd married was gone. Perhaps the Wish-Eater would take pity upon her, like it had upon the blacksmith, and ask her only for the power of her wish. Daughter knew her wish was all-encompassing. Incessant. But what if it did insist upon what she loved most? It must be her family. Guilt washed over her. She hadn't been a very good sister, as of late. Her harsh words to Josephine rang in her mind. And Sidonie...she hadn't made time to visit lately. No matter her desperation, she would never do anything that would jeopardize her sisters, or her father, or her dear sweet niece and nephew. So, if it came to that, she would just need to find another bargain. Something else to offer. She had the whole journey to come up with a plan.

"Elodie?" Sebastian asked gently.

"I'll need to think on it too." She chewed on her lip. "Agathe was strange...about the Wish-Eater. Before I left."

"You said she had the book. How'd you find out?"

Memories of her tearing around Agathe's cabin like a whirlwind bubbled to the surface. Her cheeks heated. She'd been acting like a madwoman. "I was…looking for something in her cabin. I found it in a drawer."

"You said she believes. Why did she buy it if not to use it?"

"I think to keep others from using it. She said it was dangerous."

"I don't doubt it is, if this beast is real."

"It's a risk worth taking."

"I hope you're right." She heard the doubt in his voice. Ignored it. "She said to read the book."

"Agathe has never been one to lead a person astray. If she says to read the book, then that's what we'll do."

CHAPTER 29

THUNDER

*T*wo days they rode. The foothills grew up around them, crowned by tall evergreens that towered to the sky, blocking out the sun. The forest felt still here, like an inhaled breath, but Sebastian didn't mind. For he was with Elodie, and he would ride with her into the gates of hell itself. They talked of everything, and of nothing. Their silence was as comfortable as their conversations, even the hard ones. There were only two things they didn't speak of. Willum. And Sebastian's wish.

Everything with Elodie felt alive and new. Like this was his life, and his brewery back in Lunesburg a mere dream, rather than the other way around. The feel of her soft backside nestled against him, her curls tickling his face—he memorized the feeling—carefully tucking each sensation away in his heart. Whatever happened with the Wish-Eater, he didn't regret this journey. He couldn't regret this time with her.

For Elodie's part, the time away from Lunesburg seemed to be doing her good. She was coming alive too, and he'd never tire of watching it happen. Elodie frolicking in a meadow, Corentin loping after her, his pink tongue lolling. Elodie picking wildflowers, threading them into her braids so she smelled of wild roses, tucking a sprig into the buttonhole of his vest. Elodie standing on the flat pebbles of a stream in her bare feet, her skirts held aloft around her ankles, screeching at the cold. Elodie kissed by firelight, reading the story of the Wish-Eater from the leatherbound book, the tale just as Piers had told it. Here, her cheeks were flushed, her eyes bright. Freedom looked good on her.

He tried not to let his mind wander too much, but there were moments when he couldn't help himself. In his daydreams, the flower-strewn meadow transformed itself into a soft bower in which to lay her down—to feel her lithe body yielding beneath his. The crystal stream became the perfect bathing hole, where he would undress her piece by blessed piece until she was bare before him, from her supple breasts to the tantalizing curve of her hips. The velvety sky diamond-studded with stars would bear witness to his fervent confession of his love.

With each hour that passed, holding back his feelings became harder, more of a strain. He longed to throw caution to the wind and confess it all—she had asked, after all. She was curious about his wish. But each time he came close, he resisted. When they'd left she'd been just barely holding herself together in the storm that life had thrown at her. She had a difficult decision to make, and clearly she was struggling with the options. She didn't need more complication. He wouldn't be the thing that broke her.

Late afternoon of their third day, a chill wind snarled past them, grabbing their cloaks in icy fingers. Elodie shivered before him, looking up at the slice of sky visible through the treetops.

"Some weather's blowing in," Sebastian said. "Perhaps we should stop for the day."

She nodded. "According to the map, we should be close. We can hunker down tonight and make the final push in the morning."

"Let's find a good place to camp." They rode a bit farther, until they came to a copse of trees even thicker than the rest. A fallen snag promised dry firewood and shelter. "Those branches are pretty thick," Sebastian said. "We can wait out the worst of it under there." As if on cue, thunder rumbled in the distance, the sound vibrating through his chest.

"Looks perfect," Elodie said.

Sebastian dismounted and then helped Elodie down, his hands lingering perhaps a moment too long on her trim waist after her feet met the ground. Corentin stretched and yawned.

"Should I make a fire?" Elodie asked.

"See what you can get going and gather as much wood as possible. I'll get the oil-skin tarp rigged as a shelter."

They set upon their tasks swiftly and silently, mindful of the grey clouds darkening the sky above them and the booms of thunder growing nearer. Elodie had gotten a respectable fire going and was tending to Feu by the time Sebastian got the shelter up. It was a tilted, awkward thing, strung between two trees and the ground, but it would keep the worst of the rain from them. Rain that was just starting to fall in cold, fat drops.

Elodie looked up, squinting into the rain. The drops sizzled on the wood. "I'm not sure we'll have much time to enjoy the fire."

"No. Why don't you get under here before you get too wet?"

They piled their bags and Feu's saddle under the tarp, leaving little room for two humans and one dog. They sat cross-legged, facing each other, hunched and bedraggled. "Well, this is cozy." Elodie laughed. Corentin licked her face and she scrunched up her nose against the bath. "All right, settle down."

Sebastian let the laughter roll through him, warming him. Even wet and cold and hunched under a tarp, he'd rather be here with her than anywhere else in the world.

"We have any food left?" Elodie asked, and Sebastian reached behind him to rummage through his pack. It was hard to see the contents in the gloom. The storm had brought with it an early night, dark shadows washing over them.

"Some rolls, the end of some cheese, one very smushed tart, and..." He pulled out a little flask he had packed. "Emergency rations."

He handed it to Elodie and she unscrewed the top, sniffing.

"Whiskey?" She moved her face from the smell as if the vapors burned her nostrils.

"Good to keep us warm," Sebastian said. "Just have a little."

Elodie took a sip, squeezing her eyes closed against the burn. She coughed then handed it back to Sebastian. "I don't know how people can drink so much of that stuff."

"Agreed. I much prefer cider." Sebastian took a swig.

"Me too," she said. "Not that I ever get any. Willum polishes off the bottles I buy before I get a drop." As she said the words, her hand flew to her lips. She'd broken their unspoken rule of not mentioning Willum.

"It's okay, you know," he said. A flash of light lit up the clearing around them, and they both froze. Ear-splitting thunder sounded seconds later, chasing hot on the heels of the lightning. The rain seemed to call out in answer, its flow strengthening.

"Poor Feu." Elodie peered through the rain at where the horse huddled next to a tree, head down and ears back.

Sebastian laughed. "Only you would be stuck in the middle of a thunderstorm and worry about the horse."

"At least we're out of the worst of the rain," Elodie said. "Though not all of it." Fat drops were finding their way through the seam of the tarp, dripping down onto them. Elodie pulled the hood of her cloak up, shivering.

"Are you cold?" Sebastian asked. He took one of Elodie's hands and found it as cold as ice. "Elodie!" he yelped. "You're frigid!"

"My fingers are always cold."

He took his hands and rubbed them briskly together around one of hers before bringing it to his mouth and blowing warm air on it. Then he took the other, repeating the ritual. Her fingers were still sandwiched between his hands, inches from his lips, when he looked up at her. About to ask if she felt better. But the words died on his tongue. Her blue eyes gleamed in the recesses of her dark hood, her gaze fixed upon him with an intensity he thought he recognized. A longing that answered his own. His heart leaped into his throat, mingling with the taste of whiskey into a choking concoction so powerful, he could barely breathe. The space between them grew impossibly small. As hot as a hearthstone.

Elodie still hadn't pulled her hand from his. Buoyed by the strangeness of their circumstances, or perhaps the magic in her eyes, a daring filled him. A roaring hunger. He wanted her, and by the gods, she wanted him too.

Slowly, his eyes still locked on hers, he brought her chilled fingers to his lips.

And kissed them.

Her eyes fluttered closed.

He kissed her knuckles next, the skin beneath his lips as smooth as porcelain.

He lowered her hand and pulled it toward him, painfully slowly, watching in rapt disbelief as her body tilted toward his. Her lips toward his—

Corentin let out a single bark.

Sebastian and Elodie flew apart, both of their backs rod straight.

Sebastian's roaring hunger turned to helpless fury. This was his chance. His moment. Damn the consequences, damn the right thing, damn the gods damn dog—

A crunch of underbrush sounded in the distance.

Feu snorted, tossing her head in disquiet. She'd heard it too.

"What is it?" Elodie asked. The shine in her eyes had changed to something else he recognized. Fear.

Sebastian quickly ran through what he'd heard of these woods. Predators stalked these forests. Bandits. Wolves. He wasn't sure which would be worse. No...that wasn't true. He'd prefer the wolves. He glanced at Elodie. Men brought worse horrors. "I'm sure it's just a deer trying to shelter in the storm."

"Liar," she whispered. A branch snapped, closer this time, followed by crashing through the thick underbrush. A muffled curse. So it was human predators, after all.

Corentin was on his feet now, his hackles raised. A low growl emanated from his body.

Sebastian reached into his pack and pulled out a knife. Elodie's eyes went wide, and she rustled through her own pack, retrieving a strange carved knife with a blade that looked to be made of bone. She clutched the weapon in white-knuckled hands.

"Stay here," Sebastian said.

"Where are you going?" she hissed, grabbing his arm as he started to duck under the tarp.

"I'm just going to check it out."

"We should stay quiet. Hope they don't find our camp," she said.

An explosion of lightning followed by a boom of thunder shook both of them.

Corentin barked again. So much for stealth.

"Stay put. If they're unfriendly...it's best if they think I'm traveling alone. I don't want them seeing you and getting any ideas."

Elodie paled but finally nodded, releasing his sleeve.

He scrambled out of the tent, his hands slick with dirt that was quickly turning to mud in the deluge. The fool dog shadowed him, growling softly.

Another flash of lightning illuminated the clearing.

Sebastian stiffened. There was a figure standing next to Feu. A cloaked man, impossibly tall.

But he appeared to be alone. If he wasn't friendly, Sebastian would have a prayer of a chance to defend himself and Elodie. "Hello, stranger," he called out in a loud voice. "I'm a simple traveler. May I ask what you're doing in my camp?"

The man turned from Feu and took a single, limping step toward him. A step that was startlingly familiar. Sebastian froze, the blood in his veins turning to ice. It couldn't be—

The man threw his hood back. Rivulets of water ran down Willum Mercer's face, painting his scowl like a watercolor. "I'm looking for my wife. And I think I've found her."

CHAPTER 30

UNWELCOME VISITOR

The numbing cold of the storm was nothing compared to the sight of Willum. Her husband. This deep in the woods, away from the bounds of civilization. She had no one to protect her but Sebastian. But who would protect Sebastian?

"Willum," she breathed, the word lost to a crack of thunder that echoed throughout the clearing. "What are you doing here?"

"What am I *doing here?*" He took a halting, menacing step forward. "You have the audacity to ask me that, when you're here with *him?*"

"It's not what you think," Elodie protested. "Sebastian and I are traveling together, nothing more." Their almost-kiss just moments before flashed to mind, but she shoved it to the side. "I've never been unfaithful to you with Sebastian or anyone else."

"Isn't that exactly what you'd say if you had been unfaithful?" Willum said. Water plastered his hair to his head. "I suppose I can't blame you, married to a poor, drunk cripple. Quite an upgrade with this one."

Her mouth dropped open at his suggestion.

"She speaks the truth," Sebastian said. "Elodie's never done wrong by you."

"Don't deign to tell me about my own wife!" Willum roared, advancing on Sebastian. "I've known her far better than you. In every intimate and carnal way. Do you know how she likes it when you tickle her between her thighs? I want to make sure that if you're fucking her, she's at least getting off on it!"

"Willum!" Elodie exploded, aghast.

"Don't speak of her like that." Sebastian advanced on Willum. Déjà vu pierced her, sharp and insistent. This would come to blows. Just as it had in the town square.

"I'll speak of her however I please," Willum said. "She's *my* wife!" He pounded his chest.

"I don't care if she's your wife! She deserves respect and you've been shit at showing it to her. She deserves better than you," Sebastian spat.

"And you think you'll just move in all subtle-like, with your money and your fine manners?" Willum and Sebastian were nose to nose now. "Well, I'd have to cleave her first, and it's never going to happen." He barreled into Sebastian and bore him to the dark, muddy ground.

"Willum!" she screamed. "Stop it!"

But Willum was a man possessed. He reared back and punched Sebastian, sending the other man's head snapping to the side.

Elodie leaped into the fray, throwing her arms around Willum's neck, trying to pull him bodily off Sebastian. "Stop it! What's wrong with you?"

But there was only the roar beneath her of a man driven past the point of reason into a realm of blood and fury.

Willum twisted and she tumbled to the ground with a thud, sliding across the wet ground. She pulled her face from the mud as a fork of lightning illuminated the churning sky above them, the sight of Willum beating Sebastian bloody below. Willum's fists pounded against Sebastian's ribs and stomach, ears and head.

"Stop!" she screamed again, but Willum didn't stop.

Sebastian had his arms up, protecting his face, but Willum's fury left him no space to fight back. At this rate, Willum would kill him. She couldn't let him.

Elodie looked around the clearing frantically for something, anything that could stop Willum. She had Agathe's knife, but she didn't want to kill him. Across the clearing, a fallen branch rested, small enough for her to wield like a club. She scrambled over to it, heaving it up into her hands. She staggered to where Willum continued to attack Sebastian. *Daughter forgive me.* With all her might, she swung the branch and cracked it across the back of Willum's head.

He tilted as if in slow motion and then fell to the side in a wet, muddy heap.

Elodie dropped the branch and rolled the rest of Willum's body off of Sebastian. She fell on her knees at his side. "All-father save you," she whispered in horror as she saw what Willum had done. Sebastian's lovely face was covered in blood, pouring from his nose, and a cut above his right eye, and another on his lips. "Sebastian?" She smoothed his hair back from his forehead. "Are you all right?"

He stirred at her touch. "Been...better..." he croaked.

"Can you sit up?"

With her help, Sebastian eased himself into a seated position, clutching one arm around his torso. "Feel like I've been trampled by a herd of cattle."

Elodie glared at her husband's unconscious form. "Willum has that effect."

"Did you...get him? Is he just unconscious or..." Sebastian trailed off.

"I don't much care at this particular moment. I'm so sorry, Sebastian."

Corentin sat down next to Sebastian and licked his cheek.

Sebastian hissed. "Lot of help you were. Next time, get in the fray."

The dog licked him again, as if he understood.

Elodie glanced back at Willum. She should go check on him. Willum had a thick skull, but... She got to her feet and waded through the mud to his side. He still had a pulse. A mixture of relief and regret flooded her, quickly followed by guilt. She didn't wish her husband dead. She couldn't. Even if this man lying in the mud barely resembled the man she'd married. Even if then she'd be safe. "He's alive."

221

"What should we do?" Sebastian asked. "I don't particularly want to be here when he wakes to receive the rest of that beating. Should we head back?"

"Back?" They were so close, they couldn't head back. But Sebastian was right. They couldn't be here when Willum woke up. There was no telling whether he'd be in a mood to listen to reason. "I can't leave. Not until I find the Wish-Eater. It's now or never."

Sebastian let out a wheezing laugh. "You can't be serious. It's dark as pitch and the storm is only getting worse. We don't even know where to go from here."

"I do." She could feel something tugging at her. Not toward home, but forward. Toward the unknown. "You don't have to come. You've done enough...suffered enough. But it's close, Sebastian. I have to try. Once Willum comes to, I'll have to go home with him. This is my last chance."

Sebastian sighed. "Well, there's no way in hell I'm going to stay here with him. So if you're going, I'm going."

She sprang forward and threw her arms around him.

He groaned.

"Sorry," she said. "You've been a truer companion than I deserve."

He looked at her then, his hazel eyes the only color in the dark, muddy clearing. "You deserve everything, Elodie. And more. Don't let anyone or anything tell you otherwise."

She swallowed the lump in her throat. She didn't know what to say. *Thank you* seemed woefully inadequate in the face of all he'd given her. Respect. Joy. Hope. He'd believed in her when no one else had. Believed in her wish. "Sebastian—"

"Let's just find this thing. Maybe it'll give me two wishes and I can get my ribs fixed up. I think he might have cracked one."

The rain had washed some of the blood from Sebastian's face, but his wounds looked garish in the low light. One of his eyes was already purpling with a bruise. "I should tend to your wounds before we go. Disinfect them."

"I don't want to hang around this campsite any longer than we have to. Bring whatever you have and you can do it when we stop for a break."

Elodie stood and looked at Willum, unconscious in a puddle in the pouring rain. "We can't just leave him like that."

Sebastian staggered to his feet, straightening with a wince. "You think he'd do me any favors?"

"I know it's not fair to ask. But please. Just help me move him under the tarp."

With considerable effort, and groaning on Sebastian's part, Sebastian and Elodie dragged most of Willum's sizable bulk under the tarp shelter they'd rigged.

"There." She stood. She was drenched and covered with mud. "I'll deal with him when I get back. Corentin, stay with him."

The dog let out a low whine but sat down dutifully.

They started into the trees in the direction the map had marked. "Elodie," Sebastian said quietly, clutching his side. "How do you think he found us?"

Elodie's brow furrowed. He wasn't the best tracker. "Agathe was the only other one who knew we were here, but I don't think she would have given our whereabouts willingly..." Willum wasn't in the best place, mentally, but he would never have hurt an old woman. Would he? "You don't think he hurt Agathe, do you?" she asked.

"I wouldn't put anything past him."

They walked silently through the sentinel trees, the cold and the wet numbing Elodie's worry and doubt. Her thoughts flitted between her troubles like a hummingbird. Sebastian was slowing down, his shoulders hunched. She shouldn't have let him come. He was likely in shock. She needed to get him dry. Even if they found the Wish-Eater, her life was in shambles. How could she go back? How could she stay married to such a violent man? Josephine had been right. She could never trust Willum around a baby.

They wandered for what felt like an hour, climbing over downed branches and logs, threading between thick branches. The night seemed to mirror her thoughts. Everything was a mess. She'd nearly kissed Sebastian. And Daughter help her, she'd wanted to. She still wanted to. The truth numbed her more than the incessant rain. She'd rather be drenched, lost in a dark wood with Sebastian than let Willum take her back Lunesburg. To her old life. Was it even about the Wish-Eater anymore?

Her thoughts spiraled darker. Darker. This close, she should be filled with elation. Excitement. But she couldn't shake the sense of dread that shrouded her like a cloak.

Elodie stumbled to a stop as they reached a steep ravine cleaving the forest floor. It stretched up the hillside before them, shot through with boulders and snags of old downed trees. It ran with the beginnings of a rushing river of storm runoff.

Sebastian drew up beside her. His wounds looked purple in the dim light. "We can't cross that."

Elodie bit her lip, feeling little against her numbness. He was right. Perhaps they could make it across, but it looked treacherous. And why? She had little sense that this was the way to go. They were turned around. Lost. Whatever certainty she'd felt earlier had been doused by the frigid rain.

"Elodie." Sebastian lay a soft hand on her shoulder. "We made it farther than I expected, in truth. But this isn't worth dying for. We should head back."

If they could even find the way back. She nodded, her teeth giving an involuntary chatter. "You're right. You're frozen and wounded. I shouldn't have dragged you out here."

"I'm here by choice," he said. "Remember, I had a wish too."

"I guess neither of our wishes will come true." The beginning of tears thickened her throat. Could she really have come this far, gotten this close, to give up?

But what else could they do?

In the distance a light bloomed to life. White and pure. Lovely as the sunrise.

Elodie squinted, blinking through the raindrops collecting on her eyelashes.

"What is that?" Sebastian asked.

"I don't know." She looked at him with excitement. "What if it's the Wish-Eater? It wants us to find it."

"That's quite a stretch." But his words were unsure.

"Come on. Please." She grabbed his hand. "Just one look. If it's nothing, we'll turn back."

Sebastian sighed and nodded.

Step by careful step, they crossed the treacherous ravine. Sebastian helped Elodie when her skirt snagged on a branch; she caught him when he slipped on a rock and nearly fell.

Then they were across. She jumped onto the muddy bank and offered her hand, pulling him the rest of the way.

The light was getting brighter. Elodie shoved down her impatience at his slowness as they walked the rest of the way to meet it.

She held up a hand against the brilliance. "A crystal?" The iridescent column was fused to the face of a large boulder. Elodie put out a hand to touch it and the light died, leaving them in darkness.

"What the hell was that?" Sebastian whispered.

But then another light bloomed. Distant and weak, as if partially shielded from sight. Elodie took a few steps and the boulder revealed a narrow entrance—a gap in the rock face. The light was coming from inside. "A cavern. This is a passage inside. We must be here." She turned to him, ignoring his wary expression. "Come on. This is it. I can feel it."

They stepped forward into the dark.

CHAPTER 31

HUNGRY

They walked deep into the cavern. One by one, crystal lights blinked to life in front of them, only to go dark as they reached them.

Sebastian leaned heavily against the wall. "This cavern knows we're here."

"I don't think it's the cavern doing this." Elodie couldn't bring herself to speak above a hushed whisper. She feared drawing attention to them. Yet wasn't that why they were here? And clearly, whatever lived in the place was fully aware of their arrival.

At some point, Elodie wasn't sure exactly when, Sebastian had taken her hand, and they now walked close together, their fingers threaded and tightly clasped. His palm was feverish beneath hers, but she badly needed the steadying comfort his touch brought. They had started this together. They would finish it that way.

The tunnel snaked to the left, and Sebastian pulled her to a stop. "How far do you think we go? What if what's waiting in here isn't the Wish-Eater? What if it's something that preys on the stories? On the naïveté of travelers and wishers?"

"Then it can take me. I'm not turning back now."

"Elodie—"

"No, Sebastian. We've come too far." She wouldn't be talked out of this. Not after all they'd been through to get here. All she'd been through. She would finish this.

The light behind them flickered out, but this time, no other light came to life.

"What's going on?" Something was waiting just out of reach. She could feel it. Elodie put out a hand against the pregnant darkness, fearful that her fingertips would make contact with something that wasn't stone, but flesh.

"Slowly. Here, I've got the wall."

Step by step, they inched forward.

"Did you bring any flint?"

"I have flint, but nothing to light."

"It was a distant hope." Elodie kept thinking her eyes would adjust, but the darkness was oppressive.

"I know all about those."

The cave was chill and smelled of earth and damp, and something else. A sweetness, a little like cinnamon. "Do you smell that?"

"Smell what—"

And the ground fell out from beneath them.

Down she tumbled, down what, she couldn't say. Blackness surrounded her, enveloping her senses. Arms, elbows, and knees smacked against hard rock as she fell, head over feet, her skirts tangling about her. It was some sort of steep incline. When Elodie finally came to a stop, she wasn't sure which way was up or down, or left or right. All she knew was darkness. And that the smell had grown stronger. "Sebastian?" She placed her palms on the rough earth, pushing up to hands and knees.

There was no answer.

"Sebastian." She reached out—feeling around her, shuffling through the dirt and rock to feel for him. Perhaps he had hit his head or passed out from the fall. He had been hurt already.

"Sebastian." Her voice twisted as fear lanced through her. She couldn't be alone in this place.

A noise—a shuffle of rock—sounded. Perhaps ten feet from her. "Sebastian?" Her breath came in quick burst. "Is that you?"

"It is not," a deep voice growled.

Elodie froze. "Who are you?"

"You've come so far to find me. Is that the question you really wish to ask?" The voice was low and sensuous, almost a purr. As if it had all the time in the world.

"Please," she said. "Show yourself."

"Some wish to not see," it said.

"I only have one wish I care about," she said. "But it would put me at ease."

The light bloomed, crystals all around coming to life. She squinted at the sudden brightness, holding up a hand to let her eyes adjust. She had fallen into a huge cavern that glittered with crystals, the ceiling and walls littered with them. But they were not what she fixed her eyes upon when her pupils adjusted. It was the creature before her.

It was a strange amalgamation of man and beast. Wings and claws and face and fur. It could have been drawn from a children's book with tales of centaurs and hippogriffs, but the dark eyes that blinked in its very human face were shrewd, though not unkind. Somehow, it made her trust it less.

Despite its impossible form—part beast, part man, part bird—her fear lessened slightly at the sight of it. Imagination could be worse. Her eyes focused. "Sebastian!" He lay in a crumpled heap across the cavern.

Elodie scrambled to his side and turned him onto his back. *Please, please...* A wheezing groan escaped him. Her eyes fluttered closed in relief. He was alive.

"What happened?"

She helped him to a seat. "We made it. And...we've got company."

Sebastian squinted against the bright of the crystals. His already pale face drained of color as he caught sight of the beast. "Un-Brother take me," he whispered.

Elodie straightened, facing the creature. "You are the Wish-Eater." It had the body of a lion, or at least what Elodie had read lions looked like, for she had never seen one in person. Its fur was a tumbling brindle, a calico swirl of browns and yellows and reds. From its shoulder blades sprouted two black wings tucked against its withers. Nowhere to fly in here. It stood as tall as a draft horse at least, its head nearly brushing the stalactites dripping from the cavern's ceiling. Was it confined to this small place, or did it choose to remain here? She shook off the ruminations. She needed to gather her thoughts, be careful with her words and wise with her questions. One did not trifle with a creature such as this.

"I am," it confirmed.

"I have a wish," she said. "We both do, in fact. We'd like you to grant them."

"I presumed as much. Otherwise, why would you have come?" the creature said. "I am curious. How did you find me? It has been many years since I've received visitors."

"A book. A storybook." Elodie stood and helped Sebastian stagger to his feet. He was so cold. But at least the cavern was dry and warm.

"Tell us of the price," Sebastian said. Yes, the price. The terms of the bargain were critical.

"If you have the book, then you know the cost. You must give the thing you love most in this world."

"No," Sebastian practically spat.

The Wish-Eater didn't seem surprised. "Are you certain? You've come all this way, after all, and at some cost to yourself, it seems."

Sebastian shook his head. "I won't sacrifice her."

Her? Elodie opened her mouth to ask what Sebastian meant, but the Wish-Eater interrupted her. "And you, little fair-haired one?"

Elodie was careful with her answer. She'd been thinking on it for three days, her mind spinning in circles. But she'd reached a troubling conclusion. She avoided looking at Sebastian. It was personal—raw—humiliating—but she couldn't hold back. "What if...what I love most in the world...is my wish?" Her eyes fluttered closed against the shame of it. Somehow along the way, the idea of becoming a mother had grown larger than anything else in her life. Like a blackberry vine, it had choked out the healthy growth of family, friends. Leaving only the sweetness and thorns of her wish—feeding her and tearing her apart in turns.

In an eye-blink, the Wish-Eater towered above her.

Breath wooshed from her chest at its nearness. How had it moved so fast?

"Hey—" Sebastian cried, but it held up a hand. Talons. It was incongruous. The creature's front arm started like a colossal lion's but tapered to the thick, roping digits of an eagle, affixed with gleaming claws as white as ivory. Three talons, she noticed with detached observation. One was missing. "Easy," the Wish-Eater rumbled. This close, its smell of cinnamon and cloves was overwhelming. It reached for her slowly and pressed its hand—foot—paw, she didn't know what to call it—against her forehead with surprising gentleness.

Images flashed in her mind, rising unbidden. Elodie let out a startled cry. Was the creature doing this? The pictures were not of her as a mother. Of a babe in her arms. Of her and Willum.

They were of Sebastian. All Sebastian.

Sebastian standing in the dark of Elliason's Lake, a hand out to her. Offering her tea with whiskey as the lamplight gilded the gold of his curls. Sebastian striding through the orchard, apple blossoms falling on his broad shoulders. His smile and his laugh, his selfless proposal to Josephine. Riding Feu with his warm chest behind her, his arms surrounding her, his scent of pine enveloping her.

Daughter help her. The thing she loved most in the world was Sebastian Beringer. It was as foolish and inconvenient a love as there could ever be, but as she tested the revelation, she found it was real. Solid.

Tears slicked her cheeks as she opened her eyes. She couldn't look at him. Wouldn't look at him. So she met the Wish-Eater's amber eyes, ringed with brown as deep as loamy soil. "I can't pay that price." She couldn't sacrifice Sebastian. Wouldn't. Not even to have her wish come true.

The Wish-Eater dropped its paw and paced back across the cavern, its tail flicking across her legs. It rounded on them both. Its strangely human lips were set in a thin line. "Perhaps an alternative then because it has been so very long, and I am so very hungry. Would you give the thing *he* loves most in the world?"

Elodie inhaled sharply. She had hoped the Wish-Eater might offer a different price, but this, she had not expected. She did look at Sebastian then. He hardly looked like himself, bedraggled and beaten, but she recognized the fear in his green eyes. The emotion that seemed frozen there.

For he wasn't moving.

Elodie took a step toward him. "What did you do to him?" came her garbled cry.

"Never fear. I will release him when you've made your choice. I don't want him influencing your decision. It is for you and you alone."

She eyed the Wish-Eater again warily. "Would I give the thing *Sebastian* wants most in the world, in exchange for *my* wish?"

"Yes, that is my offer." Was there impatience there?

Elodie buried her hands in her skirt, her mind whirling. Sebastian had never told her what he loved most in the world. But, he had said *her. I won't sacrifice her.* It was a person. Sebastian loved someone. Her heart stumbled over the realization. What a fool she was, loving him, when he longed for someone else. He'd been doing this all for a woman. Elodie closed her eyes against the heat of the shame. She shoved it down. She needed to focus on her decision. Sebastian had already made his choice. He wouldn't get his wish. But hers was still on the table. All she had to do was doom a stranger. Be selfish for once in her life and she would finally be whole.

She looked at him, uncertain, torn with indecision and hating herself for every greedy thought. If she took the Wish-Eater's offer, it wouldn't just be hurting a stranger, it would hurt Sebastian too. He cared about this person. And Sebastian had given so much to her. Been such a true friend. It was one thing to make sacrifices yourself. For your own wish. It was another entirely to take advantage of another. Could she live with herself if she made that decision? Would she see the cost, every time she kissed her babe goodnight? She'd come so far from who she thought she'd been—her desperate wish had driven her into a part of herself that she hardly recognized. And certainly didn't like or admire. But to do this—it would be to step fully into a dark place there was no coming back from.

Her heart seized as she shook her head, tasting the salt of tears on her lips. "No. I won't do it."

Sebastian stumbled forward then, one hand going to his knees. The other to his chest. "Thank the All-father. Elodie, I should have told you. It was too dangerous to go into this without telling—"

"And you?" The Wish-Eater snarled in displeasure. "I suppose you are too noble to give the thing she loves most in the world?"

Elodie's gasp was cut off as the Wish-Eater's paralysis overtook her. She struggled against it, thrashing against the bonds of magic that held her. But she moved not an inch. She screamed, but no sound came out.

"I will not." Sebastian answered without doubt.

The hold shackling her released, and she fell to her knees, fresh tears of relief falling. The horror of it washed over her. That the Wish-Eater had knowingly asked Sebastian to gamble with his own life. What game did this creature play?

Sebastian grabbed Elodie's elbow and helped her to her feet. "And now we must go. It was a mistake for us to come here. We're clearly not as committed as we needed to be to see our wishes granted."

"I cannot argue with that," the Wish-Eater agreed, its tail flicking back and forth. "But there is just one problem."

Elodie stepped closer to Sebastian, her fingers threading into his. "What's that?"

The Wish-Eater stalked forward. "I'm. Still. Hungry."

CHAPTER 32

FREE

A mistake. A fool-headed, addle-brained mistake.

Sebastian angled his battered body before Elodie's. He spoke with more command than he felt, his ribs groaning with the effort. "We came here in good faith. Your terms were fair, but they were not for us. Now let us go in peace." Sebastian's mind still struggled to comprehend what he was seeing. A creature like this shouldn't exist. He'd always thought he lived in a world of rules and logic, things you could see with your eyes. But here was proof that the world was a much stranger and richer place than he'd ever dreamed. A momentous realization—if that realization wasn't about to eat him.

The Wish-Eater paced the crystalline cave, its tail flicking softly. "Long have I waited here alone. Long have I hungered for the power of the wishes of men. You come here, dangle your desires before me, then think to leave? I do not think so."

"Wait—you eat—wishes?" Elodie asked. Perhaps she had thought the name was metaphorical, like he did. She stood pressed against him, as taut as a coiled wire.

"People come here to have their wishes granted, but that is not my name. The Wish-Granter. I eat them."

Sebastian frowned. It wanted to eat...their wishes? "I don't understand."

"They are my fuel. My food. What is there to understand?" The Wish-Eater surged forward, and Elodie and Sebastian scrambled back, pressing themselves against the sharp crystals glowing in the cavern wall.

Sebastian pulled a knife from his belt, holding it aloft. "Stay back!" His ribs throbbed and the cuts on his face burned in a chorus of agonies. There was no way in the Un-Brother's unholy name he'd be able to fight this thing. But he'd at least die trying. For Elodie.

The Wish-Eater's answering chuckle chilled him to the bone.

"Wait." Elodie stepped out from behind him. Her golden brows were drawn together, her face grave. "If you take our wishes, what remains?"

The Wish-Eater sat then, its powerful haunches bunched beneath it. When it spoke, it sounded as if it knew it had won. "Peace."

Peace?

"What do you mean?"

"With wanting comes the pain of not having. When the wanting is gone, the pain stops."

Elodie was silent for a moment. But when she looked up, tears shone in her eyes as bright as the crystals surrounding them. "If...if we gave you our wishes freely, would you allow us to leave this place? In safety?"

"Elodie, what are you doing?" he hissed.

"What I should have done a long time ago," she said with infinite sadness. "Laying down this burden."

"If you give your wishes freely, I will let you leave this place unharmed," the Wish-Eater said. "I swear it."

ELODIE SLUMPED TO THE GROUND, her knees hitting the dirt. Disappointment crashed over her like waves battering the shore. She had done it. Despite all odds, she had found the Wish-Eater. And it was yet another failure.

Hot tears broke from her eyes, spilling onto her cheeks. She wiped them away hastily. "You must think these human emotions very pathetic."

"On the contrary," it said simply.

She looked up at that, blinking through her tears.

"Elodie—" Sebastian started to kneel, but she waved him back.

She needed a moment. To process. To decide. "I just thought... I don't know. I hoped . . . that the Daughter had a plan. Bringing us here."

"Did She not?" the Wish-Eater asked.

She blinked at that, staring at her dirty dress through refracted tears. So many nights she had prayed to the All-father, to the Daughter, her heart crying out with sorrow. *Why did you give me this desire to be a mother if it was not your will that I would be one?* Perhaps...bringing her here was the Daughter's way of making amends. Of saying: If you cannot be happy in the way you hoped, at least you can be happy in a different way.

The past four years had been a blur, focused so intently upon her obsession with having a child. She knew so little other than the rise and fall of her hope and disappointment, as regular as breath, as regular as her heartbeat. It had begun to erode her core, hollowing her out month by month. First it had taken her joy, then her laughter. Her attention, her faith. Lastly, it had taken her gratitude.

One by one, this dream had taken the good things in her life and left behind disappointment and envy and bitterness. It had taken so much. There was little left other than the weight, and the sorrow of *not having.* Perhaps if she had been less focused on it, she would have had more time for Willum. To help him find a way out of his own sorrow. Maybe she wouldn't have let her resentment toward him turn toxic. And maybe she would have been closer to Sidonie and Hugh and little Rolo because seeing their family wouldn't have filled her with such jealousy. Maybe she wouldn't have lost so many friends, as each had gotten pregnant and she'd pushed them away. Maybe she would have been kinder to Josephine. To Agathe. To her father. Maybe she wouldn't have used Sebastian—dragging him over the countryside for her own desperate mission.

This wish had twisted her into a person she hardly recognized. It had robbed her of her light and left only shadow. And yet, it had been a part of her for so long. If she gave it up, would there be anything left?

"What is your choice?" the Wish-Eater asked, its head cocked.

Elodie's breath came in quick, short bursts as the decision coalesced. Could she truly do this? Yes. She could. She'd been so fixed on a distant, unlikely future that she'd ruined half of her past and ignored her present. Even more than being a mother, she wanted to be herself again. To be able to meet a new day with something other than trepidation and sorrow. The Wish-Eater was offering that to her. A clean slate. Maybe it *was* destiny that had brought her here. A peace offering from the All-father, for the hell he'd put her through the last five years.

Elodie pushed to her feet, her entire body shaking. But she was resolved. There was only one choice. One path forward. "I want you to eat my wish."

The Wish-Eater stood and approached.

Elodie squared her shoulders, ignoring the pounding in her chest. "Will it hurt?" she breathed.

The Wish-Eater shook its head. "Not when you give it freely."

"Elodie, you don't have to do this—" Sebastian cut in.

She leveled her gaze at him. "Yes. I do. Not for the Wish-Eater. For me."

"Speak your wish."

Elodie closed her eyes. "I wish to be a mother."

SEBASTIAN STOOD as rigid as a fence-post, watching in rapt fascination, despite his horror. A stream of white light emanated from Elodie's chest and coalesced in the air in front of her. Images flickered there, floating like dreams: Elodie swollen with child—Elodie singing to a swaddled baby—Elodie running after a golden-haired toddler as it screamed in delight.

They were beautiful, these images, so beautiful. A tear snaked down his cheek as he mourned this life she would never have.

The Wish-Eater threw back its head, its golden eyes flickering closed as it basked in the power of Elodie's wish, drawing the light into its strange form. As it consumed her very dreams.

It would be only a moment before it was his turn. Panic circled his mind and clouded his thoughts.

Could he give up his wish? The creature promised peace. Freedom. But a freedom from Elodie... What kind of a pale life was that? Did he want to be free from her bright smile, from the music of her laugh? Free of his dreams of her that surrounded him the moment he closed his eyes? Though...to be free from the ache in his heart at the sight of her...

He'd fallen in love with Elodie nearly a decade ago, back when he'd been a lad of fourteen. His love was like a vine that had twisted so tightly around his soul that he didn't know where one left off and the other began. But, for the past ten years, he had grown no closer to making her his, not really. Not in the way that counted. And what had he given up? The chance to travel, to live or work in strange new places. To fall in love. To have a family. Children.

Willum had sworn that he would never give her up, never cleave her. If they stayed married, could he truly watch her waste her life with that broken man...watch as he blackened her lovely face with bruises and she did nothing? For what purpose?

This was his one chance to have a real life, instead of this half-life he'd been living.

The choice before him was not Elodie or no Elodie. It was to continue to live as a miserable lovesick wretch, or to seize the possibility of happiness.

What advice would Dion give? He would tell Sebastian to move on with his life. To try a new path. He couldn't base his decisions on Elodie anymore. And that was what he'd done, hadn't he? For so long, he'd forgotten any other way.

Peace. Peace sounded good. And what was the alternative? To cling to his wish, perhaps at the cost of his life? He wasn't that foolhardy.

It was time to start living his life for himself.

The light between Elodie and the Wish-Eater had faded, and they both opened their eyes. The Wish-Eater glowed slightly, faint light haloing its form. "Delectable..." it purred.

"How do you feel?" Sebastian asked Elodie.

Tears slicked her cheeks as she turned to him. "Free."

The Wish-Eater licked its lips and turned to him. "And what of you? Your wish is just as strong. Stronger, even."

Sebastian cleared his throat. "I will feed you my wish. But I ask one favor."

The Wish-Eater raised one eyebrow.

He glanced at Elodie. "Let me say it in my mind."

A knowing smile curved the creature's mouth. "Very well."

"Elodie, would you please look away? When he eats it?"

She frowned but nodded. "Secrecy until the end, is it?"

"It's personal. I'm sorry."

"No need to apologize." She sighed.

"Ready?" the Wish-Eater rumbled.

Sebastian nodded, closing his eyes. *I wish I was married to Elodie Ruelle all the days of my life.*

A peculiar sensation filled him. As if a magnet was pulling the emotion out of him—calling to the tendrils of love that traversed his body—his soul. The heat of his wish pooled in his heart, growing so strong that he gasped in a breath. And then the mass was being pulled out his front—sucked like poison from a wound—leaving blessed emptiness in its wake—

A dog's bark reverberated through the cavern.

Sebastian's eyes flew open. The cherished images of his wish were hanging in the air between him and the Wish-Eater, for all to see.

"I bloody knew it," came the voice of Willum Mercer.

CHAPTER 33

DEAL

*E*lodie didn't know where to look. Her husband's sudden appearance, dripping and furious, or the images that hung in the air like visions in a crystal ball. Images of Sebastian. And her. Sebastian running his thumb across the apple of her cheek, Sebastian twining his fingers in hers as they picnicked on the shore of Elliason's Lake...Sebastian waking beside her, those green eyes taking her in with a reverence that stole her breath.

She was Sebastian's wish.

He loved her.

Sebastian Beringer was in love with her.

The images vanished like steam from a tea cup, leaving only questions, and the shocked silence of Willum's appearance, Corentin at his side. The dog must have tracked them and led Willum here.

"What are you doing here?" she asked. It was a feeble question, and not at all the one she wanted to ask, or of the person she wished to ask it. *When? How? How long? Why didn't you say something? How could you agree to marry Josephine?* Their almost-kiss under the tarp had raised questions in her mind, but it had been a strange, enchanted moment that she had brushed off as her own wishful thinking. Never had she dreamed that *she* was Sebastian's all-consuming wish. She'd taken his kindness for generosity of spirit or even pity, but never this. Never love.

Willum's presence forced her to shove the questions aside and focus on him. She knew why he was here. He'd follow her anywhere. She was his. Hadn't he said as much in the clearing? His presence chilled her even more than her sopping dress. He would never give her up.

"I should ask you the same question," Willum spat. "But I already know the answer. Running away with Beringer? It's so very predictable."

Elodie protested. "We weren't running away—"

"Was your unnatural union to be blessed by this freak unnatural creature?" Willum gestured wide.

"Stop it," Elodie snapped. For his part, Willum seemed strangely untroubled by the appearance of the Wish-Eater. Did he remember the story? Did he understand what the creature did? What it offered? Or was he taking the bizarre scenario in stride, just another facet of her betrayal?

"Willum, you need to leave. Now. We're all leaving." Elodie addressed the creature, nodding her head. "Thank you for what you've done."

The creature's low chuckle raised the hairs on her arms.

Corentin stalked forward two steps with a growl.

"But our new guest has come all this way," the Wish-Eater said. "It is his turn."

"My turn for what?" Willum barked. "I'm just here for my wife."

"But you have a wish too." The Wish-Eater's nostrils flared. "I can smell it. Just as potent as hers." The creature looked him up and down, took in the strange set of his hips, the hunched way he carried himself. "Perhaps...to be whole again?"

Elodie's mouth went dry. What was the Wish-Eater saying? It had just told them that it didn't grant wishes, it ate them. But then—what of its offer to them when they'd first arrived in the cavern? Had the creature lied to them? Or was it lying to Willum? What would have happened if she or Sebastian had taken the bargain it had first offered? She didn't understand.

Sebastian's cracked lips pressed together. He realized it too. His swollen eyes were narrowed.

"You are unfamiliar with the story," the creature said to Willum. "I will make it simple for you. I will grant your wish—whatever the fondest desire of your heart may be. In exchange—"

"For what?" Willum crossed his sizable arms before him. Even as she cursed Willum's presence here, she had to admire his boldness. His fearlessness in the face of something he'd never seen, or likely even conceived of. He seemed so certain, wrapped in his low-burning fury. So calm.

"You must give me the one thing you love most in the world."

Willum snorted. "Is that all?"

The Wish-Eater said nothing.

Elodie hissed in a breath. It had been so long since she and Willum had known each other's secret thoughts. What did he love most in the world? Who? Was it her?

"Don't," Sebastian said. "It's not worth it."

Willum took a menacing step Sebastian's way. "Not another word from you or I beat you the rest of the way dead." He turned. "Let me get this straight. You grant my wish. I give up the thing I love the most. No tricks. No fine print.

"That would be our deal," the Wish-Eater said.

Willum's dark eyes flicked to Elodie. He was a shadow of the boy she had fallen in love with—this man who now bargained with a devil. "I'll take it."

Bonds of air seized her and jerked her forward. She let out a garbled cry.

Sebastian reached out and clutched her waist, hauling back against the creature's magic.

Corentin barked furiously, the hackles on his back standing tall.

The Wish-Eater grinned, revealing sharp, white canines that glittered in the crystal glow.

"Stop it!" Sebastian screamed. His locked wrists cut iron furrows into her stomach. "Willum, don't do this. Don't let it take her!"

"Maybe it always should have been you, Beringer," Willum said. "You're a better man than me. I can't live like this anymore. If this is my chance, I'm taking it."

But then, the bonds of air released her, and she stumbled into Sebastian's arms.

Willum's eyes went wide. "What's happening? What are you doing?"

The Wish-Eater stalked forward, hissing at Corentin. With a powerful sweep of its eagle-like arm, it tossed the dog across the cavern. Corentin tumbled into the rocky wall with a yelp.

"Corentin!" Elodie cried. She blew out a relieved breath as the dog staggered to his feet, growling but keeping his distance.

"You made your deal," the Wish-Eater said to Willum, "and so have I. Many years ago. Centuries, in fact. It was unholy magic that made me, and unholy magic will unmake me. The selfish choice of man willing to give what he holds most dearly, for his own gain. It is this very selfishness that trapped me in this body—this cage—and now it is yours that frees me."

The Wish-Eater's wings went wide, filling the cavern. Elodie and Sebastian stumbled back as the creature seized Willum, its talons puncturing his shoulders. Willum let out a strangled cry, struggling against the beast.

Elodie could only watch in horror as the Wish-Eater began to pull light from Willum's body.

No—not light.

His soul.

From the Wish-Eater's body, something else came forth—something dark, and old, and hungry. The Wish-Eater's face flickered, its eyes changing from the ringed gold of agate to the deep brown of loamy soil. "No—" Elodie breathed. Willum was *becoming* the creature. It wasn't granting his wish at all. It was trapping him.

A grey sheen snaked over Willum's skin, crackling and spreading like tree bark. "What's happening?" he cried, looking at his changing hands. At fingers that were as grey as stone. At feet as heavy as lead weights, crusting to the ground. *All-father help them.* The Wish-Eater was sucking Willum's soul into its strange form, but his body was turning to stone.

"Stop it!" she screamed. She couldn't let it take him. Couldn't doom him to this sad, lonely life. A life in a cave filled with darkness, staring at the frozen remnant of his human life. His human form. He didn't deserve that. No matter what he'd done.

Elodie hurled herself at the creature, struggling to break the bond between Willum and the Wish-Eater. She pummeled its eagle-like arms. "Stop it! You tricked him!"

The creature released its grip on Willum long enough to seize her arm and toss her across the room.

She tumbled to the ground, her skirts tangling around her knees—exposing the knife in her boot. The knife she had forgotten she had. Agathe had said the creature was dangerous—she had warned her. Elodie pulled free the knife with its strange, bone-white blade. She looked from the weapon to the Wish-Eater's hand. Its three talons, where there should have been four. Could it be?

It didn't matter. She had to try.

Elodie scrambled forward and lunged at the creature.

And stabbed it in the neck.

The Wish-Eater howled with rage, dropping Willum to the ground with a thud. Its arms came up to stem the black blood gushing from its neck, bathing its brindle mane.

Elodie pulled the knife from the creature, falling to the ground. She scrambled to Willum, who had collapsed on the floor, his limbs mobile again. His skin pink and supple.

"Help me get him up," she cried, and Sebastian took Willum's other arm, hauling him to his feet.

"Let's get the hell out of here," Sebastian panted.

"How?" Elodie breathed. "We fell in here. We can't leave the same—"

The Wish-Eater let out a snarling bellow of fury that shook the cavern.

243

Elodie clamped her hands over her ears, the dagger dripping black blood still clutched in one fist.

"How dare you?" the creature seethed, shaking its massive head, advancing on them with a roar.

Elodie's knees went weak, but she held her ground, waving the knife in front of her, swiping it at the creature. "Stay back!"

It shied back with a hiss. "Where did you get that?"

"It doesn't matter. You tricked us. We're leaving."

"No one leaves this place," the creature screamed. "It is a prison!" The crystals in the cavern flared to life and Elodie threw up a hand against the brightness. The cavern stretched much farther than she had imagined behind them.

"What in the Un-Brother's hell?" came Willum's garbled curse.

Elodie shared the assessment. For the newly revealed stretch showed another human-shaped statue.

"You monster," Elodie choked, stumbling back.

The Wish-Eater moved, faster than she'd thought possible. Faster than her eyes could follow.

She couldn't comprehend as the creature bowled into her, bearing her to the ground, its great weight on top of her. Her head cracked against the stone floor, the air fled from her lungs, and the knife tumbled from her fingers.

The Wish-Eater flashed its sharp canines in a macabre grin—ready to devour her.

Her hand fumbled for the knife—

Corentin appeared out of nowhere, barreling into the Wish-Eater. The dog's jaws closed around the Wish-Eater's neck with a snarl.

The Wish-Eater reared back with a roar, its bulk leaving her...just enough... She stretched for the knife...

Her fingers closed around the solid handle and she brought the knife up, burying it in the Wish-Eater's side.

Its screeching roar sent the blood fleeing through her veins.

Arms heaved under her shoulders, pulling her from beneath the thrashing, panting beast.

"Look," Willum cried. Far across the newly revealed cavern was a dark opening. A way out. "Come on!"

Together, they ran in limping strides, enmities forgotten. United in purpose.

"Corentin!" Elodie cried as she reached the opening. The dog had saved their life.

He dropped from where he'd been latched on to the Wish-Eater like a leech, sprinting across the cavern toward them.

They piled into the opening, running from the cavern, where the Wish-Eater roared its displeasure.

The crystal lights winked out.

"There's no leaving here!" came its snarled cry.

In the darkness, their panting, desperate breaths stood out in sharp relief.

The blackness was total. All encompassing.

"I can't see a bloody thing," Sebastian said.

She felt Corentin shove past her leg and then bark.

"I think he knows the way." Desperate hope seized her.

"Follow the damn dog." Willum's voice.

Elodie fumbled out and clutched at a shirt of the person ahead of her. Willum. Too tall for Sebastian.

"Can it follow?" she whispered as they shuffled forward.

"This passage seems too small for it," Sebastian said. "But that doesn't mean it won't meet us at the end."

"Comforting," came Willum's dry comment.

"Realistic," Sebastian shot back.

"Quiet," she hissed. "Maybe we can hear it." But her panicked breath was deafening in her ears.

"I think it's widening..." Sebastian said.

A lock of Elodie's hair fluttered against her sweat-slicked forehead. *Fresh air.*

Beyond, a noise like a rushing river sounded, though she still couldn't see.

"Elodie, give me the knife." Willum held out his hand for it.

She tightened her fingers on the slick hilt, remembering how easily he had given her up. Elodie narrowed her eyes. "I think I'll keep it." Willum didn't deserve to be trapped for eternity inside a hideous mythical body, but there was no way in the Daughter's name she'd forget his betrayal, either.

At her reticence, Willum seemed to crumble in on himself. "You fought it. You tried to save me, even after what I did—" He choked on the words, and when he finally looked up at her, the expression on his shadowed face was one she hadn't seen in years. As if what had happened in the cave had stripped away all of Willum's bitterness and resentment, his anger at the world. For a moment, he was *her* Willum again, just a boy—scared and sorry. "I never deserved you, Elodie. Not even before the accident. You're good and kind you stood by me despite everything I've done, all the ways I hurt you—"

Corentin barked ahead of them. And barked again. Fear curdled her gut.

Sebastian spoke first. "It's here."

"Please Elodie, give me the knife. I'll go first and try to wound it again. It's got to be struggling after your two blows. I can buy you both time to run like hell."

"But—" They couldn't just leave him. Could they?

His brown eyes bored into her. "I was never the husband you deserved. Let me do this now. Beringer will keep you safe."

Elodie's heart spasmed. "Willum—"

But he was already snatching the knife from her hand and barreling out of the cave as fast as his limping gait could take him. Out into the open.

"Fool brave man." Elodie stumbled from the cave into the night.

On a stretch of ground to their right, the Wish-Eater and Willum grappled. The rain still poured in torrents. She could barely make out the figures through the oppressive storm.

"Come on." Sebastian grabbed her arm, hauling her away from Willum.

"We have to help him—"

"You heard him! We have to go."

They stumbled forward. Away from Willum's bellows. The Wish-

Eater's roars. Her heart writhed in her chest. Could she really abandon him? He was a drunk and a son of a bitch, but he was still her husband. She slid on the slick snarl of rocks and roots as Sebastian pulled her along, navigating around a nest of brambles.

He pulled up suddenly and she bumped against him, their sodden clothes squelching from the sudden contact.

The ground before them sloped down into the large, steep ravine they'd crossed once before. But the water from the storm had poured into the channel, turning the ravine into a churning river, whitewater bubbling down over boulders and trees, bearing debris and branches with it. Her eyes searched the tangle of grey and green, desperate for a way across.

"We can't cross." Sebastian threw out his arm. "It's too dangerous."

A flash of lightning split the sky and Elodie looked back at where the Wish-Eater and Willum wrestled in the distance. More lightning illuminated their plight as the Wish-Eater slashed across Willum's chest with razor-sharp talons. He was losing.

"We can't stay," she protested. "There's no other way to get away from it."

A clap of thunder mingled with the inhuman scream of the Wish-Eater. Had Willum wounded it again?

Corentin navigated down the bank, barking.

"Look, there! He found a way across." A thick tree had fallen across the ravine. If they forded across the river using the bulk of the trunk to hold themselves firm against the current rushing from above, maybe they could make it. "Come on." She grabbed Sebastian's hand and pulled him forward, down the bank the way Corentin had gone.

Her feet lost purchase on the slick mud and she slipped and hit the ground hard. A sharp rock split one of her palms and she hissed in pain.

"Are you okay?"

Elodie rose to her feet, pulling her skirt from a branch that had caught it. "Fine."

Lightning flashed again, but she couldn't see the Wish-Eater. Or Willum.

"Where are they?" Sebastian asked.

"Hurry." Elodie pressed her hip against the large log and waded into the water cascading down the ravine. She gasped at the shock as water filled her boots, swirling around her, tugging at her skirt. It was ice cold, numbing her instantly.

Corentin leaped onto the log, trotting across the top of it to the other side.

"Show off," she grumbled. Then she yelped as her foot slipped on a rock beneath her and she almost went down. She managed to wrap her arm around the log and right herself, her heart thundering at the exertion. The force of the water was tremendous, the rain hammering her face ever present.

Step by shaking step, they crossed until they made it to the other bank and collapsed into the mud.

The rushing of the river and the rain filled her senses. Her body was totally numb. It was like being inside a cloud, floating in a strange nothingness. Her eyes fluttered closed.

"Elodie." Sebastian patted her cheek. Harder.

She frowned at him.

"You need to get up. You're too cold. We need to keep moving. Keep your body temperature up."

Corentin barked and her frown deepened. "What now?" She sighed.

But then, through the ever-present din of the storm, she heard a cry. A human cry.

Elodie jerked straight up. "Willum." She staggered to her feet, peering through the wall of water. Where was he?

"All-father save us," she breathed, her shaking finger pointing.

The ravine. The river. The log they'd just crossed—Willum was clinging to one of its branches, below the tree. Barely holding on.

"Come on!" Elodie surged forward, only to be spun around by Sebastian's firm grip on her upper arm.

"It's suicide," Sebastian said. "We'll be swept away."

"We just crossed!"

"And barely made it. We can't pull a man of Willum's size out of the river. He'll take us down with him."

She turned back to Sebastian with steel in her voice. "We can't just let him die. He bought us time. He saved us."

Sebastian closed his eyes and hissed but nodded. "Okay. Carefully."

So they waded back into the water, the rushing cold filling her boots once again. Inch by inch, Elodie reached the spot where Willum hung on, Sebastian just a few feet behind her.

Elodie turned, her belly against the log, and dangled her arms down to Willum. "Take my hand." The sight of him terrified her. His colors were all wrong. His face was as white as death, his lips blue. Scarlet blood flowed freely from four slashes across his chest. The expression on his face was wrong too, more wrong than all the rest. Fear.

"I'm afraid to let go with one hand," Willum said. "My arms are so weak."

Sebastian was next to her then, leaning over too, his arms down. "It's okay. We'll get you together. We'll each take one of your hands and pull you up. One big push, and we'll get you out of here. Then you can rest."

Willum nodded.

"On the count of three," Sebastian said. "Pull yourself up and grab our hands. One. Two. Three!"

Willum heaved himself up, grasping first for Sebastian's wrist, then Elodie's. His fingers were as slick as a greased pig, and they almost slipped through hers, but she managed to catch his wrist with her other hand and hang on for dear life. The full weight of him felt like it would pull her shoulder from its socket. Her stomach dug into the log beneath her, a stray nub poking her like a knife.

"Okay," Sebastian said through gritted teeth. "Now we pull. One. Two. Three!"

Elodie heaved with all her might, with every ounce of strength she had left. But Willum was a large man, heavier than she could have imagined. They lifted him inches...a foot...but not enough. Not enough for him to get his arms around the log, for them to pull him to safety.

Her strength gave out and she collapsed against the log, gasping for breath, her arms hanging long. She was so numb and tired. Her hair plastered her forehead, forming a curtain before her eyes. "He's too...heavy..." she panted.

"Willum, can you maybe grasp the branch closer up to us? And we can pull under your armpits?" Sebastian asked.

Willum's eyes had fluttered closed for a moment and his grip on her hand loosened, slipping slightly.

Elodie lunged forward, grabbing his wrist again with frozen fingers. "Willum! Wake up. Come on. Snap out of it."

When he opened those chocolate eyes and met hers, there was something there she had never seen on him before. Resignation. "I'm so tired, Elodie." His voice was raw. "I'm tired of not being the man I thought I would be. The husband you deserved. I'm tired of hurting all the time. Of hurting you."

"Willum Mercer," Elodie said through a throat thick with tears. "Don't you give up on me. Don't you dare give up—" But his grip was already loosening.

"Be happy, Elodie." Willum's eyes fluttered closed.

"Willum!"

His hand slipped from her grasp, leaving her holding nothing but air.

CHAPTER 34

THE BOOK

The morning dawned as crisp and clear as a bell, as it seemed to do, after a rain. The sky was relieved of its burden—the great weight of thunderclouds it had borne. But a great weight had fallen upon Elodie.

The night had felt like a strange and terrifying dream. But it had been no dream. Willum was gone. She was a widow. The word didn't fit, like too-tight shoes. But somehow, she wore it just the same.

Sebastian had dragged her from the ravine, through the rush of cold, frigid water, pulling her up onto the bank when she was too tired and too numb to save herself. He had heaved her up into his arms and carried her through the sodden woods, back to their camp.

Sebastian had stripped their clothes from them and maneuvered her into his bedroll, pressing his body against hers—his warmth banishing the wracking chill that threatened to carry her away. She was too numb and tired and filled with grief to notice his naked body pressed to hers with more than detached observation. Her time with Agathe had taught her that it was the best way to combat the creeping cold and raise a person's body temperature. She had no doubt that Sebastian had saved her life.

He was there now, dressed in dry clothes, blowing on the start of a fire to banish the morning's chill. He turned his back respectfully as she pushed to a seat. Her body ached in every nook and crevice, her stomach churned with hunger, and her heart—well, her heart was broken. No, Willum hadn't been the best husband these last few years, and there had been times when she had yearned to be free of the man he had become, but she had loved him. And he'd deserved to be loved. Deserved to be mourned. For he had saved them too.

With mechanical motions, Elodie pulled dry clothes from her pack and donned them. She walked to the fire, putting her hands out to feel the warmth.

Corentin rubbed against her leg and she scratched him behind his overlarge ears. Corentin had saved her life too, more times than she could count. "You are a good dog," she murmured.

"How are you doing?" Sebastian asked quietly.

She looked at the sky. The sympathy twisting his face was enough to bring a lump to her throat. "My husband is dead. How am I supposed to be doing?"

"I don't profess to have known him well, and I'm still mad as hell that he bargained with your life, but it seemed like he found a sort of peace...at the end. An acceptance. That has to be worth something, doesn't it?"

It was true. The light in Willum's eyes when he'd let go of the log— it had been peaceful. He had lived in pain for so long, longing for the person he used to be. He was ready to lay that burden down.

"I'm just so angry," she whispered. Her voice was hoarse.

"At whom?"

"Everyone. The All-father. For letting that stone fall on him. Letting it injure him and ruin his future. Myself. For being so obsessed that I dragged us all out here. If I hadn't been here, he wouldn't have followed."

"You can't blame yourself. Willum made his own choices. Every step of the way."

But she did blame herself. Anger kindled inside her then, as bright and crackling as the fire that warmed her fingers. Anger was more bearable than grief. "How did we not know what we were walking into? How did I not see it?"

"How could you have known?" Sebastian asked.

Elodie shook her head. "How could Agathe not tell me? She sent me into that creature's clutches with only a stupid knife."

"She told us to read the book. She said it was dangerous, right? And the knife—it was the only thing that saved us—"

"The book!" Elodie fumed, storming back to their leaning shelter, rummaging through her pack for the bloody book. She seized it, stalked back to the fire pit, and threw it on the flames. Her breast heaved. "That book can go straight to the Un-Brother's fiery hell. It told us nothing. It didn't warn us. Agathe should have told me herself." Though that last thought rang false. Agathe had tried, hadn't she? And Elodie had stormed into the night, too obsessed to listen to reason.

Elodie watched as the greedy flames licked the book's blue leather binding, its gilded edges.

And it didn't catch.

Sebastian leaned forward with a frown. "Why isn't it burning?"

Elodie's breath caught in her throat. She crouched down to examine it, cold fingers skittering up her spine. "The title—"

Still the book sat in the fire, impervious.

"The title of the book was *The Wish-Eater*, was it not?" she asked. "Am I mad to think that?"

"You're not mad," Sebastian agreed. "So why does it now say *The Wish-Eater and Other Tales?*"

Elodie seized a stick and knocked the book out of the fire. Gingerly, she lay a finger on the cover. It wasn't even warm.

She picked it up, flipping through the first story. The Wish-Eater. It started the same. But...her eyes widened. Somehow, the book had changed. "The end is different." She sat down next to Sebastian. "Listen to this."

Once upon a time, there was a man who was born as poor as they come. He was the sixth son of a cabbage farmer, and a sickly boy at that. There was never enough food to fill all the hungry bellies and never enough wood to keep their hovel warm. When he was just six he began helping in the fields, carrying and pulling weeds where he could. But he knew no other way.

"I remember," Sebastian said gently. "The new part."

Elodie flipped forward.

Near nightfall, they came upon a cave. The old man took the heavy cuffs from the blacksmith and told him to wait at the entrance. "I go first. We had a deal."

Unease filled the blacksmith, but he agreed.

The blacksmith passed a frigid night at the mouth of the cave. Near midnight, a man in a black cloak appeared, waking the blacksmith from a sound sleep. "May I share your fire?" the man asked.

"I couldn't get one lit," the blacksmith admitted. "The wood is too wet."

"Let me try," the strange man said, crouching low. The blacksmith didn't see the flint strike, but the kindling caught and fire whooshed to life with surprising force.

The man settled by the fire, the cloak of his hood still raised. The blacksmith thought it odd but didn't want to be rude. Especially not when the man offered him a pull of whiskey, and the vintage tasted like nothing he'd ever known—the bite and the burn reminiscent of cinnamon.

"What are you doing out so far?" the stranger inquired.

The blacksmith gave a rueful laugh. "I travel with a man who is convinced a wish-granting creature lives in these woods." He shrugged off his embarrassment. "Children's tales."

"You have a wish?"

The blacksmith gave a wistful nod. "She's with the All-father now."

"The Un-Brother governs the dead," the man said. "And he's often willing to bargain."

"Who would make a bargain with the Un-Brother?" The blacksmith shook his head. "Only the foolish."

"And the desperate. I'm curious. What would you give for your wish to be granted?"

"Anything I had," the man admitted.

"Even the thing you loved most in the world?"

The blacksmith shrugged. "I already lost her."

"This other fellow. What about him? Would you give the thing he *loves most in the world?*"

The blacksmith paused. He barely knew the old man. If he could truly bring his lost love back to life... "Yes." The blacksmith thought he saw the shine of white teeth in the recesses of the man's hood.

The man stood. "Come with me, then."

"What?"

"Do you want to see her again?"

The blacksmith stood. He followed the man into a tunnel in the hillside— leading to another cave. White crystals lit their way, and when they reached a large cavern, the stranger turned.

He lowered his hood, revealing a face like a skeleton, but for his golden, glowing eyes—

"The Un-Brother made the Wish-Eater?" Sebastian interrupted.

Elodie swallowed. "Do you want to find out or not?" Her voice was small. How close they'd come to evil—tangled with it. How fortunate they were to make it out alive. But they hadn't all made it out alive, had they? She kept reading.

The blacksmith turned to run, but he found his feet were frozen to the spot. Turning hard and calcified. Turning to stone. The Un-Brother reached into his chest with skeletal fingers of magic and pulled out his soul—brilliant white and blue—tinged with darkness. Corrupted by desire.

The Un-Brother began weaving magic, creating a cage for his soul formed like a beast—a strange, inhuman beast. "The All-Father and I have an understanding, you see. He creates man, I create only beasts. He governs this world, I the underworld. Confined to the depths but for one day a year, when the veil grows thin. I am limited, in my ability to harvest souls. But you, my selfish, twisted friend, you will be my harvester."

"What are you doing to me?" the blacksmith cried, his soul struggling against the Un-Brother's unholy grip.

"They will come to you—the desperate dreamers. And you will ask them what they are willing to sacrifice. The selfish belong to me—those willing to sell out their fellow man. Only when such a man offers himself to you—offers to trade his most precious love—or that of his neighbor, will you have completed your penance to me. He will take your place, and you will be free."

"Free to do what?" the blacksmith cried. For his new form was almost complete around him. He could feel the strangeness—see through its slitted eyes, feel the weight of the wings upon his back. "You turned my body to stone!"

"When you've served your term, you'll return to your body and have your wish. Enjoy your riches, your love, your health. For you'll still be mine in the end."

Elodie cleared her throat, closing the book.

"Well, that would have been helpful before we went into the cave."

A little laugh escaped her. Followed by a tear. She flicked it away. They'd read the book cover to cover on their journey to the cave, heeding Agathe's warning. And that was *not* the story that the book had told.

"It was a trap. A honeyed trap for the desperately hopeful. And the book is the bait. It tells a story of wishes come true, not the truth of what the Wish-Eater really is, or the real cost of making a deal with it." Sebastian shook his head.

What a fool she'd been. A trap for the desperately hopeful. And she'd been one. But no more.

"What are the other stories?"

She handed the book to him. "I don't know if I can hear anymore."

Sebastian flipped through the pages. "There are—These are the names of people. Their stories."

"The Wish-Eater's victims."

"And...and not." Sebastian flipped to the end of the book and looked up in amazement. "Elodie, we're in here. Willum."

She let out a strangled laugh, tears pooling on her lashes like refracted stars. "Obsessed village woman gets her husband killed. The end."

"Agathe is in here."

She looked up sharply. "Really?"

Sebastian closed the book, tucking it under his arm. "We have a long ride back. You'll have time to read her story. I think we should get moving. Leave this place."

"All right."

"There's something I need to ask before we go."

She met his amber eyes. Her heart seized. She hadn't even started to contemplate what the previous night's events meant for her and Sebastian. She, realizing she loved him. She—on her own. He...giving away his love for her—letting the Wish-Eater devour it. Would he still want her now? The irony of her losing the one thing she loved most was too much to bear. Tears coursed down her face then, and she shoved the bundle of thoughts down deep. Willum deserved her full attention, her sorrow. She'd have the rest of her life to contemplate the exquisite cruelty of the turn their fates had taken.

"Do you want to try to retrieve Willum's body?" Sebastian asked.

She nodded woodenly. "Do you think it's safe?" she whispered. "It's not...out there?"

Sebastian shook his head. "If Willum didn't kill it, I think it's back in its cave, nursing its wounds. Besides. The Un-Brother's deal—it can only take the selfish, right?"

Those words were little comfort.

CHAPTER 35

SPLIT

*C*orentin found Willum near the bottom of the steep incline, wedged between two boulders. His face was as white as new fallen snow, the scratches and ragged furrows in his chest torn by the Wish-Eater's talons standing in stark relief.

Sebastian hadn't liked the man, even despised him toward the end, but no one deserved to go out like this.

Elodie's hands pressed to her mouth as she looked at him, her tears flowing like spring thaw.

Should he wrap his arms around her? Give her whatever comfort he could offer? But how much had she seen in the cavern? Would she think him trying to make some misplaced romantic gesture? The sight of her falling into herself should shred his heart with ragged fingers. But he felt nothing. True, there was sorrow—the sorrow one human felt toward another who had lost their life. There was sympathy for Elodie in her time of grief. But the yearning ache in his chest that he felt at her presence, her touch, her rosemary scent—it was gone.

For the first time in four and a half years, Elodie was unwed—and he no longer loved her. He had given up his wish—every desire and longing to be with her for the rest of his life. Things couldn't have gone worse if the Un-Brother himself had choreographed them. And after meeting his beast—perhaps he had. A bubble of manic laughter surfaced and Sebastian disguised it as a cough.

Elodie looked up at him, her eyes bloodshot.

Sebastian cleared his throat. "Let's go get him."

Willum had followed them on a big black mare that belonged to his friend Bellamy. With much difficulty, they retrieved Willum's body, wrapped it in a cloak and the tarp Sebastian had brought to camp beneath, and got the man up on the horse's back. By the time they finished, Sebastian was sweating through his shirt, and his ribs were on fire.

"I shouldn't have asked this of you," Elodie said, worrying her lip with her teeth.

"You didn't. I volunteered," Sebastian said as he tested the ropes that held Willum to the horse.

"You don't need to do that anymore." Elodie turned her back and walked to Feu, hauling herself up into the saddle. She was getting better at that.

"Do what?"

"Be so nice to me. Treat me different than anyone else."

With the black horse's reins in one hand, Sebastian hauled himself up into the saddle with a hiss of pain. He settled into the saddle with a groan.

"You should let me look at those ribs," Elodie said.

"Let's just get out of here." Sebastian clucked his tongue. "And I'm not treating you differently. It's common decency to help someone in their time of need."

"You're telling me all the things you've done in the last months— the trip to Rochester, Josephine, this trip...you would have done those things for anyone else, out of common decency?"

Sebastian pursed his lips.

Elodie sat before him, her spine rod-straight. Like she was afraid to touch him. She knew. Of course, she did. She'd seen those images in the cave, the secret desires of his heart. And she was disgusted by it. Afraid to even touch him. Hot shame slithered up his neck, heated his ears. He wished in that moment that he could be anywhere but here.

"Why didn't you tell me?" Elodie asked, still looking forward. Perhaps it was better to have this conversation when he couldn't see her face. When she couldn't see his.

"What purpose would that have served?"

"I...I don't know. Honesty? I thought we were friends. I thought I knew you."

"Honesty for honesty's sake is the height of selfishness. It would have lightened a burden on me by placing it on you."

"I would have wanted to know. You robbed me of that choice."

"What choice? You couldn't have left Willum."

Silence. "But maybe...I don't know. We'd almost been married five years. Maybe he would have cleaved me if I'd asked."

Sebastian's stomach swooped and dipped like a swallow on a zephyr. She couldn't be saying what he thought she was...was it possible he had misjudged her—his chances...No. "I know you, Elodie. You honor your commitments. You would never have given up on your marriage. Not with him injured like he was."

When she didn't respond, his shoulders relaxed. He'd evaluated correctly after all. "It was better to be your friend. We couldn't have stayed friends if I'd told you."

"But you didn't let me be a friend to you. How in the All-father's name could you agree to marry Josephine? If you..." She trailed off.

He let out a harsh laugh and then winced as his ribs groaned in protest. "Not my most well-thought-out decision."

"And now?"

"Now what?" he replied carefully.

"The Wish-Eater... It ate your wish?"

Yes. By a crueler twist of fate than he could imagine, yes. Tears pricked his eyes, and he fought them. Fought the invisible hand squeezing the air from his lungs.

"I see."

And by her tone, he knew she did.

"So, will you marry her?"

"Josephine?" he managed.

"Yes."

Would he marry Josephine? His heart was empty now. It was possible he could fall in love with her. It wouldn't ache to be near to Elodie day in, day out. The Ruelle family was wonderful. It would be good to be settled down. Have a child. But...did he *want* to marry Josephine? He didn't think he did. It had been so long that he'd been driven by this impulse in his heart, its beating song of *Elodie, Elodie.* What would it feel like to live without that? Who would he be without it guiding him? When he'd given up his wish, it had been the first decision in a long time he'd made just for him. And as horrible as it had turned out, it had felt good, choosing what was best for him. Taking care of himself first. "I don't want to marry her," he admitted.

"Then don't." Elodie let out a tremendous sigh. "Don't. She's too young to marry; I don't know if she'll ever really want to. You deserve every happiness, and so does she. Not some forced marriage of convenience."

"Okay, then. She'll be all right?"

"She'll be relieved. I promise."

A weight slithered off his shoulders, like a cloak falling to the mossy forest floor beneath them.

Elodie's voice cracked as she asked, "Can we still be friends?"

He swallowed his knee-jerk reaction. *Of course.* If he was taking care of himself first, though...he would need to think on it. Whether it made sense for him. Was healthy. "I hope so," he finally answered.

"I hope so too." Elodie's back relaxed a bit then and she leaned gently into him.

He let his hands rest on the saddle before her, settling in for the long ride. As the silence fell upon them, it brought a bone-tired weariness. And so he closed his eyes and let Feu's rocking gait put him to sleep.

THE TRIP back to Lunesburg was quiet and uneventful.

They said little, dozing in turns, passing back and forth what little food they had left. They didn't stop to make camp. The thought of sleeping beside Willum's decaying body was too much for either of them to bear.

It wasn't until they neared the crossroads to Rochester that Sebastian began to worry.

"I don't think we should return to town together." Sebastian finally voiced his concern. "People might think I did this. Willum's and my quarrel before we left is well known."

"His body was clearly attacked by an animal," Elodie protested. "No one would think you capable of murder."

"Even with my face like this?" Sebastian pointed to his bruises and split lip. Elodie had found some herbs along the way that had numbed the pain and spurred his healing. But still, he had days yet before he looked normal.

Her mouth compressed into a little button, which he took to mean she conceded his point. He used to think it adorable when she did that. Now, his observation of it was detached. A few times along their journey back, he could have sworn he felt some sensation there— some feeling for her that still lingered—triggered by the way the dappled light gilded her golden curls, or the way her clever fingers wound through Feu's chestnut mane. But it must have just been his memories. A familiar path his thoughts had worn smooth over the years.

"I think it would be better if I returned a few days later, when my bruises have recovered."

"Where will you go?"

"Rochester. I'll stay at Ava's."

Elodie nodded her head curtly. "Ava's." He couldn't see her expression, but her voice sounded distant. Her shoulders heaved with a sigh.

"What am I going to tell his parents?" she asked. "They're going to blame me."

"The truth?" Sebastian offered.

"That I was chasing the Un-Brother's spawn to grant my desperate wish to be a mother, and then Willum nearly sacrificed me for his own dreams before dying heroically?"

Sebastian winced. "Fair point. What reason could you have to be out in the forest?"

Elodie thought. "Perhaps...gathering herbs or supplies for Agathe. Or my business."

"The slash marks could have been from a wolf. Or a bear. The Malveille Forest is known to have both. It's a simple enough story. You needed some time alone after your fight, so you went into the woods on an errand. Willum came after you and was attacked by an animal."

"That sounds plausible."

"People don't want to believe in the strange or unnatural. Give them a half-decent explanation and they'll accept it. Tell them Willum died defending you from a vicious beast. That much is true, after all."

"You're right," she murmured.

They were coming upon the split in the road that would take him to Rochester. He reined in Feu and swung down, bones still creaking. Corentin stretched beside them as Sebastian helped Elodie slide off the horse.

"I'll take Corentin with me," Sebastian said. "What about...the other thing?"

They hadn't read the book again in their long ride. Part of Sebastian was dying to—to devour the other stories, to find out if others had managed to avoid destruction at the Wish-Eater's talons. To see how the book had recorded their tale. But the other, more powerful part of him wanted nothing else to do with the Wish-Eater or the Un-Brother ever again. He couldn't change the past. He could only start living his future. And clinging to old wishes was not the way to move forward.

"I'll take it," Elodie said. "I'll see if Agathe knows of a way to destroy it. I don't want anyone else to fall victim to it."

They transferred Elodie's pack to the black horse, tying it over the horse's withers. "Are you going to be all right the rest of the way...?" He didn't say it. Riding with Willum's body.

She nodded, tears glittering in her sky-blue eyes. "It's time for you to stop worrying about me, Sebastian."

He let out a soft laugh. "Force of habit."

She sprang at him, wrapping her arms around his torso in a hug. "Thank you, Sebastian. For everything."

He wrapped his arms around her too, kissing her flaxen head. "You're welcome."

Elodie pulled back. She swallowed. "Promise me something?"

"Anything," he said without thinking. Another force of habit.

Her request was quiet. Simple. "Go live your life. For you. Not for anyone else."

It was his turn to swallow. "Okay."

Her request rang in him like the peal of a bell, the resonance lingering in his soul long after the sound had died. He thought on it as he watched her ride away, as he pulled himself into Feu's saddle, as he rode for Rochester. As he pushed into Ava's common room hours later, weariness hanging off him in waves. There were only a few stragglers left in the inn, and the big hearth filled the room with blissful warmth. He knew what he'd do that was just for him, if he wasn't worrying about anything or anyone else.

Ava froze in the act of drying a flagon. "You look like hell." Her red curls were tied in a shimmering purple ribbon, her spotless white apron pulled tightly around her trim waist.

"Feel like hell too." He grinned, leaning his elbows onto the bar. "But..." He heaved in a breath, his whole body tingling. Was this what it felt like to be alive? To take a chance? "I thought I'd finally take you up on that offer. If it's still on the table," he added hastily.

She sat the glass down slowly and leaned forward, giving him a generous view of her glorious cleavage. "You can get a room anywhere in the city."

"That's not the offer I was referring to." His voice was hoarse, his heart hammering. Did he sound seductive, or desperate? *Please be seductive.*

Ava reached out and brushed a stray curl off his forehead. A smile curved the corner of her finely-wrought lips. "I think we can come to an arrangement."

Powerful heat raced through him. All-father, it had been a long time.

She wrinkled her nose next and leaned back, crossing her arms before her. "What about a bath first? And a hot meal. You look like you've been eating bark for days."

He hung his head with a laugh. "Yes, a thousand times yes."

"And your dog sleeps in the hayloft."

He grinned. "Ava, you are an angel."

"You just wait, Sebastian," she purred, her bright eyes flashing. "You have no idea."

CHAPTER 36

HOME

Fatigue pulled at Elodie like an anchor as the horse plodded past the familiar landmarks toward home. It was nearly midnight. When the sign for Larkhaven came into view, a sob of relief escaped her. Every bone in her body ached, every piece of her soul wept. She wanted to lie down and let sleep pull her under.

She walked the horse right up to the front stoop before pulling the reins and bringing it to a stop. She leaned over its neck and slid her one leg over the bundle wrapped across the horse's rump. Willum.

Her knees gave out as her feet hit the dirt lane; she grabbed the stirrup to keep herself from falling to the ground. She gave the horse a tired pat and summited the three steps.

Knocked.

Waited.

Knocked again, fighting the knot in her stomach. Would it be a cold reception? She'd left in a whirlwind of cruel words to Josephine. Maybe they wouldn't be able to forgive the things she'd said—

Her father opened yanked open the door, clad in his white nightgown.

"Pepa." The word creaked from her, and the dam broke.

He caught her as she fell, swinging her up into his arms. "Where have you been—" he started. She felt the sharp inhale of breath as he caught sight of the horse. The burden over its rump. "What…is that?"

She squeezed her eyes closed, salty tears drenching his nightshirt. She couldn't say it. She opened her mouth to say his name, but the word wouldn't come.

Pepa closed the door. "Josephine! Up with you! Your sister's home. We need hot tea and a hot bath."

The moments that followed were a blur. He wrapped her in a blanket on the sofa. Shoved a glass of whiskey into her shaking hands. "Drink. You're too cold."

She curled into herself, letting the warmth of the blanket cocoon her. She'd brought him home. Now she could fall apart. The tears came, sobs and ragged breaths. Her heart keened for everything that could have been. The life that had been stolen from her and Willum. The life that had been stolen from her and Sebastian too. The dream that she had given up. At least there—the wound didn't ache. It was strangely blank, when she thought of the promise of motherhood. Like a wound healed over. It had once been raw, but no more.

Elodie drifted in and out of sleep. There were murmured voices. She woke to find Josephine stripping off her stiff, cold clothes, and her father sliding her into a blissfully warm bath. She was too numb to think of her modesty, even as Josephine shooed her father out of the bathroom now that the heavy lifting was done.

Josephine undid the snarls in her hair that had once been braids, scooping warm water over her. Elodie looked at her sister, blinking her eyes to focus. Josephine was in her nightgown, but her color had returned. She looked like herself.

Elodie reached out a hand to grasp her sister's—stopping her as she went to pour water over Elodie's shoulders. "I'm so, so sorry, Jo."

Josephine nodded, pressing her lips together to stem the tears. "Me too." She nodded and then surged forward, pulling Elodie into a hug.

Josephine bathed her, dried her, and wrapped her in warm, dry clothes. When it was done, Josephine led her to the table, where she put down a bowl of hot soup and leftover bread heated on the hearth.

Elodie fell upon it, finally noticing that Pepa had returned when the bowl had been licked clean.

"I put him in the barn," Pepa said gruffly. He'd dressed and donned his boots. "Rubbed the horse down too. Bellamy's?"

Elodie nodded. "Willum rode him. He came after me."

"We were worried sick, Elodie," her father said. "Where'd you go?"

She shrugged, looking down at the swirls of wood on the table's surface. "I needed to get away. To think. After everything. I went up past Rochester. Just wanted to be in nature. Clear my head. Collect some herbs."

"Why didn't you tell us?" Josephine asked gently.

"I didn't know if you'd want to talk to me...after...how we left things."

"You're kin, Elodie," Pepa said. "There's nothing you can say or do to make us love you any less."

She swallowed, nodding. "I...know that now."

"How'd it happen?" Pepa asked. "If it was self-defense—"

"I didn't kill him." Elodie finally looked up at that.

Pepa held up his hands. "Wouldn't judge you if you did."

"We were attacked...by wolves. The night of the big storm. He fought them off, and we were running...he fell into a river. Was swept away. By the time I could get to him..."

"And you got him out of the river, all bound up and on the horse all by yourself?" His question was gentle, but incising.

Elodie looked up then, meeting his eyes. "A passing traveler took pity and helped me."

Pepa and Josephine exchanged a look.

She shook her head, a spark of anger kindling. "I loved Willum, and I was faithful to him. If you have something to say, say it."

Pepa held up his hands and shook his head. "I told him myself. There's no one truer than my Elodie. If that's how it happened, that's how it happened. I'm sorry, Elodie. That you had to go through that. All of it."

"Thank you." She rubbed her brow between her eyes. A headache was forming there. "Thank you for the bath, and the food. But I'm very tired. I'd like to go to bed."

"You can sleep with me," Josephine offered.

Elodie's heart stuttered. She and Josephine hadn't slept together since they'd been girls, since they would all pile together in one bed and talk late into the night. A stray tear snaked its way down her cheek. "That would be nice."

They piled into Josephine's narrow bed, and Elodie turned, burying her nose in the lavender scent of her sister's curls. "I don't deserve a sister like you," Elodie murmured, her eyelids dragging closed.

"I haven't done it yet," Josephine whispered in the dark.

Elodie opened her eyes. "The baby?"

Josephine nodded. "I...I'll think more about giving it up for adoption." The words were hesitant. "If you want."

Elodie paused. "What do *you* want?"

Josephine's voice twisted. "I don't want to die."

Elodie propped herself up on her arm at that, peering into her sister's face in the dark. Tears snaked down Josephine's face, glimmering in the quicksilver moonlight pouring through the crack in the curtains. "What? What are you talking about? The pennyroyal has left your system. You're fine."

"Mama died...having me. If I have the baby... I'm scared."

Elodie's heart broke anew at that. She'd never even thought of the fears that might be bundled tightly within her sister at the prospect of childbirth. Josephine was a child who'd had her mother stolen from her—who feared she'd done the stealing, through her very existence.

"Oh, Josephine." Elodie wrapped her arms around her sister, shushing her as she cried. "You don't have to have the baby. It was selfish of me to ask it of you. You'll have your time, if you want it, when you're older, when you've met a man who makes your knees weak and your heart burst with love."

Elodie licked her lips, fighting a fresh wave of her own tears. She'd found such a man. But he didn't love her anymore.

"Then, I don't want to go through it. I don't want to die and I don't want to give up my life. I never should have been with him. I should have known better—"

Elodie shushed her sister. "It was his fault, Jo. You're young and he preyed on you. He knew it. Don't blame yourself. I should have never put that guilt into your head."

"I don't know how it all became such a mess." Josephine sighed.

"That's life," Elodie said. "It's messy and surprising and never goes according to plan."

"How do you stand it?"

Tears slipped down Elodie's cheeks. "I don't know. I haven't been doing a very good job at that."

"But...I know you're sad about Willum, but...you seem better somehow. More peaceful."

Elodie thought on it. "I guess...I let go. I thought I could control it all, and life kept reminding me I couldn't. All I can control is how I respond. So I'm going to try to do that."

"Hmm."

Elodie smoothed the hair off her sister's forehead, and they settled back down, Elodie with one arm wrapped tightly around her sister, their bodies fitted together like nestled spoons.

"Does this mean I don't have to marry Sebastian Beringer anymore?" Josephine asked. "Pepa tried to convince me to accept him the entire time you were gone."

Elodie let out a soft laugh. "No. You don't. You never did. That was crazy."

"So crazy!" Josephine said, joining her laughter. "He's too serious and responsible. Boring."

"Right. Perfectly boring." Her heart twisted. "It would have been a terrible match."

"I would have driven him mad."

"I don't doubt that."

"He didn't really want to marry me, did he?"

"No, not really," Elodie admitted.

"Then why did he ask?"

"Because he thought you and the baby needed someone to take care of you. And he was willing to do it."

Josephine was silent. "That's...so nice. I should say thank you."

"That would be a good thing to do."

Elodie's eyes were closed again, consciousness drifting away.

"Elodie?"

"Hmm?"

"I'm sorry about Willum. I...I always really liked him. When he wasn't drinking."

Elodie sighed. "Me too, Josephine."

CHAPTER 37

FIGHTER

*W*ith the morning came visitors. And food. Sidonie and Hugh with a roast, Justus Gregoire with a pot pie some village woman must have concocted for him, Alder Landry and Delphine with tarts. Margery with a basket of bredele flowers. Elodie took each, accepting their condolences and platitudes.

She felt like that statue in the Wish-Eater's cavern, present in body, though not in spirit. She missed Willum—his presence had brought her a comfort she hadn't recognized until it had been gone. Its absence was like a familiar tree cut down. But, All-father help her, she missed Sebastian more. He was the only one whose arms she wanted to fall apart in. And he was the one whose arms she couldn't.

After a lunch which she chewed and swallowed mechanically, a knock sounded on the door.

Elodie looked up with half-interest as her father went to the door.

A moment later, Agathe burst into the living room and pulled Elodie into a fierce embrace.

Relief flooded her. She hadn't ruined things with Agathe. That would have been a loss too great to bear. "Can we go sit outside?" Elodie murmured into Agathe's silver hair.

Agathe pulled back, her eyes shining with sympathetic tears. "I think some fresh air would do you good." She seized Elodie's hand and pulled her to her feet and out the back door.

"Agathe, you were right, about everything." The words spilled out of Elodie's mouth. "I'm so sorry. I was awful—"

"Hush. All is forgiven." She put her hands on Elodie's shoulders. "Are you safe?"

"We wounded it badly. Maybe killed it."

Agathe shook her head. "I don't think it can be killed."

"You saved my life. The knife you gave me..." Elodie trailed off.

Agathe led her to a bench warmed by the sun. "Why don't you start at the beginning?"

So Elodie did. She told her everything. Right down to Willum slipping through her and Sebastian's fingers.

Agathe took it all in stride.

"How are you feeling, with it all?"

"Okay, considering," Elodie said. "None of it feels real."

"That's normal," Agathe said. "The mind goes into shock in times of great loss. A defense mechanism. It will break soon, and it will feel overwhelming. But you'll get through that, too."

"I keep thinking about those last moments," Elodie said. "I should have fought harder for Willum. To keep him with me."

"It wasn't your job to fight for him. It was his to fight for himself. And he decided he was done fighting. That was his right to choose."

"I think he just wished the pain would stop. It was killing him, wishing things could be different."

"Do you think he found peace?"

"Yes." Elodie closed her eyes briefly, enjoying the sun on her face.

"Then we should be glad for him." Agathe paused. "And what of you? Have you found peace?"

Had she? Her heart cried out over how close she and Sebastian had come, mourning a love that could have been. But she had spent so long wishing for things to be different—wishing for something she didn't have—something she had no control over. It had nearly destroyed her. That wanting *had* destroyed Willum. She was done with that. Done with letting the wanting control her. Run her life. It was time to live the life she'd been given. The hand she'd been dealt.

"I think I have," Elodie admitted. "Or at least I'm determined to find it. For the first time in a long time, I feel like I have time. Space. To think about what I want my life to look like." She drew in a deep breath and let it out. "I feel guilty even saying it. But...it's freeing."

"I suggest you dispense with feeling guilty. Wretched emotion. Just eliminate it altogether. Life is much more pleasant."

Elodie closed her eyes. "How does one even begin to do that?"

"You realize that you're not supposed to be anything other than you are. Anyone else. Feel anything different. It's all valid. It's all you."

"I'll try." She regarded her mentor—saw the wisdom encapsulated there. Would she ever be so wise?

"Do you regret it? Giving up your wish?"

Elodie shook her head. "I thought I would, but it's a relief, honestly. Like I had this weight bearing me down into the deep, and now I'm finally surfacing. Breathing air for the first time in so long."

"Good."

Agathe asked carefully, "Do you think Sebastian regrets giving up his wish? I knew that boy had a sweet spot for you."

Elodie shrugged helplessly. "We haven't spoken of it. I don't think we will. It's done, right? What's the use of agonizing over it?"

Agathe started to speak and then shook her head.

"What?"

"Nothing. You *have* grown, haven't you?"

"Only took me about four years too long."

"Nonsense. You're right on time."

"I wanted to ask you about the book."

"Do you still have it?"

Elodie nodded.

"Did you read it like I told you?"

"I did, but it...changed. Before we went into the cave, it was an innocuous children's story. After...the story had changed. And there were more. Stories of people who had sought the creature."

"Crafty bastard," Agathe spat. "The Un-Brother knows the darkness that lurks in our hearts—the part that wants to deceive ourselves. The book must have molded to be what you wanted to see."

"We tried to destroy it."

She shook her head. "It can't be destroyed. I've tried. The best you can do is bury it. I threw it in a lake, but clearly, that wasn't enough. It surfaced and found its way back into the world."

"We didn't read your story. It seemed too personal. But I am curious. The dagger—was it made of one of its talons?"

Agathe grinned. "Oh, yes."

"Will you tell me your tale?"

"You don't want to read it?"

"I'd rather hear it from you."

Agathe leaned back, her eyes growing distant. "I told you I was married when I was young, to a brute of a man. The Wish-Eater's book found its way to me, and I made the journey. It was my wish to be rid of my husband, but when the time came to make the trade, I couldn't. I loved my mother most in the world, and I wasn't going to sacrifice anything else for that man. Even to be rid of him. I resolved to grant my wish myself. But the Wish-Eater didn't want to let me leave. It attacked me, trying to eat my wish. But I wouldn't let it. I clung to my wish, fighting with every fiber of my being. One of the men who had once journeyed to that cave had dropped a sword, and I seized it. I sliced the Wish-Eater through, severing its talon. I don't think it had ever been wounded before. Or had anyone fight back. It recoiled but quickly recovered and came at me, knocking the sword from my hand. I grabbed the only thing I could as it tried to suck the wish from me. Its own claw. I slashed at its face, wounding it worse. I ran. I made it out of the cave with my life, still clinging to that talon.

I returned home, more determined than ever to grant my own wish. And my husband beat me within an inch of my life for leaving without telling him where I was going. Bloody, nearly unconscious, I found that talon on the floor. I stabbed him with it, right in the heart."

"Agathe!" Elodie breathed, shocked by the tale. "How did you avoid punishment?"

"I ran. I staggered out of that town and never looked back. I'll never regret fighting for my life. No woman should. I had the knife made from the creature's claw to remind me of the type of person I want to be. A fighter."

"I lost it," Elodie admitted. "I'm so sorry."

"Nonsense. It served its purpose. It brought you home. It showed you what I always knew. You're a fighter too."

Elodie let the word settle atop her like a mantle. Or a crown. A fighter. Yes, she was. It had been she who'd first stabbed the Un-Brother's spawn, not Sebastian, not Willum.

"I guess you're right," she finally said. She'd been fighting for her wish for so long, but only in laying down the fight had she found any semblance of peace. Maybe...there was a time to fight, and a time to rest. And knowing the difference—that was the real wisdom.

"I owe you an apology too, you know," Agathe said.

"For what?"

"Some of the things you said, the night before you left...they stung, but there was truth there. I've been keeping you close for a long time now, hoping you would take over for me someday. But that wasn't fair. I know it's not your path. Your gifts lie in healing plants, not people."

"It is what I love," Elodie admitted.

"The reason it took me so long to get here today is because I was in Wouraux. I've started the process to adopt one of the girls from the orphanage."

"Adopt?"

"Her name's Odette. She's precocious. She wants to be a healer and I need an apprentice. It's a perfect arrangement."

"I remember her. As skinny as a bean pole?"

"That's the one."

"What a wonderful idea," Elodie said. And she meant it. Agathe would be a tremendous mother.

"I think we'll be good for each other."

"You ready to parent a teenager?"

"Daughter help me! I'm sure your father will have some lessons from the front lines to give me."

"He'll be able to regale you with stories for hours, I'm sure. We three are the cause of all his grey hairs, as you hear him tell it."

"Men are so dramatic."

Elodie's spirits plummeted as thoughts of Willum rushed to the forefront.

"I'm sorry, "Agathe said, sensing her change in mood.

"Don't be. I forgot there, for a moment or two. It wasn't all I thought of."

"Those moments will grow, in time."

"Is it awful of me, to find moments of contentment when Willum is gone?"

"Nonsense. He would want it for you. And if not, he never deserved you."

Elodie smiled. "I think he would want it for me. He just didn't know how to show it."

Agathe wrapped a thin arm around Elodie's shoulders and Elodie settled into her side.

"What of you, Elodie? What is it you want to do?"

"Now that I'm out of a job?" She eyed Agathe sideways.

"You know we can work together as long as you like—"

But Elodie waved a hand. "I want to rebuild my mother's greenhouse and grow my herbs there. I want to focus more on my business. I think I could help farmers with their crops... I don't know exactly what it would look like, but I just...see it."

"It's a fine idea. A plant doctor."

"Exactly."

"And will your father allow you to take over the greenhouse?"

"I'll handle him. This is one of those times to fight, I think."

CHAPTER 38

TO LIFE

*S*ebastian stood in his brewery, looking about. He had passed four days at Ava's—four days burying himself in her comfort and warmth, reveling in her softness beneath his fingertips, her sweetness on his lips. Four days of not thinking about what he had lost. What he had given up like a fool. He didn't deserve Elodie. He had given his love away.

It had been yesterday that Ava had finally taken his face in her hands, laid a gentle kiss on the yellowing bruise shadowing his eye, and said, "It's time. You are always welcome here, but this is not your home. Or your life. Whatever you've been avoiding, you are strong enough to face it." And she was right.

Grinchaux sat on the stairs up to the loft meowing balefully. The cat didn't like how long he'd been gone, and he definitely did not like that Corentin had returned at Sebastian's side. "You got bacon for breakfast," he told the cat. "What more do you want?"

The brewery was none the worse for wear for his absence, though he had orders to fill and several batches that were ready to be bottled. Nothing was out of place—but everything was wrong.

His time with Ava had numbed the pain of his loss, held the

thoughts at bay. Now that he was back home, they rushed in—powerful and insistent.

He turned around slowly, feeling the despair building within him. "It's not fair, Corentin."

The dog cocked his head.

"This should have been my chance. I'd waited so bloody long and this was my chance. And I *gave up my wish.*" The place where his feelings once lived was a quiet, empty space now, but that didn't mean his mind didn't remember the twisted turn of events. That it didn't seek to remind him at every turn.

Someone pounded on the door. "Bas!"

Dion barreled through the door as soon as Sebastian opened it. He wore a fine charcoal grey suit and hat, with a waistcoat of burgundy beneath.

"How'd you know I was back?"

"Word travels fast in a small town, my friend."

"Why are you all dressed up?" Sebastian asked.

Dion gripped Sebastian's shoulders, excitement written across his face. "Because I am going to Willum Mercer's funeral!"

"You seem a bit cheerful to be attending the funeral of one of your townsfolk."

Dion let out an exasperated gasp. "I'm cheerful for you, my friend! Because of what this means for you! You've been waiting patiently for years and now your day has come! Yes, it's a tragedy, but all things have their time. Willum's time had run down, and now it's yours!" He clapped Sebastian on the arm.

All-father help him, it was even worse hearing it from Dion's mouth. Sebastian closed his eyes. Wait, why was he praying to the All-father? The all-mighty bastard had done nothing for him except set him up for the worst kind of fool.

"Why do you look like someone died?" Dion crossed his arms over his chest.

"Someone *did* die," Sebastian countered.

"Right, your lady love's abusive husband. Why is this not good news? What am I missing here? Don't tell me this is some sort of misguided Beringer code of chivalry where you can't court her because she's a widow—"

"She *is* a widow! Chivalry is not misguided—"

"Screw chivalry." Dion poked him in the chest. "You worry too much about everyone else. What others want. What's proper. I'm not going to let you talk yourself out of this one. Elodie is far too beautiful to remain a widow forever. If you don't start courting her soon, someone else will—"

"I don't love her anymore!" Sebastian roared. "All right? I don't love Elodie anymore." He dropped his head into his hands.

"We talked last week. You loved her then. You've loved her for ten years. You're telling me the minute—"

"I know!" Sebastian threw up his hands. "I know all of it. I just..." He sighed. "Do you have time for a drink?"

"I think I better make time." Dion took his coat off.

So Sebastian told him. The entire mad story. The Wish-Eater. Giving up his wish. Willum. It was one thing that he had always appreciated about Dion. Nothing fazed him.

When the tale was told and both of their cups were in need of refilling, Dion let out a whistle. "You do have some uncommon bad luck, my friend."

"You're telling me." Telling the story had drained some of the despair from him, leaving him feeling as limp and rung out as an old dishrag.

"So just fall in love with her again," Dion suggested.

"It doesn't work that way."

"How do you know? There's nothing left in there? You feel nothing for her?"

Sebastian shook his head. "There's something, but nothing like it was before. I think it's just respect. Platonic love, like I feel for you or Delphine, or the damn cat."

"Platonic love can grow. I am fairly irresistible—"

Sebastian snorted. "I'd sooner court the cat."

"I'm serious. Plenty of people marry and then grow into love."

"I'm not sure Elodie would agree to that type of arrangement."

"You don't have to tell her."

"Are you suggesting that I just...fake it?"

"Why not? You enjoy each other's company. There are worse matches."

"I couldn't do that to her. If she marries again, she deserves to find someone who can love her the way she deserves."

Dion rolled his eyes. "There you go again, being selfless to a fault."

"Is it such a bad thing?" Sebastian shot back.

"No, it's not," Dion admitted. "Though sometimes I do think you worry too much about how your actions affect others. You can't tiptoe on eggshells all your life. You need to seize what you want."

Sebastian deflated. He'd thought as much himself. It was why he'd given up his wish, and look where that had gotten him. "I did stop by Ava's in Rochester for a few days." He looked up with half a smile.

Dion's eyebrows rose. "The buxom innkeeper you told me about?"

Sebastian nodded.

"There you go. We need more of that. Look, are you actually smiling instead of brooding?" Dion pointed at him.

Sebastian rolled his eyes. "I smile."

"So, if not Elodie, then what *do* you want? It's not Josephine, right? Rumors are still swirling about that engagement."

"Daughter, no. I need to put a stop to that."

Dion blew out a breath. "Let her down easy."

Sebastian nodded. "I think...I want to build my tasting room. Maybe travel a bit. And then...who knows? Maybe marriage. A family. I just need to start living. I've been standing still for too long. Waiting." He didn't say the rest. He didn't need to. Waiting for Elodie. Unable or unwilling to cleave her from his life. His heart. And though he still fumed at the injustice of the timing, when he set that aside— there was a sort of calm within him. Where a desperate yearning once twisted at him, eating him away from the inside, now there was —peace.

Dion took the flagon and poured them both more cider. "That's the best thing I've heard you say in years." He held up his glass. "To life, my friend."

Sebastian smiled. "To life."

———

DION CONVINCED Sebastian to attend the funeral. So he found himself dressed in his own suit of grey, walking into town beside his friend. The sky was as bright as a blue-bell above them, the sun quickly warming him in his wool jacket. He adjusted his tie, trying to let a little more air in.

"You're doing the right thing," Dion murmured, nodding to Madam Rouleux as they passed. "It would look odd if you weren't there."

"It feels wrong to pay my respects. I'm partly to blame for his death."

"From what you told me, he got himself into that mess, and you almost saved him. Don't blame yourself."

An image flashed to mind of Willum's pale face, bloodied and slick with rain, as he slipped into the rushing river. He shivered. "I don't want to think about it."

They crossed the bridge and walked into the town's square. Delphine was standing near the church entrance, babe in her arms.

"I should go." Dion hurried to meet her, and Sebastian hung back. He was here, but that didn't mean he wanted to talk to anyone. Not that it seemed he would get his wish. Talia was striding across the square toward him. He squared his shoulders and took a breath for whatever dressing down was about to come. Perhaps it was for the best. He needed to make things right with Talia, and he couldn't avoid her forever.

Talia stopped before him, looking lovely in a dress of light grey trimmed with white ribbons. "Seems like too fine a day for a funeral, doesn't it?" she said, squinting up at the perfectly blue sky.

"No day is a good day for one," Sebastian said cautiously, "but you're right."

"Sebastian—"

"Talia—"

They spoke over each other, then laughed nervously.

"Let me first, if you don't mind," she said. "I owe you an apology."

"Oh?" His eyebrows flew up.

Her fingers knotted and untwisted, her gaze fixed upon them. "The things I said about you having feelings for Elodie... That was none of my business. And I just want you to know, I didn't tell anyone my suspicions...at least not on purpose." She stumbled on. "You see, I did tell Delphine because she's my best friend, and she knew I was spending time with you, and I was confused, and I think we were overheard. But I would never purposefully gossip about you or your business. I think it's terrible form—"

"Talia." He held up a hand. "It's all right. Whatever you did or didn't do, I forgive you."

She looked up at that. "You do?"

He nodded.

She blew out a breath. "I'm so glad. And if you want to marry Josephine Ruelle—"

"I'm not marrying Josephine."

She paused. "You're not?"

He shook his head.

"Thank the Daughter. That would have been a terrible idea, Sebastian." She let out a relieved laugh.

"You're not the first person to say so. The truth is, I did once have feelings for Elodie. Not that it's something I ever wanted to advertise. Especially on a day like today."

"Of course."

"But I was in a cage, and it was stopping me from moving forward."

"And now?"

Sebastian rubbed his jaw as realization dawned. "Now... Now I'm free."

A smile broke across Talia's face. She had a very pretty smile, with straight, white teeth. He'd never really noticed. "I'm glad." Her smile faltered as her eyes flicked to something over his shoulder.

He turned. It was Elodie and her family coming up the road. Her father, Frederick, her sisters, and Sidonie's husband, Hugh, and their son all walked in a tight cluster, clad in the dark grey of mourning. Elodie held herself stiffly, her eyes set on the stones before her, her strawberry-blonde curls pulled into a tight bun behind her head, her marriage shawl wrapped around her like armor.

He should go to her, give her a word of comfort. After all, he was the only one who truly understood what had happened…

No. He shook off the impulse and turned back. Elodie wasn't his to comfort or aid. Her problems weren't his to fix. True, his heart twisted at the sight of her, but it wasn't the sharp pang of longing he remembered. She had the comfort of family around her. That was what she needed right now. And what he needed was to move on.

A screech sounded from the front of the church.

The commotion was Willum's mother, crying out like a she-devil, lunging at Elodie, held back only by her husband.

"You did this!" she cried. "You killed him! If you hadn't been out there in the woods, he never would have come after you! He never would have died!"

Elodie's father stood partially between them. "Eugenia, accidents happen and they're nobody's fault. Elodie is heartbroken over Willum's loss. Don't make this harder than it is."

"It wasn't an accident," Eugenia cried. "She wanted him gone! She did this!" The crowd gasped, and Elodie's face seemed to crumple. But then she squared her shoulders, fire sparking to life inside her. She stepped up beside her father, facing her mother-in-law. "Willum was his own man, with his own mind. He always was, right up until the moment he died. He made his own choices. He lived by them, and he died by them. If you don't acknowledge that fact, you dishonor his memory." Elodie's voice was strong and unwavering. "Now, this is supposed to be a celebration of Willum's life. And part of that life is me, his wife. I know you never liked me, but I would hope you could set that dislike aside for a few hours. For Willum's sake. For the fact that, if nothing else, we both loved him. And we have that in common. Now if you can keep yourself together, come inside. Otherwise, I think you should leave."

Frederick put her arms around Elodie's shoulders, Sidonie on one side, Josephine on the other. They stared down Eugenia Mercer until she huffed and strode inside the church without another word.

The commotion over, he turned back to Talia, closing his mouth, which had fallen open.

"I never envied Elodie her in-laws," Talia murmured.

"No," he agreed.

He struggled to gather his thoughts, scattered like stray sheep at the sight of Elodie and her family. Talia watched him cautiously.

"Where was I?"

"Freedom."

"Right. I'm sorry if I ever led you on. I don't know if there will ever be anything romantic between you and me, Talia," Sebastian admitted. "I don't know when I'll be ready for something like that. But I'd very much like to be your friend, if you'd have me."

Her eyes softened, and she smiled again. "Friends would be nice."

Sebastian offered his arm, and she threaded her elbow though his. They walked into the church together.

CHAPTER 39

GREENHOUSE

*I*t was a strange thing, to not have to worry about Willum. The funeral was done, the wake complete, his body laid to rest in the cemetery on the banks of the Weiss River. A lovely headstone picked out. She had gone through his minimal belongings, giving some to his parents, keeping a few items for herself, donating the rest to the church for those less fortunate. There was…nothing left to do. A life wound up neatly.

Except for the threads still tied to her heart, wound around it in impossible knots. If she were being honest with herself, she hadn't been in love with Willum for a few years. But she still loved him. She was still filled with sorrow at the fact that his life had been cut short.

Elodie sat on the bench in Larkhaven's garden, soaking up the sun, letting the calm of nature soothe her. She'd had a lot of time to think, in the four days since Willum's death. Despite the funeral arrangements and the steady stream of people coming by, she'd had time. And one conclusion was as clear as day. She'd been wasting her life, living in a future that may never come to pass. Willum was gone. Her mother had died just a few years older than she was now. It was time to stop wishing and start living.

The funeral service had been lovely, the pews filled with people and flowers. Willum hadn't liked big crowds after his accident, but Elodie chose to think of him how he had once been in his youth. When he'd loved the attention. Blossomed in it.

The garden bench that had become her refuge creaked slightly, and she opened her eyes to find her father sitting next to her, settling in with a groan.

"Your arthritis acting up?" she asked.

"No," he said.

"Ruelles aren't very good liars," Elodie said.

"Tell that to the ten silver missing from my moneybox," Pepa said.

Elodie froze, her heart leaping into her throat. "You knew about that?"

His wrinkled face was kind. "You know if you ever need anything, you only need ask."

She squeezed her eyes shut for a moment. "I know. I was too proud to ask."

"Another thing we Ruelles aren't very good at. Humility. Did you get what you needed with it, at least?"

She considered. "Yes."

"Good."

"I'll pay you back every copper. I promise."

"You owe me nothing, child. I can think of nothing better to spend it on."

"You don't even know why I needed it."

"I don't need to. If you needed it, it was for a good cause."

Elodie chewed her lip. She needed to ask her father about the greenhouse, but she'd been delaying the awkward conversation. She couldn't put it off forever. "Pepa, I need to talk to you about something else."

He sighed. "The greenhouse."

"It would mean so much to me if you'd let me fix it up. I just don't understand why you're so resistant."

Her father stroked his long beard, staring into the overflowing garden rows. "She designed all of this, you know. It was just a ragged patch of grass. She tilled the rows, even helped me set the fenceposts. She was a force of nature."

Elodie said nothing, not wanting to break the spell.

"When she came to me about the greenhouse, I didn't want to build something way out there, so far from the house, but she said the soil was better, the light, on and on. I couldn't refuse her anything. So I built it, and she adored it. She was out there, when her labor came on with Josephine. Out there alone. She'd started bleeding, things were going badly, and she couldn't make it back. It wasn't until near dark that I realized she should have been back and went out to find her." He shook his head, tears sparkling on his grey eyelashes.

"If she'd been closer, if I'd gotten to her sooner...maybe..." He turned to look at her then. "On some level, I blamed that place for killing her. It was easier...than blaming myself."

"Oh, Pepa," Elodie said softly. She didn't know what to say.

"It wasn't fair to you girls. To keep that piece of her to myself. Willum may not have been my favorite son-in-law, but there was good in him. At his core. And a good man's death brings some things into perspective. I've kept too much of her to myself. When I'm gone, you girls won't have any of her left. That isn't right."

"What are you saying?"

"I want you to fix up the greenhouse. And I want...to talk...about her. It won't be easy, but I need to share with you the pieces I have left."

Elodie wiped a tear from her cheek with the heel of her hand. She settled against her father's side, resting her head on his big shoulder. "I'd like that."

They sat like that a moment when Rolo came screeching into the garden, leaping onto Pepa's lap. Sidonie and Hugh must have arrived for dinner.

"Oof!" he said, catching the lad.

"Auntie Elodie!" Rolo cried. "I learned to rhyme!"

"Oh?" Elodie arched a brow. She stood, pulling Rolo off of her father. "We'll have to see if we can find some rhymes! A fat cat perhaps? Or a round hound?"

Rolo giggled with glee as they walked into the living room, where Hugh was pulling out a chair for Sidonie.

Josephine hollered from the kitchen. "Dinner's on, Sid. Come help me carry it in?"

Elodie put Rolo down and shooed him toward his father. "I'll get it."

Hugh waved her down. "Let me."

Elodie watched his retreating form with surprise, turning to her sister.

"His training is coming along nicely," Sidonie said with a grin as she bounced Chantall in her arms.

Elodie laughed.

Josephine and Hugh carried the food into the dining room, setting it on the table. Like magic, the family materialized around the long, wooden expanse, filling the chairs. They dished up the food: steaming roast, potatoes, squash and green beans, fresh bread from the oven with sweet cream butter.

Pepa finished pouring the wine and stood, raising his glass. "To family gone, but never forgotten. To Willum."

Elodie pressed her lips together as she raised her glass, nodding in thanks to her father.

He sat down, and they dug into the meal, all except little Rolo, who seemed intent upon shoving his food around his plate. "So, my question," Josephine said. "Elodie, are you going to move out of that sad, little flat and back in here?"

Her father looked up with hope in his eyes. "You know you're always welcome."

"I was thinking about that," Elodie said. "And I'd like to move back in for a time. While I fix up the greenhouse. After that, we'll see."

The clatter of forks stilled as everyone looked to Pepa. He nodded slowly. "I've already told Elodie I think it's a fine plan."

Elodie grinned.

Josephine squealed. "I can't wait to see you every day!"

"You won't have much time," Elodie said. "You'll need to be on the potter's wheel every day to make enough inventory for the store I plan to open."

"Store? What's this now?" Pepa said.

"I plan to open a store to sell my herbs. I'll put some of Agathe's remedies in there, and with Josephine's pottery, there will be plenty of inventory."

"Now let's not—" Pepa started, but Sidonie shushed him. "The winds of change are blowing, Pepa. Best you just let them bear you along."

Pepa turned to Hugh for support, who just shrugged. "Haven't you learned by now, sir, that there's no stopping the Ruelle women when they get an idea in their head?"

"You get that from your mother," her father grumbled, but Elodie could see he was softening.

"Right, Pepa," Josephine said. "Because you don't have a stubborn bone in your body."

He threw up his hands. "We'll try it. But if it doesn't work, no coming crying to Pepa!"

Elodie stood up from the table, coming around to kiss her father on the head. Josephine came around the other way and kissed his cheek. "Women!" he growled. "Surrounded by women. Hugh, you watch that little one. You're already evenly matched, two to two."

Hugh took Sidonie's hand, giving her a quiet, adoring smile. "I realized I was outmatched years ago."

"Smart man," Pepa said. "Smart man."

Elodie returned to her seat across from Josephine and winked at her sister.

Despite all that had happened, for the first time in a long while, the future looked bright.

ELODIE AND JOSEPHINE were clearing the dinner plates when a knock sounded at the door.

"Hasn't everyone already fawned over us enough?" Pepa growled, heading for the front.

But when he returned with Sebastian, Elodie's breath stilled.

"What are you doing here?" The question tumbled out of her mouth before she could stop it.

Sebastian worried his grey hat in his hands, turning it about. "Actually, I'd like to talk to Josephine, if I may."

Josephine appeared from the kitchen, taking off her apron and handing it to Elodie. They walked into the front sitting room to talk.

"What do you think that's about?" Pepa murmured.

"The engagement, I presume." Elodie stacked the last of the dishes. Her gut had churned at the sight of him. She'd seen him at the church, sitting in the back next to Talia. Were they dating again? Now that he was free of his troublesome love for her? He looked achingly handsome despite his healing bruises, his golden hair curled around his ears, his strong form clad in a smart, grey suit. She shook her head, trying to rid herself of the thoughts, the feelings that swirled through her like autumn leaves. It wasn't to be. He wasn't hers to want. To have. She'd turned over a new leaf, and she would stick to it.

No more yearning for what couldn't be. There was only being grateful for what was.

Josephine returned to the kitchen and donned her apron, picking up a dish rag.

"What did he say?"

"He broke off the engagement." Josephine rolled her eyes. "Not that it was ever real to begin with."

Elodie released a breath. "Are you all right?"

Josephine turned to her. "You're still okay with...what we talked about?"

"You taking the tincture?" Elodie nodded. Her heart twisted at the thought of the life that would be lost, but the ache—the weight—she had once felt was gone. This was Josephine's decision. And she would support her sister.

"Then I'm all right." Josephine picked up a glass and started drying.

Elodie's hands stilled in the soapy water. Sebastian wasn't hers, but there was one last piece of unfinished business between them. "Give me a minute." She turned and jogged through the house and out onto the front lane. Sebastian was most of the way back to the brewery.

"Sebastian!" she called after him.

He stopped. Turned.

When she came to a stop before him, her tongue seemed tied in knots. His hazel eyes, ringed with blue, peered into her, so earnest, so kind. She put a hand to her stomach to still the butterflies there. How had he done this for so many years? Loved her without ever giving up a clue?

"It was a nice service today," he said.

"Thank you."

"I saw...what your mother-in-law said."

Ugh. That.

"It's not my place, but for what it's worth...I'm proud of you...for how you handled it. Standing up for yourself."

"I appreciate that. There's something about facing down a mythical monster that makes your mother-in-law seem a little less scary."

Sebastian laughed. Such a bright, genuine sound. Elodie could live in his laugh. She shoved the thought down. "I spoke with Agathe about destroying the book. She said it can't be done."

"Bad news."

"She suggested we bury it. Is...that all right with you?"

"It's your book, Elodie. Do with it what you want."

"All right. Somehow, it seemed like both of ours. I just wanted to ask before I did it. Do you want to come with me? Close the chapter, so to speak?" She gave him a weak smile.

He hesitated. "I think I'll pass, actually. I think it's best...if we go our separate ways. Being around you... It reminds me..."

"I understand," she said softly. "Thank you for everything, Sebastian."

He nodded. "Goodbye, Elodie."

Elodie stood and watched as he walked up the lane to the brewery, as he disappeared inside the door. Savoring one last glance—one last taste of what might have been. And then she carefully tucked those feelings deep inside, turned, and walked away from Sebastian Beringer.

CHAPTER 40

THREE MONTHS

The summer passed in a blur of plans and lumber. Sebastian poured himself into the addition to his brewery, and the tasting room materialized with remarkable efficiency. It was the first weekend in September when finishing touches were finally done, and Talia decided to throw a Grand Opening party.

Their relationship had transformed from uncertain friends to comfortable business partners as the months had progressed. There had been one mistaken kiss between them, but they'd both agreed after that the spark had been missing—and Sebastian had gratefully let her settle into the role of his energetic head of marketing. Soon after, a solicitor from Oberhaven passing through town had started courting her, a man whom Sebastian liked and Talia was over the moon for. It had unfolded perfectly.

The Grand Opening party this afternoon had been all Talia's doing. There would be bredele flowers from the bakery and fresh spiced sausages and cabbage cooked on an outdoor stove. Musicians in the corner and fresh flowers decorating the tables.

"Hello!" A bright female voice muffled by an armful of fresh blooms breezed through the open front door.

"Elodie!" Talia hurried over, taking some of Elodie's burden. "These are beautiful. Thank you so much!"

Elodie sat the rest down on a table and leaned down to greet Corentin, whose tail thumped against her leg with enthusiastic insistence. The sojourner hadn't returned for the dog, and Sebastian had become quite fond of him. "Who's a good dog?" She leaned down and scratched behind Corentin's big ears.

"Hello." Sebastian came over, arms crossed before him. He and Elodie hadn't spoken much since their encounter with the Wish-Eater; their exchanges were always polite but a bit formal. Part of him regretted what he'd said to her the day of Willum's funeral, pushing her away. He did miss her friendship and the easy way it had been between them. But it wasn't good for him to be around her. To dwell on the past. It reminded him too much of his old feelings. Sometimes he almost felt like they were there, lurking in the dark recesses of his heart. He needed to keep looking forward. Moving on.

"This place is stunning." Elodie craned her neck, taking in the tall, wooden rafters, the sleek tables. "It's been fun watching it come to life. I'm glad to finally see the inside."

"I feel the same about the greenhouse," Sebastian said. "It shines with new life out there. And the flower garden you planted—it's amazing how quickly it's grown."

"It's been good to keep my mind off things," Elodie admitted. "Focus on the business. Though I think I will have perpetual dirt under my fingernails."

"Life of a gardener."

"Exactly. There are worse things."

"Business going well?"

"It is. In fact, I'm in the process of negotiating with Margery and Paul to lease the retail space next to the bakery for a shop for me and Josephine. There's an empty flat above it too. I think we may move into it."

"The two of you? That's wonderful."

"I'm excited. Although Pepa keeps complaining about being abandoned in his big, old house." She rolled her eyes. "He's as dramatic as an old lady."

"He'll come around."

Elodie nodded. She looked lovely today, clad in a dress of dusty pink, cinched with maroon ribbon. Her figure had filled out a bit as well. Gone were the sharp, bird-like clavicles of last winter, the hollow-eyed expression. "You look good, Elodie," Sebastian said. "Happy."

"You too." Her blue eyes grew wistful for a moment, holding his own. His breath caught in his throat as he struggled against the feeling that there was something more between them—something unspoken and unending and as deep as the sea. And then she clapped, and the spell was broken. "Now I should get to work making you some bouquets." She turned. "Talia, where are the vases?"

The two women busied themselves with filling vases, and Sebastian returned to the bar to finish setting up the glasses, goosebumps pebbling his skin despite the warmth of the day. He shook his head. This was why it was better to keep his distance. Even now, being around Elodie confused him. The remnants of his old wish were burned into his memory, though the substance was gone.

Talia appeared before him, her hand on her hip, her brow furrowed.

"What?" Sebastian straightened. "What's wrong?"

Talia huffed and towed him outside into the bright yard. "It's none of my business, so I'd resigned myself to staying out of it, but I just can't. I can't let you waste your life any longer. I'm officially meddling."

"What are you talking about?"

"Elodie!" Talia hissed. "You're obviously still in love with her! Her mourning period is over. Ask her to dinner."

Sebastian took a step back. "Why would you think that?"

"Because you stare at her the way I stared at you for months. I don't know why you decided you were over her. If it was for me, I'm flattered, but things aren't like that between us, and it's time to be honest with yourself. People don't fall out of love like that."

Sebastian sighed. "You don't understand."

"Then help me understand."

He rubbed the back of his head. *Well, Talia, one of the Un-Brother's mythical minions was trying to eat me and I gave up my wish in exchange for freedom...* "It's complicated."

"Then uncomplicate it. Because you love her, and she loves you too."

His head jerked up. "What? Why do you say that?"

Talia rolled his eyes. "Is she looking at you right now?"

Sebastian glanced to the interior of the tasting room, where Elodie was arranging flowers in a vase. Their eyes met and she averted hers quickly. "Yes," he breathed. He shook it off. "That could have been a coincidence."

"It's not a coincidence. Call it women's intuition, or whatever you like. But I've done my part now, Sebastian. I've said my piece. The rest is up to you."

Talia strode back into the tasting room, leaving Sebastian open-mouthed in the sunshine.

Talia was wrong. She had to be. She didn't understand what had gone on with the Wish-Eater. It had taken his wish. Gobbled it up completely. He glanced at Elodie again, then shook his head. It didn't matter what Talia thought. If Elodie had feelings for him. He didn't love her. He didn't. He shoved the thought down mercilessly.

"Damn it," he growled. "How the hell am I supposed to throw a party now?"

SEBASTIAN DID his best to focus on his guests, on their hugs and hand-shakes, on the congratulations and laughs. The entire town had come out for the party. The tasting room and the wide stretch of lawn outside was filled with happy families and people.

Dion was on his third glass of cider when he stood on a table and made a particularly embarrassing toast to Sebastian, the "best brewer in all of Astria."

Despite the sea of faces, it seemed Elodie was everywhere he looked. Elodie chatting with Delphine and cooing over their baby, Elodie spinning her nephew around in the grass until he tumbled down in a fit of giggles. Elodie chatting with Bellamy, who seemed just a tad too friendly with his old friend's widow. Anger flickered to life inside him on her behalf. Her husband was not three months in the ground and—

"Can an old lady get a refill?"

Sebastian blinked. Agathe was before him, waggling her glass.

"Of course. And you're not an old lady." He took the glass from her, setting it beneath the spout. He handed it back to her when it was full. "There you are."

She hesitated, examining him. "This is a party, you know. I believe it's supposed to be fun?"

He let out a harsh laugh. "The host never has fun, right?"

"I suppose."

"I just have a lot on my mind. Don't worry about me," Sebastian said.

"Old lady prerogative. But I'll leave you be." She turned to leave, and he called out after her.

"Agathe—"

She turned back.

He stepped closer, running a hand though his hair. This was madness. He just needed to put Talia's comment to rest. Get it out of his head. "Can I ask you something? About a certain—" He looked about. The noise of laughter and conversation filled the room, so no one would be able to overhear what he was about to say. "Mythical creature?"

She took a sip. "This sounds good."

"When it eats a wish, it's gone, right? All the way?"

"Well, that's a matter open for some debate. Some might say *yes*. It's gone for good. Some, myself included, believe that a strong wish can never really be gone. A seed always remains. And it only takes a seed to grow an oak tree."

A numbness swept over his body. *A seed remains.*

"And still others might say, in the case of a certain wish, namely, yours, that love is not a wish."

His comment came out hoarse. "What do you mean?"

"Love is not a wish. It is stronger and more enduring. Desire—the desire to make someone yours—that is a wish, that can be whisked away. But if you truly love someone, those roots run deep, far deeper than even the Un-Brother himself can touch."

Her words were like a swift punch to his gut. "You think...that's true?" he wheezed.

"The question is, do *you* think it's true?" Agathe took another sip.

Sebastian's mind was pinwheeling into open air. "I need—I need —" He staggered back, out the door into the hot afternoon. People surrounded him. Noise and movement.

"Sebastian?" he heard Talia call after him, but his feet staggered forward.

Stumbled.

He needed to be alone, needed space to breathe—to think—

His feet bore him down the lane toward town. But he didn't want town. Normally, when he needed to think, he would go to the orchard, but it was open to the public today, filled with picnickers and running children.

Down the lane to Larkhaven, around the back, down the path, now lined with smooth stones and bright flowers.

To Elodie's greenhouse. Sparkling like a diamond amongst the greens and browns of the countryside. A jewel—a gem among the mundane. Just like Elodie.

He staggered against it, stripping off his tie, unbuttoning his vest and his top two buttons.

Air. He needed air.

His wish. His dream. His love for her, which had consumed him for so long, only to be robbed from him the moment he needed it most. Was it really gone? He searched within himself, desperate, clawing. The little phantom pains he still felt when he looked at her, when she walked by on the street—was it a seed? Was it his love, its roots tangled deep in the fertile soil of his soul? Did he still love her?

He sank down onto the ground, his back to the greenhouse, his spinning head in his hands.

You look at her the way I used to look at you.

Love is not a wish.

Had he given up too soon? Resigned himself to the fact that the wish had been cut out of him, surgically excised? When in fact, his love for Elodie remained?

And if he truly loved her, what did it mean for them? Did she share his feelings? What if he professed his love for her, and she didn't feel the same?

"Sebastian?" A quiet voice interrupted the maelstrom within him. He whipped his head up.

Elodie.

She stood there, uncertain, more beautiful than the first rose of spring, more precious than the last summer sunset.

"I just saw you rush off, and..." She threaded her fingers together. "It's a good place to fall apart." She nodded to the greenhouse. "You were there for me once, when I needed you. I thought I'd return the favor. If you need. But if you want to be alone, I'll go."

"I don't know what I want," Sebastian whispered. Here, in this place, just him and her alone, he could feel the throb of something insistent within him. Something familiar—and *new*.

He got to feet as shaky as a newborn foal's, his heart beating so hard, he feared it would burst from his chest. He stepped forward.

So long he'd been cautious—careful. Worried about everyone else but him. He'd never been the kind of man who saw what he wanted and seized it. The kind of man who insisted upon the life he deserved. But he wasn't that man anymore. There was only one way to know if he truly loved her still.

"I think..." Another step toward her. Then another.

Blood rushing in his ears. Energy coursing through his veins.

Toe to toe, he faced her, reveled as she looked up at him with those doe eyes filled with hope...

"I think what I want is you."

Then he kissed her. One hand threading through her silken curls, the other pulling her close. Their lips met and his love burst forth within him, a kaleidoscope of sensation and color and sound no longer held back by a shaky dam of doubt and misunderstanding.

Elodie's body melted against his even as her arms tightened around him, and those silken lips parted with a little sigh.

His spirits soared even higher, to a place of light and love he'd never thought possible.

Because he loved Elodie Mercer.

And she loved him too.

CHAPTER 41

KISS

Sebastian is kissing me.

The thought blazed through Elodie like a comet, leaving a trail of delicious warmth.

She had so many questions—so many things to say—but she didn't want to break the spell of the moment. She never wanted his mouth to leave her own.

The questions could wait.

Elodie curved her body into his own, weaving one hand through his golden locks, as soft as lamb's wool.

His lips on hers had started out gentle—so exquisitely tender. Tasting of honey and apples, his lips explored hers, his tongue flicked between, darting against hers, sliding like silk.

But still he held back—as if he wanted to take his time, to memorize and savor the moment, to roll the taste of her about his tongue like the finest wine.

Heat pooled deep within her. It had been a long time since she'd wanted a man as desperately as she wanted Sebastian.

A little moan escaped her and she tightened her hand in his shirt, the other in his hair. She didn't want to savor him. She wanted to devour him, indulge her senses in a gluttonous feast of every piece of

Sebastian. She wanted to see the stretch of his tawny skin, taste every inch of it. Feel the length of him—as soft as velvet, yet as unyielding as steel.

Sebastian sensed her eagerness and his kiss deepened, his fingers in her hair tightening, angling her head so he could explore her mouth all the more. He spun her and in three steps her back hit the side of the greenhouse, a breath hitching from her.

His body pressed against the length of hers, and hers sounded an eager response—her breasts tight, her breath ragged.

Sebastian's mouth left hers and trailed across her jaw and to her ear, where he nibbled and kissed, each touch of his lips kindling the fire within her even hotter. "I can't believe this is really happening," he murmured into her skin. "You have no idea how long I've wanted this."

"It is," she gasped in reply. "And I do."

There were too many clothes between them. She pulled his jacket from his broad shoulders. It dropped to the ground. She ran her hands over the muscles of his arms, his back. Daughter help her, she'd wanted to touch him like this for so long. Ached to. She pulled the tails of his shirt from his belt—

His lips left the curve of her shoulder, where he'd been lavishing his affections, and he drew up. He put one hand on the side of the greenhouse, creating space between them. "Elodie," he panted. She loved hearing her name on his lips. Like music. Like water cascading down the pebbles of a stream. "Are you sure...? We don't have to rush anything—"

She seized his face in her hands, marveling that she was allowed to do so. Her heart sang at the new world opened up to it. Only hers to explore. "For once in your life, stop worrying about everyone else, and take what you want."

A smile curved his lips, sending flutters of pleasure through her belly. "I'll never stop worrying about you, Elodie. But point made." He seized her beneath the rear, pulling her legs up around his waist.

A gasp of surprise escaped her, and she wrapped her arms around him, letting him carry her inside.

He set her down on the wooden workbench, his lips finding hers again—insatiable. She enclosed her legs around his hips, drawing him closer.

And then he stopped, drew back for a moment. She could feel his hazel eyes tracing the lines of her nose, her cheeks, her lips. "All-father, you are beautiful, Elodie."

She ran her fingers through his disheveled hair. "I was thinking the same thing about you."

They crashed together like waves on the shore, toppling a few pots of chamomile on the bench next to her. "Sorry," he gasped, and she just laughed. "Stop worrying."

"Force of habit," he said through his kisses.

"Fewer words," she panted.

And he complied. His fingers found the laces of her bodice, his hands the swell of her breasts, and she arched into him, every sensation driving her higher, filling her with a kind of disbelieving joy she'd only dreamed about.

The greenhouse around them was verdant and warm, the smells of herbs and spices and warm tomatoes on the air. Sunlight slanted through the glass panels, limning Sebastian's supple form as he pulled his shirt over his head. As he lowered her gently to the floor.

Sebastian undressed her with reverent care, worshipping every newly exposed part of her body with fingers and lips. By the time he pulled his trousers off, she was quivering with desire, desperate to join with this man who made her feel so alive.

"Sebastian, please," she whispered, clawing at his back as he dipped back down to kiss her stomach again.

His eyes twinkled as he lifted his head. "See, words can be helpful."

But no more words were needed.

For so long, she had been a cairn, a woman buried under the stones of her disappointments. Her failures. But she had clawed free—gasped her way to fresh air and oxygen and the hope of new life.

Sebastian transformed her now to something even more. No longer a statue, a likeness of a woman. Now she was a pyre—blazing bright enough to light the sky.

AFTERWARD, they lay with Elodie's dress draped over them, an empty burlap seed sack for a pillow.

"That wasn't at all how I expected this afternoon to go," Sebastian admitted as he kissed her brow.

Elodie chuckled, settling her head on his shoulder. "Disappointed?"

Sebastian considered. "What's the opposite of disappointed? Disbelieving, pinch-yourself-this-can't-be-real, ecstatic? Yes, that's what I think I am."

Elodie couldn't wipe the silly grin off her face. Couldn't stop touching him. "Me too. It feels like a dream, doesn't it?"

Sebastian sat up slightly. "This isn't a dream, right?"

Elodie gave his firm stomach a gentle pinch. "Don't think so."

"Thank the All-father."

Elodie propped her chin on his chest, gazing at him. "I have so many questions."

"Ask away."

"What changed? You've barely said two sentences to me these past few months."

"I thought the Wish-Eater ate my love for you. So I resigned myself to making the best life I could without it, and that meant staying away from you...because it was too hard otherwise."

"I understand."

"But then Talia today said I was still in love with you. I said that was crazy, but I couldn't dispute that I still felt...*something* when I saw you. I'd thought it was just an echo of the wish, but Talia's comment made me doubt that. Then I talked to Agathe. It was her opinion that the Wish-Eater couldn't wipe out love because love is more enduring than just a wish. Once I started thinking about it, realizing it was a possibility, it all just...rushed back to me."

Elodie sat up then. Breathless. "That makes sense. Why didn't we think of that?"

"It was too hard to talk about, maybe?"

Elodie nodded. She examined one of her curls. "I realized how I felt about you right before it took your wish. When it asked me whether I'd give up what I loved most in the world..." She cleared her throat. "I know it's wrong because I was still married to Willum, but I realized it was you."

Sebastian stroked her brow and her eyes fluttered closed. She leaned into his touch. Light, his hands were magic. "I don't think how we feel can ever really be wrong. Because we can't help or change it. It's what we do with it that counts, right?"

She nodded. "When you gave up your wish, and then Willum passed, I was so angry."

"Me too. It was shit timing."

"The worst!" Elodie laughed. "I felt like the All-father was mocking us."

"Or the Un-Brother."

"Or him. But...I'd spent so long wishing to be a mother, and I was finally free of that. I wasn't going to spend any more time wishing for things that couldn't be. You didn't love me anymore, and I needed to live my life as best I could."

"And you have. I'm so proud of all you've accomplished. Look at this place."

She cleared her throat again, fighting tears. Looking at him then, laid out before her. A miracle. "But I never stopped loving you. I've missed you so much."

Sebastian's voice was thick when he responded, "I've missed you too."

She kissed him, soft and sweet. She lay her head back down on his chest, settling in. She never wanted to move from this place, to break the magic of this moment. There were questions and complications, but in this moment, everything was absolutely, breathtakingly perfect.

"I guess visiting the Wish-Eater wasn't a total bust," Sebastian said.

Elodie's heart twisted. For Willum, it had been. But for her and Sebastian...perhaps giving up their wishes had been exactly what they needed. It gave them the space to move on, clearing the way for something new to bloom. "Maybe we should dig up that book," she joked, pointing through the glass. "I buried it right under that big oak tree."

Sebastian shuddered. "I think it's best if the book stays buried. After all, we granted our own wishes, after a fashion, didn't we?"

She threaded her fingers through his and closed her eyes. Perfectly content. Exactly where she was supposed to be. "Yes, we did."

EPILOGUE

*S*ebastian stood next to Elodie's family, watching as the Baumai parade wound its way into the square. Not Elodie's family, he reminded himself. *His* family. Minus Josephine, who was in Rochester for six months, studying under a stoneware master there. Corentin's tail beat a steady rhythm against his shin.

He spotted Agathe's old horse, Maven, as he trundled around the corner, then Agathe and her skinny apprentice, Odette, then... His heart seemed to sigh at the sight of her. Elodie. Clad in a new dress of lavender trimmed in white, her curls threaded with white ribbons and miniature roses. A bright smile on her face. One hand on the swell of her belly, the other waving to the crowd. Elodie Beringer. His wife.

"At some point, you have to stop getting misty-eyed when she walks in a room," Sidonie remarked, standing next to him. She bounced her daughter, Chantall, who had just turned one year old, on one hip. Frederick had been towed away by Rolo, who wanted to explore some wagon or other.

Sebastian's cheeks heated. "I'm working on it."

"Nonsense," Hugh said, massaging his wife's shoulders. "Let the man enjoy being a newlywed."

"Does six months wed still qualify?" Sidonie arched a brow.

Hugh and Sebastian exchanged a look. "It's a year, right?" Sebastian asked. "We can be disgustingly sappy at least the first year?"

"Agreed," Hugh said. "At least."

"Just wait until the baby comes." Sidonie gave her daughter a peck. "The honeymoon will be over then."

"I don't think there's anything that could change how I feel about Elodie." Sebastian caught her eyes over the crowd and she grinned, waving.

Sidonie rolled her eyes. "The worst part is, I believe him!"

Hugh kissed Sidonie's cheek. "Leave the man be."

Agathe's wagon was circling the fountain now and Elodie peeled off from it, skipping across the square to meet him. "Blessed Baumai."

"Baumai blessings, my love." He gave her a kiss.

"I have something for you." Her cornflower-blue eyes were sparkling, her cheeks rosy pink. Pregnancy looked good on her. Happiness did.

"Oh?" Sebastian asked. "A gift?"

She revealed a flower crown from behind her back, threaded with greenery and tiny bluebells.

Sebastian threw back his head and laughed. "For me?"

"You seemed to like the first one."

Sebastian drew her into his arms. "It was when I first fell in love with you."

She trailed her fingers up his arm and placed the crown on his head. "Well, then, I better keep them coming."

THE DAY WAS FILLED with food and laughter and music and dancing. Elodie said Sebastian didn't actually have to wear her crown, but he insisted. He was a fool for Elodie, and he didn't care who knew it.

The sun was dipping low when both of the casks of cider ran dry.

"I've got one more in the wagon." Sebastian shoved to his feet, extricating himself from the bench.

"Need any help?" Frederick asked.

"Don't trouble yourself," Sebastian said. "I've got a cart." He kissed the top of Elodie's head. "Be back in a minute."

Corentin trotted along beside him as he made his way to the alley behind the church, whistling softly.

He pulled the cider barrel off the wagon and maneuvered it into the cart when a shadow fell across his path.

A tall, scruffy man stood shaded in the lamplight. His clothes were dirty and worn, his long beard and hair tangled and unkempt.

"You startled me," Sebastian said, his senses firing. He'd never seen the man in the village before—

Then the lantern light flashed in the copper of his hair, the gold flecks of his eyes. The freckles on his dingy face.

Sebastian's blood ran cold. "Piers?"

The sojourner stepped forward and the light lit something else. Silver. A knife in the sojourner's hand.

"What are you doing here?"

"You let me rot in there," Piers rasped. "You said you'd return with the money, and you never came. Ten months I sat in that cell. Ten. Months."

Sebastian stepped away, his back flush to the wagon. He had no weapon, not even something to club the man with.

Corentin growled softly at his side. The dog had defended them against the Wish-Eater, but would he recognize his former master? Turn on Sebastian?

"I'm sorry. We found what we needed. I didn't need the information anymore."

"I can see that. Been watching the square for a while. Everything's worked out nicely for you, hasn't it? That pretty lass's brute husband is gone, you slid right into his spot. Baby on the way. Picture of domestic tranquility. It's almost like all your wishes have come true. You found it, didn't you? It's real."

Sebastian licked his parched lips. "What do you want?"

The sojourner held out a hand. "The book. I lost everything in that fire. Look at me! It's time my dreams came true. And I want my dog, too."

"We destroyed the book."

Piers advanced on him, bringing the knife up between them. "I know that's a lie. The book can't be destroyed."

"The Wish-Eater... It's not..." Sebastian swallowed his word of caution. This man had robbed Elodie. He had taken advantage of Josephine. Now he came here, threatening Sebastian with a knife?

This was exactly the type of man the Wish-Eater sought. Whom the Wish-Eater deserved. And the Wish-Eater was exactly what Piers deserved, too. If the sojourner wanted the book so badly, he could have it. Sebastian wasn't about to endanger his family trying to convince the man it was a bad idea. Perhaps his magic would protect him.

Sebastian looked up, straightening his shoulders. Meeting the other man's hostile gaze. "Outside the village, on the way out of town, is an estate called Larkhaven. Take the path around through the garden, and you'll come upon a greenhouse. There's a great oak tree shadowing it. The book is buried under its branches."

Piers nodded and stepped back, sheathing his knife. Back was his easy smile, his slick mannerisms. "Sorry I had to go about it this way. But as you can see, I have need of a turn of luck."

"You'll find it," Sebastian said flatly.

Piers patted his leg. "Come on, Corentin."

The dog stayed put, sitting down beside Sebastian. Whining softly.

Sebastian rested a hand on the dog's head. "The journey to the Wish-Eater's cave covers difficult terrain. Why don't you leave Corentin here? You'll move faster without him. You can come pick him up when you return."

Piers frowned.

"As you can see, he's well cared for."

Piers shrugged his shoulders. "Very well. One less mouth to feed."

"Exactly."

"But I'll be back for him," Piers said, starting down the path away from the square.

Would he? Maybe the sojourner would do the right thing and his conscience would spare him from the Wish-Eater's clutches. Or maybe he would prove exactly the wretch he seemed to be. Whatever the outcome, Piers' fate was in his own hands now.

Shaking off the unease of the interaction, Sebastian retrieved the cart with his last cask and started up the cobblestone street. Dog at his side, whistle on his lips. Back toward the light and life of the square. Back toward the one whose light would always guide his way home.

FROM THE AUTHOR

I was raised to believe that I could achieve anything I put my mind to. And thanks to healthy doses of hard work, good fortune, and privilege, that proved true for most of my life. Until 2016, when my husband Mike and I decided it was time to start our family.

Cue the solid brick wall. The next three years were some of the most heartbreaking, challenging times of my life. The months ticked by without a pregnancy, followed by obsessive googling, tracking, doctors visits, acupuncture, diet changes, IVF, and illness. Tears and fights, sleepless nights and existential crises and so much money down the drain. But the wish had taken hold. I wanted to be a mother so damn bad that it had become a part of me. A part of me that was killing me and keeping me alive at the same time.

There was no exact cathartic moment, only a slow realization that my wish was draining the joy and happiness from my life. If I wanted to go on, somehow, I had to let the wanting go.

So the Wish-Eater was born. Every book has pieces of the author woven into it, but this book is my heart. I wrote the story I needed with the moral I needed to remind myself of, time and again. Obviously there are differences—most importantly, Willum is not modeled after my husband, who has been my stalwart companion through this dark territory. But Elodie, sweet Elodie. I know her pain, and she knows mine.

This book is for all of you who have longed for something so badly you thought it would break you. Who have had to figure out how to go on without that dream, that hope, that wish, that person. *Especially* those of you facing the pain of infertility. For me and for Elodie and Sebastian, letting go was our road to peace. I know you'll find yours.

ABOUT THE AUTHOR

Claire Luana grew up in Seattle reading everything she could get her hands on and writing every chance she could. Eventually, adulthood won out, and she turned her writing talents to more scholarly pursuits, going to work as a commercial litigation attorney. But it turns out that's not nearly as much fun!

Since returning to her more creative roots, Claire has written and published five fantasy series: The Moonburner Cycle, The Confectioner Chronicles, The Mythical Alliance, The Knights of Caerleon, co-written with Jesikah Sundin, and The Faerie Race, co-written with J.A. Armitage. Her stand-alone novels include *Orion's Kiss* and *The Mesmerist*.

She lives in Cle Elum, Washington with her husband and two dogs. In her (little) remaining spare time, she loves to hike, travel, binge-watch CW shows, and of course, fall into a good book.

Connect with Claire Luana online at: http://claireluana.com

OTHER BOOKS BY CLAIRE LUANA

Moonburner Cycle
Moonburner, Book One
Sunburner, Book Two
Starburner, Book Three
Burning Fate, Prequel Novella
Moonburner Cycle, Box Set

Confectioner Chronicles
The Confectioner's Guild, Book One
The Confectioner's Coup, Book Two
The Confectioner's Truth, Book Three
The Confectioner's Exile, Prequel Novella
Confectioner Chronicles, Box Set

The Knights of Caerleon, with Jesikah Sundin
The Fifth Knight, Book One
The Third Curse, Book Two
The First Gwenevere, Book Three
Gwenevere's Knights, Box Set

The Faerie Race, with J.A. Armitage
The Sorcery Trial, Book One
The Elemental Trial, Book Two
The Doomsday Trial, Book Three
The Faerie Race, Box Set

The Mythical Alliance: Phoenix Team

Phoenix Selected, Book One

Phoenix Protected, Book Two

Phoenix Captured, Book Three

Phoenix Trafficked, Book Four

Phoenix Revealed, Book Five

Phoenix Betrayed, Book Six

Mythical Alliance: Phoenix Team, Box Set

Orion's Kiss

The Mesmerist

Writing as Jae Dawson:

Moonlight & Belladonna

Heartbeats & Roses

Snowflakes & Holly